I0588345

MIDNIGHT LULLABIES

IT'S DARK OUT THERE ...
AND IT LASTS A LONG TIME ...

Midnight Lullabies: Unquiet Stories & Poems is a collection of the horror short stories and poems—both old and new—by *NY Times* bestselling author and five-time Bram Stoker Award winner, Jonathan Maberry.

In the darkest hours of the night the natural world yields to the creatures who dwell in the dark. A serial killer who adopts orphaned children during the apocalypse; a heartbreaking reconciliation of two estranged brothers; a paralyzed MMA fighter receiving an offer he can't refuse; strange voices crying out from the heart of a collapsed mountain; a little girl who enlists the aid of the monsters in her closet to battle cosmic horror; a delicious revenge by a refugee from the death camps; rednecks battling zombies; a terrified child whose family has become monsters; Earth-borne horrors taking hold on an alien world; and more! Plus new horror tales and eerie poems.

With a foreword by *NY Times* bestseller Joe R. Lansdale.

MIDNIGHT LULLABIES
UNQUIET STORIES & POEMS

JONATHAN MABERRY

WFP
WordFire Press

MIDNIGHT LULLABIES: UNQUIET STORIES & POEMS
BY JONATHAN MABERRY
Copyright © 2024 Jonathan Maberry Productions

All rights reserved. No part of this book may be reproduced or transmitted in any form or by any electronic or mechanical means, including photocopying, recording or by any information storage and retrieval system, without the express written permission of the copyright holder, except where permitted by law. This novel is a work of fiction. Names, characters, places and incidents are either the product of the author's imagination, or, if real, used fictitiously.

The ebook edition of this book is licensed for your personal enjoyment only. The ebook may not be re-sold or given away to other people. If you would like to share the ebook edition with another person, please purchase an additional copy for each recipient. Thank you for respecting the hard work of this author.

EBook ISBN: 978-1-68057-694-8
Trade Paperback ISBN: 978-1-68057-695-5
Dust Jacket Hardcover ISBN: 978-1-68057-696-2
Library of Congress Control Number: XXXXXXXXX
Cover design by **(REQUIRED)**
Cover artwork images by **(REQUIRED)**
Kevin J. Anderson, Art Director
Published by
WordFire Press, LLC
PO Box 1840
Monument CO 80132
Kevin J. Anderson & Rebecca Moesta, Publishers
WordFire Press eBook Edition 2024
WordFire Press Trade Paperback Edition 2024
WordFire Press Dust Jacket Hardcover Edition 2024

Printed in the USA
Join our WordFire Press Readers Group for
sneak previews, updates, new projects, and giveaways.
Sign up at wordfirepress.com

This is for Kathy Grove and Frank Donohoe—two of my English teachers from Frankford High. Thanks for encouraging me to write creepy fiction ... even if it gave you the chills.

And, as always, for Sara Jo ...

CONTENTS

Foreword   xi

The Door Between Us   1
A Small Taste of the Old Country   18
The Queen of Thorns   41
Being Emily-Claire   44
Calling Death   71
Cooked   87
Gavin Funke's Monster Movie Marathon   103
Doctor Nine   123
Lullaby   124
The Things That Live in Cages   142
Invasive Species   165
Monk   173
Road Beers with Norm and Tank at Twitchy's
Hatchet House   177
Saint John   212
Son of the Devil   243
The Scream   268
When You See Millions of the Mouthless Dead
Across Your Dreams in Pale Battalions Go   283
Jonathan Maberry's Published Works   303

About the Author   313
Other WordFire Press Titles by Jonathan Maberry   315

FOREWORD
BY JOE R. LANSDALE

Jonathan Maberry is a writer I admire. He is versatile, clever, and from what I can tell, able to write anything. That's my kind of writer.

I don't remember when I first met Jonathan, or what I first read of his, but he is the sort of writer that immediately demands attention. He has one of those unique powers that many writers would like to have but don't have.

He's a storyteller. He is a plotter as well. I admire that. A writer like Jonathan is popping with ideas. If you can imagine hearing popcorn popping, then you may have some idea what's going on inside his creative head. Lots of kernels of ideas heating up and exploding into something enjoyable. He loves writing and his enthusiasm is like a baseline in his fiction. It's so strong it's almost something you can pat your foot to.

I can see hints of other writers in his work, the way you might spot a fragment of banana or strawberry in a blended fruit shake. But there are ingredients in Jonathan's concoctions you can't spot. Some sort of seasoning that comes from the mixer of the blend. A seasoning all his own and one that other scribblers of stories don't have and wouldn't recognize if they were searching for it. He doesn't have to search. He's found it.

It's the *IT* factor. Story charisma. Originality.

He can do traditional and make it seem fresh, he can do nontraditional and make it seem dangerous.

Jonathan can see around corners. He can write stories where you can only see the tip of the iceberg but can sense what's beneath the water. At other times you can see the whole damn iceberg adorned with dancing penguins operating a lemonade stand. They might be leading you to a delicious drink, or into iceberg disaster. Jonathan and his penguins are tricky.

In this super collection you will have some, shall we say, unusual experiences. You'll meet an unusual baker whose goods have a taste of the Old Country about them.

You will encounter the uncommon contents of a girl's school locker.

You will hear unsettling sounds on the wind. Sounds that some will lock their doors against and try to drown out with radios and TVs turned up loud.

You will spend some quality at a rare movie marathon. Light and shadow, but mostly shadow.

But enough of the hints. I fear giving something away. I think it's important that the reader not know all that is in a story, what it is about. Oh, a glimpse of this and that maybe, but beyond that, it's not up to me to pull the curtain.

Jonathan Maberry will do that. Once you're in your seats, of course, eyes trained on his production. Once you are comfortably seated, a great curtain will slide away and a page full of words will fill the stage. As you read, those words will leap off the page and into your brain, and soon they will miraculously become people and atmosphere.

Keep your eyes on the stage. You're safer that way.

And though you are seated, oh, the places you will go.

—Joe R. Lansdale
August 2023

THE DOOR BETWEEN US

—1—

He sat on one side of the bathroom door.
It crouched on the other.
Two inches of wood between them.
Worlds apart.
He wept.
It growled.
And the night refused to end.

—2—

It hadn't looked or felt like that kind of night when he went to bed.

Maybe, Danny reckoned, they never start like that.

He was six but he remembered some of the worst nights he'd had. None of them ever started with thunder or lightning. There was no fog or anything like that. Twilight melted the sun, and it got dark, and that was all normal.

Until it wasn't.

Danny remembered.

He had gone to bed with a real sense of excitement because the next morning was the first day of school. Danny liked books, and Mom had already picked up his textbooks. *Introduction to English. Introduction to Math. Introduction to Geography. My First Reader.* Easy stuff. Way easier than what he'd been reading on the Net, in comics, and like that. He liked sports, so gym seemed like it would be cool. He didn't even mind math. Numbers didn't scare him.

Girls did, but not too much.

And the other kids didn't scare him at all, because he'd always been the biggest kid. In pre-school, in kindergarten. In the neighborhood.

So he was excited. So excited that it took a long time to get to sleep at all. But then he sank down into dreams about everything being new and shiny on the first day of first grade.

Then he heard the phone ring. At first it was something in the dream, a phone ringing down the hall at school. Faint, muffled, like it was in someone's office with the door shut. Then it got louder, and that pulled him up to the surface of his dream where he lingered, his attention being drawn to the rings as they became more real. They became the sound of Mom's cell phone.

The rings stopped.

He was more than half awake by then and he heard her voice. He couldn't hear any of the words even though his bedroom shared a wall with his parents' room. But he could tell it was Mom talking. Dad was working nights three days a week, driving some stupid Uber until way late.

Mom's voice changed, and that brought him all the way up to consciousness. Not just because she was talking. Or even because she was talking loud.

No, what changed was when she started screaming.

And she screamed a long, long time.

Danny almost did not get out of bed. He wanted to know and absolutely wanted *not* to know. Grandpa was old, and his knees were really bad. He'd fallen a few times, getting hurt each time.

Gramma had that thing that made her stop talking normal and forget things. A stroke? He was pretty sure that was the word. So, the call could be about either of them.

Danny did not want to go in there and hear something bad. Not Grandpa or Gramma. He did not think he could take that. Not on the night before school started. Not ever. Not really. Not now.

The scream punched all the way through the wall.

And it went on and on and on.

Danny heard sounds. Corinne coming out of her bedroom. Yelling. Calling for Mom. Asking what was wrong. Corinne was fifteen. She was older, smarter. She knew everything. She was tough. Corinne took tae kwon do and could break boards and beat people up. She was like a superhero. Like Black Widow or Wonder Woman. Tough like that.

But then ...

Corinne started screaming too.

Danny cringed beneath the covers.

Why was *Corinne* screaming? She was always cool. Even on Christmas morning she was chill. Nothing ever bothered her. Dad always said that she was fifteen going on thirty. She didn't even yelp at monster movies. Corinne just wasn't the kind to ever scream.

But her scream was as loud as Mom's.

Maybe louder.

Yes. Louder.

It was a word that she screamed. One word pulled out of her so hard that it filled all corners of Danny's room.

No.

Nooooooooo.

That. Louder, longer.

Danny started to cry.

He didn't know why. He just knew that whatever was making Mom and Corinne scream like that was too big for him to know about. He grabbed the ends of his pillow and pushed them against his ears. Fat pillow, lots of foam stuffing.

It muffled the screams.

It didn't stop them.

And somehow that was worse.

—3—

The screams went on and on.

Danny could hear them asking questions.

Why? Why?

Over and over again, and when either Mom or Corinne asked the question, the other would answer with No.

Danny cried into the pillow. His nose was running, but he did not want to move, even to get a tissue.

No.

Why?

No, he couldn't move.

Why would he? He was safe right there.

No, he didn't want to know what made them so upset.

Why would he want to know if it was Grandpa or Gramma?

Dad would be home soon, anyway. Wouldn't he?

Yes. Of course he would.

Dad would come home, and he'd make it all right. He was good at that. Even when he was tired from working at the garage or driving the Uber, he always fixed things when he got home. The toilet, the garbage disposal, the light in the yard. He was able to fix anything. Everything.

He'd fix this, Danny knew that. Dad could fix anything and everything.

So, why didn't Mom call him?

Why didn't Corinne? She had her own cell phone.

Danny wanted to get up, stand on his bed, pound the wall, and yell at them to call Dad. They *knew* he could fix whatever was wrong.

Why didn't they call him?

Why?

Why?

—4—

No.

Danny didn't want to understand why they didn't call.

He refused to understand.

It made no sense. It was wrong. It was stupid.

It was ...

It was just *no*.

He lay there, half smothering himself with the pillow.

I'm not getting up, he told himself. Thinking it loud enough to try and drown out the screams. *No way. I'm not getting up. No. No. No.*

Noooooooooo.

Silence.

Had he said that out loud? Or was it Corinne?

Very slowly, very quietly, Danny eased the tension of the pillow. Just on one ear. The ear closest to the wall. But he kept the corner of the pillow knotted in his fist just in case he had to put it back. Just in case there were more screams. Or maybe something worse. Like hearing them talking. Like hearing them *saying* why they were screaming.

He held his breath as he listened.

Corinne wasn't screaming anymore.

Neither was Mom.

There was no sound at all.

—5—

Until there was.

But it wasn't a good sound.

No.

Not at all.

—6—

Really there were a bunch of sounds.

One after the other. Not quick, but slow.

They ate up time as he lay there. His arms were aching from holding the pillow. His hands were sore from squeezing the ends. His chest hurt because he kept not breathing because he wanted to hear.

There was nothing to hear.

Not on the other side of the wall.

Outside, sure. There was the creak of the chain that held the tire swing. There was a car sound for a moment—passing, though, not stopping. Not Dad coming home.

There was the sound of trees. It was still all day, with summer refusing to go. But then when the sun started to set it got cool. Almost cold. And the wind began. There were trees on all four sides of their house. Big, bushy ones. Two oaks out front, one on each corner. And two elms at the back corners. The one elm, the one closest to his room, had the tire swing. The other one had bits and pieces of a tree fort that was Dad's when he was a kid. Grandpa had built it, and a storm killed it when Danny was two. He didn't even remember.

Except the lightning. He remembered that. It was his oldest memory, and it was the loudest sound he'd ever heard. His memory of it was weird. Like something that was always there, but with no details. Just the noise.

That's why he was afraid of thunder. And loud noises. The first memory in his head was something so loud that it left a mark on him. In him. In his head.

A scar, he thought.

But this wasn't a storm outside. It was just the wind.

Blowing through the trees. Making the rustling leaves sound like waves on the beach. He hadn't noticed that before last year, when Mom and Dad took them to the beach in New Jersey. To Sea Isle City. It rained nearly the whole time they were there. He and

Corinne and their cousin, Lisa, sat on the big porch and played games. Corinne taught them how to play Monopoly and blackjack, but they were dumb games and after the first day they just played games on their phones. Well, Lisa and Corinne did. Danny had a Fire HD that was made for kids. Had movies and games and stuff.

As he played through the rainy weekend, he could hear the waves on the beach a block away. That sound and the sound of wind through the leaves were the same.

He wished he was down the shore. Even if it was rainy. That would be okay as long as they were all there. Mom, Dad, Grandpa, Gramma, Corinne, Aunt Helen, and Cousin Lisa.

All of them. Safe and sound and far away.

The wind made the trees sound like waves. It made them sound safe and far away.

But then that changed.

Why did the wind do that?

Now it sounded like fingernails scratching on the glass. He cringed back from it, not liking that sound any more than the silence from Mom's room.

Danny had no idea what to do.

He needed to pee, but the bathroom was in the hall, on the other side of Mom's room.

Why had they stopped screaming?

No, why were they so quiet now?

Both of them.

Quiet.

Too quiet.

Only the scratchy-scratchy trees were making real noise. Louder than the breaking waves rustle of the leaves. Closer too. Right by his bed. He did not dare look, though. Just in case it wasn't branches making the clawing sounds.

Danny lay there, trying not to pee the bed. It made his stomach hurt so bad.

But he would not pee the bed. No. Not anymore. He'd stopped

doing that two years ago and was proud of it as much as he was ashamed for having ever done it when he was little. Mom and Dad hadn't said anything. They hadn't yelled. Mom stroked his hair and helped him clean up. Dad took the sheets and blankets down to the washer in the little room off the kitchen.

Corinne had made a face, though. She had not said anything, but there was that wince that was half disgust and half a smile.

Two years ago, but he remembered it as if it was last night.

So, no. He would *not* pee the bed.

No.

Never.

His stomach hurt so bad, though.

—7—

He couldn't hold it anymore.

Getting out of bed, though, was so scary.

His room was full of shadows, and they all seemed wrong. Weird. Not the right shapes. And the closet door was open. Not much. Just a little. Too much, though.

Driven by need, Danny reached down with one foot until his toes brushed the floor.

Cold hardwood.

Icy cold.

It made him need to pee even more.

Danny held his pillow like a club in case something reached out from under the bed. Not that a pillow could do much. Even at six he understood that. But it was what he had.

He scooted to the very edge of the mattress and let his toes act as bait.

And waited.

Waited.

The wood beneath his toes warmed up a little. Taking warmth from him. Giving solidity in return. He understood the concept without being able to frame it in his mind. Knowing was enough.

Nothing grabbed him.

No slimy fingers or scaly palms or sharp claws.

Nothing.

After about a thousand years, Danny put his other foot down, the pillow raised and ready.

The wood was there. Firm and normal. Nothing made a grab for him.

It was a tremendous relief.

He stood up, still holding his weapon. The shadows that were supposed to be his dresser, his chair, his art table, his box of toys, his pile of clothes ... they stayed where they were.

He discovered that he could actually breathe again.

Danny took a few careful steps. None of those shadows suddenly jumped at him.

"Stay there," he whispered.

It sounded silly to him, and he was embarrassed by being afraid like that.

He stopped and listened.

The tree still scratched, scratched, scratched at the window glass.

There was nothing—not a single sound—coming from the other room. He thought about that. His embarrassment at talking to a pile of clothes on a chair—of even being afraid of it—steadied him. That fear was silly.

What about his other fears?

The silence bothered him. But ... why? Maybe it was just that Mom and Corinne had gone downstairs. The living room was in the front of the house, and he could never hear much from there. Not up here, not in his room. It was a really big house.

Maybe he was just being stupid. Being a baby. Corinne accused him of that sometimes.

"Danny-baby! Baby Danneeeee."

She didn't do it much. And not so much lately as before. Last year and before that.

He almost wished he could hear her voice now. To say

anything. Really, because anything would be better than the silence.

Danny took another step. There was one board in his floor that creaked and he almost—*almost*—stepped on it. But didn't. He caught his balance and made the step bigger, longer, setting his raised foot down on the far side of the wide oak plank.

But he stepped onto the edge of a little area rug, and it shot along the floor, turning his step into a lunge, and the lunge into a crashing fall. It was so loud.

And it hurt.

He landed on his butt and suddenly there was a fiery burning pain in his tailbone. Danny yelled. He couldn't help it. The fall, his yell, all of it was beyond control. All of it was loud. So loud.

He lay there and froze. He stopped breathing and fought back his need to scream because the pain was really bad. He could feel it like a line of fire ants from his tailbone all the way down to his heels.

And he still had to pee. Worse than ever.

Silence.

Danny listened to the night and the wind and the scratching trees and the voice of the house. There were the old creaks that happened all the time, and especially when the wind was blowing this hard. There was the rattle of the loose shutter on the attic window. There was ...

"*Danneeeeee.*"

He heard it.

From the other side of the wall.

Corinne's voice. Or, at least, he thought so. It wasn't exactly right, though. Like she was trying to hide her voice and pretend to be someone else. Like a game.

Except he knew it wasn't a game.

"*Danneeeeeeeeeeeeeeeeeeee.*"

Danny felt tears in his eyes. They burned and itched at the same time.

He got up as quietly as possible. Driven by fear. Driven by hope. Driven by the need to pee. Driven by ...

By what?

That voice was Corinne's.

Wasn't it?

He tiptoed to the door and listened, his ear pressed against the wood. There was no sound in the hall.

"*Danneeeeeeeeeeeeeeeeee.*"

That was coming from Mom and Dad's bedroom. The sound came through the wall. Not through the door.

Cold tears ran down his hot cheeks.

No, he thought, leaning into the word as if it could make things so. *No, no, no.*

"*Danneeeeeeeeeeeeeeeeee,*" called the voice.

Was it Corinne's?

Now he wasn't sure.

There was something weird about it. Something ... He fished for the word.

Strange?

Scary?

Wrong?

He paused. Yes. That was the word.

Her voice was wrong.

It took so much of Danny's courage to reach for the doorknob. And all of it to give it a turn.

There was only a small *click*, but he froze anyway, sure that it was the loudest sound in the whole world.

"*Danneeeeeeeeeeeeeeeeee.*"

The sound was coming through the same part of the wall. Closer to where his bed was. To where Mom and Dad's bed was. Not over by the door.

Danny opened the door a quarter of an inch. Barely wide enough to look into the hall. It was dark, with just a little light coming in from outside. This was the back of the house, so the light was the one on the Coopers' fence. The motion detector light. It came on when someone was moving around back there. Or something. The Rileys' dog, Conan, set it off a week ago. Before that it was a fat raccoon on the fence.

It was on now.

What, he wondered, set it off this time?

"Danneeeeeeeeeeeeeeeee."

The voice was the same each time. Only the first time was shorter, but then it was like something repeated. Like a sound thing from his tablet. Just replaying. And that did not feel right, either.

And why wasn't Mom saying anything?

His need to pee fought past his need to hide or even to be careful, and he stepped into the hall. He knew where every creaky board was between his room and the bathroom at the end of the hall.

For a moment he considered going downstairs to the little bathroom near the living room. But there were four stairs that *always* squeaked. Really loud too. Dad always joked about it.

"Someone's playing my tune," he'd say when anyone ran up or down the stairs.

Danny did not want to play that tune. Not now. No way.

He moved in slow motion down the hall, edging as far away to the other side of the hall as he passed Mom's room. He saw something that nearly made him scream.

The door to the bedroom wasn't closed all the way.

"Danneeeeeeeeeeeeeeeee."

This time he heard it from the open door.

Then he heard something else. A soft banging sound, and he turned and peered down the stairs. He couldn't see the front door, but Danny knew the noise it made when it was left open. It sounded exactly like that. The wood of the door thudding against all the coats on pegs just inside.

That's the sound he heard.

There was more. A breeze coming up the stairs, as cold and silent as a Halloween ghost. The door was completely open.

He paused for a few moments, despite his bladder screaming at him and the whisper from the bedroom. Danny looked down the stairs and saw something he didn't understand but knew he had to.

There was something wet on the stairs. With almost no light everything was in black and white and a million shades of gray, but he knew some of the stairs were wet.

What with, though? It didn't look like water.

It almost looked like chocolate syrup. Thick and dark like that.

But Danny knew it wasn't that. He knew it.

"Danneeeeeeeeeeeeeeeeeee."

He tore himself away from the wet stairs and the ghostly wind and the open door and hurried to the bathroom.

Just as he shut the door—doing it sooooo quietly—and turned the lock, he heard a new sound. A creak. Hinges.

Like every other sound in the house, this one was different from all the others, and he knew them all. This was a bedroom door sound. His parents' bedroom door. Opening slowly.

No. Slowly wasn't the right word. As he pulled down his pajama bottoms and began to pee—almost unable because he was so scared—he fought to find the right word.

Not slowly.

It was ... sneaky.

That was it. A sneaky sound. It was someone trying not to let the hinges creak. Someone trying not to let the hinges *warn* him.

Danny finished peeing, his body trembling with relief, but his head swimming with new fear. He pulled his pants up and closed the lid but did not dare flush. He'd already made too much sound peeing even though he aimed for the porcelain and not the water.

Without even pausing to wash his hands—something he always did—Danny hurried to the door and checked the lock. Still locked. He leaned against it to listen.

"Danneeeeeeeeeeeeeeeeeee."

He jerked back with a cry.

The sound was right outside the door.

Not down the hall, not in Mom and Dad's bedroom. Right there. Inches from his ear.

Danny staggered back, clamping his hands over his ears.

"Danneeeeeeeeeeeeeeeeee," cried the voice that was almost, but not quite, Corinne's. *"Come out and let's play."*

He stood there. Trapped. Shaking all over. Crying. Terrified.

He needed Mom.

He needed Dad.

He needed the *real* Corinne.

"Danneeeeeeeeee ... open the door."

The doorknob rattled.

Then he heard another sound. Other *sounds*.

The soft scuff of feet, both right on the other side of the door and farther down the hall. Soft. Secret. Sneaky. And ... clumsy too. Draggy, like someone limping.

"Danneeeeeeeeeeeeeeeeeee."

He heard the sound of something scraping on the door. Very slow. Going from high and almost all the way down to the floorboards outside. A woody sound. Like a nail or pin scratching the wood.

No. That wasn't quite right, was it? Not a nail. Not a pin. Not metal.

Scraping. Scratching. From top to bottom, then a pause. It started again. Top, almost to the frame and then very, very, very slowly down to just above the floor.

Not metal.

Nails.

Not like building nails.

He knew what it was, and it made him want to scream.

It was the sound of fingernails on the wood just on the other side of the door.

"Won't you come out and play with me?" asked that awful voice.

He spoke out loud without meaning to. It just came out.

"I want my daddy ..."

Danny caught himself, clapping hands over his mouth as if he could somehow stuff those words back inside.

I want my daddy.

But the words were already out. They were said. And they had been said loud enough to be heard.

There was a soft gasp.

Then there was more of the scuffing sound. More than two feet could make. Was it Corinne and Mom?

Was it something pretending to be Corinne and Mom?

"Danneeeeeeeeeeeeeeeeee."

"Danneeeeeeeeeeeeeeeeee."

Two voices, one overlapping the other.

Corinne and ...

"Mom ...?"

There was a pause, then a new sound. A soft, sneaky, oily, wet laugh.

"Open the door, Danny," said the second voice. Not his mom's voice. Not his mom's voice. Not Mom's voice. Not Mom.

"Let us in, Danny," she said.

Then she laughed.

They both laughed.

He heard a new scratching sound. Low. Down at the bottom of the door. Danny stared at it, seeing shadows moving just beneath the edge of the door, in that half-inch gap between door and floor. Shadows moving and the sound of scratching.

"I want my daddy!" he cried, almost yelling it.

The laugh again. And those scratches.

"Open the door and we'll help you find Daddy," said both voices.

The scratching. The moving shadows.

Then ...

Then.

Something slid under the bottom of the door.

Fingers.

But not. Not really. Just fingernails.

Long.

Black.

Tipped with red.

Wet with red.

Dripping with red.

Clawing at the bottom of the door.

"*Danneeeeeeeeeeeeeeeee, open the door so we can play.*"

He knelt down and stared at the fingernails. The claws. The red, wet claws.

"*I want my daddy!*" he screamed, and he screamed really, really loud.

There was a pause. A very long pause.

"*Daddy's coming,*" said the Corinne voice.

"*Daddy's coming right now,*" said the Mom voice.

There was more of the scuffing, dragging sound. It seemed far away and for a moment—a single bright moment—he thought they were leaving. Going away. Going back into Mom's bedroom. Going back to shadows and wherever they came from.

"I want my daddy," he said very softly now, the words cracked by sobs. "Please, I want Daddy."

The scuffing, dragging noises got louder.

No, not just louder. They were getting closer.

Whatever it was ... was coming closer. Up the stairs. Down the hall.

Soft footsteps.

Then they stopped.

Something hit the door. It was a strange noise, both hard and soft. There was force but it was as if someone hit the door not with a fist but with a loose hand. Like that.

"*Danneeeeeeeeeeeeeeeeee,*" said the Corinne voice and the Mom voice at the same time.

"Go away! I want my daddy."

Another soft but heavy hit. Definitely a hand. He could hear the knuckles, but not like someone knocking. It was just a loose hand hitting the bathroom door.

"Please," begged Danny. "I want my daddy."

There were two thuds, like someone dropping to their knees right outside. He could hear breathing down near the gap between door and floor.

"Danneeeeeeeeeeeeeeeee."

Danny heard the voice.

Danny screamed.

The voices outside laughed. Sneaky, playful, nasty.

Corinne.

Mom.

And one more. A man's voice.

Daddy was home.

"Danneeeeeeeeeeeeeeeee," called his father. *"Open the door."*

Danny sat down and put his back to the door and wrapped his arms over his head and tried not to listen.

He tried.

He tried ...

A SMALL TASTE OF
THE OLD COUNTRY

—1—

Campanario Cantina
El Chaltén Village
Santa Cruz, Argentina
October 31, 1948

"Would you gentlemen like something fresh from the oven?"

The two men seated at a small table by the window looked up with wary eyes. The question had been asked by a very old man with a face that seemed to be composed entirely of nose and wrinkles from which small, bright-blue eyes twinkled. He held a wicker basket with a red cloth folded over the heaped contents.

"No," said the older of the two seated men. He was about forty and had very black hair. His mouth was a hard horizontal slash bracketed by curved lines. Laugh lines, perhaps, though he was not smiling at the moment. "We did not order anything." His Spanish was rough and awkward, fitted badly around a thick foreign accent.

"I'm sure you will both enjoy what I have." The intruder nudged the basket an inch closer.

The rest of the cantina was quiet; a few clusters of men bent close for discreet conversation over tall glasses of beer. There was no laughter in the place. No music. No one who entered did so with a happy laugh or with a boisterous call to a friend. There was a large fire in the hearth because the temperature had dipped during the cloudy day, and stiff winds blew inland across the Falkland Current.

The second man at the table was a young bull with blond hair and huge shoulders. "Does the landlord know that you're peddling your crap here?"

"Sir," said the old man, "I am a baker, and the landlord is a regular customer."

The black-haired man leaned a couple of inches toward the basket, then cut a look at his friend. "Did you smell this?"

"Smell what?" said the younger man, whose chair was set on the far corner of the small table.

Encouraged by the expression on the black-haired man's face, the baker said, "I have something here that you might enjoy, my friends."

"I doubt that."

"May I show you?" asked the baker, his smile obsequious but earnest. "I can guarantee you both that this is something you cannot get here. Not even in the houses of your friends who understand such things. Alas, no. The recipe is an old family one and is, perhaps, too regional and specific to be popular among the locals here. It is something that you probably thought you would never smell or see again, and certainly never taste again. Not truly. Not, if I may be allowed a liberty, *authentically*."

"Oh, very well," grumbled the blond. "Show us and be done with it."

The intruder bowed, plucked a corner of the cloth and folded it back with great ceremony to reveal small loaves of dark bread. Steam rose in soft curls, and a delicious aroma filled the air. The black-haired man smiled and let out a long, soft breath. His friend's eyes widened.

"Schwarzbrot ...?"

"Indeed, my friends," said the baker. "A recipe handed down from my grandmother's grandmother. The very best wheat and rye blended with caraway, anise, fennel, just a little coriander. And, of course, a touch here and there of allspice, fenugreek, sweet trefoil, celery seeds, and cardamom. I grind each of the spices by hand and then grind them again together and mix them into the dough. Everything is done the old way. Everything is done right, because such things deserve precision, do you agree?"

The men nodded absently, their eyes fixed on the hot bread. They both swallowed over and over again as their mouths watered.

"Baking is a tradition as worthy as any other," continued the baker. "The recipes for making *schwarzbrot* are jealously guarded by each family, withheld even from next door neighbors. Go on, my friends, try them."

The men exchanged a brief look and a briefer shared nod, and then they each took a loaf of the black bread. They sniffed and then took tentative bites. The baker watched their eyes, saw the eyelids flutter, and he smiled as the men chewed, swallowed and took larger bites.

"Mein Gott," murmured the black-haired man. "This is heaven. This is pure heaven. I'd never thought ..." He stopped, shook his head and took a third bite, leaving only a nub pinched between his thumb and forefinger.

The young blond man ate the entire loaf without comment and then eyed the basket. "How much for another?"

The baker smiled and placed it on the table. "Consider these a gift. It is a great pleasure to know that you not only enjoy them, but also truly *appreciate* them. So, please, enjoy a small taste of the old country."

Each man snatched seconds from the basket and bit into them. After a few moments of undisguised gustatory lust, the black-haired man looked up, his jaw muscles bunching and flexing as he chewed. "Which *old* country would that be, exactly? We are Argentinians. Santa Cruz is our home. We are from here."

"Of course," agreed the baker, returning the nod and adding a small wink. "We are all clearly Argentinian."

"Yes," said the black-haired man.

"Yes," said the blond. "I have never been out of the country. Born and bred here."

"Of course," agreed the baker.

They all smiled at one another. When the two younger men finished their loaves and explored the basket they found it empty, and their faces fell.

"I have more in my shop," the baker said quickly. "It's near here, on a side street off the square. Becker's Breads and Baked Goods."

"And you are Becker?"

"Josef Becker, sir," said the old man. "And you gentlemen are ...?"

The black-haired man said, "I'm Roberto Santiago and this is Eduardo Gomez."

Becker looked amused. "Santiago and Gomez? Of course."

Santiago eyed him. "Your name is not Spanish. Are you *Deutschargentinier*?"

"No," said Becker, "I am not a descendant of immigrants, as I imagine you are."

"Sure," said Gomez without conviction. "That is what we are."

"I was born in Hallstatt in Austria," said Becker. "Perhaps you have heard of it? Such a lovely place in the Salzkammergut, located on the southwestern shore of a lake. Those of us from Hallstatt, there is great pride in who we are, and what we are, and what we have endured."

"I have never heard of Hallstatt," said Gomez in a guarded tone.

"Have you not?" said Becker, looking sad.

"We are Argentinian," insisted Santiago. His eyes were hooded.

"Of course, of course," Becker soothed. "As are so many here in Santa Cruz, and in Buenos Aires, Misiones, La Pampas, Chubut, and a hundred small villages."

The men said nothing.

"We are all Argentinians because it is such a lovely place," continued Becker amiably. "A lovely and very safe place to be. The brisk and breezy nights, the tequila ..."

Santiago and Gomez sat very tense, very attentive, and their eyes were hard as fists. Becker gave them an understanding nod and the slightest suggestion of a wink. "It is a very large world, my friends, and even here in lovely Santa Cruz we can all sometimes feel very far from home. I know I do."

"You talk a lot," said Santiago.

"I'm old," said the baker with a shrug, "and old men like to talk. It reminds us that we are still alive. And ... well, the world has emptied itself of so many people that I knew that I often have only my own voice for company. So, yes, I talk. I rattle and prattle and I can see that I try your patience. Why, after all, would men as young and healthy as you, my friends, care to waste time listening to the babblings of an old man?"

"That question has occurred to me," said Santiago. "I am utterly fascinated to know why you feel that it is appropriate to interrupt a private conversation."

Gomez turned away to hide a smile.

The little baker was unperturbed. "I take such a liberty, my friends, because tonight is the second day of *Allerseelenwoche.* — All Soul's Week. Do you know of it?"

Gomez began to answer, but Santiago stopped him with a light touch on the arm.

"No," said Santiago, "we don't know what that is."

"Of course not. You have never been to Austria, as you have said. Let me explain. In Austria we do not celebrate Halloween, as the Americans and Irish do. For us this holiday is about reflection, about praying for those who have been taken from us, for making offerings to the spirits of our beloved dead. And we all lost so many people during the war."

Gomez kept his gaze locked on Becker, but Santiago looked down at his hands.

"The war is over," said Santiago softly.

"Is a war ever truly over if people are alive who remember it?" asked Becker mildly. "Can it be over if people are alive who remember the world before the war, and can count the number of people and things they have lost? Family members, cities, friends, dreams, promises ..."

The corner of the room was very quiet now.

Becker pulled out a chair and perched on it. "Allerseelenwoche was never a time of celebration, and now that the war has run its course we are left to tally the costs. We honor our dead not only by remembering them, but recalling what they stood for, and what they died for."

Santiago nodded and lifted his beer glass. He stared moodily into it, nodded again, took a long swallow, and placed it very carefully back on the table.

"Why do you talk of such things?" asked Santiago.

"Because it was always a custom of my family to celebrate Allerseelenwoche. My family was very ... ah ... dedicated to custom and tradition."

"'Was'?" asked Gomez.

"Was."

The two younger men looked at him, and although they did not ask specific questions, Becker nodded as if they had. Answering in the way that many of the pale-skinned residents of Santa Cruz did these last few years.

Becker touched the curved handle of his wicker basket. "We love our dead. Their having died does not make them less a part of our family. We can see the holes carved in the world in the shapes of each one of them. You understand this?"

The men nodded.

"We believe that during Allerseelenwoche," said Becker, "the spirits of our loved ones come and sit beside us at our lonely tables. We know that the dead suffer. We know that they linger in the world between worlds because the church tells us that all souls are in purgatory awaiting judgment. The priests tell us that only the perfectly pure are then raised to heaven but the rest must wait for their sins to be judged and their fates decided. It is what all souls must endure, for—after all—was anyone ever without sin? Jesus, perhaps, but who else? No one, according to the priests with whom I have spoken."

The men offered no comment, nor did they chase Becker away.

"The priests say that when Judgment Day comes then the souls of all the dead will be either raised up or cast into the Pit. Until then, they linger and linger. So it is up to those of us here on Earth to care for them, to remember them, to pray that their sins be forgiven, to offer what comforts we can. That is why we have this holiday. It reminds us to remember them. And to remember that they *remember* being alive. They may be dead and may have no earthly bodies that we can see except when the veils between worlds are thin—as they are this week—but they *feel* everything. Hunger and thirst, joy and despair, ecstasy and pain. And fear. Yes, my friends, they know fear very well. During Allerseelenwoche we leave bread to ease their hunger and water to soothe their thirst. We light lanterns so that the dead know they are welcome in our homes and, for a week at least, not be so alone, and so that they will not be afraid of the dark. These are good customs because they remind us of our own compassion, and of our better qualities, mercy among the rest. And that is why we have traditions, is it not? So that we remember what is *important* to remember? That is why we go to church so often during that week. We go to pray for the dead, and to beg God to call them home to heaven."

Santiago began to speak, but Gomez touched his arm. The young blond man gave Becker a fierce and ugly look. "Perhaps it is in your best interest to go away now."

"No, please, a moment more," begged the baker. "I did not come here to tell ghost stories and spoil your evening."

"Yet that is what you are doing," growled Gomez.

"I said all of that in order to say this," Becker said brightly. "I opened my little bakery here in order to preserve more than the recipes of my family. I opened it to celebrate who I am and where I come from. After all, I may live the life of an exile here but I am Austrian, now and forever. Surely you can appreciate that."

Gomez and Santiago nodded but said nothing.

"So," said Becker, "in the unlikely event that you might be interested in tasting more of my family's old world recipes, why not come by my shop tomorrow night? I would be happy to make you a traditional dinner with all of the delicacies for which my family was famous."

Gomez cocked his head to one side. "Like what? I mean ... I have, ah, *heard* of Austrian cuisine because of the number of Austrian and German expats living here, but have never tasted any."

"How sad," said Becker, then he brightened. "Well, my friends, I would be delighted, indeed honored, to introduce you to *tafelspitz*, which is lean beef broiled in broth and served with a sauce of apples, horseradish, and chives. Or, if you prefer, there is *gulasch*, which is a lovely hotpot that should best be eaten with *semmelknödel*—a dumpling for which my mother was rightly proud."

Santiago closed his eyes for a moment and breathed slowly through his nose.

"You can have *selchleisch* with sauerkraut and dumplings. And for after," said the baker, "you can try my aunt's recipe for *marillenknödel*, a pastry filled with apricots and mirabelle plums. The dumplings are boiled in lightly salted water, then covered in crisply fried breadcrumbs and powdered sugar, and baked in a potato dough."

"*Gott im himmel,*" murmured Gomez, and there was no trace

of Spanish in his accent. Becker did not comment on that. "You're killing me."

"Will you come?" asked Becker eagerly. "Will you allow me the great honor of making such a meal for men who, I have no doubt at all, will truly appreciate it. Here, in this town, I am a simple baker. Most of my day is spent making local goods. *Aljafor* and *chocotorta* and—God help me—*tortas fritas*. That's what my customers want, and because I need to make a living it is what I sell. But it is not who I am. It is not the food that I understand, and I cannot sell Austrian goods to the public. Not even here. Not openly, anyway. That would present so many problems and, unlike you gentlemen, I have no papers that say I was born here. Everyone knows that I am Austrian. To hostile and suspicious eyes I am German, and these days everyone hates the Germans."

Gomez turned and spat onto the floor.

"Argentina is a haven in name but not in fact," said Becker, lowering his voice. "People are *looking* for Germans. For certain kinds of Germans. No, you do not need to say anything because I know you are men of the world and understand such things. My point—and I admit that like all old men I wander around before I approach the kernel of what I mean to say—is that I need to be a *good* German if I am to live safely. That means letting go of so much of my culture. To abandon it and forswear it and pretend that it never mattered to me at all."

Becker paused and dabbed at the corner of his eye, studied the moisture on his fingertips and wiped it off on his shirt.

"I have had to become a stranger to the man I used to be," he said. "So much so that my family, were any of them still alive, would not know me were it not for the things I prepare in secret. For me. For them. That is why I ask you fine gentlemen to come to my shop after it is closed and share a feast in celebration of Allerseelenwoche ... to remember all of those who we loved and who died in the war. Will you grant me that kindness? Will you tolerate further the company of a talkative and sad old man who wants nothing more than to offer that taste of home. Of ... my homeland? Can I entice you? Will you taste what I so eagerly want to prepare for you?"

It took a long time for either of the men across the table from him to answer. Eventually, though, Santiago croaked a single word.

"Yes."

—2—

El Chaltén Village
Santa Cruz, Argentina
November 1, 1948

The knock was discreet, and Josef Becker answered it at once.

He opened the door, stepped past the two tall men and looked quickly up and down the crooked street. There were no streetlights, but cold moonlight painted the cobblestones in shades of silver and blue. A dog barked off in the distance and a toucan—very far from his jungle home—sat on the eave of the shuttered jeweler's across the street. There were no people at all, though the chilly breeze brought the sound of laughter from some distant party in a house around the corner.

"Come in, my friends," said Becker and he patted the backs of the men as they passed through into the bakery. When they were all inside, Becker pulled the door shut and locked it with a double-turn of a heavy key.

The shop was small, but the space had been used with care. There was a long glass-fronted counter in which were set square platters of baked goods. There were small cakes dusted with powdered sugar, round chocolate double-wafer cakes, cornstarch biscuits covered with coconut, glistening cubes of quince, vanilla sponge-cake ladyfingers, and many other delicacies particular to Argentina. There were French and Italian cakes and sweets, too, and even some pastries of American invention.

But what dominated the store were the breads. So many of

them. *Aajdov Kruh*, the Slovenia bread made from buckwheat flour and potato, dark Russian sourdough and crisp Japanese *melonpan* made from dough covered in a thin layer of crispy cookie dough, *michetta* from Italy and *taftan* from Iran, and dozens of others from dozens of places, including a whole tray of sugary *pan de muerto*. And, of course, central to all, were the breads from Austria and Germany. The light *semmeln oder brötchen* wheat rolls, whole grain rye *vollkornbrot. dreikornbrot* rich in wheat, oats and rye, five-seed *fünfkornbrot*. Even thick, dark, salted *brezels*.

The two guests stood staring through the glass, eyes wide, lips parted with obvious hunger.

"Gentlemen," said Becker, beaming with pride, "I can say without fear of contradiction that there is no finer selection of baked goods to be found anywhere in Santa Cruz."

"Anywhere in this entire godforsaken country," breathed Santiago.

Becker chuckled. "Pride is a sin, they say, but if so I will accept whatever punishment is awarded me for I am very proud."

Gomez kept licking his lips like a child. "May I ...?" he began, then stopped and gave Becker a quick look. "Are these for sale?"

"Nothing here is for sale," said Becker, then laughed aloud at the crestfallen looks on his guests' faces. "I am only teasing! Nothing is for sale to you because you are my guests. Which means that everything you see is yours for the asking. Come, come, we will eat dinner and then have some wine and conversation, and when you go, I will overburden you with bags and bundles of goodies to take back to your home. Come, gentlemen, come into the parlor and let us sit."

Still chuckling, Becker passed between the folds of a drapery hung over a doorway and waved for the two men to follow. They did, and within minutes they were all seated at a large wooden table set near a crackling fire. A fine linen cloth had been placed upon the table and places set at each chair. Santiago frowned across the table at three additional settings.

"Are we expecting others?" he asked.

"Hmm?" murmured Becker, then he smiled. "Ah, remember that this is Allerseelenwoche, my friend. I have set an extra place for each of us so that we can offer food and drink for those we have lost and perhaps bring them here to share our feast and be warmed by the fire and by our company."

Santiago looked uneasy, but he nodded. Gomez briefly looked down at his empty place.

"Would you gentlemen prefer a local red wine or something from *my* country?" Becker leaned on the word "my" and it brought the two men to attention.

"What do you have?" asked Gomez.

"Yes," agreed Santiago, "if it is from your country, I would be interested to take a taste and judge it."

"How delightful," said Becker, springing up and fetching a heavy bottle from a large terracotta wine cooler. He uncorked it and filled all six of the glasses on the table, then uncorked a second and third bottle and set them close by. "This is a *Riesling* from the Wachau region of Austria. You will notice, perhaps, just a hint of white pepper."

"This will do very well," said the black-haired man after a sip.

"What shall we toast?" asked the baker. "Or, may I suggest something?"

"It's your house," said Santiago, "the first toast is yours."

"Most gracious," said Becker. He raised his glass and said, "*Genieße das Leben ständig! Du bist länger tot als lebendig!*"

Always enjoy life! You are dead longer than you are alive!

His guests paused for a moment, then they nodded and drank.

After the glasses had been refilled, Becker vanished into the kitchen and returned with the first of what proved to be many courses. Not only had he prepared the delicacies with which he had tempted the men to join him, but he had gone farther and set dish after dish on the table. More than any three men could hope to eat. More than a dozen men could manage. With each course, the baker served his guests first and then placed small portions of every dish on the plates set aside in honor of the dead. Soon those untouched plates were heaped high with slices of rare meats, with strong cheeses and steaming vegetables; and bowls of soups and stews were set in place beside the plates.

Gomez picked up his fork and then frowned. "Excuse me, but I do not have a knife."

"Do you not know the custom?" asked Becker, raising his eyebrows. "On Allerseelenwoche many people hide their knives so as not to tempt evil spirits to acts of mischief. Granted that is usually only done on Halloween night, but in my town we hid the knives all week." He sighed. "Strange, though, how mischief found us regardless."

After only a brief pause the guests attacked their food and soon thoughts of knives were gone. As promised, the slices of roast beef and boiled pork and baked chicken were so rich and tender that their forks easily cut through the flesh. The men devoured the food, often in long periods where there was no conversation and the only sounds were that of chewing and crunching, swallowing, and sipping; of forks sliding along plates and spoons scraping along the rims of soup bowls. And throughout there were gasps of delight and sighs of contentment. Bottles of wine were opened and emptied. The faces of the three men grew rosy and flushed, and their eyes took on a glaze as bright as that on the cooked hams.

It was only when the feast began slowing that conversation began. At first it was questions about ingredients and origins of the recipes. Becker told them about how one aunt would prepare a dish and how a cousin would do it differently but equally well. He spoke of town fairs and Christmas feasts and wedding banquets and funeral luncheons, and the menus appropriate to each. Then, as he refilled their glasses once more, he sat back and said more wistfully, "But that is all what was, not what is, my friends. We speak of ghosts, do we not?"

"Ghosts?" inquired Gomez, his mouth filled with a large bite of a schnitzel that was so spicy that sweat beaded his upper lip and forehead and glistened along his hairline.

"Surely," said Becker. "The ghosts of everyone who created the recipes on which we dine. None of them are my own, of course, but were crafted by members of my family. Sisters and aunts, cousins and nephews, and my dear mother and grandmother. Even my father was a veritable demon in the kitchen. The *schweineschnitzel* you seem to be enjoying so much was his personal recipe. It was as if he stood beside me in spirit as I prepared it, as if the ghosts of everyone I loved were with me in my kitchen, guiding my hand. I often feel them with me, though perhaps because of the holiday I feel them more acutely this week. And I have no doubt they each added a touch of this and that when I was not looking."

Gomez swallowed and picked up his glass, sloshing a little of the wine as he did so. "Then let us drink."

"*Ja,*" said Santiago, "*Zum wohl!*"

"*Zum wohl,*" growled Gomez, and Becker echoed it as they all raised their glasses in the direction of the empty side of the table and downed the wine to the last drop. Becker filled the glasses again.

Santiago stared at the plates of uneaten food across from him, and he slouched back in his chair, chin down on his chest. "What happened to them?" he asked. "To your family, I mean."

The baker sighed. "They died during the war."

Gomez frowned. "In Hallstatt? I did not know that city had been bombed."

"Oh, none of them died from bombs," said Becker as he pushed back his chair and stood. "Let me clear away."

Gomez looked down in dismay at his plate and seemed surprised that the heap of food was gone.

"Time for something very special," said Becker as he stacked the plates and set them on a sideboard. "I hope you saved room. A little room, at least."

Santiago discretely unbuttoned the top of his trousers to ease the pressure on his swollen stomach, while Gomez looked eager to start the whole feast again. Becker vanished into the kitchen and returned a few moments later bearing a small silver tray on which was a pyramid of small cakes. They were each round and about a quarter inch thick. Pale, with a hint of gold baked in around the edges, and each was marked by the indentation of a cross cut across their surface. Steam rose from them as if they had come straight from the oven, and the smell was wonderful, enchanting, hinting at nutmeg and cinnamon and allspice.

"Every village has its own recipes for soul cakes or soul bread," said Becker as he placed the tray in the exact center of the table. "Some prefer to bake loaves of it, while others make cookies. My mother's recipe was for little cakes like these. Crisp at the edges but soft as butter in the middle, and light as a whisper on the tongue."

The two guests stared hungrily at the pile of cakes.

"I remember so many times helping my mother as she baked a hundred-weight of soul cakes to give to the poor children who came knocking at our door all through Allerseelenwoche. You see the crosses on each? That means they are alms, and are therefore righteous gifts given freely to any who ask. That was so like my mother—she would open the door at anyone's knock and welcome them inside. She could not bear the thought of turning someone away hungry, especially when we—as bakers and cooks —always had enough."

Becker placed his fingertips on his chest over his heart the way some people did when touching crosses, but he wore no jewelry of any kind.

"We were luckier than most for we never knew hunger. We knew *of* it, of course. We were all aware of the horrors of hunger, of want, of unbearable need. Of having no place and being unwelcome and having doors closed to us. So when my ancestors settled in Hallstatt and opened the doors of our bakery, how could any of us turn away someone who came to us asking for something to eat? A crust of bread is nothing to those who have so much, but it can feed a starving child or keep a man alive to work another day in hopes of providing for those he loves. These cakes? They might be all that a starving child might eat that day. How could anyone with a beating heart turn a deaf ear to the knock, however weak and tentative?"

"Good for you," said Santiago.

"No, not good for me," said Becker. "Good for my mother. She was the kind heart of my family. She was like her mother, and her sisters were like her. Kind and generous, in part because it was their nature and in part because they remembered hunger and want."

"These cakes smell delicious," said Gomez.

"Do they? My mother would be pleased that you think so."

"Then let us each have one in honor of her," suggested the big blond man.

"Of course, my friend, of course." Becker leaned across the table and picked up a cake, careful not to crumble the delicate crust between his fingers. He set it on a small plate and placed it in front of Gomez. He repeated the action for Santiago. Then he took one for himself and sat down.

Santiago nodded toward the empty side of the table. "Aren't you forgetting something?"

Becker glanced at the untouched plates of food. "Ah. So courteous. But, no, my friend, soul cakes are for the living."

"Oh," said Santiago, clearly not following.

"One more thing," said Becker as the other men began reaching for their cakes. "A last bit of seasonal ceremony, if you'll indulge me. I like to follow the traditions in form as well as spirit." He crossed to a cabinet and removed a small lantern, checked that it was filled with oil, and brought it to the table. "Do either of you have a match?"

Gomez produced a Lucifer match from a pocket, scraped it alight on the heel of his shoe, and leaned the flame across to Becker. The old man's eyes twinkled with blue fire as he guided Gomez's hand toward the lantern wick. The flame seemed to leap from match to wick and at the same moment Gomez twitched with a deep shiver.

"What's wrong with you?" asked Santiago.

"I ... nothing," said Gomez. "Just a chill. It's gone now."

Becker adjusted the flame and placed the lantern on the table close to the untouched plates of food. "So the souls of the dead can find their way here to join our feast."

"Forgive me, Herr Becker," said Santiago, his faux Spanish fading in favor of cosmopolitan German, "but isn't that a bit ghoulish?"

"Do you think so?" asked Becker, looking surprised. "How perceptive."

"What?"

"Nothing. A joke." Becker refilled their glasses with the last of the final bottle of Riesling. He placed his palms flat on the table and let out a long, satisfied sigh. "Now, my friends," he said, also speaking German. "Before we partake, let me tell you something of these cakes. There is magic in baking. A special sorcery that can transport us to other places and times with a single bite. That is why I invited you both here."

"What do you mean?" asked Santiago. "Why us?"

"Because you are no more Argentinian than I am, nor even *Deutschargentinier*. You are sons of Germany, as I am a son of Austria. No, please don't deny it. We are all friends here. We are safe and alone here, and we may be who we are. There are no spies here. No Americans or British. No hunters from the new state of Israel. We have nothing to fear from each other and that allows us to take a breath, to be real, to be ourselves."

"And what if we are German?" asked Santiago, his tone dangerous, his eyes cold.

"Then I am among countrymen," said Becker. "I invited you here to share my holiday feast because I knew—I *knew*—that you would appreciate it as only sons of the Fatherland could."

"How do we know you are not a Jew?" demanded Gomez.

"Because I have eaten pork with you," said Becker. "And beef with cream sauce. Because I say that I am not a Jew. Because if I was a Jew there would have been a dozen armed men waiting for you in here and not a feast and good wine and hospitality."

"He's not a Jew," said Santiago.

"No," agreed Becker. "I am a baker from Austria, and my family has lived in Hallstatt for generations." He touched the surface of the soul cake on his plate. "I asked you here to share in this special and sacred celebration. To break bread with me, to feast with me and the spirits of my family because I am alone and lonely, and I knew you would understand. Neither of you have families here, either."

"No," said Santiago. "Mine were killed in Dresden."

"*Um Gottes willen*," blurted Gomez, but Santiago shook his head.

"Enough, Erhardt," said Santiago. "He is right. We are alone here. We are safe here, if nowhere else."

"I ... I ..."

Santiago turned to Becker. "My name is Heinrich Gebbler, and this is Erhardt Böhm, and we are happy to share this table with you. God! How good it is to be myself, even for a moment."

Gomez—Böhm—cursed and slapped the table hard enough to make the wine in all of the glasses dance. "Then be damned to all of us. Yes, yes, I am Erhardt Böhm. There, I said it. Are we all happy now?"

"Very happy," said Becker. "And I thank you for your trust. Believe me when I say that it is a secret that I will take with me to the grave."

"You had better," warned Gebbler. "We are taking a great risk."

"Now can we eat these damned cakes?" asked Böhm.

"Wait, wait," pleaded Becker. "Everything must be done exactly right, as I have said. To eat a soul cake is a very serious matter, especially in such a moment as this. After all, we have each seen our world burn. We have each lost so many of those we loved during the war, have we not?"

The two Germans nodded.

"Then should we not honor the dead by inviting them to join us at this table?"

"Sure, sure," said Böhm, "invite Hitler and Himmler and Göring for all that I care. The dead are dead, and I am hungry."

"The dead are dead, but they are hungry, too, Herr Böhm," said Becker. "I have lit the lantern so that they can find us, and I have prepared food for them, because the dead are always hungry. Always."

"You're being ghoulish again," muttered Gebbler.

"Perhaps." He gestured to the cakes. "Did you know that the moment grain is milled it's possessed of its greatest life-giving potential? The dough for the soul cakes must be made when the flour is fresh and alive. It must contain life in order to be worth consuming."

"I don't follow," said Böhm.

"You will," said Becker. "Now, please, try the soul cakes."

The Germans shared another glance, then shrugged, and picked up the cakes. They each took small tentative bites.

"This is delicious," said Böhm.

"I've never tasted anything so good," said Gebbler.

"How delightful!" cried Becker, clapping his hands. "Have another. Have as many as you like."

Böhm pulled the plate over and pawed four more of the cakes onto his plate, then offered what was left to Gebbler. Despite the heavy meal, they ate with relish, their faces dusted with sugar and crumbs falling onto their shirts. While they ate, Becker spoke quietly of the holiday.

"During Allerseelenwoche," he said, "the souls are released from their graves, and they wander the Earth as hungry ghosts. Lanterns like this invite them to dine with us in the hopes that they can feast well enough to ease their hunger and gain a measure of peace."

"So you keep saying," said Gebbler, pausing with a fresh cake an inch from his mouth, "but quite frankly, Herr Becker, I am not a very good Catholic. I never was, and less so since the world fell apart. Everything that I cared about burned down. The damned Russians and British and Americans have taken it all from us. Our hopes and dreams and every single thing of worth that we owned. *We* are the ghosts haunting a world in which we no longer truly live."

Becker nodded. "To be equally frank, Herr Gebbler, I am not a very good Catholic, either."

"But not a Jew?" asked Böhm, his cheeks bulging with soul cake.

"Not a Jew."

"Then if you're not Catholic," asked Gebbler, "why do you go to such lengths to follow these rituals?"

"Because I am a *kind* of Catholic," said Becker. "My people tend to adopt the customs of wherever we live. It is how we survived all these years. Well ... how we once survived. Clearly we did not blend in well enough. They still came for us and rounded us up and took us away. It's not really something that can be blamed on the war, though. My sisters and brothers, uncles and aunts, cousins ... they all died far from the battlefields. I doubt they ever heard a shot fired or saw a bomb fall."

The two Germans suddenly paused in the act of chewing and looked at him with sudden suspicion.

"What does that mean?" demanded Gebbler quietly.

"It means that I am not a Jew or a homosexual or a Pole or a Slav or any of those groups, nor were any of my family, and yet they all died in the camps. In Bergen-Belsen and Sachsenhausen, in Buchenwald and Dachau, in Mauthausen and Ravensbrück." He leaned slightly forward and smiled a sad little smile. "I am Romani."

"A damn gypsy!" Böhm spat the half-chewed cake onto the table. "This is a trap. He's poisoned us."

Both Germans shot to their feet.

"No, no, no," said Becker, holding his hands palms out. "I would never pollute my family's recipes with poison. There is nothing hidden in the meat or bread or anything else. Did I not eat it along with you?"

"You didn't eat the cakes," snarled Gebbler. He took a threatening step toward the baker.

"No, but not because they are poisoned, which they are not," protested Becker, still seated, "but because they were made specially for you. For tonight. They were made in celebration of Allerseelenwoche."

"This is a trap, Heinrich," said Böhm. "Let's see how much of him we need to cut off before he tells us who else knows about us and—"

"No," said Becker. "You will not need to do that, Oberscharführer Böhm. Oh, don't look so surprised. Do you think I picked you at random? I came here to this town to find you and Obersturmführer Gebbler. I came looking for both of you because you were at Mauthausen, where my mother and grandmother were taken. You took the gold from their teeth and cut the rings from their fingers. You worked for the commandant, Franz Ziereis, and under his direction you worked them and starved them until they dropped, and you buried what was left of them in mass graves. My brothers and sisters too. And my father. All of them. Starved to death and buried like trash."

Becker's voice was soft, quiet, unhurried.

"So they died," sneered Gebbler. "So what? You Romani are trash and you have always been trash, and the world is better off without you. You're worse even than the Jews. At least they never renounced their faith even when we held their children above the flames of a bonfire. You gypsies would forswear anyone and anything to try and survive. Your mother probably offered to spread her legs for us and maybe did."

"Maybe she did," said Becker. "Maybe she begged and maybe she said that she renounced her faith, her culture, her people. What else could she say? Why would she—or any of them—not try anything in order to survive? What is a proclamation of renouncement except words? How is that more ignoble than slaughtering innocent people by the hundreds of thousands? By the millions?"

His tone never rose beyond that of mild conversation, and he wore a constant smile of contentment.

"We'll see what you are willing to promise," said Böhm, reaching for a serving fork with two long tines.

"No," said Becker. "We won't. Or, rather, it won't matter. Nothing you can do to me will matter at all. Not now. Not anymore."

Böhm and Gebbler glanced toward the windows and doors.

"Don't worry," said Becker, "no authorities are coming. Argentina doesn't care who or what you are or what you did. That's why so many Nazis came here. It was a safe haven. However, 'safety' is a funny word. It is conditional on assumptions about how the world works."

"You're babbling," said Gebbler.

"No," said Becker, "I'm explaining. The assumption is that you are politically safe, and you are. The assumption is that you cannot be extradited, and you can't be. The assumption is that no earthly power is likely to harm you here, and that is almost certainly correct."

"Then what the hell is this all about?" demanded Gebbler.

"The fault in the assumption," said Becker, "is that I have any interest in relying on earthly powers to punish you. I don't. I have no faith at all in governments and agencies and courts."

Böhm pointed the fork at him. "Talk plain or—"

"Shhh," said Becker. "Stop for a moment and think about where you are and what I have said. Think about the time of year."

The Germans stared at him.

"My lantern is not very bright," said Becker, "but it is bright enough. Oh yes, it is bright enough for the spirits of my beloved dead to follow, even though their bones are buried on the other side of the world. What is distance to ghosts?"

The lantern flame suddenly danced as if whipped by a breeze, but all the windows were closed. It threw strange shadows on the wall. Becker smiled.

"I have been a good host," said the baker. "I have prepared the very best dishes from the recipes of my family, and you have fed well. Very well. Some celebrations require fatted calves, but I think fatted pigs will do nicely."

Böhm shivered again, and now Gebbler did too. Their breaths plumed the air of the dining room. The flickering shadows on the wall looked strangely like silhouettes of people. Many people. Old and young, short and tall, male and female. Everywhere, all around the table.

"The dead are always hungry," said Becker. "And you will be, for them, a small taste of the old country."

He sat back, still smiling, and watched as the shadows fell upon the two German officers. It was a quiet street, and the windows were shuttered, and if anyone heard the screams they did not come to investigate.

THE QUEEN OF THORNS
A POEM

Who, except the Gods, can live time through forever without
pain?
Agamemnon
Aeschylus

She is called the Queen of Thorns.
She is down there, somewhere.
Down there beneath a million tons of weight and worry,
buried deep in the dark, moist folds of unlighted rock, of ruin,
clasped in the arms of dirt and
discarded bones.

She hasn't been alive for a thousand years, but she has never died.

In the buried darkness, the Queen of Thorns does not sleep.

She is incapable of sleep,
incapable of dreaming.
Incapable even of nightmares, madness.
Hers is a terrible and unflinching, unrelenting clarity of mind.

Hers is a hunger beyond the aching of a thousand bloated
children,
a need more searing than any savior trying to pass on a poisoned
cup.
Impaled, defiled, stripped to ragged bones and forgotten
even by the holy butcher priests
who were sworn to watch for her return.

She is part of the soil.
Blind white grubs are her jewels.
Chips of cracked coal are her eyes.
Her fingers are the roots of petrified trees in which no sane birds
will sit.
Her hair is the delicate webs of spiders' silk and velvety fungus,
woven into the fabric of the Earth.

She is the Queen of Thorns.
She is hunger.

You have never known hunger.
Not like hers.
You have hungered for sustenance of the body,
that transient satisfaction of caloric heat.
You've hungered with your hands for the weight of gold,
or the crispness of green paper.
You've hungered for love that would inevitably die anyway.

You've hungered for acceptance and approval from drunken
fathers
and cowed, humiliated mothers.
You've hungered for the sweating and pumping and spurtings of
simple lust.
You've hungered like the human animal has always hungered.
The hunger of the beast.

But hers is the hunger of the soul.
Deep hunger.

Hers is the hunger that only the Queen of Thorns
can ever understand.

Only her and her attendant ghosts
So willing, so hungry for her grace.

BEING EMILY-CLAIRE

—1—

Emily-Claire had monsters in her closet.

But then, who didn't? That's what closets were for. Well, mostly. The closet also had a lot of clothes in darker earth tones, grays and black. She wasn't Goth like a lot of the girls at school, or didn't think she was. Emily-Claire was just herself, and she wasn't interested in relating to the other kids. Those colors let her fade into the background. Where it was quiet. Where it was safe.

There were shoes in there—old sneakers she wore in gym, heels her sister said she could save for prom. As if. And she had some good walking shoes because Emily loved to walk. Hiking shoes, ditto. Lots of old toys in there as well; stuff people gave her when she was little. Back when they thought she was the kind of kid who played with those sorts of toys. Her aunts and grandparents stopped giving her Barbies and Baby So Sweet when they saw what happened to them.

There were shouts after that, Mom crying, Dad on the phone to therapists. Whispers behind closed doors. Tests and scans. Emily-Claire told a pack of lies, and after a while they stopped looking at her like she was a new species of toad. Not that being a toad would be a bad thing, but since people like her parents didn't like toads, the looks weren't happy ones.

She didn't tell them that there were monsters in her closet. Even when she was little—six or seven—Emily-Claire was too smart to make that mistake. Young did not mean stupid. Not for her.

So, yes, she had monsters in her closet. Once in a while one of the monsters would hide in the curbside mailbox, waiting for her to reach in and get the mail. That was nice.

She was so happy they were there. Without the monsters, where would she be? It was a question that weighed on her. Because, truly, without them, where *would* she be?

The real problem was that there was a monster in her school locker, too, and that thing wasn't one of *hers*.

—2—

Emily was thirteen, an age she wished she could be for the rest of her life. Thirteen was, after all, her lucky number. Fourteen was looming, though. Fourteen would be dull. Fifteen too. Maybe sixteen would be okay, though, because she planned on getting her license at the earliest possible moment. Old Mrs. Willow three doors down said that she would sell her car to Emily-Claire for a dollar and a crow feather when she got her license. Emily-Claire had tried to give her a crow feather on account, but the crone asked for the dollar instead.

"Crow feathers are special things, little witch," said Mrs. Willow. It didn't matter that Emily-Claire was not a witch. The old lady called her that because *she* was a witch. Not a pointy-hat kind, but a real one. Positive magic, crystal energy and wisdom that ran miles deep. *Wicce* was an Old English word for sorceress. A word people always got wrong, using *Wicca* instead, but that was the masculine. On the other hand, the Middle English word *wicche* could be used for men or women. But no one ever used it.

In either case, "witch" was just—according to the old lady—a "term of convenience."

"What's that mean?" Emily-Claire had asked. She was nine at the time.

"It means that there isn't any word in English that really fits," said Mrs. Willow. "There's no word in any language you could fit into your mouth that suits who you are. Or what you are."

Even at nine, Emily-Claire thought she understood that. Even so, she didn't call herself "witch." Instead, she preferred another of the old lady's favorite words.

A *sensitive.*

Yes. That fit her very well.

The car the old lady said would be hers was an ugly, lumpy AMC Gremlin that hadn't been pretty when it rolled off the assembly line in 1978. Some maniac had painted it a lurid shade of dark orange that was nearly, but not quite, pumpkin. Emily-Claire thought it was magnificent. Named for a monster, and as ugly as a gargoyle. Despite its age, Mrs. Willow whipped around town in it way too fast. A few times Mrs. Willow had taken Emily-Claire out to strange little stores in parts of the city she could not afterward find on a map.

There, on side alleys off of Boundary Street, Mrs. Willow and Emily-Claire had gone shopping in tiny, crowded stores filled with crystals and dried herbs and decks of hand-painted tarot cards, and cones of incense that smelled like memories rather than smells. The owners of the store were always old ladies like Mrs. Willow. Some were so ancient their faces looked like collections of wrinkles rather than skin. Except for the eyes. All of them had young eyes. Or ... maybe it was that their eyes were so old they looked young. Emily-Claire rather thought that was the right way to think about it.

She wanted to go find those stores on her own. In that car. She was certain the Gremlin would remember the way. She wanted to get to know those old ladies. Maybe grow up and grow old and be like them. That sounded wonderful to her, and she was sure her closet monsters would approve.

If, of course, she lived that long.

Right now, things weren't looking good.

Even the monsters had their doubts.

—3—

She first realized that there was a problem when something in her locker at school tried to eat her. Well, maybe not *eat*. But grab. It definitely took a grab. And it wasn't at all nice about it.

It was a Thursday, which was no surprise to Emily-Claire. Thursdays tended to suck on a regular basis.

It started in the girls' bathroom.

Emily-Claire was washing her hands after a really fun biology class, where they dissected pig fetuses. She'd told Mr. Boykin that she "forgot" to wear the blue protective gloves. Really, she liked to feel the skin and the organs. Even though the pig had never been born, it had a lot to tell her. Memories borrowed from her mother and from other pigs going way back. Like as far back as when there were no people and the pigs were being hunted by saber-toothed cats—*smilodon fatalis*.

She always learned so much from blood and skin. Nearly as much as she learned from rotting vegetables and decaying trees. They were fading away and wanted to tell her their stories; and she always wanted to listen. Though, it was listening with touch and smell and sometimes taste. It wasn't an ear thing, and, for some reason, smell didn't connect her to anything except what it was in the moment. If she smelled a chocolate chip cookie it told her it was a chocolate chip cookie. She had to actually break it up between her fingers before she learned about the fields and forests where the wheat and cocoa grew.

So, her hands were messy, and Mr. Boykin told her to clean up before her next class. Emily-Claire always washed slowly and thoroughly, because good soap broke the connection and let her come back to the now. Otherwise she'd be jumping at shadows thinking a saber-toothed cat was about to eat *her*.

The two other girls in there were at the far end of the line of sinks. Unlike her, they *were* Goth, though not the same kind of Goth as each other. Cynthia Harper—who demanded that people call her Syn—was a full-blown traditional Goth who only listened to Goth punk from the 1980s. She wore a lot of chains, fishnet stockings—often hidden under her jeans so she didn't get yelled at for dress code stuff—and had bats and skulls on every item of clothing or personal possession she owned. She was a ninth grader, which made her a senior at John Paul Jones Junior High. She began applying a fresh layer of black lipstick while talking to Naomi Pelembe, who was still a Baby Goth. Naomi hated that people called her that, but she was a seventh grader who still wore Disney princess T-shirts on the first day of school. Syn had very pale skin that Emily-Claire figured was mostly makeup. Naomi's parents had emigrated from Mozambique before she was born, and she had beautiful dark-brown skin.

Emily-Claire tried not to look like she was eavesdropping, but she caught a name that made her want to hear. Syn mentioned something about Jonah.

That really caught her attention. Emily-Claire had only recently started thinking seriously about boys. Well ... *boy*. Jonah Allyn was the best-looking human being she had ever seen. Tall and thin and pale, with icy-blue eyes that looked like he'd not only *seen* things but had spent enough time thinking about them to understand what he'd seen. That mattered a lot to her. When he looked at her, which he did more and more often this year, his eyes seemed to open up a little door in her head and peer inside. Like he not only saw her but wanted to see more. To know more. About her.

Her.

The fact that he had curly blond hair, great teeth, and smelled good had absolutely nothing to do with anything.

They had spoken a bunch of times. Always about books. He

was one of those guys who didn't read fiction. It was always nonfiction stuff. History and philosophy and geography. Jonah said he wanted to become an archaeologist, digging up the bones of history to understand why people did what they did. His blue eyes turned kind of misty gray when he talked about the past. It made her wonder if he was a sensitive too. Not with dead or dying things, but with old stone and wood and things people owned when they were alive. It was a question she'd been working up the nerve to ask, but hadn't gotten there yet.

"... said they saw him in social studies," Syn was saying, "but then he just like bugged out. Left his bookbag and even his cell phone."

Naomi gasped, horrified. "He left his *cell*?"

"I know, right?"

"So, where'd he go?"

"That's just it," insisted Syn, "nobody knows. That skanky old backpack he uses as a book bag was on the floor by his locker. Door was closed and locked and all. His cell was in his backpack. But he wasn't there, and nobody's seen him."

"And he didn't come back for his phone?" Naomi seemed unable to get past that part of the story.

Syn, who was always looking at Jonah—like *all* the time—seemed hooked on the strangeness of it all. She looked around to see if anyone was listening even though it was only the three of them in the bathroom. Syn looked right through Emily-Claire. People did that a lot. Maybe it meant that it didn't *matter* if someone like her heard, because Emily-Claire didn't have any friends. Probably, but she didn't care. School friends were never a priority for her. There were other conversations worth having. Mrs. Willow. The ladies on Boundary Street. The trees in the yard. Dead pigs and crushed beetles. Something was always dying in the world, and dying things always wanted to share. They were better conversationalists too. They spoke about old things, deep things. Important things.

In an exaggerated conspiratorial whisper Syn said, "I heard

that they called his mom, and she freaked out because Jonah never came home. And my friend Jilly who's an office aide told me that Jonah's folks are going to file some kind of missing persons thing."

"Why?" asked Naomi, clearly confused. "He's not missing. He just didn't come home."

"That's the same thing, genius," snapped Syn. "They think maybe he ran off."

"Ran off? That's crazy," cried Naomi. "Who would run away and not take their phone?"

Emily-Claire wanted to tell her to shut up about the phone, but she kept her mouth clamped shut and listened.

"I don't know," admitted Syn, "but it's really weird, don't you think? It's not like Jonah was a freak or anything. I don't think he was into anything. He's not a druggie or any of that."

"I still don't understand why he'd up and take off without his phone," muttered Naomi as the two girls walked past Emily-Claire like she was a hole in the air.

The door closed with a bang, and then it was completely silent in the bathroom. No water dripping, no sounds at all from the hall.

Emily-Claire frowned at herself in the mirror.

"What?" she asked her reflection. The short, pale, thin, wisp of a girl looking back at her had no answers.

—4—

Emily-Claire began asking questions.

As she saw it, the whole school was weird. There were very few of what might be called "normals." Only a handful of the cheerful kids in trendy clothes and this year's hair. The school dances were mostly played out with clumps of kids standing talking about other clumps while a DJ played EDM that like four people danced to. The whole school vibe was fringe, but not in a fun way. There were more varieties of Goth than anything else—

vampire Goth, metal Goth, fairy Goth, Candy Goth, J Goth ... A long list, but none of them mixed, except for a few Baby Goths, who were sucked into one tribe or another by the end of seventh grade. There were the retro grunge skater kids. There were the ghosts, the ones who drifted through the halls without saying a word to anyone. Like ... ever. There were some in the hip-hop crowd, but they usually had earphones in, even at dance parties. There were the school cliques—choir, chess, art, band, stage— who seemed to view anyone outside of their circle as beings from another world.

And then there was Emily-Claire, who was not a ghost or a Goth, and did not consider herself a freak or a geek. She was who she was, and liked being exactly that.

She talked to some people. She had no actual friends, but there were other kids she sometimes talked to. They, unlike she, were actively withdrawn. Either because of social anxiety issues or being told too many times that they were freaks, they'd washed up against the fringes of school society. Saying little, not even to one another. Pale or dark, skinny or fat, pretty or plain. It didn't matter. They were different in all the ways that mattered to kids like Syn and Naomi.

The people who she knew would talk to her didn't have a lot to tell her. The story spread that Jonah was missing. There were rumors that he'd been abducted, though why and by whom changed from one story to the next. Drug cartels, human trafficking, a death cult, the government, and aliens were all suggested. Emily-Claire didn't think any of those theories made sense.

She sought out Syn's friend, Jilly, who worked in the office. Jilly was the kind of person who got high on gossip, and Emily-Claire guessed that's why she volunteered to be an aide. Jilly liked to vaguebook and sly-tweet all sorts of stuff. Most of it was all hype and no meat, but she was sometimes right.

"Hey, Jilly," said Emily-Claire, catching up with her going into another bathroom. Jones had a lot of bathrooms and all of them looked like the one from Harry Potter. Emily-Claire suspected that all school bathrooms were haunted, and that was fine. "Did you hear about Jonah?"

Jilly turned, already smiling, eyes alight with secret knowledge. She was in the same Goth clique as Syn, but dressed more "normal" because of working in the office. Even so, it was black on black on black. No dark lipstick or eyeliner, though, and she had auburn hair that wasn't dyed black.

"What did *you* hear?" Jilly asked as they went inside. It was her standard opener, wanting to know what someone else knew so she would never get hit with a "Yeah, I know" response.

Emily-Claire told her what she overheard from Syn, and some of the theories floating around school. Jilly made a face of haughty disdain. "Oh, girl, you're way behind the times. Jonah isn't just *missing*; the police were here twice and sent one of those CSI teams to check out his locker."

"Why?"

"Because of the blood, silly," said Jilly with a happy leer, "why else?"

"Wait ... blood?" Emily-Claire's heart slammed to a frozen halt in her chest. "What blood?"

"On the inside of the locker." Jilly managed to say everything as if the other person was somehow mentally deficient. Emily-Claire never minded; that was Jilly's thing. Jilly took a breath and explained that the vice principal and the school security officer decided to open Jonah's locker to see if there was anything that might provide a clue as to what happened to him. The locker, however, was completely empty. No textbooks or papers, no smelly gym clothes or pictures. "You know what *was* in there?" Jilly added.

Emily-Claire's heart was an icy stone. "What ...?" she asked, her voice hollow and small.

"*Three drops of blood*," said Jilly with ghoulish triumph.

"Three ...?"

"Drops of blood. Yes. That was all, but I mean ... it means something nasty happened."

Jilly said more, but Emily-Claire wasn't sure she heard any of it.

Blood.

"No," she whispered.

Jilly sniffed indignantly. "What, you think I'm lying?"

Emily-Claire jerked upright. "What? Oh! No, that's not—"

"I don't just make stuff up," snapped the other girl, clearly offended.

"No, sorry, I—"

But Jilly went into a stall, banged the door shut and locked it.

Emily-Claire fled.

—5—

The next thing Emily-Claire did was go straight to Jonah's locker. It was in a corner of the basement hallway, down the hall from the boys' gym. The lockers were a million years old, with dented doors covered in band stickers, scratched graffiti, and grime. She did not have to look hard for 117, but she couldn't get to it.

There were five orange traffic cones set in a wide half circle around it, and the locker itself was sealed with black and yellow tape. Crime scene tape, though there were no words on it. The tape sealed all four sides of the locker and clear plastic had been placed over the dial combination. Signs were taped up that read: POLICE: DO NOT TOUCH.

She edged close, leaning over a cone, reaching out to touch.

A locker was a closet, and closets had shadows. Monsters lived in shadows, and they were her friends. Were there monsters in Jonah's locker? If so, would they know what happened to him?

She knew his combination because they'd been talking once while he opened it, and Emily-Claire noticed things like that. Left three, right fifteen, left thirty-seven.

She was beginning to reach for the knob, sure she could turn it even with the plastic cover, when she smelled it.

The stink.

Such a stink.

Like rotting fish. It was awful. The kind of smell from a cellar where something bad happened. Worse than the smell of a beach after something washed up. This didn't have a normal odor. It was wrong. Very, very wrong.

Then something thumped inside of the locker. She jerked back, staring.

But there was only silence now.

Did that just happen?

There it was again. It sounded wet and heavy and the fish stink was worse. Not just stronger, but the stink no longer felt quite dead. No. Now it felt completely alive, and in all the wrong ways. She yelped and nearly ran.

Nearly.

What stopped her was the voice. It spoke in a soft whisper, like the way her closet monsters did. But it wasn't the same. This voice was lower, deeper. Sneakier.

"Open the door," it said.

"Wh-what?"

"Open the door," repeated the voice. "I know you want to. I know you *can* ..."

It was like a closet monster voice, but she knew—she *sensed*— that it was a lie. A trick. Her own monsters had coaxed her into opening her closet door when she was little, speaking in soft whispers too. She'd been too young to be really afraid of monsters. The unknown was never scary to her. She always wanted to touch it and listen to it and taste it.

Once she'd opened her closet the monsters had reached out with their strange hands. Claws and scales and fur. Touching her small hands. Touching her face. They could have torn her to pieces because closet monsters are very, very strong. But none of them ever left so much as a scratch on her. Not then, and not since. And she had spent so many hours on so many days and nights, sitting in the open closet doorway, listening to their stories in their whispery voices; and she telling them her own stories.

But this was different. She could feel that without even touching the locker. And yet she wanted to dial that combination and open the door and ...

And what? she asked herself.

Jilly said they'd found blood. She'd touched human blood before. It spoke to her the way those kinds of things often did. Telling the things that happened to the body in which it used to race like red fire through the veins. There had never been a reason to touch the blood of someone who'd died. She'd only done that with animals. Like the pig fetus in biology.

Jonah's not dead, she shouted inside her head.

"No," agreed the silky voice, as if it could hear her thoughts. Or, that one at least. "Jonah's not dead. He's in here with us."

With us.

Us. Now it was saying that there was more than one thing in the locker. How many? And what kind of monsters were they? She knew, from the stories *her* monsters told her, that not all creatures were kind, even though they were all dangerous. Most were not dangerous to little girls. Or to teenage girls. Or to boys, for that matter. Not unless those kids were mean to the monsters. They never forgot and never forgave, but they were loyal and kind too.

"Open the door, E.C.," said the voice.

Emily-Claire nearly screamed. Only one person ever called her E.C.

"J-Jonah ...?"

"Yesssss," hissed the voice, drawing the word out so that it turned to hot steam. It kind of sounded like Jonah too.

She backed up a step and was about to go when she saw something that made her pause. There, on the lower corner of the door, was a smudge. It was dark and nearly invisible against the band stickers. She saw it, though. She knew that the CSI people had missed it.

Blood.

The tiniest smear of it. Not quite dry.

"C'mon, E.C., go ahead and open the door. It's cool," suggested the voice, and now it was talking exactly like Jonah.

She stuffed her fist into her mouth and stood there, wide-eyed, wet-eyed, shivering.

Then she reached out a trembling finger toward the smudge.

"What are you doing, E.C.?" asked the Jonah-voice.

"N-nothing," she lied, though her voice quavered.

"Don't touch that," said the voice. "There's a metal splinter there. You can't see it, but it's there. Touch it and you'll get cut."

It sounded so reasonable now. No longer slippery, but the real Jonah. Reasonable, normal. It made her doubt for a long moment, the vulnerable pad of her finger only half an inch from the smear.

"Why don't you open the locker instead," said the voice. "That way you can have whatever you want."

She didn't move.

"You can have me, E.C.," said Jonah. "We can—y'know—hang out and stuff."

"I ..."

"You know the combination," he said. "I saw you watching ..."

A tear broke from the corner of her eye and rolled like acid down her cheek.

"Jonah," she breathed.

"I'd love to hang out, E.C.," he said. There was such warmth, such kindness in his voice. "You're pretty cool, you know that? I think you're hot and—"

She touched the blood.

It did not speak to her.

It *screamed*.

Then a teacher came out of a side room, saw her, began walking toward her, and she whirled and ran away, trying to outrun her horror. Trying to outrun her broken heart.

—6—

She ran upstairs and down the empty halls and back to the bathroom. Into a stall. Door slammed, lock turned. Emily-Claire stood wide-legged as if the floor tilted under her and she did not want to slide down into a screaming place. She braced her hands on the metal walls and clamped her teeth shut and squeezed her eyes closed.

The horror, though, and the heartbreak was in there *with* her.

It was Jonah's blood. She was absolutely sure of it. Positive beyond any doubt. But it was wrong too. The blood was—she fished for the word—*polluted*. His and not his. Jonah's but not completely Jonah's. She wasn't sure if she could explain it, even to herself, but she absolutely knew. Something had happened to him, and whatever was in his locker had taken him. Or ... taken him over. She wasn't sure. His blood was mixed with something else. It stank of fish and rot and life and—

Not death, though.

Jonah was gone, but she did not think he was dead. He was *gone*. Taken. Something had stolen him away, maybe pulled him into his locker when he opened it. Tore him through that narrow opening, leaving behind nothing but a few drops of polluted blood.

She did not ask herself why. "Why" was a stupid question. It was naive, because monsters didn't have the same wants or needs as people. They were, after all, monsters. And this one was a kind she'd never encountered before. Not in dreams and not in any of the closets in her family's big house. None of them smelled of fish and wrongness. Her monsters smelled of compost and rich earth and worms and skin and old bones and darkness.

Bells rang and suddenly the whole world seemed to be doors banging out, sneakers on floorboards, laughter, gossip, hurrying, shouts and yells, the ringing of cell phones. The noises swirled around. Girls came into the bathroom, chattering like pigeons, used the facilities, left. Then silence fell again.

She wanted to be home. To fly there. To suddenly *be* there. Home where the shadows were her friends. Home where the monsters in the closet were.

She wasn't.

Emily-Claire was in school and something was horribly wrong.

—7—

It took her a long time to come out of the bathroom. The halls were silent and empty once more. The old, polished floors gleamed with light that slanted down through the big windows at each end of the hall.

Emily-Claire hurried along like a small ghost, sticking to the shadows, until she reached her own locker. She wanted to get her stuff and then go home. Maybe talk to Mrs. Willow and see if she had any idea what to do.

She dialed her combination and pulled open the door. She never stopped to consider the smell. The wrong smell. The fish smell.

As the lock clicked, the door suddenly whipped open and something dark and green lashed out at her. Something that glistened wetly. Something that uncurled from the shadows inside her locker. For a moment she thought it was a snake, but it wasn't. Snakes did not have big suckers in rows on their bellies. Suckers rimmed with rows upon rows of sharp little teeth.

One of the tentacles slapped across her face as she dodged away. It did not catch her but it did cut her. She felt it burn, but even that was wrong. It burned too much for so shallow a cut. It was more like an actual burn—intense and shocking. She backpedaled all the way to the opposite wall as the thing chased her, reached for her, and only when she slammed against the soccer team trophy case did she realize what it was. Not a snake. Not an arm.

It was a tentacle.

Long and swollen and slimy, with suckers on the bottom and barnacles on the top, as if it had lived deep in the water for a long time. Way too long.

A second tentacle wriggled behind it, trying to crowd through the narrow opening. And a third. More.

Back there, deep inside the shadows that stretched much farther than her shallow locker, was a beast of some kind. Incredibly huge. Ugly. Obscene. And it wanted her. It wanted to drag her inside, the way it had dragged Jonah. The way it might eventually take all of the kids here. One at a time.

What then? What would happen when it had fed on all of the kids in her school? Would it be strong enough to break through the whole wall of lockers, tearing its way from wherever it lived down so deep that sunlight couldn't reach it?

"No!" she shouted.

"Yesssssss," it whispered, no longer pretending to be Jonah. Being itself. "Come inside, child of flesh and bone. Let us show you the infinite stars. They go on forever and forever and forever. We will open your skin and fill it with stars. We will—"

"No!" she bellowed again, then whirled and ran.

It was two miles to her house, and Emily-Claire ran all the way.

—8—

No one was home. Mrs. Willow was out too. Emily-Claire called the numbers for the little shops on Boundary Street, and no one answered.

She pounded up the stairs to her room and lunged for the doorknob of her closet.

But there she froze.

What if it was *here* now too? What if it followed her home, just like it followed from Jonah's locker to her own? What if it chased away all of her own monsters? Or worse, hurt them. Killed them. Just to get to her?

Hopelessness was a punch to the stomach, and her knees buckled. She dropped down so far her knees thumped painfully on the rug.

"Please ..." she begged.

She reached up to the knob. If her monsters were gone, then what?

Then I'll let it take me too.

The thought was a knife in her mind. Cold and sharp. She looked around the room as if she could see the whole house. No one was home. Where had everyone gone? Had they opened the wrong doors too? Was that how it was all going to end? People opening doors to lockers and closets and offices and bathrooms, expecting things to be what they ought to be. Not expecting ancient monsters. Who would be prepared for that?

Had her family already been taken? Had Mrs. Willow and the old witches on Boundary Street? Was everyone she cared about gone?

Something shifted inside the closet. Heavy. Soft.

Fresh tears rolled down her cheeks. She wiped at them, and her hand came away red, and for a moment she couldn't understand it. Then she remembered her sliced cheek.

Another thump.

"Please," she said again, and reached for the doorknob.

If they're all gone, then it can have me too.

The knob turned easily with a nearly silent *click*. She held the door shut still, dangling on a moment of terrible doubt.

Then Emily-Claire opened the door.

—9—

The thing inside reached for her. It had a long, long reach because it was stretching out from much farther away than the clothes hanging inside her closet. It reached through worlds of shadows.

The reaching hand had long, long fingers, and each one was

tipped with sharp, sharp claws. Those claws were black as midnight and sharp as thought. Those talons spread wide as it reached for her shoulder. She bowed her head as tears fell onto her thigh.

The fingers closed on her shoulder.

Very, very gently.

—10—

Emily-Claire went back to school. She had a fresh Band-Aid on her cheek. It had little pictures of the Bunny Beasts from the *Blood C* anime she liked. Her hair was brushed and pulled back into a ponytail, and she wore clean clothes.

She carried a box with her. Small, wooden. Something she'd made in an arts and crafts class. A shadow box. The teacher had tried to explain to her that it *wasn't* a shadow box because real shadow boxes were actually very deep picture frames with glass lids. They were for putting 3-D stuff into, like dried flowers and dinosaur bones and swarms of dead butterflies. Emily-Claire had only smiled and built the box her way.

"But," said the exasperated teacher, "it's just a *box*."

"With a hinge," she said.

"Well, sure, but—"

"And it's full of shadows," Emily-Claire told him. The teacher gave in, because he was wise enough not to argue about such things with a girl like Emily-Claire.

The shadow box was made of maple and hickory and painted with images of night-blooming jasmine. The wood was heavy, but she managed. It did not have dinosaur bones or dead insects in it.

When she got to the front steps of the school she stopped and looked up. They looked the same, as did the school itself, but the world had changed for her. Her cheek tingled; not so much with pain but with a reminder that Jonah was gone and there was something in there, hiding in the beautiful shadows, that was ugly and wrong. Something that didn't belong. Something she now knew was actually sleeping and only *dreaming* that it was here in her school.

That's what the monsters in her closet had told her while she sat there, weeping, resting her cheek against the scaly wrist of the thing that lightly gripped her shoulder. It was her first monster, the oldest one. The one she'd met when she was three. It whispered to her of things even older than itself. Creatures so incredibly old that people thought they were immortal. Beings so strange and powerful that whole civilizations on dozens of worlds worshipped them as gods.

Except they were not gods. They were monsters and they were aliens, but not gods.

The monster in her closet was very specific on that point. Once they were servants of vastly powered Elder Gods and over time came to believe that *they* were gods themselves. Some of them rebelled and committed terrible sins across a thousand worlds. To the civilizations they conquered they were the Great Old Ones. Feared as demons and worshipped as gods, they drove their own worshippers insane.

The Elder Gods smashed them down, but even they were not powerful enough to destroy the creatures they had created. So, they locked them away. One of the most powerful of the Great Old Ones was an incredibly powerful and evil being who embraced the terror of his aspect and fed on the fear that his monstrous form and incredible power created. Whole worlds died for him—sometimes in war, sometimes in waves of mass suicides.

When Emily-Claire heard that, she wept. Strange as she was, and as in love with the voices of dead things as she'd come to be, suicide was the worst thing she could imagine. Being alive meant that there were so many things to see and know and learn and sense and taste and experience. Even a girl as alone as she was— or maybe because she spent so much time alone—she was in love with life. The idea that a creature with so much power *enjoyed* tricking billions of people into killing themselves for him made her so furious that she got up and walked round her room and kicked things, punched things, screamed at the top of her lungs.

The monster, patient, waited for her to sit back down.

"What's the thing's name?"

The monster paused as if unwilling to speak it aloud, then he drew a breath and whispered the name. "Cthulhu."

The very sound of that name hurt her ears to hear it and her brain to know it, and she shook her head, sorry she'd asked.

When she could speak—and it took a while—she asked, "If this *thing* is that strong, then what can we do? It's going to eat all of us!"

"The universe was born from chaos," whispered the monster in a voice as soft as rabbit fur, "but there is a beautiful balance to it. Cthulhu, for all his power, was thrown down and imprisoned in a city beneath the waves. In the nightmare corpse-city of R'lyeh he sleeps and only dreams that he is awake."

"Wait ... *what*? That makes no sense at all."

"Life is a dream," whispered one of the other monsters from deeper in the closet, and others picked it up and chanted it for a few moments. The line from the old nursery rhyme came to her ... *Row, row, row your boat, gently down the stream ... merrily, merrily, merrily, merrily ... life is but a dream.* It had been a silly song when she was little, but now it chilled her.

"We are all dreaming," said her patient monster. "When we believe that our dream is the only reality then we stay asleep forever. But when we open our inner eye to look around, we see that the universe is like the ocean and we, in the bubbles of our dreams, swim there. Together sometimes, or alone. Cthulhu believes that his dream is the *only* one, and he is so old, so powerful that he is trying to force that dream into *your* world, Emily-Claire. Into this world. Jonah has already become lost in that dream. Cthulhu fed on his dreams, and he wants to feed on yours. On the dreams of your friends at school. If he feeds enough then the sleeper will awaken and the dream of this world will become a nightmare."

She shivered as if a cold, damp wind was blowing through her bedroom. She fumbled for the monster's hand and clutched it, pressing it to her hammering heart.

"What can we do? How do we fight something that strong? I mean, how was he even stopped before?"

"With magic, of course," said the monster. "With magic so old the names for the spells were lost before your sun caught fire. Old, *old* magic. The Elder Gods had many servants and not all of them rebelled. Cthulhu used evil and ugly magic, but the magic of the loyal servants was cleaner. It was a terrible fight, though, and worlds were destroyed in the conflict. In the end, their dream of beauty was enough to overcome his dream of horror."

"Clean magic? Like the Jedi," suggested Emily-Claire.

The monster in the closet chuckled. They had watched those movies together when she sat in the open doorway and played the films on her laptop. Many other monsters had clustered around.

"Like the Jedi," it agreed, "though ten billion times more powerful."

"And this Cthulhu thing was like the Sith?"

"If you like," said the amused monster. "The struggle was terrible and lasted for a thousand years, but in the end the loyal servants cast a great spell that sent Cthulhu into a deep, deep sleep. They imprisoned him beneath the ocean where no one could find him or free him. There the evil has slept for thousands of years."

She remembered the stink of rotting fish and wrinkled her nose.

"But Cthulhu dreams," warned the monster. "Oh, he dreams, and his dreams are so deep, so powerful that they intrude into *this* world. Into many worlds, and many times."

"He's asleep and he's that strong?" asked Emily-Claire, amazed.

The monster made a sound. Maybe it was a laugh. "Coming here, to your school, stealing your friend, attacking you ... that is not power, my little princess. That is a whim in a dream. But if he *feeds enough* to wake up ... then you will see power. Then worlds will fall as his rage awakens."

"But ... but ... what about those good guys? Won't they just—I don't know—knock him out again?"

"The universe has changed much since then," said the monster with a sad shake of his head. The others in the closet shifted and muttered. A breeze like a dry wind blew out of the closet door. It smelled of sadness and fear, which she had never felt before here.

"We have to do something," insisted Emily-Claire.

"Yes," said the monster. "You do."

It took her a half second to realize that he said "you."

She asked, "What ...?"

"There is a reason evil has come to your school, your friends, to you ..."

"But ... I'm just a girl. I'm only *thirteen*, for Pete's sake. What can I do?"

The monster said nothing.

"*You're* all monsters," she yelled. "Can't you fight him for me?"

"We are sent to watch by the Elder Gods, but the world as it is now is vastly different from the world as it was when we were brought here. Our shadows once roamed free beneath a ceiling of clouds, but your kind rose up and built structures—tombs and temples, castles and houses, and in their rooms we became trapped, retreating from the clearing skies, fleeing from the sun, finding safety in rooms without windows."

"Like closets ...?"

"Like closets," said the monster. "We live in your closet, Emily-Claire. The shadows here are the darkness in which *we* dream. And so, we remain, monsters in your personal shadows. Bound to you, Emily-Claire."

"But ... but ..."

In the open doorway, the shadows roiled and swirled as the other monsters clustered to watch.

To watch her.

She stared back at them. At their forms, which changed constantly as if moved by winds only they could feel.

And she smiled.

Then she said, "Ah."

And all the shadows swirled faster and faster.

Which is why Emily-Claire went back to school.

—11—

It was late, and the last class was about to let out.

Emily-Claire went to the auditorium, which doubled as the theater for school shows. She'd worked crew for two productions and knew every inch of the backstage area. There were prop rooms and changing rooms, and rooms for pieces of set and band instruments. She snuck into a costume room, locked the door from the inside, set the box on the floor, then sat down to wait.

She heard the bells and the banging open of doors and the herds of footsteps. She heard the building come alive and, gradually, fall quiet again. There was no window, and the only light was from her cell phone.

Waiting was hard. It was scary. But it was also exciting.

The minutes gathered into bunches and slowly—so slowly—withered and fell away. She texted her mom, who—to her incredible relief—responded. Everyone was back home now. Emily-Claire lied and said she was staying late for a school thing.

Well, not really a lie. This was the school, and there was a thing.

Her mom filled the screen with emojis, told her to be home as soon as it was over, and that was that.

"Over," echoed Emily-Claire. "Sure. If I can."

—12—

When she was sure the building was completely empty—there were no night watchmen at John Paul Jones Junior High—Emily-Claire unlocked the door and crept out, carrying the heavy box.

The halls were dark and so quiet that even her careful footfalls made a racket. Echoes chased her as she tiptoed down the stairs and along the hallways to her locker. A spill of yellow light from one of the sparse security lamps fell across the floor, and she saw —scuffed by a hundred shoes—a few smears of her own blood. She set the box down and touched her cheek.

She left the box on the floor and went to the janitor's closet around the corner, returning quickly with a long-handled push broom.

"Sorry," she said to the school as she swung the broom with all her might and shattered the security light, plunging the hall into nearly total darkness. Emily-Claire tossed the broom away and knelt to touch the spots of blood. Sniffed it, rubbed it between her fingers. There was nothing to learn from it because she was still alive. Living things didn't speak to her in the same way. She was relieved to find that there was no fish smell, either. Not that she expected any, but it was a relief nonetheless.

A sound made her jump, and she whipped around to see her locker door jiggling. It was weird to her that the small hinges and cheap combination lock could trap a monster like that.

"Cthul—" she began and bit down on the last syllable. Even so, a tentacle slammed so hard against the locker door that cracks whipsawed up the wall above it and two acoustic tiles fell from the dropped-ceiling. Emily-Claire yelped and clamped her hands over her mouth.

The hinges on her locker creaked ominously.

Emily-Claire felt sweat burst from her pores and soak her clothes. She had never been this frightened before. What if she was wrong? What if her plan was stupid?

What if the thing who lived in the shadows here had fed on more than Jonah? What if all he needed was one last Emily-Claire-sized bite?

She licked her lips, set her teeth, and walked carefully over to the locker.

The combination was twelve ... two ... thirty-seven. She dialed right, then left, and then past zero to the right and all the way to thirty-six before she paused. The locker trembled, but not as if struck. More like the thing was right there, directly behind the thin metal, trembling with the anticipation of that last click.

"Please," she said aloud. It was not a prayer. It was a plea. The kind one would make to a friend.

She took a breath and turned the combination lock one tiny bit to the right.

Click.

The door burst open as three massive tentacles squeezed out, coiling in the air to try and wrap around her. If they had caught her she would have been dead—or lost—on the spot, but by then Emily-Claire was moving. As soon as she turned the dial to thirty-seven, she whirled and threw herself into a long dive. One full semester of gymnastic club hadn't taught her much, but she could tuck and roll. She tucked and she rolled and the tentacles crushed the empty air inches above her.

Emily-Claire came out of her roll badly, rising too fast and pitched too far forward. She tried to grab the sides of her wooden box and missed completely, hitting the top with her chin, biting her tongue, and nearly breaking her jaw. Blood welled in her mouth and she gagged, but she fumbled for the box, grabbed a corner as she fell, clawed it toward her as one of the tentacles smashed down on the floor. The old polished floorboard cracked apart in a spray of splinters. The shock knocked the box out of her hands again, and it went sliding down the floor. With a cry she scrambled to her feet, ducked under another tentacle, and dove again.

A fourth lashing tentacle caught her, lifted her, and smashed her against the base of the trophy case. The display glass shattered, showering her in glittering razor-sharp debris. She covered her face with her arms, but felt a dozen burning points of pain ignite on her skin.

Then she lunged again, throwing herself along the floor like a seal, reaching for the box. One tentacle tried to curl around the box—maybe sensing its danger—but Emily-Claire clamped her hands on the lid, gritted her teeth, and tore it open.

All of the shadows in the box spilled out.

All of the monsters who lived in those shadows—her monsters—spilled out too.

The monsters she had gathered into her light-proof little shadow box and carried all the way to school. A simple act that she could do and they could not.

Emily-Claire had brought her shadowy friends to school with her, and in the darkened hallway, she let them out to play.

The tentacles paused, confused as the shadows spread out and grew and expanded, because size does not mean the same thing in all dimensions. Not at all in a world of shadows. Emily-Claire snatched up the broom and held it like a war club, but she knew that it was not the weapon to win this fight.

Her monsters were here. With her. For her. *Because* of her.

Her monsters.

Hers.

She faced the waving tentacles. "You took my friend," she said. "You can't have me. And you can't have my school."

The shadows gathered around her. The tentacles whipped back and forth, furious and threatening.

"This is *my* world," she growled. Emily-Claire reached up a hand and touched the shoulder of her first friend. He was a thing of horror and of beauty. Tall, covered in scales and spikes, with enormous fangs and eyes that blazed like black fire. "And these are my friends."

Her friends howled as they attacked.

—13—

School was closed the next day. It was on the news. Someone had broken in and smashed the trophy case, broken some lights, tore open a whole row of lockers and even ripped up floorboards. The police were called in. The principal was on the news to growl about hoodlums and gang members.

Emily-Claire sat on the floor in the open doorway of her closet and watched. Her laptop was propped atop her shadow box. She was eating a bowl of fresh sweet strawberries, and every now and then a hand with long claws would reach out of the darkness of her closet to pluck a fat one. Monsters liked strawberries too.

CALLING DEATH

"It weren't the wind," said Granny Adkins, rocking back and forth. "Weren't the wind at all."

The young man perched on the edge of the other rocker, head tilted to lift one ear like a startled bird, listening to the sound. He was stick thin and beaky nosed, and Granny thought he looked like a heron—the way they looked when they were ready to take sudden flight. "Are you sure?"

"Sure as maybe," said Granny, nodding out to the darkness. "The wind fair howls when it comes 'cross the top of Balder Rise. Howls like the Devil himself."

"Sounds like a howl to me," agreed the young man. "I mean, what else *could* you call it?"

Granny sucked in a lungful of smoke from her Pall Mall, held it inside for a five count, and then stuck out her lower lip to exhale in a vertical line up past her face. She didn't like to blow smoke on guests, and there was a breeze blowing toward the house. A chime made from old bent forks and chicken bones stirred and tinkled.

She squinted with her one good eye—the blue one, not the one that had gone milky white when a wasp stung her there forty years back—and considered how she wanted to answer the young man.

Before she spoke, the sound came again. Low, distant, plaintive. She left her initial response unspoken for a moment as they sat in the dark and listened.

"There," she said softly, "You hear it?"

"Yes, but it still sounds like a—"

"No, son. That ain't what I meant. Can you *hear* the sound? The moan?"

He licked his lips and leaned into the wind, tilting one ear directly into its path. "Yes ..."

"Now," said Granny, "can you hear the wind too?"

"I ..." he began, but let his voice trail off. Granny waited, watching his face by starlight, looking for the moment when he *did* hear it. His head lifted like a bird dog's. "Yes ... I hear it."

They listened to the moan. It was there, but the wind was dying off again and the sound grew fainter, thinner.

"That, um, 'moan,'" the young man said tentatively, "it's *not* the wind. You're right."

She nodded, satisfied.

"It's a separate sound," continued the young man. "I—I think it's being carried *on* the wind." He looked to her for approval.

She gave him another nod. "That's another thing about living up here in the hills," she said, tying this to their previous conversation. "When you live simple and close to the land, you don't get as blunt as folks in the cities do. You hear things, see things the way they are, not the way you s'pose them to be. You notice that there are more things around you, and that they're there all the time."

The young man nodded, but he was half distracted by the moans, so Granny let him listen for a spell.

His name was Joshua Tharp. A good name. Biblical first name, solid last name. A practical name, which Granny always appreciated because she thought that a name said a lot about a person. She would never have come out onto the porch if he'd had

a foreign-sounding name, or a two-first-name name, like Simon
Thomas. Everyone Granny knew with two Christian names was a
scoundrel, and half in the Devil's bag already. However, this boy
had a good name. There had been Tharps in this country going
back more generations than Granny could count, and she knew
family lines four decades past the War of Northern Aggression.
Her own people had been here since before America was America.

So, Joshua Tharp was a decent name, and well worth a little
bit of civility. He was a college boy from Pittsburgh who was
willing to pay attention and treat older folks with respect. Wasn't
pushy, neither, and that went a long way down the road with
Granny. When he'd shown up on her doorstep, he took off his hat
and said "ma'am," and told her that he was writing a book about
the coal miners in Pennsylvania and North Carolina, and was
using his own family as the thread that sewed the two states
together.

Now they were deep into their third porch sitting, and the
conversation wandered a crooked mile through late afternoon
and on into the full dark of night. Talking about Granny and her
kin, and about the Tharps here and the Tharps that had gone on.
Joshua was a Whiskey Holler Tharp, though, but there was no one
left around here closer than a third cousin with a couple of
removes, so everyone told him to go see Granny Adkins.

"Hell, son," said Mr. Sputters at the post office, "Granny's so
old, she remembers when God bought these mountains from the
Devil, and I do believe the good Lord might have been short-
changed on the deal. You want to know about your forebears—
and about what happened when the mine caved in—well you go
call on ol' Granny. But mind you bring your full set of manners
with you, 'cause she won't have no truck with anyone who gives
her half a spoonful of sass."

Granny knew that Sputters said that because the old coot
phoned and told her. Wrigley Sputters was a fool, but not a damn
fool.

Come calling is exactly what young Joshua did. He came

asking about his kin. That was the first day, and even now they'd only put a light coat of paint on that subject. Granny was old, and she was never one to be in a hurry to get to the end of anything, least of all a conversation.

Joshua's people, the true Whiskey Holler Tharps, were a hard-working bunch. Worked all their lives in the mines, boy to old man. Honest folk who didn't mind coming home tired and dirty, and weren't too proud to get down on their knees to thank the good Lord for all His blessings.

Shame so many of them died in that cave-in. Lost a lot of good and decent folks that day. Forty-two grown men and seven boys. The Devil was in a rare mood that day, and no mistake. Guess he didn't like them digging so deep.

Granny cut a look at the young man as he sat there studying on the sounds the night brought to him. He was making a real effort to do it right, and that was another good sign. He came from good stock, and it's nice to know that living in a big city hadn't bred the country out of him.

"I can't figure that sound out," said Joshua, shaking his head. "What is it?"

Granny crushed out her cigarette and lit another one, closing her eyes to keep the flare of the match from stealing away her night vision. She lit the cigarette by touch and habit, shook the match out, and dropped it into an empty coffee tin that had an inch of rainwater in it.

She said, "What's it sound like?"

That was a test. If the boy still had too much city in him, then there would be impatience on his face or in his voice. But not in Joshua's. He nodded at the question and once more tilted his head to listen.

Granny liked that. And she liked this boy. But after a few moments, Joshua shook his head. "I don't know. It's almost like there are two sounds. The, um, *moan*, and something else. Link a faint clinking sound."

"Do tell?" she said dryly, but with just enough lift to make it a question.

"Like ... maybe the wind is blowing through something. A metal fence, or ... I don't know. I hear the clink and the moan, but I can't hear either of them really well." He gave a nervous half laugh. "I've never heard anything like it."

"Never?"

"Well, I—don't spend a lot of time out of doors," he confessed. "I guess I haven't learned how to listen yet. Not properly, anyhow. I know Granddad used to talk about that. About shaking off the city so you could hear properly, but until now I don't think I ever really understood what he was saying."

Another soft moan floated over the trees. Strange and sad it was, and Granny sighed. She watched Joshua staring at the darkness, his face screwed up in concentration.

Granny gestured with her cigarette. "What do you think it *might* be?"

"Is it ... some kind of animal?"

"What kind of animal would make a sound like that, do you suppose?"

They sat for almost two minutes, waiting between silences for the wind to blow. Joshua shook his head.

"Some kind of cat?"

That surprised Granny and now she listened, trying to hear it through his ears. "It do sound a might like a cat," she conceded, then chuckled. "But not a healthy one. Was a broke-leg bobcat got caught in a bear trap once and hollered for a day and a night."

"So—is that what it is? A wounded bobcat? Is that clinking sound a bear trap?"

Granny exhaled more smoke before she answered. "No, son, that ain't what it is."

"Then ...?"

She chuckled. "It'll keep. You interrupted your ownself, son. You was asking me a question before we heard yonder call."

He nodded, but it was clear that he was reluctant to leave the other topic unfinished. Granny felt how false her smile was. The mysteries out in the dark would keep. Might have to keep without the other shoe ever dropping.

"I ..." Joshua began, fishing for the thread of where they'd been. "Right ... we were talking about the day Granddad left for Pittsburgh. He said it was because there was no work, but he never really talked about that. And when he moved to Pittsburgh, he always worked in a foundry. He never wanted to go back to the mines."

"No ... I daresay old Hack Tharp would never set foot in a mine again. 'Specially not in these hills, and probably nowhere. Lot of folks around here with the same thought. Those that stayed here gave up mining. I know men who wouldn't lift a pickax to go ten feet into a gold mine, not after what happened. Hack was one of 'em."

"Tell me about him. He died when I was ten, so I never had a grown-up conversation with him. Never got to really know him. What was he like?"

Granny smiled, and this time the smile was real. "Hack was a bull of a man, with shoulders from here to there, and hands like iron. A good man to know and a handsome man to look at. Hack worked himself up to foreman down in the Hangood Mine. Swung a pickax for twenty long years down in the dark before he was promoted, and still sucked coal gas for twenty more as the foreman. The men liked him, no one crossed him, and his word was good on anything he put it to. Can't say as much about a lot of people, and can't say half as much about most."

Joshua nodded encouragement.

"But Hack up and moved," sighed Granny. "He was the first, and over the years more'n sixty families have left the holler. Ain't no more than a hundred people left on this whole mountain, and I know of four families that are fixin' to leave before long. Might be that I'll be the last one here come next year, if *I'm* even here a'tall."

"People started leaving because the mine closed?"

"They started leaving *after* the mine closed. This place went bad on us that day, and it ain't ever gone to get better."

The moaning wind and the soft metallic *clank* drifted past the end of her statements almost as if it were a statement itself.

Joshua cleared his throat. "Do you remember when Granddad left? I got the impression it was pretty soon after the disaster."

"It were on the third Sunday after the cave-in. Hack packed up only what would fit into that old rattle-rust Ford pickup of his and drove off. Never came back, never called, never wrote. But ... before he left, though, he came to say goodbye to ol' Granny." She sighed. "'Course I wasn't Granny back then. Just a young, unmarried gal who thought the sun rose in the morning 'cause it wanted to see Hack Tharp."

"Pardon me if this is rude, but ... were you and Granddad sweethearts?"

Granny blew out some smoke, thought for a moment, and gave a small shrug. "There was no official understanding between us, as you might say. Every girl in five counties wanted to catch Hack's eye, but for a while there I had me some hopes. Maybe Hack did, too, 'cause I was the only one he lingered long enough to say farewell to. And—I blush to say it to a young feller like you —but I was something back then. You wouldn't know it now, lookin' at this big pile o' wrinkles, but I could turn a few heads of my own. Thought for a while that Hack might have been charmed enough to stay 'cause I asked him, but the cave-in plumb took all those thoughts out of his mind. He was set on leaving, and he knew that I never would."

"Even if he'd asked?"

She sighed again. "There are some things more important than love, strange as it sounds. At least I thought so back then. You see ... I had a talent for the old ways. With a talent for dowsing and a collection of aunts who were teaching me the way things worked in the world. Herbs and healing and luck charms and suchlike. Some folks call us witches. Even seen it in books. Mr. Sputters at the post office showed me a book onest called *Appalachian Granny Magic*. And I guess it's fair enough. Witch comes from some older word that means 'wise,' and that's all it is.

Women who know such and such about things. My Aunt Tess was a fire witch. She could conjure a spark out of green wood with no matches and only a word. My own mammy was the most famous healer in the holler. People'd come from all over with a sickness, or send a car for her to deliver a baby."

"I heard about that. Granddad told me a little. He said you could find water when no one else could."

She nodded. "I been known to do that now and again. Mostly I make charms to ward off badness and evil. Half the rabbits in these hills walk with a limp since I started selling they's feet to ward off ill luck. And you can walk for two days and not find a soul who ain't wearing one of my snakeskin bags on their belts. Real toad's eyes in 'em, too, because fake charms don't stop nuthin'." She smiled. "Does that scare you, young Joshua? All this talk about witches?"

"Not as much as that sound does," he said, nodding to the night. "It's really creeping me out."

Granny puffed her cigarette and only smiled.

Joshua cleared his throat. "You were telling me about how Granddad came to say goodbye."

"So I was. Well ... Hack Tharp stood foursquare in my yard, not two paces from where I sit right now. 'Mary Ruth,' he said, 'I'm gone. I can't live here no more, not with all the dead hauntin' me. My brothers, they never had a chance. They was so obsessed with earning that bonus that they went crazy, picking and digging like the Devil was whipping them, and then that whole mountain just up and *fell*. And it went down fast too. Killed 'em before they could git right with God. I was right outside taking a smoke when the mouth of Hell opened up and swallowed those boys. I haven't had a night's sleep since it happened. And I won't ever sleep a night if I stay here.'"

"'Weren't your fault,' I told him. But Hack shook his head. 'I ain't saying it is. And I ain't losing sleep 'cause I feel guilty about being on *this* side of the grave when all my family was taken by death. No—the bosses killed all those men—killed my own brothers, two of my cousins. Killed 'em sure as if they blew the mountain down with dynamite. Killed 'em by digging too deep in a played-out mine. Killed 'em by greed, and that's an evil thing. Greed's one of the bad sins, Mary Ruth, one of them seven deadly sins, and it made my brothers sell their souls to Old Scratch himself.'"

"I didn't know Granddad was so religious. He never went to church when I was a kid. Not even on Easter and Christmas."

"I suppose," said Granny, "that he lost the knack. Seen a lot of it after the collapse, just like I seen a lot of folks suddenly hear the preacher's call before the dust even settled. Since then, though ... well ain't no one in this holler don't believe in the Devil anymore, so the unbelievers have started believing in God by default."

"Was there an investigation?" asked Joshua. "Did the authorities ever determine that the mining company was at fault?"

"Investigation?" Granny laughed. "You got a city boy's sense of humor, son. No, there weren't no investigation. And even if someone wanted to investigate, there weren't no way to do it."

"Why not? I've read a lot about mining, and a structural engineer could do a walk-through look at the shoring systems, the drill angles, the geologist's assessment of the load bearing walls of the mountain, and—"

"No one's ever going to do any of that."

"Why not?"

"'Cause they'd have to cut through a million tons of rock to take that look."

"They could just examine the areas dug out when the bodies were removed."

Granny studied him for a moment. "Your granddad didn't tell you?"

"Tell me what?"

She sighed. "Those dead men are still there, son. The company never dug them out. *Nobody* ever dug them out. That whole mountain's a tomb for all those good men."

Joshua stood up and stared at the darkness again, looking toward Balder Rise. The wind blew from that direction, carrying with it the soft moan. "God," he said softly.

"Oh, God didn't have nuthin' to do with what happened that day," said Granny. "Your granddad spoke true when he said that it were the evil greed of the mining company that brought the ceiling down. They dug too deep."

"That's something Granddad said a couple of times, and now you've said it twice. What's that mean, exactly?"

"The mining company was fair desperate to stay in business even though most of the coal had already been took from old Balder. They kept pushing and pushing to find another vein. Pushed and pushed the men, too, tempting 'em with promises of bonuses if they found that vein. Understand, boy, miners are always poor. It's really no kind of life. Working down there in the dark, bad air and coal dust, it's like you're digging your own grave."

The moan on the wind came again, louder, more insistent. The black trees seemed to bend under the weight of it.

"The company kept the pressure on. Everybody needed that vein, too, because the company *owned* everything. They owned the bank, which means they held the mortgage on ever'body's house and that's the same like holding the mortgage on ever'body's souls." She shook her head. "No, a lot of folks thought the Devil himself was whispering in the ear of ever'body, from the executives all the way down to the teenage boys pushing the lunch trolleys. Infecting them good-hearted and God-fearing men with their own greed. Spreading sin like a plague. Makin' 'em dig too hard and too deep, with too much greed and hunger."

"Digging too deep, though—you keep saying that. Do you mean that they over-mined the walls, or—?"

"No, son," she said, "that ain't what Hack meant, and it ain't what I mean."

"Then what—?"

The moan came again, even louder. So loud that Joshua stood

up and placed his palms on the rail so he could lean head and shoulders out into the night. Granny saw him shiver.

"You cold?" she asked, though it was a warm night,

"No," he said, without turning. "That sound ..."

Granny waited.

" ... it sounds almost like a person," Joshua continued. "It sounds like someone's hurt out there."

"Hurt? Is that really what it sounds like to you?"

"Well, it's something like that. I can *hear* the pain." He shot her a quick look. "Does that sound silly? Am I being a stupid city boy here, or—?"

"You don't sound stupid at all, son. That's one of the smartest things you've said. You know what's happening?" she asked. "The city's falling clean off you."

He studied her.

"It's true," she said. "Your daddy might have been born in the city and you might have been born and raised there, too, but you still got the country in you. You still got some of the hills in you. You get that from ol' Hack, and I bet he was always country no matter how many years he lived in the city—am I right or am I right?"

"You're right, Granny," said Joshua. "No one would ever have mistaken Granddad for anything except what he was. He ... loved these mountains. He talked about how beautiful they were. How they smelled on a spring morning. How the birds would have conversations in the trees. How folks were simple—less complicated—but they weren't stupid. Always said how he wished he could have stayed."

Granny closed her eyes for a moment, remembering Hack. Remembering pain. Remembering the horror of that collapse, and all the things that died that day. Those men, her love, this town.

"Is something wrong?" asked Joshua.

She opened her eyes and rocked back so she could look up at him. "Wrong?"

The moan cut through the air again. Louder still.

"I suppose you could say that nuthin's been *right* since that mine collapsed," she said, and Granny could hear the pain in her own voice. Almost as dreadful as the pain in that moan. "Close your eyes again and listen to that sound. Don't tell me what it ain't. Listen until you can tell me what it is."

Joshua closed his eyes and leaned once more on the rail, his head raised to lift his ears into the wind.

After a full minute, he said, "It sounds like a person ... and that clinking sound ... that's definitely something metal."

She waited.

Joshua laughed. "If it was Christmas, I'd say it was Old Marley and his chain."

When Granny did not laugh, Joshua opened his eyes and turned to her.

"That's from the—"

"I know what it's from, son. And it ain't all that far from the mark." She sucked in some smoke. "Not a chain, though. Listen and tell me I'm wrong."

He listened.

"No, you're right. It's, um ... sharper than that. But the echoes are making it hard to figure it out. Almost sounds like a bunch of little clinks, almost at once. That's why I thought it was a chain; you know, the links clinking as it blew in the wind."

"But it ain't a chain," she said, "and it ain't blowing in the wind. Ain't echoes, either."

There was a stronger gust of wind, and the moan was much louder now.

Joshua pushed off the rail and walked down into the yard. He stood with his hands cupped around his ears to catch every nuance of the sound. Granny dropped her cigarette butt into the empty coffee tin and lit another.

The moaning was so loud now that anyone could hear it. So loud that anyone could understand it, and Granny watched for the moment when Joshua understood. She'd seen it so many times. With friends, with her own daughter—who screamed and then ran inside the house to begin packing up her clothes and her babies. She hadn't come back.

Granny had seen a parade of people come through, stopping as Hack had stopped, wanting to say goodbye. Only one of them ever came back. Norm McPhee wandered back to the mountains after spending the last fourteen years in a bottle somewhere in Georgia. He came back to the holler, back to Balder, back to Granny's yard, and he stood there for an hour, his eyes filled with ghosts. Then Norm had walked into the woods, found himself a quiet log to sit on, drank the rest of his bottle of who-hit-John, took the pistol from his pocket, and blew his brains all over the new blossoms on a dogwood tree.

Granny smoked her cigarette and wondered what Hack Tharp's grandson would do, because she could see the set of his body changing. He was slowly standing straighter. His hands fell slowly from behind his ears. His eyes were wide, and his mouth formed soundless words as he sought to speak the thoughts that his senses were planting in his head.

Joshua turned to her. Sharp and quick, but his mouth wasn't ready to put voice to the thought that Granny could now *see* in the young man's eyes.

"I can hear them," he said at last.

Them.

"Yes," she said.

"It's not just one sound, and it's not an animal. There are a lot of them."

"Yes," Granny said again.

Something glistened on Joshua's face. Was it sweat?

"Granddad said that forty-nine people died that day. Mostly men, a few kids."

"Yes," she said once more.

"All of them digging down in the earth," said Joshua, and his voice sounded different. Distant, like he was talking to himself. Distant, like the wind. "All of them, digging like crazy." His eyes glistened. "What did Granddad say? You just told me ... that those men were so obsessed with earning that bonus that they went crazy, picking and digging like the Devil was whipping them."

"And then that whole mountain just up and fell," agreed Granny softly.

"It killed them fast. Killed them before they could get right with God."

She nodded.

"Like the mouth of Hell opened up and swallowed those boys," Joshua said, his voice thick, his eyes filled with bad, bad pictures. "God."

"I already said it," whispered Granny, "God didn't have nuthin' to do with what happened."

The moans were constant now. The voices clear and terrible. The metallic clinks distinct.

Joshua laughed. Too quick and too loud. "Oh ... come *on*! This is ridiculous. Granny, I don't mean any disrespect, but ... come on. You can't expect me to believe any of this."

"I never asked you to."

That wiped the smile off his face.

"Granddad left because of this sound, didn't he?"

Granny didn't bother to answer that.

The moans answered it. The clank of metal on rock answered it.

"No," said Joshua. "You want me to believe that they're still there, still down there in the dark, still ... digging?"

Granny smoked her cigarette.

"That's insane," he said, anger in his voice now. "They're dead! They've been dead for years. Come on, Granny, it's insane. It's stupid."

"Son," she said, "I ain't told you none of that. I ain't told you nuthin' but to listen to the wind and tell me what *you* think that is."

The voices on the wind were filled with such anger, such pain. Such hunger.

The incessant clanks of pickaxes against rock were like

punches, and Joshua actually yielded a step backward with each ripple of strikes. As if those pickaxes were hitting him. More wetness glistened on his face.

"Granny," he said in a hollow voice, "Come on …"

Granny rocked in her rocker and smoked her cigarette.

"All these years?" asked Joshua, and she could hear how fragile his voice was. It had taken three weeks of the sound before Hack had up and left. A lot of folks played their TV or radio loud and late to try and hide the sound.

One by one, people left the mountain. Took some only months; took others years.

Joshua Tharp stood in the yard and winced each time the wind blew.

He won't last the night, she thought. *He'll be in his car and heading back to the city before moonrise.*

"All these years … digging …"

His eyes were suddenly wild.

"Has … has … the sound been getting *louder* all these years?"

Granny nodded. "Every night," she said. "Every single darn night."

"'Every night,'" echoed Joshua. He stood his ground, not knocked back by the ring of the pickaxes this time. Granny thought that either he had found his nerve or he had lost it entirely.

"I 'spect one of these days they'll dig they'sselves out of that hole." She paused. "Out of Hell."

The picks rang in the night. Again and again. Over and over and over again.

Then there was a cracking sound. Rock breaking off. Or breaking open.

Joshua and Granny listened.

There were no more sounds of pickaxes.

There were just the moans.

Louder now. Clearer.

So much clearer.

"God ..." whispered Joshua.

"God had nuthin' to do with the collapse," said Granny. "And I expect he's got nuthin' to do with this."

The moans rode the night breeze.

So loud and so clear.

COOKED

Billy Sparrow was high.

Almost high.

The "almost" part was a bitch. It was a heartbreak.

He needed to get high enough to fly away, like Cooter promised they could do.

But he wasn't high enough for that.

For Billy the high used to start before he even clicked his lighter to smoke the ice. Meth was always like that, you even think about it you get a tingle in the balls and a flutter behind the eyes. High before you're high, that's what Cooter used to say.

Cooter used say a lot of stuff.

Cooter was pretty funny. He had Billy laughing the first time they smoked meth. Called it methandfriendofmine. That was funny.

He and Cooter would smoke so much they'd get pipe-drunk and then everything was funny. Peeling wallpaper was funny. A cockroach swimming in his cereal bowl was funny. Even watching Carla, that scratchity-ann crank hoe, pick at her blisters was funny.

That was a long time ago.

The anticipation wasn't the same.

The high wasn't the high anymore.

Now, when Billy popped a lighter under the quartz all he felt was bad stuff. His stomach was full of bees, and there were thorns in his head. Even when he sucked in that first lungful and the world fell off its hinges. That used to be epic. That used to be the fucking *it*.

Now it was like opening a door into a haunted house.

Cooter was in that haunted house too.

Sitting there, grinning at him with crooked teeth surrounded by charred skin, staring with eyeballs that had been boiled white in the fire.

If Billy smoked too long he could see Cooter die all over again. It was like a big DVR playing the scene over and over again in his head. Surround-sound and everything. No amount of smoke could bury that, and the deeper into the high Billy went to hide from it, the clearer the picture got.

—2—

They'd come in a couple of Escalades. Farelli and his posse of six wiseguy wannabes from Newark, rolling up to Cooter's little place on DeFrane Street. White boys dressed like they thought *The Sopranos* was on the Fashion Channel. Pointy shoes and tight pants and shirts open to show Neanderthal hair on their chests. Acting tough, hoping to be noticed by guys who *are* tough. Talking trash.

Carrying baseball bats and gas in red plastic cans.

Billy was in the attic, huddled over the last fumes in a pipe. He heard the shouts, but at first that didn't mean shit to him. You get high, you hear stuff. Some highs are good, some highs blow. People steal shit from each other. There are fights. It's no big deal.

But then the shouts turned to screams.

Screams weren't part of it. Meth doesn't take you down that

avenue. Billy staggered to his feet and looked down the attic stairs. There were no doors anywhere. Billy remembered he and Cooter taking them off, but he couldn't remember what that had been about.

The screams were loud enough to poke holes in the envelope of his high.

He crept down to the second floor and leaned over the banister.

There they were.

The dickheads from Seventh Avenue. Farelli's thugs were like a pack of dogs. Billy lost count of the number of times they beat him up. Rubbed his face in dogshit. Kicked him in the balls. Always laughing about it. Always grabbing their own nuts and yelling "Eat me!" every time they saw Cooter. Always calling Cooter faggot or nigger or other shit.

Worse than a pack of dogs, Billy thought. Dogs won't fuck with you for no reason. Billy Sparrow didn't hate very many things, but he hated Farelli and his crew.

Farelli lived in the house with all those statues of the Virgin Mary on their lawn. The virgin and a bunch of dumbass plastic pink flamingoes.

Billy had a vague memory of him and Cooter stealing some of them the other night. Or was it last night? What the fuck did they do with them?

They stole all sorts of shit. Flamingos, those goofy little lawn gnomes, a statue of a black guy dressed like a jockey. That one really pissed Cooter off. Billy didn't know why. Sure, Cooter was black, but he wasn't a jockey. But it pissed Cooter off, and when Cooter gets pissed, he gets funny.

Billy remembered what they'd done with the stuff they stole. The gnomes and flamingos were all on the front lawn here, with the Virgin Mary and the lawn jockey snuggled down in the crab grass together. Cooter couldn't take their clothes off—they were statues, after all—but the way he laid them down said it all. With the gnomes and pink birds watching. It was fucking hilarious.

Afterward, when they were about to get high, Cooter said that he'd have to move that shit before his uncle saw it. Uncle Conch Boukman was a hard-headed, short-tempered old man who moved to New Jersey after his village in Haiti was destroyed in that earthquake. Cooter was his only relative, but to Billy they were so different that it was hard to tell that there was any connection.

But Uncle Conch brought a little money with him, and he paid the mortgage off on Cooter's pad.

The screams from downstairs punched Billy in the head, and it shook him out of the memories of last night.

Farelli and his goon squad were all there. So were a whole mess of Cooter's friends. Couple of kids Billy knew too. Maybe ten people, hanging out, getting high. One guy—the uptown kid who brought some quality ice with him—with the shorts down around his knees so Carla could give him a courtesy BJ. But Carla wasn't blowing him. Or anybody. Billy looked at her and saw her face burst apart as a baseball bat hit her.

She screamed, and the bat hit her, and she couldn't scream anymore. Carla fell back, and she fell weird, like she had no bones in her neck.

That's when it all went crazy.

That's when Farelli's thugs went apeshit. Bats and chains.

Farelli stood in the center of the living room and even from upstairs Billy could see that there was a bulge in Farelli's pants. He was rock-hard watching this shit. Billy knew about that. His old man had been like that sometimes. Getting serious wood because using a belt on Billy and his sisters felt that good. Made him feel that jazzed.

That's when Billy heard Cooter come crashing into the room, swinging a mop handle and catching Farelli's cousin, Tony, right across the forehead.

There was a moment when Billy thought it would all be over right there and then. Everyone and everything froze solid. Even the screaming stopped for just a second.

Billy wanted to scream a warning. He wanted to shout at Cooter and everyone else. Tell them to run, tell them to get the fuck out.

While there was still a chance.

—3—

But there was no chance.

Cooter knew it when he came charging out of the kitchen with the mop.

Farelli and his goons knew it before they loaded into their Escalades. They knew it when they stopped at the Lukoil to fill up their red gas can.

Even the zoned-out stoners knew it. Carla probably knew it, too, right up until the bat knocked her head loose on her neck.

Billy knew it. Billy knew that all of them—greaser or meth-head—were born into this. Into this moment, like they were all bowling-balls thrown down polished wood alleys but all the alleys were designed to converge into one spot. No pins. Just a bunch of bats and a gas can and a mop handle.

The moment became unstuck when Farelli laughed.

The right kind of laugh will do that.

Cooter looked at him and Farelli looked back.

Billy screamed then.

Nobody heard him, because everyone was screaming. The bats went up and down and around and around, and somebody kept painting all of the drowsy, doped-up, screaming faces with red.

Cooter tried to run.

They splashed him with gas.

Farelli flicked a cigarette at him.

Cooter made it all the way to the second floor. Billy tried to help him. Swatting at the flames that were wreathed around Cooter's face. Billy shoved him into the bathroom, knocked him down with burned hands into the tub. Turned on the water.

But by then there were flames coming up through the floor.

The water filled the tub, but fire reached up with long yellow fingers between the floorboards and drove Billy back. From the bathroom doorway he watched the inferno heat boil the water in the tub. Where Cooter was.

When Billy dove through the second-floor window, he saw three things.

The Escalades driving away, laughter tumbling out of the open windows.

The faces of pink flamingos and lawn gnomes and the mother of Jesus staring up at him with plastic eyes.

And then the hedges reaching up and tearing at him with a thousand green fingers.

Billy got out of the hospital the day they buried Cooter.

He was the only one at the graveside. Billy and the priest, who didn't even look at him. And a brass urn full of ashes.

Billy's hands were burned. He had bandages around his face and under his clothes. Billy felt the fire still burning in his skin and the screams still burning in his head. They would have kept him in the hospital, but despite everything they say about providing medical coverage if you don't have money, they will kick a meth-head out after a couple of days. He didn't have any money, so he walked home. Back to Cooter's.

The house was a blackened shell. The fire department had been able to save the front steps. The rest was cinder.

Billy sat down on the top step, rested his elbows on his knees, hung his head, and cried until there was no moisture left in his body. The urn sat next to him. No one had claimed it, so they'd given it to him, and he carried it all the way back.

He stayed there all day, talking to Cooter in his head.

Cooter didn't say shit, though.

Two days later Billy bought some rock. Smoked it. Saw

Cooter. They slopped on the couch and played video games. They talked about living and dying. They hung out.

When the rock was gone and the high broke apart into little pieces of reality, Cooter went back to sleeping in his urn. Billy went back to the burned-out house, sat down on the step next to the ashes. And cried.

That was life.

That was every day.

On the sixth day after the funeral, on the long downslope of a high, Billy sat on the step with his head in his hands. He heard a car pull up and stop, but he didn't look up.

"You that white boy," said a voice.

Billy looked up slowly. Moving fast hurt. It broke blisters. So, Billy moved like he was old. Uncle Conch stood on the soot-covered little bit of pavement that ran between the two halves of the front lawn. He wore a black suit and a shirt the color of snow. His hat hid most of his face so that only his chin and mouth were in the light. He had dark lips and cigarette-yellow teeth.

"You that white boy," he repeated, his thick Haitian accent making everything sound like a song. "You was friends with Cooter."

"I guess," said Billy. He realized that his nose was running, and he sniffed. Tasted some tears, so he wiped his eyes.

Uncle Conch looked down at the urn. "That my Cooter?"

Billy nodded. "You weren't at the funeral, so they said I could have his ashes."

"Yeah," said the old man, "I'm too close to the grave my ownself for me to want to visit a boneyard."

That made sense to Billy, and he nodded.

After a while, Uncle Conch said, "You and Cooter always doing the drug."

He never said "doing drugs" or "smoking meth." Doing the drug.

"I guess."

Uncle Conch stepped a little closer. He had bad legs and leaned heavily on a cane that was carved with snakes and skulls.

"Why you do the drug?"

"What?"

"The drug. Why you and my Cooter always do the drug? Where it take you?"

Billy thought about that. "Away, I s'pose."

"You suppose? You don't know?"

"Away."

Billy stared down at the lawn. The heat had withered the grass to brown strings, and the fire hoses had turned that to clingy seaweed. The tendrils were wrapped around the legs of half-melted flamingoes and the throats of charred gnomes.

Another shuffling step closer. "Tell me," he said.

Billy squinted up. "Why do you want to know about that stuff?"

Uncle Conch lowered himself down to the step. It took a long, painful time for the old man to do it. Billy tried to help, but he was too badly burned. When he was down, Uncle Conch took a minute to catch his breath, and he produced a spotless white handkerchief and mopped his brow. Billy was pretty sure he'd never seen anyone use a handkerchief before, not outside of a movie.

"Tell me, boy," wheezed Uncle Conch, "why you and my Cooter always want to go away? What you want to get away from?"

Billy looked past him to the street, but what he was seeing was the open mouth of the grave before they lowered the box. The mound of dirt was a brown heap that they didn't bother to cover with one of those green AstroTurf mats. Nobody gave enough of a shit even for that.

"I don't know."

"Tell me, boy. I got to know."

Billy looked at him. "Why? What does it matter now?"

"It matters to me. Cooter may not be a saint, but he all the family I had left. Tell me what he wanted to do. Let me carry that for what time I got left. Give me that much so I don't bury his dream too."

Billy stared at Uncle Conch for almost a minute before he could answer. "You were in Haiti when we were growing up," he said. "Cooter and me were always getting kicked around, you know?"

"No, I don't know. Tell me."

"I don't know ... I saw Haiti on the news and stuff. I know that you guys had it worse down there than we had here...."

"Poor is poor is poor," said Uncle Conch. "Kid starving in the street don't measure his hunger 'gainst some other kid he never met. Kid still hungry. Kid still cries when he hungry."

"Yeah, but it wasn't just that. Cooter's mom was pretty cool— she was your daughter?"

Uncle Conch shook his head. "My sister's daughter. Only one of us to leave Haiti in a hundred years."

"Until you."

The old man shook his head. "I live here, boy, but I ain't ever left Haiti. Haiti is home. I'm a Boukman—you know what that mean?"

Billy shook his head.

"My great-great-many times-great granddaddy was Dutty Boukman, a *houngan* from Jamaica who settled in Haiti. Let me tell what a *houngan* is," said Uncle Conch. "That's a sorcerer, a priest of the old religion. Dutty led the first slave revolt in Haiti. He that strong. He that fierce a man. Once Dutty shucked off his chains no man could put them back on again. Them French they had to shoot him a hundred times to bring Dutty Boukman down. Why so many times? Because Dutty was filled with the *loa* of Kalfu—and that is one powerful spirit. Kalfu is the *loa* of the crossroads and every slave who ever died had to stand before that spirit and tell Kalfu how they died and who killed them. Kalfu got so angry he looked for the right man, the right slave, to open a doorway in his soul, to let him come through. That's what Dutty

Boukman did. Dutty's heart was so filled with hate for the slavers that he opened up the door in his soul and let Kalfu come walking through. Oh, now Kalfu is not Casper. You know Casper, the friendly ghost? Like on TV? No, Kalfu not like that. Kalfu controls all the evil forces of the spirit world. He bring bad luck and hard justice. Dutty was filled with that dark magic, and when he told all the other slaves to rise up, they rise up. That was 1791. By 1794 slavery was abolished in Haiti. That's how strong Dutty Boukman was. That's the blood that flows right pass the crossroads. The river of dark blood that flows over the years from him to me." He paused and sadness filled his eyes. "And to Cooter. And that river of blood end with Cooter, but it don't make the little boy strong. All that river did was wash him away, and up in heaven his mama is singing a sad song."

The birds in the tree seemed to echo that music.

"I live here, but Haiti is in me." Uncle Conch touched his chest. "When I die here, my soul will be buried in Haiti."

Billy nodded. That was something he could understand. "Cooter and me always wanted to find a place that we could call home. My mom died when I was two, so I never got to know her. Cancer. Sucks, but I was over Cooter's all the time. His mom was so great, you know? She was always singing songs."

"Little Bird," said Uncle Conch, and there was a smile buried down inside the wrinkles on his face. Sad, and deep and real. "That's what we called her. Little Songbird."

"She was great. She was the best. But ... you know, she died too. A bus hit her. I mean, how random and fucked up is that? How does God allow a bus to hit someone like her? Fucking bus should have hit my dad. Or Cooter's dad. Those two assholes should have had a fleet of buses hit them. Fuckers."

Uncle Conch nodded. "I didn't know that about her husband. Not until I get a letter and she tell me. I was putting money together to come here and talk to that man when I get the other letter. 'Bout the bus."

They sat and thought about it.

"You didn't come, though," said Billy. It wasn't an accusation. He was putting it out there to see what it looked like.

Uncle Conch nodded. "I didn't come. Not 'til after the quake."

"Yeah."

"I think the quake was a judgment on me."

Billy looked at him. "What?"

"The *loa*—they know what kind of man I am."

"Cooter said you were a priest too," said Billy. "They said in your village back on the island people thought you could magic and stuff. Tell the future, cure all sorts of diseases and raise dead people. He said you were a good guy."

The words were kindly meant, but Uncle Conch looked sad. "What Cooter know? All he knows is what his mama, Little Songbird, tell him, and what she know? Over here her whole like, just hearing 'bout things in letters. No ... it's the *loa* who know the truth. They know that I carry Boukman blood—hero blood— and they know I studied the ways of the *houngan,* but they also know I ain't done much with it 'cept make myownself happy. Drink and pussy and some deviltry to make the long nights scream. Yeah, you can fool your family but you can't fool the *loa*." He paused and Billy did not interrupt. "Maybe I'm a bad man, white boy. Maybe I'm a bad man like Cooter's dad. Like your dad."

Billy said nothing.

But then Uncle Conch shook his head. "No, not like those cockroaches. I don't put my hand on a woman, and I don't put my hand on a baby. Even so ... I'm a bad man. I done bad things." He nodded to the rhythm of his own thoughts. "Haiti a bad place. Hard place to be a good man. Easy place for a bad man to be a bad man. Bad is more fun."

"I—"

Uncle Conch laughed. A deep, rumbling laugh that had no humor in it. "Don't worry, white boy, I ain't going to do bad things to you."

"You weren't bad to Cooter."

The old man sighed and ran his fingers along the outside of the brass urn. "I wasn't good to him, neither."

"You paid his bills, man. You gave him a place to live."

Uncle Conch turned and looked at the charred walls behind him. "All I gave that boy is a place to die, and I think he was dead before they cooked him in there."

But Billy shook his head. "No, man, that's just it. Cooter and me ... we could always get free. We could get away anytime we liked."

The old man's brows knitted. "How? How you and my Cooter get free?"

When Billy didn't answer, the old man nodded.

"The pipe," said Uncle Conch.

"I guess."

"That got you away?"

"Yeah."

"All the way away?"

Billy thought about it. "At first, yeah."

"What happened at first?"

"At first, man, we'd light a pipe and take one hit and we were gone. Really gone. We were flying." He closed his eyes to summon the memory, and his body swayed as if he was gliding on the winds, riding the thermals, high above it all. "That's how we escaped, man."

"Escaped?"

"Cooter's dad. Mine. When Cooter's dad went to jail, we sailed so high that night. Oh, god, we were all the way up. Flying like birds."

When he opened his eyes, Uncle Conch was not looking at him. Instead he was studying the soot-blackened flamingoes.

"That why you got these birds all over the lawn?"

Billy sniffed back more tears. "That was Cooter's idea. He said that maybe if we got high enough we'd fly way up in the sky, like the flamingoes. You ever see them? They soar up there, not a care in the world, just floating on the wind like nothing beneath them matters. Nobody can touch them up there. They're so high. And so free." He looked at the melted wings of the pink plastic birds. "Now Cooter's gone and all the flamingoes are dead. Cooked, man. It's all cooked."

A sob broke in Billy's chest, and he hugged his ribs with bandaged hands as he wept for Cooter.

Uncle Conch laid a hand on Billy's trembling shoulder.

"Why'd they have to do that?" sobbed Billy. "Why'd they have to do all that? So we stole their yard stuff. So we took some stupid pink birds and stupid gnomes and that other stuff. If they were mad about it, most they should have done was mess us up a little. They done that plenty of times. All they had to do was knock us around a little and take their stuff back. And, look, man, they didn't even take their shit. All that stuff's still here. What was it all about, man? What's the point of anything if they didn't even take their stuff back?"

He kept crying, and his voice crumbled beneath the weight of it. The only word he could manage was, "Cooter ..."

Then Uncle Conch bent close and whispered in his ear.

"Now you listen to me, boy," he said, "I told you once that I'm a *houngan* and the blood of Dutty Boukman run through my veins. Told you that my many-times grandfather got so mad, so damn mad, that he opened up a door in his soul and let something evil come right on through."

"Kalfu," said Billy.

"The *loa* Kalfu, lord of the crossroads, bringer of hard justice." Uncle Conch picked up the urn. "I just 'bout pissed on everything good there was in the Boukman name. I left my Little Songbird to get knocked around by a weak, bad man. I let her boy die trying to fly away from this shithole. I done that. I could have changed it, but I didn't, so I done that."

Billy shook his head, but Uncle Conch was staring at the urn. He opened it and looked at the soft gray nothing that was Cooter.

"I done this," he murmured. "I got no one else alive on this Earth who is blood kin to me. The Boukman name, proudest blood of my people, dies when I die. And if I die this moment, right now, then that blood turns to piss that ain't worth hosing off the street."

He drew a long breath.

"But I got me a little breath left and a little blood yet, and I got me a heart that is so full of hate that it wants to burst open and break the world. So what you think I should do?"

Billy said nothing. His eyes were huge and round.

"You 'member Cooter said I could magic, white boy. Pretend I'm a genie in a bottle and you can ask one wish. What that wish going to be?"

Billy looked at the urn and down at the melted flamingoes and then up at the endless blue sky. "I guess I'd want two wishes," he said.

"What wishes, boy?"

"I'd want to see Cooter again. He's my best friend, you know? He's the greatest, Cooter's the king. I'd want to see him again. Not with burns on him, though. Like he was yesterday morning. Laughing and happy, singing to himself like the way his mom used to. That's what I'd wish for."

A tear broke from Uncle Conch's eye and wandered over the million seams and lines in the old man's face, burning like hot silver.

"And what's your second wish? You want me to burn those boys who burned Cooter? You want me to raise the devils of Hell to burn them? Or how about I call the *loas* of vengeance and we turn these melted gnomes into a pack of monsters to hunt *that* pack of monsters. I could do that. That's dark magic. I call Kalfu and I could do that."

But Billy shook his head. "No ... if I only had one more wish after that, I'd want Cooter and me to fly out of here. Far away. Like flamingoes, but not melted ones. Not fly like we're smoking ice, but really fly. All the way into the sky. That would be the shit, man. That's what Cooter would want."

Uncle Conch stared at Billy for a long, long time.

"That's all you want? You can have all the revenge you want and instead you want to fly away with my Cooter like a couple of birds?"

Billy closed his eyes. "Big pink flamingoes, man. So high ... so free ..."

—5—

Billy thought he said more to Uncle Conch, but he couldn't hear his own words. Another sob hitched his shoulders.

But it wasn't a sob, of course. He knew that. When he opened his eyes, he knew that much.

Far, far below the Passaic River curved along the edge of Newark, but from up here it looked like a blue ribbon. Billy turned to say something to Uncle Conch, but it wasn't the old man. It was Cooter. Big and pink and riding free. Billy called out to him, but his voice sounded different. It didn't sound like his voice. And it didn't sound wrong. It sounded right. It sounded too right.

Billy closed his eyes and he laughed in that strange new voice as he and Cooter flew free.

—6—

Uncle Conch took his time getting to his feet. He was old but parts of him were even older, used up before their time. He braced himself on his cane and began lumbering toward his car.

In his chest, his heart hammered like old drums. Fast, insistent, powerful. Pain darted up and down his left arm.

But he hummed as he walked to his car. He knew that he wasn't going to die in the next five minutes. Not that soon. When he got to the curb he turned and looked at the debris in the yard. The flamingoes were gone, and that made him smile. For just a moment. It would be the last of Uncle Conch's smiles to touch that face.

Then his eyes fell on the little singed and half-melted gnomes.

Nasty looking little things. Stupid things. White man's idea of what looked good on a man's lawn.

The eyes that looked on the gnomes was Uncle Conch's for one blink longer. Then with the next blink the eyes changed from dark-brown to fiery red. The smile on the old mouth changed, became broader, brighter. No longer the pained smile of a dying man but the vital smile of something far more powerful. In his chest the old heart began hammering to a rhythm that was many times older than the body around it. A rhythm many times older than the pavement beneath the scuffed shoes. Many times older than the country in which he stood. As old as hate, and that was so very old.

"Rise up, my brother spirits," said the voice that was no longer Uncle Conch's. Nor was the language English, or French or Creole.

On the lawn, there was a small sound, a tiny groan, a rasp of plastic. One of the lawn gnomes raised its singed and sooty head. The white beard was streaked with ash, the eyes were melted holes. The mouth was stamped into the plastic. But then the plastic lips trembled and the whole body trembled with effort and finally there was a *popping* noise as the mouth opened. Broken, twisted plastic in a zigzag gash. The little creature smiled, and its wide and wicked grin was exactly the same as what was now stretched across Uncle Conch's mouth. The mouth that had belonged to Uncle Conch, when there had been an Uncle Conch.

"Rise up, brother spirits," repeated Kalfu, using Uncle Conch's borrowed mouth. Each word was exhaled on a hot breath that blew through the open door of hate in the ancient body. "They are serving dinner on Seventh Avenue. White meat, served rare. All you can eat."

One by one the melted gnomes opened empty eyes and ripped open jagged mouths. Hungry mouths. They rose unsteadily to their feet, tottering toward the open car door beside which Kalfu, their brother, waited.

GAVIN FUNKE'S MONSTER MOVIE MARATHON
(BRING THE WHOLE FAMILY!)

—1—

Gavin Funke sat in the dark and watched his monster movies.

One after the other.

All day.

Well into the night.

He had the theater mostly to himself. The popcorn was fresh and the smell of it filled the entire theater with buttery goodness. The Coke was cool, not cold, but that was okay. Making ice was a luxury, and he needed as much juice as the generators would give him to run the projectors and the air conditioning.

The theater was nearly quiet. A few people made some noise, but there was always a little of that. Over in the corner, in the darkest and most private spot in the auditorium he could hear soft moans.

Gavin didn't care about that. He was not that kind of voyeur.

He sat with his feet wedged between the backs of the two seats in front of him, his sneakers parted in a Vee so as not to obstruct his view. On the screen a black man in a stained white shirt was hammering boards over the windows of a farmhouse. There were bangs on the doors as clumsy fists pounded on the doors and walls. Anyone with half a brain could tell those boards weren't going to stop anyone. Even if Gavin hadn't seen this movie a dozen times he'd know that. They were nailed crookedly and in haste. And they were straight-nailed, not toe-nailed. Not screwed securely. Wouldn't take much at all.

"Dumbass," he yelled at the screen.

But the actor playing the guy in the movie with the monster didn't listen. None of them ever did. They did stupid things because they were stupid characters. And they died. A lot of them died. Sometimes all of them died.

But not Gavin Funke.

No sir.

He was the star of *this* movie and he was not going to make any mistakes at all. Not one.

Sure, there had been a learning curve, but the point was that he *did* learn.

He dug into the tub and pulled out a fist of popcorn, not caring that some of it fell onto his shirt or lap, or onto the floor. That was what brooms were for.

A foot kicked his chair, but he didn't bother turning and instead said, "Mom! Shhhhh!"

Another kick.

"Mom, *c'mon*—how 'bout it?"

Kick.

Gavin abruptly stood up, shot his mother a lethal glare, and moved to the row in front. Not the perfect distance, but still good. And no kicking.

He ate the popcorn more slowly, and it lasted all the way up until the hero got killed. He kept hoping the movie would—just for once—end differently. But it stubbornly refused to do so.

—2—

Gavin slept in because he hated morning. That's why he arranged the movie marathons to go well past midnight. Last night was zombie night. From one yesterday afternoon until the last credits rolled up a minute after five a.m.

He was bloated with popcorn and Milk Duds and Night & Day and some shady off-brand beef jerky because, hey, he needed protein and all the good stuff was gone. Marathons were good for the soul but hard on the colon, and he spent a bad hour in the chemical toilet out by the dumpsters. Gavin was wise, though, and daubed Vicks on his upper lip to kill the smells. He read nearly three chapters of an autobiography by an actor with a huge chin. It was pretty funny, and laughing helped his colon do its business.

Then he went inside, took a shower, dressed in new clothes that came from JCPenney. The belt was a tighter fit than it should have been, and he wondered if all that candy was nudging him up a size. That could be a problem because all he could manage was off the rack.

"No more Milk Duds," he promised. But that was a low bar because he didn't have that many boxes left anyway. No way he'd cut out the Night & Day because the licorice helped him move things along.

Gavin turned the house lights up and cleaned the theater floor. Nothing worse than walking on all that sticky mess. As he worked he listened to Tom Waits songs on his Bluetooth earbuds. He liked Waits's older stuff, back when it was more dramatic and melodic. Currently "Tom Traubert's Blues" was breaking his damn heart, like it always did. Gavin had his own theories on what the lyrics meant. They were timeless. People leave, things end, hearts get broken. Hardly mattered what the singer intended. That guy was dealing with his own blues. While he knelt down to fish under a chair with a dust brush he wondered if Tom Waits was still alive. Probably. Guy like him would find some way to figure things out. He'd get his crap sorted. Gavin was sure of it.

Maybe one of these days he'd take a drive north to find out. He thought Waits lived in Pasadena or someplace like that. Up that way. But the singer had been raised right here in San Diego, Gavin thought.

The song ended, and Gavin paused to push the buttons to play it again, but then he stopped, looking down at the debris his last brush sweep had gathered. There was some of his own popcorn, and a stray Milk Dud that still looked good.

And a ring.

Gold. Slender. Very pretty. With delicate old world Viking tracery that twisted all the way around the band. He picked it up and sat back on his heels. The ring was dusty, as if it had been there a long time.

Had it? Could he have missed it the other times he cleaned the floor?

It made his heart hurt, and the tears ambushed him. He didn't even feel them coming but suddenly they were there. Shoving their way out of him, choking him, kicking at the walls of his lungs. He caved forward so suddenly his forehead banged against the floor. It hurt, but he didn't care. Not one bit.

He closed his fist around the ring and tried to push the fist into his chest. If he could have managed that he'd have buried the ring in the tear-moist soil of his heart.

"Mom ..."

The single word escaped his lips. He blubbered it, and the word slipped free and fell onto the dirty floor.

—3—

It took a lot for Gavin to get up off the floor.

It took so much more for him to return the ring to his mother.

He didn't know how he actually managed it, but he was aware of the cost. It was more than he was able to afford.

Getting to his feet was like jacking up an unloaded truck. He was only 5'9" and stocky though not yet fat, but his body felt like it weighed three or four tons. Even lifting his head away from the dirty floor was almost too much, and for a while he knelt there, stupid with pain. His nose was thick with snot and it ran, diluted by tears, over his lips and chin, hung there in pendulous strands, and felt unheeded to his chest.

"Mom ..."

He felt something on his face and brushed at it, and watched bits of popcorn and a strand of half-chewed red licorice whip fall away. He frowned at the red candy. How long had *that* been there? He couldn't remember the last time he'd had any, and yet it had been swept into the light by the same brush that discovered the ring. What the hell was under that chair? A black hole? The Bermuda Triangle of lost theater stuff?

The ring was tiny but heavy in his hand.

"Mom," he said again. His voice sounded a little less broken to his ears, and that gave him the courage to try and stand.

Standing. Yeah. Jesus.

That took forever. He braced one hand on an armrest of a seat. The wood was polished and cool and only mildly sticky. He fixed his eyes on the red fabric that covered the seat and back. Did every theater everywhere in the world use that same stuff? Was it a rule? A regulation? He didn't know.

He flexed the muscles in his arm and shoulder and chest and pushed.

His body resisted, as if it and gravity were conspiring to keep him down on his knees. The traitors.

But ... no.

This was not an act of betrayal. It was a mercy. To help him in this effort was to be complicit in more self-inflicted harm. Finding the ring was bad enough. Looking too closely at it was foolish, because seeing meant *knowing*. Knowing meant understanding and accepting.

He wanted to scream. To hurl a string of the most obscene words he knew—and after all the movies he'd seen, Gavin knew them all—but that would be wrong. Mom would hear him. She never liked it when people cursed. The only time she'd ever hit him growing up was when he'd dropped an f-bomb by accident after stubbing his little toe on the edge of his bedroom door on a Christmas morning when he was nine. He'd come bolting out, all happy and filled with Yuletide greed, having already peeked after his weary parents had gone to bed. There was a mountain of brightly wrapped boxes stacked like a city of goodness around the base of the glimmering tree. Gavin hadn't been able to sleep a wink, then when he heard his parents' door open, he'd whipped back his own and rushed into the hall. His little toe hit the corner and folded sideways with a sharp *crack*. Mom hadn't heard that, though. All she heard was him howling that word over and over. And she'd given him a hearty slap.

As he knelt there, preparing for another try to stand, he thought about that morning. Instead of opening presents, he'd fallen, clutching his foot. The toe was standing out at the wrong angle, and the whole foot starting to swell and darken. With a shock of horror Mom understood what had happened. She screamed. Dad came running. Then there were hugs and kisses and apologies. They bundled Gavin into the car and drove straight to the urgent care, leaving every gift unopened and forlorn. When they'd returned around one thirty in the afternoon, Gavin was half dopey with painkillers and his foot was swathed in protective gauze, with the broken toe buddy-taped to the next one.

Mom had been so contrite and embarrassed for having hit him that his own infraction for the use of that word was never spoken about. Then or ever again. She never hit him again. In retrospect, he realized that she'd simply been exhausted by sitting up until three wrapping all those presents, and then been startled by the dramatic opening of his door and him rushing out and curses filling the hall. A perfect storm that made the morning a disaster, but became a much-sanitized anecdote for years and years after. It was even told at the reception at Aunt Joan's house after Dad's funeral.

It put a small smile on Gavin's face. He could feel it, but the fact that it was a smile—given the circumstances—made him angry. He ground his teeth together and pushed.

—4—

Gavin tottered over to where Mom sat. Her eyes were alert, but they always were. They watched him approach with unfiltered anger. More like hate.

It had become hate, born of resentment and disappointment. He knew that but tried to build layers of personal misdirection over it. She'd had a hard life. Five kids. No chance at a job until the last one, Jimmy, was in school, and by then she was in her forties. Always jostling for crappy jobs with kids not much older than her oldest. Twenty-something managers at temp jobs who really didn't give a crap about her or anything. Dead minds overseeing numb employees in a nowhere job. The economy kept tanking, and then all that political stuff. More wars killing young men and women from town who went to serve and came home in boxes. Or, if they lived, came home damaged in body or soul. More diseases to be afraid of. Mom used to joke that her life was as frustrating and complicated as George Bailey's in *It's a Wonderful Life*, except that there were no adorable guardian angels and no heartwarming third act where everyone who was a pain in the ass came to save her.

Gavin could see echoes of all of that in Mom's eyes. Even now.

He raised the ring and showed it to her, angling it to catch the glow of the house lights.

"Look what I found under the seat," he said.

Mom said nothing. She glared.

He sighed.

"I'm sorry, Mom," he said.

Nothing.

Gavin took a half step toward her, and she bared her teeth. Or, tried to. The gag didn't really allow that. She tried to reach for him, but her thin wrists were snugged tight to the armrests by turn after turn of duct tape. Her ankles were similarly bound, and more of the tape held her torso to the chair-back and crisscrossed her body. He'd found pink duct tape. For her. For Mom.

Her fingers were free, though, and they flexed and twitched and clawed at the armrest. It took Gavin nearly five whole minutes to capture one of those desperate fingers, clumsy the ring onto the proper finger, and snug it in place. She was not at all cooperative. She thrashed and cried out and stabbed him with those hateful stares.

He sagged back, sweaty, gasping.

Crying.

He looked down the row to where Gavin's youngest brother and sister—Jimmy and Allison—sat, with Aunt Joan next to them. Uncle Pete was next to her, and their twins—Abby and Deedee—at the far end of the row. Gavin had not yet caught up with the rest of the family. His other two sisters, Connie and Gail, and all the various and assorted cousins, nephews and nieces. There were a lot of Funkes in San Diego County. It was a Funkey place, his dad used to say. This was all he had now. Each of them tied there. Each of them his guests, however unwilling, for his nightly movie marathons. Each of them trying to break free and escape. Each of them wild with hatred.

Gavin turned away and sat on the step beside her row, put his face in his hands, and wept again. Not as hard this time, but longer. The minutes crawled over him like ants.

—5—

As soon as he trusted his legs to carry him, he got up and staggered out of the theater and stood in the concrete yard out back. The big dumpster was near to overflowing and he could hear rats moving inside of it. He heard them crunching on discarded popcorn. They were movie-house rats, though, and he didn't mind. If they ever snuck in, though, he'd catch them and then they'd be sorry.

It was a bright day and the sun seemed nailed to the blue sky. He had plenty of time before he had to be back at work. Gavin walked around the dumpster to where his big white commercial van waited for him. It was gassed up because he always did that before he came home. And, because he was anal and was okay with it, he opened the back doors and made sure he had everything he needed. On the lefthand wall was a pegboard covered in hooks from which his many rolls of duct tape were hung. Below those were knives, clubs, brass knuckles, hatchets, a sledgehammer, bone saws, a scythe, a fire axe, coils of rope, and several canvas hoods with Velcro neck bands. On the righthand side were sturdier hooks and some eyebolts, along with a huge bundle of plastic zip-ties for restraining bound wrists and ankles. There were boxes of big black industrial trash bags, a stack of rubber body bags, and a pile of precisely cut pieces of cloth and leather belts. He always wrapped the leather belts in T-shirt cotton because he was mindful of comfort. Gags did not have to be nasty.

He also had a wheelbarrow and a decent hand truck, both of which were fitted out with bungee cords. He'd learned from experience on that. As he had with all of it. Everything was a work in progress for Gavin. But he was smart and patient and diligent and focused.

The last thing he checked was his toolbox. It was a big red Craftsman, stocked with excellent tools for any task. Drills, hammers ... all of it.

He closed the doors, patted them for luck, got behind the wheel, used the remote to open the gates, and drove out. Being careful. Always careful. Last thing he wanted to do was get caught.

The city was always quiet on Sunday mornings. He saw some people, but even though they looked at the big white van he just kept going. He didn't know any of them, and had no interest in inviting total strangers to one of his marathons. He had a big one planned for Wednesday. Wacky Wednesday, as he thought of it. Always a hodgepodge of movies. He had a totally eclectic blend in mind. Start off with trailers and a bunch of cartoons. Even the cartoons were a blend—old Woody Woodpecker, an episode of

Lippy the Lion and Hard-de-Har-Har; then a Porky Pig one, some Disney stuff, and wrap it up with one of the earliest Popeye shorts he could find. It was a good thing his theater had been renovated a few years ago to show high definition Blu-ray DVDs instead of actual film. There were two big multi-disk banks. That was great for archived funnies and old trailers. But the real heart of his projection room was the digital streaming capabilities. He had thousands of hours of movies on an Apple MacBook Pro networked to an eight terabyte external drive. Plus software that would keep the movies playing endlessly until he turned it off. Gavin could play movies until the cows came home.

After the trailers and cartoons he'd start soft, with kind of a retrospective of cinema history. First up was a digitally remastered and ultra clean version of *The Gold Rush*, Charlie Chaplin's masterpiece. After that he'd jump to an early Marx Brothers flick, then onto *Abbott and Costello Meet Frankenstein*. From there it was John Wayne in *She Wore a Yellow Ribbon*, and the Gene Kelly, Donald O'Connor, and Debbie Reynolds classic, *Singing in the Rain*. He had a lot of variety after that. Comedies by Mel Brooks, one of Orson Welles's lesser-known pieces, a John Huston adventure, and on to William Friedkin, and so on. The marathon would be an education as well as a celebration. The monster movies wouldn't start until sunset, and would again go silent with 1927's *Nosferatu*, through some of the Universal and RKO catalog, onto the Hammer flicks, more of the George Romero oeuvre, and through the darkest hours of the night. He had *Silence of the Lambs* inserted in the block of horror rather than mystery because Gavin considered it a horror film and could go toe-to-toe with any film history snob who argued otherwise.

He smiled to himself, and his heart thumped happily as he thought about the marathon. It was going to be the last word in such showcases of cinematic artistry.

Gavin put in his earbuds, turned up the music—Adele this time—and went about his business.

—6—

Gavin drove up Route 5 to the Shell station in Carlsbad. The day before he'd rigged a small generator to power an electric siphon. He checked to make sure no one was around, then got out of the van and went over to view the gauge on the single-tank truck. The needle was buried in the green, and the generator was silent, its automatic shut off triggered by the anti-spillover float in the tanker. He climbed up onto the truck and double-checked with the big stick he'd set there for that purpose. The whole tank was filled to capacity. Three thousand gallons.

Smiling, he climbed down and uncoupled the vapor and fuel hoses. He went over the whole truck to make sure every setting and fitting was correct, then climbed in and drove it back to the theater, waited until the street was clear, opened the gate, and backed it in.

He took his mom's old Honda back to his van. She wouldn't need it again, so he left the keys in it and got back into his old vehicle.

It didn't take long to get to Solana Beach, where his two sisters lived in a beach cottage. Connie owned it and rented a room to Gail. They called the place Party Central and it was indeed that. A steady stream of buff surfers or bearded hipsters. The kinds of parties Gavin would never have been invited to. The kind he only ever saw when he peeked through windows. Connie was the most promiscuous, but Gail was hardly a nun.

He spent an hour looking for them. They were not at home. Not at the Starbucks down the block. Not in the taco bar on the beach. They were nowhere. It saddened him. He was hoping they could join the movie marathon. He wanted the whole family there. He sat in his van and stared at their cottage, feeling the loss of them. Connie and Gail were always a bit silly. Flighty, Mom often said. But he loved them. They both seemed to find something funny in any situation. They even shared some giggles behind their hands at Dad's funeral, which had made that afternoon somehow bearable.

"Damn," he murmured. The pain and weariness in the sound of his own voice hit him like punches. Not jabs, but deep blows to the chest and stomach. Fresh tears tried to burn their way out of the corners of his eyes, but he pawed them away. He didn't want to cry again. Gavin was afraid he might not stop this time.

He realized that it was Gail more than Connie that did this to him. She was the baby. She was the one who seemed to be filled with life and sunshine. As a little girl she was always smiling. At everything. A falling leaf, a snoring dog, a hummingbird. She wasn't beautiful, but she'd always been pretty. Gavin understood the difference. People didn't necessarily fall in love with her, but everyone wanted to be around her. Strangers wanted to know her. You felt good when Gail was around, and when she laughed then everyone laughed. Even the real sticks-up-their-butts types had to smile. Gail was always alive. Gail *was* life.

If she was gone—then there was always going to be a Gail-shaped hole in the world through which sunshine and happiness and optimism would be slowly sucked away.

He sat there for a long time. Hands locked around the steering wheel. Fingers constrictor tight on the knobbed leather. Eyes burning as he stared and tried not to cry.

Gavin sat there for a long, long time.

And Gail was not there.

—7—

Until she was.

—8—

It took a lot for Gavin to drive back to the theater.
Too much effort.
Too much pain.

Too much time.

The sun had somehow rolled across the table of the sky and then tumbled off behind a wall of twilight clouds. There were shadows seeping out from under every car, and leaning out from the sides of homes and stores. The streetlights did not push back against this tide of darkness because they had lost that fight more than a year ago. Instead, they stood in a silent vigil as the day burned down like a dropped match.

Gavin knew that he'd lost time. Hours.

It was like that sometimes, but never as bad as this. No. Not even with Mom.

Gail, though.

As his mental circuits came back online with great reluctance, he turned to look behind him, into the bay of the van. With the doors closed everything back there was muted to vague shapes.

He could see Gail, though.

He could hear her.

She was strapped to the hand truck by a dozen bungee cords. Her wrists and ankles were secured with duct tape. Not pink. He hadn't been able to think things through enough for that. When he saw her simply walk up to his van, Gavin lost most coherent thought. He'd managed to grab her, though. To wrestle her down to the ground, put the hood over her, tie her up, attach her to the hand truck, and get her into the van. The hand truck was locked in place against one wall, held by industrial metal clips. It wouldn't fall over. He didn't want Gail to get hurt.

All of that had been done, but it must have been sheer autopilot because Gavin could not remember any of it. Not one bit. There was nothing in his head from the moment he and Gail locked eyes through the windshield of the van and now, waking up out of whatever it was. A fugue? Maybe. He thought that was the word. Even now he wasn't entirely back to himself. Not even close.

He was almost all the way back to the theater before he realized that he was hurt.

Gavin slowed and stopped for a moment in the middle of a side street and looked down at his hand. It was covered with dried blood. Not actively bleeding, though, which was something. But Gail must have fought. They always fought. Even family. Or, maybe especially family. Aunt Joan had really put up a fight. So did Mom.

He hadn't expected it from Gail, though. Not her. Not sunshine and smiles Gail.

He flexed his hand. It hurt, but everything seemed to be working. The bite wasn't bad, and it hadn't bled that much. No major arteries cut. Or, maybe there were no arteries in the hand. He wasn't sure. But the bones weren't broken, and the muscles didn't seem to be damaged.

So, Gail had fought back, had gotten him—probably when he was trying to get the gag on. He had to accept that the smiling, laughing mouth had turned savage in defense. Maybe in his fugue state he hadn't been able to reach her, to explain what he wanted from her. Maybe he'd been so messed up that he forgot to tell her that Mom was there, and Aunt Joan, and the others.

"Damn, Gail ..." he said, and heard the whine in his voice. Like how he used to say that when she played a prank on him when they were little. Before her smile made him smile back.

The sun was almost down now. He should have started tonight's movies already.

But he lingered a moment, resting his forehead on the steering wheel. She'd *bitten* him. *Gail* had bitten *him*.

It was so unfair. So wrong.

She'd never once been mean to him her whole life.

The bite, though.

That was very mean.

"That wasn't very nice, you know," he said, and the words rose to a shout.

Gail thrashed and howled and definitely would have done worse to him if she could.

"No," he said as he lifted his foot from the brake and pressed on the gas, "that wasn't very nice at all."

He drove the rest of the way to the theater, feeling the hurt burn through him, like acid in his veins.

That wasn't very nice at all.

—9—

He parked in back and had one hell of a time getting the hand truck down from the van. His hand was hurting now, and it was starting to throb.

Crap.

He nearly dropped her, and it would have served her right for what she did. But Gavin was quick and caught the handle of the hand truck just in time, steadied it, and saved the day. Then he wheeled her inside.

There was some real drama getting her into a good seat. Gail was a lot younger than either Mom or Aunt Joan, and even though she lived like a slacker, she had surfer muscles. Gail fought him every step of the way. He tried to reason with her but gave it up and saved his breath for the task of getting her from the hand truck to the seat. It took forty minutes and about a gallon of sweat.

Then he staggered over to an empty seat and collapsed into it. He was aware that every eye in the place was on him. Including Gail, not that the hood was off. Those big blue eyes. Even the spray of sun freckles across her nose and cheeks looked somehow angry, despite how pale she was. Her suntan was faded to a pale yellow.

"Not exactly a bronze sun bunny, are you?" he yelled, then felt immediately ashamed of himself. That was unkind. She couldn't help that. Not anymore.

None of them could. Mom was so pale she looked gray. Or ... maybe *was* gray. The house lights in the theater were too weak to show clearly. Aunt Joan looked positively jaundiced. The rest were a mix of milk white, ash gray, pee yellow.

Gavin looked down at his hand. Wrestling with Gail had opened the wound, and it bled sluggishly. He lifted his arm and angled it into the spill of light. The blood wasn't exactly red. Too dark, and too thick. Brick-red at best.

Even though he knew what Gail was—what she had to be—it was a shock.

Or, maybe it was the last thread holding up his denial. His hope.

He looked around the theater. There were eleven members of his nuclear and extended family here. And about thirty other people. His favorite teacher from the eighth grade. His neighbors —the nice Muslim couple from upstairs who were always sweet to him. The two guys from the game store. The cute girl who ran the concession stand in this very theater. Others. The people who mattered to him. The people who filled his world. All of them seated in chairs. Held in place. As comfortable as he could make them.

But ...

Not all of them.

Connie wasn't here. Some of his favorite cousins weren't here. His niece, Emma, wasn't here. He missed her a lot. So tiny. Seven weeks old when this all happened. There wasn't enough of her left to bring to the theater. Not after Aunt Joan had ...

Well.

He'd hoped to find more of the family.

To keep him company. And for the marathon.

The marathon.

Damn.

He looked at his hand. There were small black lines radiating out from the bite. At first he thought it was just lines of dried blood, but now he knew. Gavin fished around inside his own feelings, looking for evidence of the change. It was there.

A small thing, but there. His hands and feet were cold, and he was never cold. He rarely even slept with blankets. But they were like ice.

Is that how it would be? Just getting colder and colder until there was no warmth left in him? He hoped not. This was sunny San Diego and people came here because it was warm all year round. Not really hot, just nice. Gavin didn't want to be cold forever.

He got up and stood there, swaying a little, feeling sad and lost.

Everyone looked at him.

He saw the same hunger in their eyes that was always there. But now, for the first time, he thought he understood it. A little.

Gail tried to snap at the air between them, but the gag didn't permit it. Would she chew through it eventually? Mom did that once. She even ate part of the leather. It was cow, after all. Maybe they'd all have a last meal together. Leather. Cotton, too, but so what?

An ache opened up in his stomach. That was the best way to describe it. Opened. As if his whole body was a mouth. He thought about the popcorn and the Milk Duds. No. He didn't really want those anymore. Maybe not even the beef jerky.

He knew what was happening. Gavin understood what he was getting hungry for. It was happening so fast, though. Or ... was it fast? How long had it really been since Gail bit him? Hours. He closed his eyes, and in the darkness behind his lids he saw his veins drain of their redness and go dark. His face was starting to get cold too.

He felt two tears break and roll down his cheeks, but when he wiped them away and looked at his hand, he saw red-black smears.

The hunger was getting bigger. It was becoming insistent.

Gavin looked at his family and friends.

"I've got some stuff to do," he said thickly. "I'll be back as soon as I can."

He turned and hurried out, and he only fell twice.

—10—

It was dark out, so he turned on the exterior lights. He rarely did that because it drew other hungry people. That didn't matter anymore, though.

Gavin worked as fast as he could, attaching the hoses from the tanker truck to the line of generators he'd networked together. They chugged and hummed and poured electricity into the cables that ran like snakes across the ground and into the back of the theater. A lot of power to operate the industrial projector. He tested the system and checked the redundancies. Everything was working perfectly, and he managed a smile. Or, thought it was a smile. It felt weird, though, and his teeth clacked together.

As if biting.

That frightened him, so he hurried. His fingers were so cold, and his feet were blocks of ice. Walking was getting hard because the cold was in his knees and hips now. It hurt too. All his joints did.

Gavin set up the laptop in the projection room, opened the master file of movies and started the software running. Then he peered out at the house, seeing the screen display appear, announcing a few trailers. Another smile. Another *clack*.

"Hurry," he told himself, but the word didn't sound like a word. Just a sound. A moan.

He double and triple-checked everything, then he dimmed the house lights and shambled down to the theater. He picked up one of the big rolls of duct tape. Blue. Nice. His favorite color.

Gavin shuffled sideways along the row and sat down in the empty seat next to Mom. She stared at him, but now her eyes were different. No hate anymore. It startled him, and he looked around. Everyone was studying him. No one was glaring. No one was thrashing as if trying to lunge at him. No one was trying to bite.

They just *looked* at him.

He stood there, watching them watch him.

"Mom ...?" he said tentatively.

There was no reaction. At least nothing like what she'd done every other time since she died and he brought her here. He raised his hand—the one with the bite—and held it close to her nose. She sniffed at it. And that was all. No anger anymore. No hostility. Sniffing his hand as if sniffing his newest cologne, or a bunch of flowers he brought her on Mother's Day.

Something else opened in his chest. Not a hungry mouth this time, but something beautiful. She was Mom again. Okay, not really, but as much Mom as she could be. More than he ever expected her to be.

Gavin bent and kissed her cheek. Not even a flinch.

The coldness was growing inside of him, and despite the lovely glow inside he knew that the hunger was going to take him soon. It would make him want to go outside looking for something to eat.

"No," he said, forcing him to shape that word. To make it sound like a real word and not a moan.

Gavin sat down. It took so much of what he had left to peel off strips of the duct tape. So much to bind his ankles together. So much more to wrap it around and around his stomach and chest and the back of the theater seat. He looped zip-ties around each wrist and bent to use his teeth to pull them snugly. The left was a little too tight, but he knew that soon it wouldn't matter.

On the screen the trailers ended and the cartoons began.

He made it all the way through them. He thought he even laughed once or twice. But he wasn't really sure. The rest of the family and friends sat with him. They were all watching. The last time he looked around he saw that they were staring at the screen. Entranced by the people moving there. By Charlie Chaplin.

Gavin settled back to watch the movie marathon.

It played for hours.

For days.

For weeks.

As far as Gavin and his family were concerned, it played forever.

DOCTOR NINE
A POEM

Ragged birds in dangerous trees
clawed feet snarled by
ugly bark
Wings twisted into
the visceral vines.

In these trees no birds sing
they wait.
as they have always
waited.

Crouching
Ready
Waiting for Doctor Nine
to need them
again.

LULLABY

—1—

The realtor said, "Well, of course, you know it's *supposed* to be haunted."

He made it a joke. Saying that it was absurd. He didn't actually give them a wink, but it was implied.

"Haunted ...?" echoed Jillian. She looked up at her husband, but Matt was smiling like a kid.

"*Cool*," he said. "Who died there?"

"Really?" demanded Jillian. "*That's* your question?"

"Well ... I mean ... haunted house, sweetie. You have to admit that it's pretty great."

She gave him two seconds of an icy death stare, but it passed through him and left no mark on his goofy grin. This was pure Matt. He was smart, strong, educated, and a respected graphic designer, but at heart he was twelve years old and probably always would be.

Jillian, three years younger, had always been the adult in their relationship. Though it was an uphill slog to try to nudge him away from monster movies, comics, and video games and toward a transformation into a homeowner, husband and—in a month—father.

The realtor upped the wattage of his smile as Matt opened the gate on the whitewashed picket fence and took a few steps toward the house. It was gorgeous, and the agent began reciting the details, which was like giving tastes of crack to an eager addict.

"The Catskills are the perfect place to get away from it all. And this place has it all. Five bedrooms, three full baths, thirty-eight hundred square feet, a two-car garage, a two-story horse barn that can be converted into a gym or office. You're an artist, Matt? That space would be a great studio. Wood-burning fireplace in the living room and another in the master suite. Four-point-two acres of land including woods."

"And a ghost," said Jillian coldly.

"Oh, we have to say that. Yes, someone once heard something go bump in the night. And even though it's been newly renovated, it's an old house, full of charm and personality. There are always creaks and groans, and you're surrounded by a wonderful lush forest."

She stood her ground, not wanting to go even a single step closer. The house *was* beautiful, and—yes—charming, but even so. She absently touched her heavy belly and shook her head.

The realtor leaned close and added, "We *have* to tell you if someone reported it as haunted. Silly, I know, but there's a law. *Stambovsky v. Ackley.* They call it the Ghostbusters Law. Isn't that hilarious? You can look it up. Not trying to hide anything. Full disclosure. But, let's face it ... you've seen those ghost-hunting shows. Do they ever find anything? No. Have they ever found proof that ghosts even exist? Of course not! It's hype and nonsense. All it does, folks, is lower the price of beautiful houses like this one. You couldn't come within a million miles of a place like this for the price they're asking. Brand-new kitchen, security system, hot tub ..."

"Works for me," said Matt with so much raw enthusiasm that

Jillian knew she wasn't going to win this fight. Then a mother doe and two small fawns stepped out of the woods not a hundred feet away. The babies walked on spindly legs and the mother, patient and calm, stood watch as they began to eat wildflowers.

She sighed.

"Okay. We can look inside. But no promises."

"Of course not," said the realtor and beamed a barracuda smile.

Jillian wondered if this was what fish felt like when they bit down on the juicy worm and felt the hook go deep.

—2—

The house *was* beautiful.

Big rooms, high ceilings, and a warmth that seemed to have sunk into its bones. Jillian had researched every detail of the place and read the story in a back issue of the local paper about the so-called "ghost." The story was silly and lacked even a shred of credibility. Matt laughed about it and kept bragging that some creaking timbers saved them three hundred thousand dollars.

It was a quick sale because they had a loan for a much more expensive place, which left them plenty for some upgrades. A better security system, central air, and the conversion of one of the bedrooms into a nursery adjoining the master suite. Jillian had baby cams installed throughout, and Matt—delighted to have this place—didn't blink. He was busy converting the barn into an art studio, and his eyes were alight with possibilities. He had been doing graphic art and interior illustration for years, and like a lot of pros in his field, he was a better artist than his job required. Now, he'd have a studio to do some painting. Three days before the baby came, he began a beautiful landscape canvas of the woods spilling down to the lakefront.

At night they sat in the living room with the drapes open to the spray of diamonds scattered across the night sky, and a fire crackling comfortably in the hearth.

Jillian sat with her head on Matt's chest and baby Hope asleep in her arms. She looked up to see Matt smiling down at the little body wrapped in a pink blanket with a pattern of sunflowers.

"I thought babies were supposed to be noisy," he said. "She hardly even cries."

"She cries," Jillian assured him.

"Not much. Everyone I know who has kids kept warning me about not getting a full night's sleep for at least a year, and then the kid crying for no reason no matter what we do, but ..."

Jillian touched his cheek, and then they both looked down at Hope. The little girl was so completely asleep that she was a boneless bundle of warmth.

"She's an angel."

A log shifted in the fireplace, sending a swirl of sparks up the chimney. Outside a nightingale was singing, with counterpoint from a nightjar and a chorus of crickets. The moon would be up soon, and it looked like it was overflowing with silver that spread in a gleaming sheet across the lake's calm surface. Maybe Matt would paint that one of these days. Something to help Hope sleep through the nights. Every night.

Jillian watched her baby, doing what parents have done for thousands of years—making sure the tiny chest rose and fell.

Everything was perfect.

—3—

The full moon rose above the water, but streamers of clouds sharp as knives cut it to pieces.

A cold breeze whipped down from the north, chasing the birds back under the leaves, bending the treetops, promising winter's early arrival with frosty brutishness. The flowers in the window boxes huddled back but, trapped against the cold window glass, shriveled and died. The crickets fell silent, wondering where the day's warmth had gone. None of them would live to see the dawn. Even the grass in the yard around the house grew stiff with icy fright and paled to a deathly yellow.

The wind probed at the house with crooked fingers, finding little places where the renovation had been done poorly, or the builders hadn't thought to look. Tendrils of cold writhed along the attic floor and crept down the stairs, hunting for warmth.

Finding it.

Jillian was only half awake when she realized she was shivering.

She'd been deep inside a dream of being lost in her own house. Of wandering from room to room, finding doorways leading to yet more rooms she didn't know were there. She kept walking faster and faster, calling Matt's name. Calling Hope's name. Looking for them, and then finding one door sealed shut. She twisted the knob, but it would not open, and when she looked around in panic there were no other doors in the room. It was a small room, cluttered with stuffed toys caked with dust and hung with mobiles of mermaids and unicorns and happy animals— broken and discolored. As if the room had been closed and locked never to be opened. She whirled and looked down at the cradle set against a window. Her breath was ragged, her heart punching at the inside of her chest as she approached to see if her baby was okay.

There was a small bundle in the cradle, swathed in blankets.

But frozen air rose up as if the tiny figure beneath those pink blankets was the source of all the coldness in the world.

Jillian cried out and reeled back ...

... and woke up.

She lay there on the very edge of the bed, curled into a fetal ball, her body shuddering from the frosty air. She sat up, fighting for balance, scooting back toward Matt, who was always hot, even on nights like this.

That's when she caught sight of the small screen on the baby monitor.

It showed the cradle which was in the room next door.

The cradle was rocking very slowly. *Was it moving in the wind? God, could there be a window open?*

Jillian started to get up but then froze completely ... locked into the moment by what she saw on that monitor.

A hand.

The shadow of a hand. Long and thin. Too long. Too thin.

Reaching out to touch the top rail of the cradle. Curling fingers around it.

Rocking it.

Back and forth.

Very slowly.

And then, through the speaker on the cam and through the open nursery door, Jillian heard the gurgling laughter of her baby.

She leaped out of bed, tripping over a blanket that coiled around her ankle, fighting free, running, screaming for her husband. Screaming her baby's name. Just screaming.

The nursery was eight steps from the side of her bed, the cradle another seven steps. It felt like a mile. She burst into the small room, fists balled, ready to hit someone. To fight. To kill.

The cradle rocked slowly as a stiff breeze blew through a two-inch gap between frame and sill.

She skidded to a stop and snatched up her baby and hugged Hope to her chest. The baby burst into tears and screamed.

Then Matt was there, his face puffy with sleep but his eyes wild with fear. "What's wrong?"

Jillian turned, clutching the wriggling form. "There was someone here."

Matt stopped, eyes snapping wide. "What? Who? *Where?*"

"I saw it on the baby cam. I saw someone touching the cradle."

He looked around quickly. "Where'd they go?"

"I ... I don't know."

The nursery was small, open to the bedroom but with a door to the hall that was closed. Matt rushed past Jillian and the baby and snatched that doorknob. It rattled but did not turn—just like in her dream. Matt paused, frowning at the small dial lock above the handle. He turned it, and the door clicked open.

"Locked from inside," he said, his confusion turning the statement into a question. He opened the door and peered out into the hall, head tilted to listen. His frown deepened as he turned back to Jillian. "Did he go through the bedroom ...?"

"I ... I don't ..."

Her words trailed off because she'd seen him unlock the door from the inside. And no one could possibly have come through the bedroom without her seeing them.

"I'll check the house," Matt said, and she loved him for that. For not making her wrong, even if she was. "Is the baby okay?"

Jillian soothed Hope, who was still crying, but less stridently. She brought her into the bedroom and placed her on the mattress, checking her completely. There was no trace of a mark. No bruise, nothing. As she lay there, Hope calmed down, and the cries turned to hiccups.

"Yes," Jillian breathed, picking her up again and patting Hope's back.

Matt nodded, clearly relieved. He pulled on a sweatshirt and left. She heard him thump down the steps, intentionally making noise. Matt was a big guy, but he wasn't a fighter. He'd rather scare someone off than fight them.

Hope burped, ending the hiccups. Jillian kissed her sweet head and then movement on the baby cam caught her eye. The hand was there again, reaching for the cradle.

She nearly cried out.

And then a cloud moved away from the moon as the reaching hand became the shadow of a branch from the tree outside. Long, crooked fingers of wood, devoid of leaves. Wearing a disguise to fool her in the dark of night.

Jillian laughed. She almost sobbed.

She called for Matt.

He almost laughed too. Almost.

The night was black and cold, and their house was a long way from anyone. Neither of them really felt like laughing.

—5—

The baby slept between them all night in their locked bedroom.

She slept with them for the next ten nights. October continued to crumble away, and the wind off the lake was full of knives. On the eleventh night Matt rebelled. They had a queen bed in a room big enough for a king and he liked to sprawl.

It took a lot for Jillian to agree, but after Matt promised to go through the house and triple-check every window and door, she caved. They put Hope down together, took turns kissing the sleeping baby's cheeks, and then walked hand-in-hand back to bed. They held each other for a sleepless hour, both of them listening to the wind and to the bedroom, Matt sometimes looking over her shoulder at the baby cam.

The night passed, followed by a dozen more. They all slept through the cold darkness.

—6—

A storm rolled in. There was no snow, just wind and thunder of the kind that belonged in a summer gale and had no decent place in autumn. The booms punched the house, rattling every loose board and threatening the windows. One huge crack jerked Matt and Jillian awake at the same moment, and they both immediately looked at the baby cam.

And saw the shadowy hand rocking the cradle.

"Jesus Christ," cried Matt as he vaulted out of bed and raced for the nursery with Jillian a half step behind.

The cradle rocked back and forth.

And the room was empty.

Of course it was empty.

Except for the shadows of tortured and bare tree limbs scratching at the wall. As the echoes of the thunder rolled away between the trees, they heard a sound that chilled them both to the marrow.

Hope was laughing.

Her tiny hands were up, clutching at the darkness the way she always did when one of them was bending to pick her up. Except she was not looking at Jillian or Matt. Her eyes were fixed on the flickering shadows on the wall.

She laughed and laughed and laughed.

—7—

All next day Matt worked on the house while Jillian guarded Hope like a dragon.

Matt checked every window and door. Again. He bought fifteen additional baby cams and paid more than he wanted to for a man to come out and install motion detectors. The handyman looked at the trees and shook his head a lot.

"Got to set these at the right angle or every time the wind blows one of those branches your lights will go on."

"Just do it," said Matt in a voice that betrayed nerves and lost hours of sleep. The installer gave a philosophic shrug and set to work.

Matt bought a new set of deadlocks for the front and back door and put those in himself. The kind that needed a key from both sides, and with long screws that bit deep into the hardwood frames. He put a hefty padlock on the metal doors of the outside entrance to the cellar. The barn and garage were separate from the house, but he reinforced them too. As he worked—no matter *where* he worked—he kept looking back at the house. Jillian texted him a hundred times, and he was fine with that.

When all the work was done, and the sun was hanging off the

edge of the world, he and Jillian sat with the baby in the living room, a fire burning bright to chase back the shadows.

"It was just tree branches," said Jillian with a self-deprecating laugh.

"Of course it was," said Matt, flapping a dismissive hand.

They smiled at each other.

The smiles might as well have been made of plastic. Neither of them said a word about what the realtor had told them about this house and why it was on the market for so low a price. Jillian felt like her smile was stapled to her mouth. Matt's looked every bit as false and fragile.

When they went to bed they kept the baby with them all night. And for a week after that.

—8—

The rains came that night.

Cold, hard rain that slanted down with bullying aggression. The sound of it filled the house with a noise worse than thunder because there was no pause in it. Jillian turned on some music and cranked it up. But not Beethoven, Adele, or the Rolling Stones could shout the rain down.

Jillian sat feeding the baby by the fireplace while Matt walked the house, checking doors and windows. Looking for leaks. Feeling for wet breezes trying to sneak in through some crack he missed. The house, though, was snug. It creaked and complained, but it was built with good bones and it was meant to endure worse than this. Outside, the trees groaned and reached for the house as if trying to get in where it was warm and dry.

The branches closest to the house were crippled, though. Matt had seen to that with a pole saw. He collected the skeletal debris and burned it in a barrel behind the shed. Jillian stood in the bedroom window, watching and nodding. She wondered how much it would cost to cut those trees down and haul the timber away. Somebody would want it. No way she'd ever want a chip of that wood to burn in her hearth. No damn way.

"Everything's snug and dry," said Matt as he came yawning back into the living room.

"You're sure?" she asked, setting the baby on the thick blanket they'd spread on the floor. "You checked everything? The kitchen door? The—"

"I checked everything."

There was a howl of heavy wind, and the lights flickered. Jillian gasped and took a step toward the baby.

"Don't worry," said Matt quickly. "The lights and security have battery backup and I have flashlights like ... everywhere. And before you ask, they all have fresh batteries. If the lights go out we can camp out here in the living room. We have enough wood to keep the fire going all night."

"I—" she began and there was a huge wet crack from somewhere outside as an unseen tree succumbed to the brutality of the wind, and then the whole house was plunged into total darkness.

It took their eyes a second to adjust because they were looking away from the fireplace. Then a downdraft knocked a log loose and the blaze flared, painting the room with flickering yellow light.

Jillian knelt quickly beside the baby while Matt hurried over to get a flashlight. The exterior security lights flashed on, but they flickered as the wind drove the rain in persistent waves.

"Matt ... are we okay?" she asked in a desperate whisper.

"Of *course* we are, honey," he said, grinning in the firelight. "It's just a downed wire. With all the new stuff we put in, we couldn't *be* safer."

His response fell in the cracks between reassurance and condescension, and Jillian studied his eyes, afraid to find the fear that had to be in her own. But the movement of the flames from the burning logs danced shadows across his face and hid any true feelings.

Jillian touched Hope's cheek, then smoothed the little thatch of brown hair over the soft skin of her head. Without looking up at her husband, she said, "I hate this house."

Outside the night winds howled.

The lights stayed off, but after an angry hour the thunder went grumbling away to the east. The rain, however, intensified and fell so hard that peering out the window was pointless. Matt closed the blinds and drew the drapes shut.

"Let's go to bed," he suggested, but Jillian only shook her head. Matt frowned. "Why not? It's late and by the time we wake up it'll be light out."

She looked at the stairs that ascended into blackness and shook her head. "I'm not taking my baby up there."

My baby. *My.* Matt tried not to wince at that. He turned away and sighed, and Jillian felt bad for her clumsy words, but it was a mother speaking from her heart. Hope had come to life inside of her, grown in her womb, passed through her into the world. Yes, thinking the baby was *hers* was selfish and inaccurate, but right now she felt like a mother bear or tiger. Defensive, angry, ready to fight her own fight if she had to.

Matt got up from where he'd been sitting and poked at the fire.

"Okay," he said, keeping his tone neutral. "I'll go get some stuff. Will you be okay here?"

"Yes," she said, and again there was more bitterness in her tone than she intended, but she did not know how to control it. Not on a night like this.

"'Kay," he said. "Be just a minute."

He flicked on a flashlight and followed the beam upstairs, returning twice. The first time with a huge armful of blankets and pillows, and then grunting as he clumsied the cradle down the wide wooden staircase.

"She can't sleep on the floor, but we want her close to the fireplace, so ..."

Jillian got up, helped him position the pretty cradle, then took

Matt in her arms and kissed him breathless. Afterward she stood with her forehead against his chest.

"I love you," was all she said, but it was enough. They tucked Hope in, kissing her and smiling at the small, trusting pink face. Then they used the blankets and comforters to turn the floor into a campsite, with the cradle's frame within easy reach.

"Safe," she murmured, but by then Matt was asleep. She snuggled into him, and weariness pulled her all the way down.

—9—

Jillian woke to the sound of the cradle rocking.

She felt like her body was still more than half asleep, so all she could manage was to open her eyes just a slit. The cradle, there at the edge of the pile of blankets, moved back and forth very slowly, very gently. Her pulse began to quicken, but then she saw Matt's hand on the corner of the frame, guiding the soothing movements.

"Did she wake up?" whispered Jillian. "Was she crying?"

Matt groaned and turned over and suddenly Jillian snapped awake. Matt was on her left, curled into a ball, with both of his hands held in loose fists by his chest.

Jillian's head snapped back toward the cradle and saw the hand still rocking it.

For a fragment of a second.

And then she screamed.

Because the hand was not Matt's, and it seemed to be made of nothing but darkness.

Matt jerked awake and actually jumped to his feet, flinging the covers away. Clearly he had been tense in his dreams and now he was ready to hurt something—*anything*.

"*It was back!*" cried Jillian, and despite the impossibility of it, Matt knew exactly what she was talking about.

They crowded together over the cradle and stared in abject horror.

The entire cradle was awash in rain water. It dripped from the plastic mobile, it ran in crooked lines down the slats and spattered on the floor and puddled around Jillian and Matt. The baby lay there, soaked to the skin, blue with cold, shivering and coughing.

Jillian snatched Hope up, and Matt grabbed a blanket and whipped it around them both. They took Hope closer to the fire and warmed her, breathing on her tiny hands, kissing her, crying and saying her name. Telling the shivering infant that it was all right. That Mommy and Daddy were there. That everything was fine.

It wasn't.

Two minutes later they were in the car and heading to the hospital. Matt drove in that range between blind panic and fear of hurting his family. Jillian held a swaddled Hope and called the doctor. Reassurances from the hospital staff and the doctor were not, in fact, at all reassuring. The rain started up again.

"How the hell?" muttered Matt as he drove. "There was no leak in the roof. There was nothing. How the hell?"

There were no answers at all.

The car punched through the rain and the blackness.

Hope wriggled sluggishly in Jillian's arms. "Hurry, hurry, hurry ..."

Ahead the lights of the hospital gleamed like a promise through the slanting rain.

The doctors and nurses were waiting. They were calm, confident, capable. They said reassuring words, they acted as if this was nothing.

They took Hope with great gentleness and Jillian ghosted along behind, feeling as if she was being dragged through a nightmare. Matt was there in her periphery, holding her hand but lost in his own terror.

Jillian heard snatches of conversation between the professionals huddled around her baby.

"... acute inflammation of the lung parenchyma ..."

"... respiratory distress and hypoxia ..."

"... Streptococcus pneumonia ..."

And on and on.

The word *pneumonia* punched her in the gut and knocked all the air out of the world.

That night went on and on.

—10—

They admitted Hope.

"Just for a night," said the doctor. "Just until we get her fever down."

That was on the twentieth of October. *Just for the night* became "a few days," then "over the weekend." After that they stopped giving Matt and Jillian any guesses.

A few days became a week. A week became a month.

They waited. They slept in chairs beside her bed. They began snarling at each other for the smallest thing. They held each other and wept.

At ten o'clock on a crisp and bright Thanksgiving morning they took her home. Hope cried off and on all the way.

Cried. Did not cough.

Jillian and Matt washed her and kissed her and put her to bed in a brand-new cradle they bought online. The old one was smashed to splinters out behind the barn.

They spent a lot of time just watching her breathe.

That tiny chest, rising and falling without a hitch, without a tremble. Rising and falling with a beautiful regularity.

"She's beautiful," said Matt.

"She's perfect," said Jillian.

The baby smiled in her sleep, nestled in her blankets in the new cradle. Well away from windows or pipes. Matt and Jillian knew the location of anything that could possibly leak. The floors and walls and ceiling were marked with lines of tape, mapping everything.

"I hate this house," Jillian said, echoing what had become a mantra for her.

Matt nodded, trying not to engage on that because it usually ignited a fight.

Jillian said, "He *told* us it was haunted."

Another nod.

"The house hates us," she said.

Matt thought about all the time and money they'd put into the place. He thought about the incredible studio he'd set up in the barn and the flawless beautiful views of forest or lake from every window. He thought of how perfect the place was.

He took a breath. "Then we'll sell it and move."

Jillian studied him for a long time, then dabbed at her eyes. They watched the baby sleep. Near midnight, they moved from their chairs by the cradle to the bed, and sat holding hands. Happy and weary.

"Every test came back negative," said Matt for the tenth time since they got home.

"I know," said Jillian.

"She's completely clear."

"I know."

She turned and took his face in both her hands and kissed him sweetly on the lips. It was their first real kiss in six weeks. She had tears in her eyes. So did he.

They made love on the bedspread. It was a sweet and gentle act. It was an affirmation of life.

They could not hear the baby's slow breathing.

And so they did not hear her breath when it stopped.

—11—

The winter lasted for ten thousand years.

When spring came, the house was silent and seemed determined to hold onto the chill.

Matt worked in his studio more and more, and sometimes he

slept in there. It was where his paints were. It was where he kept the bottles that got him through the nights. His canvases were strange now. Landscapes still, but they were of blighted places. Fields grown dark with rot, diseased trees, stagnant water beside forests where no flowers grew.

One canvas, smaller than the others, was of a quiet corner of a country cemetery. A plot with fresh sod and a stone with a name that now seemed like a horrible joke.

Hope.

That single canvas remained unfinished.

In the house, Jillian sat in her chair on the days when she found the energy to get out of bed.

"Hope," she said aloud at least a dozen times a day. But the house was empty, and the word echoed in dusty rooms.

The cradle was in the nursery. They hadn't destroyed this one. It wasn't the cradle, after all.

They both knew it was wasn't the cradle.

The baby cams were still on. Everywhere in the house.

She could see it best from her chair beside the bed. Because she could also see into the nursery. The cradle was as still and silent as if it was in one of Matt's paintings. Frozen into the eternal moment of that quiet house.

"Hope," whispered Jillian.

—12—

Matt heard the sound and for a moment he thought it was a seagull over the lake.

Until it wasn't that at all.

Until it was a scream.

His whiskey glass dropped from his hand and smashed on the ground as he dashed for the door, kicked it open, ran like mad toward the house. The screams were so high-pitched they sounded raw and wet and so very, very wrong.

He slammed through the front door and took the stairs three at a time.

"Jillian!" he roared, but her screams were too loud.

He tore down the hall and bashed the bedroom door open. Jillian stood in the corner. She was as white as death and there was blood on her lips from the terrible screams that ripped their way out of her. She punched her own head as if trying to smash away what she saw.

"What's wrong?" he demanded.

She could not speak. That was impossible. Her screams needed to come out.

All she could do was point.

At the baby cam.

At the screen.

He stopped and stared at it. At the cradle in the nursery. At the slowly rocking cradle.

At the hand that rocked it.

Jillian took a breath between screams, and that's when Matt heard the sound. Through the speakers and coming from the nursery.

The creak of the rocking cradle.

And the high, sweet sound of a baby laughing.

Jillian screamed again.

So did Matt.

THE THINGS THAT
LIVE IN CAGES

—1—

Dillon saw the punch floating toward him and knew that there wasn't a goddamn thing he could do about it. The Cuban kid had battered his arms for three rounds and Dillon could no more raise his hands to block that punch than he could have sprouted wings and flown away. His legs were over-cooked macaroni and his heart was beating against the walls of his chest like a hummingbird trying to push through the windows of a burning house.

The punch was going to end him.

He knew it.

Time seemed to have slowed down so he could appreciate that fact. Dillon's corner man was screaming at him to block. The crowd was yelling like they were at the Roman Circus. Mike Dillon couldn't see at all out of his left eye and his right was smeared with sweat, blood, and Vaseline.

Dillon tried to duck his head down, to take the punch on his forehead instead of his nose. That might give him a chance. If the Cuban kid busted a couple of hand bones, then maybe his corner guy might toss a towel into the ring, or the ref might stop the fight.

Yeah, and maybe bright-blue pigs'll fly outta my ass, thought Dillon.

Even so, he closed his one good eye and ducked.

He could feel the exact moment when time snapped back to full speed. The fist seemed to fill the whole world. There was a huge sound inside his head. It was so loud that it muffled the sound of the Cuban kid's knuckles hitting bruised flesh and cracked bone.

Dillon felt the shock moving at an angle from the point of impact through his sinuses and eye sockets, past the back of his mouth, the surge of power shifting his head, tilting the opening at the back of his skull toward the brain stem.

There was a cracking sound. Sharp, wet, deep. Dillon knew that it wasn't his skull. It wasn't his jaw. The sound was immediately followed by a feeling of immense emptiness, as if his entire body had been hollowed out—nerves and skin and bone and blood. Everything below the level of his collarbones became a blank.

"I'm dead," said Dillon.

Or maybe he thought it.

He couldn't feel himself fall.

He didn't feel the flat of his back hit the mat.

He didn't feel anything.

All he was aware of was a huge black mouth gaping wide as death leaned forward to swallow him whole.

—2—

"You're awake," said a voice. "Good."

Dillon wasn't sure that the voice was real. Mostly because he was pretty sure that he was asleep. Or, maybe *unconscious* was the right word. It's not like he drifted off in his La-Z-Boy in front of the big screen. He hadn't opened his eyes though, so he wondered how anyone could tell he was awake.

His mind was filled with gutter water and debris. His thoughts were broken things that lay scattered around inside his head.

He knew that he'd been in a fight. This wasn't the first time he'd awakened in a hospital bed. A fight. Sure. Okay.

But which fight?

Who beat him this bad?

And how bad was it?

He could feel his head, which hurt so much that Dillon wanted to let the darkness take him back down into the dim nothingness.

He tried to move his arms.

Nothing.

His legs.

Nothing.

Shit, he thought, but beneath that thought there was a second and less articulate thought. It was more of a sense of how bad things might be, but his mind rebelled against putting it into words.

Got to think, he told himself. *Got to get my shit together and think this through.*

Dillon lay there, letting some internal hand flick on the light switches one by one.

He didn't try to speak. He wasn't sure he could.

There was a soft *ping-ping* sound behind him. He knew that sound. One of those hospital machines that never seemed to do anything but make soft noises. There was a dull pain in the back of his right hand. He didn't need to look to identify that. IV.

Fuck.

Unless he was dead and this was some kind of holdover memory.

"Mr. Dillon—?"

The voice again.

Male. He could tell that much. Nobody he knew. If it was Saint Peter waiting for him to make his case for entrance through the Pearly Gates, then Dillon wasn't interested. Dillon didn't want to have to explain to Saint Pete that he didn't believe in any of that shit. Heaven, wings, halos, paradise. None of that shit.

And if it wasn't Saint Pete and it was that other guy, then fuck you to him too. Dillon *did* believe in Hell, and as far as he was concerned Hell was better known as Trenton, New Jersey. Any other place, even if it was all fire and brimstone and shit, would be an improvement.

There was a rustling sound. Like newspapers. Whoever was there didn't speak again and Dillon figured the guy was reading the paper.

Fine. Whatever. Hope he had a comfortable seat because Dillon wasn't in any hurry to wake up and rejoin the world. Any world.

He settled back and let the darkness take him again.

His last thought before he passed out again was that nothing hurt. Everything should have hurt, though, so that was a little weird. The Cuban kid had beaten the shit out of him for seven two-minute rounds. Dillon had gotten two good shots in—a roundhouse kick to the ribs and a spinning backfist that emptied the kid's eyes for a few seconds, but that was back in round one. Dillon had come out hard and heavy the way he always did. That was his thing—he wrapped up the fight in the first round or he generally got his ass handed to him. Different when he was young, but Dillon was a lot of miles away from anyone's definition of "young." Cage fighting was not a sport for middle-aged guys, as the Cuban so eloquently proved. After that first round, Dillon hadn't scored a single point that mattered. And the Cuban made him pay for those early hits.

He wondered why it didn't hurt.

Darkness whispered in his ears, but it gave him no answers.

The lights in his mind dimmed and the last thing he saw, or thought he saw, was a figure—a man? A woman? He couldn't tell

—move toward the IV stand, a small plastic needle in one hand. The figure inserted the dagger-point of the needle into a port on the IV. Dillon thought he saw some ruby-red liquid, some exotic medicine, flow from the needle into the IV.

Then the darkness in his mind flared with red shadows and he was gone again.

—3—

When he woke up again Dillon knew that he was actually awake. Not dead, not floating in limbo or purgatory or trying to run a shuck on Saint Peter outside the gates. Alive.

Balls.

He knew from the way he felt that he'd been asleep for a long time. Easiest way to tell was by how much the painkillers had worn off. They don't keep giving you that shit unless you ask for it. Not in crap hospitals in Trenton. Not with his health plan.

And every-damn-thing hurt. His face felt like it had been hand-carved from his skull, diced into little bits, run through a Cuisinart, and put back on, piece by piece, with staples. His teeth felt loose and his hair hurt.

His body hurt, too, but not as intensely. That pain was distant, like an echo.

It took him a while to figure out how to move his hand, but finally his fingers twitched like the thick legs of some obscene spider and slowly crawled across the sheets. He fumbled for the button that would call the nurse, couldn't find it, and then froze as someone pressed the control into his hand.

"It's the top button," said a voice.

It took Dillon a few seconds to make sense of that. Then he remembered the voice that had called his name earlier. Was that today or last month or a year ago?

Dillon decided to open an eye and look at whoever it was.

One eyelid refused to budge. It felt like it weighed twenty pounds and was cemented shut. That was the one the Cuban kid had wailed on every single goddamn round. Fucker had a thing for that eye.

The other one wasn't as badly puffed, but opening it was like jacking up a truck.

He said, "Ow."

It took a few seconds for his eye to focus. The hospital room was small and cheerless, with furniture that was purely functional and clearly intended to make people want to leave the hospital as soon as possible. There was a window that gave a wonderful view of a brick wall streaked with pigeon shit. There were no cards or flowers on the dresser. The TV was off.

Dillon turned his head very, very carefully to look at the person sitting in the visitor's chair. He was a total stranger. Young white guy. Twentyish. Rail thin, but thin the way models and art dealers are. Like he enjoyed looking like a rake handle. Dark hair combed back, dark eyes, red lips that Dillon thought were painted with lipstick, but weren't. Expensive suit, expensive watch and rings.

"Who the fuck are you?" croaked Dillon.

The man gave him a bland, friendly smile that curled his lips without showing his teeth. "My name is Viktor Petrov."

"Russian?"

"Russian."

Dillon tried to pry open the file cabinet in his brain. Did he owe anything to one of the Russian bookies? He didn't think so, but it wasn't impossible. The Russians had taken over the kind of mixed martial arts matches Dillon fought in. They'd crowded the Brazilians out a couple of years ago because they were more ruthless but also more organized. And, let's face it, Brazilian street thugs—no matter how tough they were—weren't going to get into any serious pissing contests with guys who were ex-Spetsnaz and ex-KGB. The Russians were ass-deep in muscle who were ex-special forces.

Dillon said nothing. His tendency toward smartass remarks did not extend to deliberately pissing off the Russians.

"Are you in very much pain?" asked Petrov.

Dillon licked his lips. "It's ... not too bad."

"Can you move your legs?"

The question scared Dillon, but when he tried to move his feet, they moved. Not well, but they moved.

Petrov nodded. "Good."

"Why ... did I hurt my back?"

"You had a neck injury," said Petrov. "But it's nothing permanent. Some discomfort for a while."

"Did they have to operate?"

"No."

"I ... I thought I saw ... I mean, did *you* inject something into my IV?"

Petrov took a while before he answered. "Yes."

"Are you my doctor?"

"I am ... part of the treatment team," said Petrov. "A consultant."

"My head's all messed up," said Dillon cautiously, "so sorry if I'm a little slow here. But ... do I know you? Have we met somewhere?"

Instead of answering, Petrov said, "I've seen you fight."

"You mean you saw that Cuban kid kick my head in."

"Well, that, too ... but I've seen you in better days."

Dillon laughed even though it hurt his chest to do it. "Then you got a long memory, friend, 'cause my better days were so long ago dinosaurs were running the world."

Petrov smiled at that. His face looked like a moray eel when he smiled. "It wasn't that long ago, Mr. Dillon. I can well remember when you were the up-and-coming thing. A real martial artist in a league that has become glutted with brawlers whose only talent is that they haven't evolved enough to feel pain. Mouth-breathing Neanderthals."

"That Cuban kid had some moves," said Dillon.

Petrov shrugged. "Five years ago you would have beaten him."

Dillon said nothing. He wanted to give a nonchalant shrug,

but that would involve using too many brutalized muscles. "Kid had some moves."

"He had youth and the stamina that comes with it," said Petrov, dismissing the Cuban with a wave of his hand. "Five years ago he wouldn't have lasted four rounds with you. Ten years ago he would never have made it past round one."

"Yeah, well everyone gets old. One of these days some kid will be handing the Cuban kid his ass. Way of the world."

Petrov crossed his legs and arched an eyebrow. "Way of the world," he echoed, taking his time, tasting each word.

"Fighters aren't built to last," said Dillon. Then he sighed. "But, yeah, once upon a time I had the juice. I was always hard to hurt. Hardly ever bled, which keeps the refs from stopping the fight. And I could take a punch off of anyone."

"And you are trained as a true fighter. A warrior. *Daitō-ryū Aiki-jūjutsu* if I'm not mistaken. For how many years?"

"Started when I was six," said Dillon, and for a moment he felt a flush of pride. "So call it thirty-five years and change. Started cage fighting when I was eighteen. Twenty-three long damn years ago."

"I know. Ninety-two fights. Fifty-seven wins, two ties, thirty-three losses. You knocked out or choked out forty-three of your opponents, and you were only carried off four times counting last night."

"So?"

"So, you know more about martial arts than most of the fighters in your league put together. Real martial arts. The deep knowledge, the genuine skills. The kind of knowledge that should be preserved but which is fading in obscurity with each new generation."

Dillon sighed. "Yeah, no shit. I opened a bunch of dojos over the years. Traditional stuff, very old-school, but no one wants to spend the time to learn the old stuff. They want a few flashy moves, a quick belt promotion, and then they want to call themselves 'masters.' Breaks my heart."

"Mine too. I have very little appreciation for *new* things, Mr. Dillon. I'm very much an old-fashioned kind of person."

Dillon had to restrain himself from snorting. The Russian looked like he was two or three years out of high school.

"It's a shame," continued Petrov, "that you can't use those old-school skills in your matches."

"Ha! I wish. But the league don't let guys like me bring our A game."

"Pity."

"Got to have rules, I guess," said Dillon bitterly. "You can't really unload on a guy, even in a cage match. People'd get killed."

Petrov smiled, and he slowly traced the outline of his sensuous mouth with the sharp tip of one manicured fingernail. "That's not what they tell the rubes. The league's advertising goes to great lengths to declare that this is no-holds barred, that everything is legal, that this is—what's the phrase they use all the time? 'Fighting as real as it gets.'"

He gave a derisive snort.

"What do you expect?" asked Dillon, unsure where this guy was going with this. "This is a sport. It ain't Spartacus and shit."

Petrov sighed. "Alas, no. Those were the good old days."

You're a fucking weirdo, thought Dillon, but he kept that to himself.

"I bet you'd give a lot to fight the way you truly know how to fight. With subtlety, with ruthless efficiency, with a deadly grace."

"I wouldn't go that far," said Dillon. "You don't need to kill people to have a good fight. There are a lot of old-school techniques that I could have used ..."

"Why didn't you?"

Dillon shrugged. The action was painful, and Dillon winced. "Bad timing. If I knew what I knew now back when I started in this league, it'd be a whole different thing. But even setting aside the lethal stuff, the moves that would neutralize a bull like that Cuban kid doesn't take insane amounts of strength, but it does require speed and control. Thing is, the more damaged your muscles get, the less precise your control is. That's where the problem comes in. The older you get the more you know, but the older your body gets the less able you are to use that knowledge. It's proof that the universe likes playing sick jokes."

"I supposed you would like to have your old speed and control back last night."

"No shit. But ... if wishes were horses," murmured Dillon sourly.

Petrov uncrossed his legs and leaned forward. "Suppose you could get your mojo back?"

"Very funny, ha ha."

"I'm serious."

"Seriously about what?"

"About getting back in the ring for *real*. Wouldn't that be great? Wouldn't that be worth anything? To be at the top of your game, to be Killer Dillon once again?"

"Killer Dillon? Christ, nobody's called me that in years. That was from my old boxing days. Corny name—"

"No," said Petrov quickly, "it's not. It's a name filled with great promise. It's a name that used to give your opponents serious pause, and one that could strike genuine fear into anyone who steps into the cage with you."

Dillon laughed even though it hurt his face to do it. He raised the hand with the IV drip and waggled it back and forth. "I'm five years past my expiration date, son. I should've quit after I lost the split decision with that Polish son of a bitch from Detroit. What was his name? Lenny "the Breaker" Sepulski. That bastard fair beat the white off my ass. Should have realized he was trying to beat some sense into me, but I was too far into my own shit. Back then I still believed all the hype; I was still high off of my win-loss stats from ten years back. And, man, there's nothing sadder than a cage fighter who's losing every fight and still blaming it on a bad streak that's going to end soon. It's not a streak, it's a downward slide, and it *doesn't* end. But by the time you realize that you've lost your punch and your reflexes are shot from muscle fatigue, nerve damage and too damn many miles on the odometer, you're already into the phase of your life where you're nothing but a punching bag for younger, better fighters and a punch line to the guys who knew you when."

Petrov was nodding while Dillon spoke. "Yes," he said softly, "but I've seen how you fight. You always make the right choice— kick or punch or takedown. You knew ten times what the Cuban fighter knew. That was true of your fight with Breaker Sepulski. You were the better fighter."

"I lost those fights. And damn near every fight over the last five years."

"You lost because your age and the amount of damage you've sustained over your career have slowed your body and made your reflexes betray you."

"Yeah, well, that's why they call this a young man's game."

"No, that's why this game has become polluted, Mr. Dillon," said Petrov sternly. "When these matches first got started there were some real fighters in there. Men and women who knew the martial arts. Now what do you have? Thugs, barroom bouncers, brawlers—goons who don't understand the martial arts, not in any real sense. Men who don't *care* about the martial arts. This is just a game to them, and for many of them it's the only work they could get because they lack the raw intelligence even to work in construction, and they take themselves too seriously to go into professional wrestling." He sniffed. "At least the professional wrestlers call it 'sports entertainment.' They make no pretense about it being a genuine sport. These thugs have so crowded MMA competitions that they've become the standard for excellence. People look at them and think that these are the masters of unarmed combat."

"It's as close as you're ever going to get to having real masters climb into the cage," observed Dillon. "Most of them are too smart to risk getting wailed on. Most of them are too old. By the time they really qualify as masters they're too old for full-contact sports. Sure, they could kick ten kinds of ass in a street encounter, but self-defense against a junkie with a knife or a couple of gangbangers is one thing. The techniques you'd use in those situations come from a whole different toolbox than the stuff we're allowed to use in cage matches. And just from the point of view of recovering from injuries—I'll bet that Cuban kid won't even show a bruise by Tuesday and my face'll look like a tropical sunset for two weeks. And I'll be walking like an eighty-year-old man for at least that long." He shook his head. "No, this is a young man's game. The real masters either aren't interested in showing off in the ring or they can't see how the risk-reward thing tilts in their favor. Too much to lose, not enough worth winning."

He fumbled for the remote and hit the button for the nurse. But she still didn't come. "God damn it …"

"Not necessarily so," said Petrov.

Dillon, distracted by the lack of a nurse showing up, had lost the thread of the conversation. "What?"

"I said that, while I agree with your assessment, there is more to the equation than that."

Dillon squinted at him with his one good eye. "Like what? The only way a master—some guy who's spent forty, fifty years going all the way deep into a martial art—is going to last more than a round with a twenty-something gorilla who can barely feel pain."

Petrov said nothing; he folded his hands on his lap and gave Dillon a bland smile.

"What?" asked Dillon. "You're saying you know someone willing to take that kind of a risk?"

No answer.

"You're nuts," said Dillon. "Look, it's not even worth it from a purely financial perspective. Guy who's spent his life training to become a master—a real, genuine master of a martial art—he's got a school, or maybe a chain of schools, filled with students who look to him as the icon of martial arts skill. Now understand, all of this belief is based on what they see in class and a kind of *faith* that their master could go all Jet Li on the bad guys in a real fight. But these kinds of guys don't *get* into real fights. Avoidance is a big part of their lifestyles. They're passive, they'll walk away from an insult rather than fighting over it. So their ability to deliver the absolute combat goods is never seen but deeply believed by everyone from the newest white belt to the most senior assistant instructor. Now ... if one of these masters does something as dumb as climb into a cage to fight someone like Breaker Sepulski or the Cuban kid, he risks losing. He knows he can't match the younger fighters for stamina, and he probably doesn't have anywhere near the same protective muscle mass, which means he's jousting without armor. He also knows that he can't use his best stuff. He can't dip into his black bag of tricks and do shit like rupture the spleen, smash the hyoid bone, shatter the knee, burst ear drums, pop an eyeball or anything else that he might use in a real street defense. He's facing a fighter who spends all of his time preparing to be hit, and whose arsenal are those strikes and kicks allowed in the cage. It would be like taking a master-level swordsman from Renaissance Italy, giving him a fake sword, and then putting him in the ring with a Viking who has a sharpened war axe. It's an unfair contest on too many levels. The only way it could be fair—and this is pure fucking fantasy here—is if you could take all of the knowledge and experience from the old masters and somehow put it into the heads of the young Turks. Then, even though there would still be some restrictions on certain techniques, you see what master-level martial arts are like when it goes whole-hog. But ... that's a pipe dream."

"Ah," said Petrov, holding up a finger. "That is exactly my point. That's the tragedy right there."

Dillon frowned. "Huh?"

"At no point in this 'sport' that we both love so well are we seeing anything approximating the kind of fair fight you postulate. The game is skewed, the rules are fractured. This is why these matches draw the worst kind of gambler." Petrov laughed. "You are right to feel a measure of disdain for the kind of brawlers who dominate the sport; but I have equal disdain for the breed of gambler attracted to these kinds of blood sports. They are the same lowbrow crowd who bet on cockfights and dogfights. They bet on animals fighting animals."

Now it was Dillon's turn to remain silent. He was smart enough to recognize the insult buried inside that comment, but at the same time he couldn't really take offense. He was a dumb hulk fighting in a league of dumb hulks. No better than chickens or pit bulls except in being smart enough to know that this was no kind of life at all.

Petrov adjusted his cuffs and necktie. He was dressed very well. Expensive clothes, but good taste expensive rather than fuck-up expensive. Attention to quality rather than for display. Russian mafia guys often dressed nice. You never saw them in those damn tracksuits the Jersey goombahs wore. None of the open-shirted satin-finish sports coats of the Cuban players. This guy could be selling expensive watches or showing you four-million-dollar homes with a view.

When it was clear that Petrov wasn't going to say anything either, Dillon cleared his throat and said, "So where's that leave us other than lamenting what I don't have? I ask, because I hurt too much to lie here singing the blues."

Petrov nodded as if that was the right thing to have said.

"I was at your first fight," he said.

"You saw that?" Dillon narrowed his eyes. "Where? On tape?"

"No, I was at the Princeton Stadium when you fought two matches on the same card. Leroy 'The Lion King' Sanders and then Sonny Daye."

"Bet you don't remember much. That was twenty-three years ago. You were—what? An embryo?"

"A lot older than that," said Petrov with a chuckle. "And I remember both fights as if they happened this morning. The so-called Lion King went down in the very first round. He threw two punches and then tried to sweep your leg. You kick-checked his sweep that I bet no one past the first row saw, and then you hit him with a back-wrist strike to the floating ribs that sent a shockwave through his abdomen which caused his diaphragm to spasm. Very, very subtle. The judges scored it as a backfist because they were too dense to know what they were looking at. And your finishing blows? A two-knuckle tap to the left sinus that had to fill his eyes with tears and cause enough shock to the eustachian tubes to make him gag. Then you hit him with a tight looping palm that only four martial arts styles teach. It hit the precise point on his jaw that snapped his head around far too fast for his body to follow, which created a corkscrew twist of the brain stem. He was out before he began to fall."

Dillon narrowed his eyes. "Who told you all that? The blow-by-blow in the fight magazines called that last combination a jab-hook punch combo."

"The trade magazines are staffed by hacks who don't know a hammerblow from a blow job."

"Fair enough. But that doesn't explain how *you* know what I did."

"I told you, Mr. Dillon, I was there."

"Not a chance in hell. Even if you're older than you look you couldn't have been more than five or six years old. Only an advanced pro would have recognized what I was doing."

Petrov shrugged. "The second match lasted two rounds," he said.

"Sonny Daye was a better fighter. It was only 'cause someone else dropped that I wound up on the card with him. Nobody expected Lion King to go more than a round."

"Sonny Daye was the full-contact fighting champion of the Deep South. Forty-four wins, one loss and that was a split decision."

"Like I said ..."

"I remember watching that fight," Petrov reminded him. "Daye only tagged you twice, both with jabs while you were feeling each other out. After that he never scored one single point that mattered. By the end of the second round he was out on his feet. You delivered a series of blows to acupressure points that systematically shut down his ability to defend himself. You could have taken him down halfway through that round and choked him out. He had nothing left."

"He might have hurt bad if I tried. Get a guy who's that dazed he might not have enough marbles left to tap out. Better to dance him a little and let the corner man and the ref stop the fight."

"Which they did."

"Sure."

Petrov leaned his elbows on his thin knees. "You were a superior fighter, Mr. Dillon. If you'd have been able to get into the better leagues and better venues while you were still young enough, you could have been a contender. You might have been the champion."

"Lot of good guys up on that level."

"Few of whom are as good as you. Few of whom know as much about real martial arts. Few of whom *care* about real martial arts. There are people who still bet on you, despite your recent stats, because they know that you have more knowledge, more real skill, than the apes who dominate the league. I've made several such bets. If you were to win one of these fights, the return on the bet would be considerable."

"Then you got money to burn, 'cause even I don't bet on myself anymore. See these knuckles, the way they're too large. That's arthritis. I got osteo from old damage and now I'm getting rheumatoid. You want to bet on me in a cage match against old age?"

Dillon pushed the button for the nurse, who still didn't come.

"The fuck!" growled Dillon. The pain was getting worse. His whole body felt like it was about to catch fire.

Petrov reached out and closed his hand gently around Dillon's wrist. Dillon immediately flinched back from the man's touch. The Russian's skin was as cold as ice and clammy as a locker room wall.

"Don't worry about the nurse," he said.

Dillon tried to pull his hand away, but the Russian's grip was bizarrely strong. That was weird because even beat up and half-dead in a hospital, Dillon outweighed Petrov by ninety pounds and none of those pounds were fat. At forty-one, Dillon was rock-solid. Maybe past his own prime, but stronger than this pencil-neck.

Except that he wasn't.

Petrov's hand was like an icy cuff locked around Dillon's wrist.

"Please, Mr. Dillon," said the Russian in a soft voice. "Please. We're having a nice and very productive talk. Let's continue to have that talk."

"Let go of me, you freak."

After a long moment, Petrov opened his fingers. Dillon snatched his arm away and immediately began massaging his skin, which was cold and sore.

"What the fuck, man," he growled.

"I'm sorry for the discomfort," said Petrov.

"Shit, you almost broke my goddamn arm."

"I'm sorry, but—"

"What the hell, you're a frigging stick figure. What the fuck are you taking? Steroids? Meth?"

Petrov's smile turned sly. "Ah."

"Ah ... what? *Is* it meth?"

"No."

"Then what? You're on something. A skinny young prick like you shouldn't be that strong. What are you on?"

"What I'm *on*, to use your word, is part of why I'm here. And before we get to that, I want to correct a small mistake."

"What?" asked Dillon uncertainly. If he wasn't so thoroughly flattened by injury and painkillers he would have bolted for the door. He cut quick looks at the door anyway, wondering if he could make it to the nurse's station.

"How old do you think I am?" asked Petrov, and the question was so weird and unrelated to anything that was happening that it jolted Dillon and made him whip his head around.

"What?"

"You keep saying I'm *young*, and I admit that I look young, but how old do you actually think I am?"

"Who gives a—"

"I ask, because the reason I'm so strong and the reason I look so young are both side effects of what I'm 'on.'"

Dillon had no idea where this was going so he said nothing.

Petrov fished in his wallet for his wallet and produced his driver's license. "I am fifty-seven years old," said Petrov. "And before you ask, I have never had a facelift or any Botox injections."

Dillon stared at the license and then at Petrov. "Bullshit."

Petrov put the wallet away.

"That's bullshit," insisted Dillon.

Petrov spread his hands. "Listen to me, Mr. Dillon, and give me an honest answer. What if there was a way for you to get back your youth, your strength, your speed? What if that process also repaired any damage, no matter how old, and which also helped you heal at an accelerated rate from any new damage?"

"You're definitely on something. Magic mushrooms or something."

Petrov ignored that. "What if you go back into the ring with all of the knowledge you currently possess but with your body and reflexes at the very peak of conditioning. Stronger, faster, more durable, less vulnerable. Can you lie there and tell me that you wouldn't want to climb into the ring again without age and scar tissue and disease hanging around your neck like a ton of bricks?"

"That's a stupid question," snapped Dillon. "Of *course* I would. Who wouldn't? But the league dope tests us all the time. I come up positive for steroids or something, I'd be out on my ass, stripped of all my titles, barred from even stepping foot into—"

"This isn't a steroid."

"Or coke or some designer meth. They test for everything."

"They don't test for this," said Petrov. "Or, rather, they *can't* test for this. I can show you if you're genuinely interested."

Dillon studied him. The things the guy was saying were

wacked out, but his tone and body language were calm. There were no crazy lights in his eyes. It was Petrov's calm rather than his words that kept Dillon's own emotions in check.

And ... well, Dillon was curious. Really curious.

He was too old not to want to know.

He was too badly hurt, too sore and spent not to want to know.

And the warrior in his soul, the one that time and damage and arthritis were turning into an impotent old joke, wanted to know.

Dillon licked his dry lips.

"Okay," he said, "show me."

Petrov nodded and reached into the inner pocket of his suit. He produced three hypodermics. One was filled with a dark-red liquid; the other two were empty.

"I anticipated your interest," he said softly. "I've already begun the treatment."

"What?" croaked Dillon. "What the fuck!"

"Shhh," soothed Petrov. "Just listen. There are three steps to the process. All very antiseptic, all done with the greatest of care." He held up one of the empty syringes so Dillon could see that there were trace amounts of red liquid in it. "For step one I drew a few cc's of your blood."

"Who gave you permission, you son of a—"

"Please, Mr. Dillon, we both know that we are not talking about an approved medical procedure. It was totally safe, so you have nothing to worry about. And it's already done. So, please, bear with me."

Dillon lapsed into a tense and angry silence. However, fear gnawed at him. What had this maniac done to him?

Petrov said, "I injected your blood into my arm."

Dillon's mouth hung open in shock.

"Then, after a wait of a few hours, I drew off two syringes of my blood. I injected one syringe into you via the port on your IV. I believe you were semi-conscious at the time. Do you remember?"

Dillon did remember, and his fear began growing into terror.

Petrov showed him the third syringe, the one that was still filled with red liquid.

With blood.

God, thought Dillon.

"Why, for Christ's sake?"

Petrov's smile faded. "Because, Mr. Dillon, the injury you sustained in last night's fight was far more serious than you know. The Cuban hit you with a powerful blow at an unfortunate angle. It cracked two cervical vertebrae and the broken bones caused a deep laceration to your spinal cord. The doctors are discussing their options, but so far it is their belief that you will be a quadriplegic. Everything from the neck down *died* last night, Mr. Dillon. You were destroyed in the ring."

Dillon thrashed backward from Petrov's words, his feet kicking at the sheets, fingers stabbing the device to call the nurse.

"Fuck you!" he roared. "Fuck you. I'm not crippled, you stupid bastard. Look! I'll kick your ass!"

Petrov sat where he was, the syringe held between two slender fingers. He waited for Dillon's tirade to wind down. Dillon flopped back, gasping.

"I'm not crippled," he snarled.

"Of course not," agreed Petrov. "But you *were*."

Dillon opened his mouth but nothing came out.

"Before I injected my blood into you, you were dead from the collarbones down. Machines breathed for you, machines pumped your heart."

Dillon raised his hands and looked at them, totally perplexed. "But ... but ..."

"It's not a drug," said Petrov. "It's blood. There is a very, very old biblical saying: 'Blood is the life.' That is so very true."

"What are you talking about?"

Petrov waggled the full syringe between his fingers. "The process is simple. I consume your blood, you consume mine. Writers have mythologized the process in all sorts of absurd ways, but in simple terms it's an exchange of certain key biological materials. A virus, a very ancient virus, activates dormant DNA in you, and that begins a process whereby certain biological and genetic changes take place. The initial stages of the process occur very quickly. The complete transformation, however, takes years."

"A ... virus ...?"

"Oh, don't get hung up on that part, Mr. Dillon, this will be the very last virus that will ever affect you. After this, no more colds, no more flu, no cancer, no arthritis, not even the heartbreak of psoriasis."

"You're insane."

"Not at all." Petrov got to his feet and came to stand close to Dillon. He plugged the syringe into the port, but did not depress the plunger. "If I do nothing, the effect of the first injection will eventually wear off and you'll be exactly where you were last night. A head attached to a lump of dead meat. The first injection is self-reversing. So, if you want me to walk away, then I'll go."

Dillon said nothing. He could not compose a single sentence, not even a single word, that made sense.

"However, if you give me permission, then I will inject the second dose of my blood and within forty-eight hours you will *walk* out of this hospital. You'll probably feel so good you'll want to run. Within seventy-two hours you won't be able to find a single trace of any of the injuries you sustained in that fight. Within a week no X-Ray, MRI, or CT scan will be able to find a trace of arthritis or scar tissue."

"Who are you?" breathed Dillon. "What *are* you?"

Petrov smiled, but unlike his earlier smiles, this one was a broad grin that showed lots of white teeth.

Lots of sharp white teeth.

"I think you know what I am," said Petrov.

Dillon wanted to scream. He tried to shrink away, but his body was sluggish, as if the numbness he'd felt last night was creeping back. The sight of those terrible teeth filled his mind with horror-show images of pale creatures rising from graves and tearing the throats out of the innocent. He wanted to shout a word, to put the label on the monster that stood above him, but he could not force himself to say that word. It was an impossible thing. To say it might make it real.

"Why are you doing this to me?" he hissed.

Petrov blinked as if surprised. "Why am I saving your life? Why am I giving you eternal youth and strength and health? I thought we already covered that."

"Be ... because of the fights?"

"I already told you that I was very old-school, Mr. Dillon. I, and those like me, appreciate only the finest things. Immortality tends to cultivate more sophisticated tastes, as I hope you'll discover. I've always been a fight fan. Even before I became what I am. I want to stop being a spectator and get involved more deeply in the sport. As a manager, as a promoter. But I don't want to trot out one mouth-breathing thug after another. Just as this process will elevate you to a higher level, I want to elevate the sport of full-contact fighting to a level it has never before been able to reach. A class of masters."

"Are there others ...?"

"Like you? Not yet. I want you to be the first. I want you to cut a swath through the brawlers currently in the game and then make room for a new breed of martial arts competitor. Immortal masters. Come now, Mr. Dillon, tell me you wouldn't give everything to see fights where both competitors could use their greatest skills, to showcase the elegant beauty and sophisticated science of the real martial arts? Tell me that doesn't stir your soul."

Dillon stared at him but said nothing.

His arms and legs began to tingle again. His fingers were already going numb.

Petrov caressed the plunger of the hypodermic with one pale thumb.

Tears broke from the corners of Dillon's eyes. "I don't want to be a monster," he said softly.

"We are not monsters," said Petrov with surprising

gentleness. "We are elevated beings. Call it the next step in evolution. Call it whatever you want. We don't fear the cross. We don't hunt the innocent. None of that. So, tell me, Mr. Dillon—*Master* Dillon—what's your choice? Ordinary or extraordinary? A broken man dying in a forgotten hospital ward ... or the champion you were born to be?"

Dillon could not feel his hands and feet.

"Do it," he whispered.

INVASIVE SPECIES

—1—

We stood outside and none of us wanted to go in.

The ship was one of those old-school colony things. Ponderously slow, built when we all thought Einstein was right about the possibility of faster-than-light travel. Dumond and Chung tore holes through that maybe sixteen years after the last colony ship was launched. Somewhere way out in the black are forty-three tubs as big as the one we found on Elliot's Moon. Six earlier ships have been found, either crashed somewhere or drifting.

This one, *The Anthem*, was the seventeenth to launch. No one heard either jack or squat about it since the 2130s, and that was a long time ago. Way before my grandfather was born.

Now here it was.

Nudged up against a slope on Lemuria—formerly Kepler 62e —a super-Earth exoplanet 330 parsecs from what remained of Earth. Big, blue, with a heavy cloud cover that hid most of the land masses scattered throughout its vast oceans. We didn't know Lemuria even *had* land masses, and sure as hell didn't know some of them were forested. Now we do.

Our bird, a VB-530 tunnel rat doing long-range recon for rare minerals, squatted just outside of the shadow of *Anthem's* shadow, looking like a ladybug next to a beached sperm whale. The scale is about right. We'd drilled through the dark matter gateways, riding one of the less-explored routes in the galactic network, following data interpretations from the astronomical spectroscopy to what we hoped would be sizable deposits of palladium, rhenium, molybdenum, and tungsten.

Instead we found this big son of a bitch of a colony ship.

It lay there, its back broken from a bad landing. The hull pitted and rusted from its travels.

"How?" asked Collins, my copilot.

"I don't know."

He'd asked that question at least fifty times. *Anthem* and ships of its class could not—absolutely could not—have come this far out. There was no way. Before the first transduction tunnels were built it was a laughable concept. *Anthem* was fast, but she was sublight. At top speed she should just now be closing in on Alpha Centauri, which is only 2.4 light-years from Sol. There's simply no way she could have crossed *990* light-years. Not without a tunnel. It's folded space or it's centuries of travel; that's the new math. It's the core of what we know about FTL travel.

And yet.

"I don't know," I said again.

—2—

The screen display inside my helmet kept trying to convince me that the atmo was 87.2 percent of Earth normal.

That, at least, made some sense. Kind of.

The colony ships were built to land on alien exoplanets in the goldilocks zones of star systems. More than 90 percent of the ship was a terraforming processing plant. We could hear the hum of machinery. We could feel it beneath our feet. All of the scanners told us that, damaged as she was, *Anthem's* machineries were running full-tilt to transform the planet. We'd seen evidence of it while we descended from our ship, *Hera IV*, which was orbiting at seven hundred klicks. We saw vast stretches of forest that had withered and died as the mixture of gasses changed. And we saw huge new forests growing outward from the wreck site—forests with genetically-modified Earthlike pine trees, cereal grasses, fruit trees, hardwoods, and shrubberies.

There were insects in the air all around us—modified honeybees, beetles, even a species of leather-winged butterflies. Scanners told us that there were worms and spiders and other animals in the soil beneath our boots. We were even picking up thermal signatures of small rodents, squirrels, birds, and a kind of deer adapted to this kind of world.

Since we'd cracked the science of folding space, Earth has terraformed just shy of three hundred moons and seventeen planets. There were some so far along that the colonists didn't need to wear pressure suits.

None of the colony ships had done that, though, because until now we thought that none of them had been out there long enough to set up shop.

Anthem proved all that wrong.

Don't ask me how, because I simply do not know.

"This is freaking me out, Dix," said Collins as we walked slowly toward the ship. The sun was rolling toward the horizon and darkness was coming. "This looks like they've been running the processor for at least fifty years. Given how big this planet is, they've already impacted it. The old biosphere is in active collapse, and the new one is spreading fast as hell. How?"

"You keep asking me as if I could know," I said. "Only thing that makes even a little sense is somehow they jumped way out here and got the terraforming going as soon as they crashed. If that happened sooner than later, it means this could have been running for better than ninety years."

It was true enough. Just from the size of some of the towering hardwood trees this had to be in motion for better than half a century, and the ninety-year mark seemed likely.

"Bottom line is," I said, "we may never know how they got all the way out here."

Collins held a scanner up and moved it from end to end along *Anthem's* hull. "Picking up thermal signatures," he said, but then paused, his lips pursed.

"You mean there are survivors?" I asked. For some reason I had been expecting the processor to be running on automatic. There were no shelters, no signs of orderly cultivation. No recent signs, at least. The fruit trees had clearly been hand planted, but everything around them was overgrown. Same with the smaller crops. On the way from our bird we walked through planted fields of some rough-looking gray cabbages, pumpkins, potatoes that—when pulled from the soil—looked stunted and mushroomy. There were other crops, too—salad greens, herbs of many kinds, and long rows of radishes and garlic.

Lots of garlic.

Collins had knelt to study one of the cloves. "Pretty pure," he said. "Close to Earth normal. And they have a lot of it." Then he added, "That makes sense. Garlic has lots of healing qualities, and it's a blood purifier. Useful in any new or modified biosphere."

We took samples, but I tapped Collins and nodded to the sky. "Computer model says twilight is short here. Tilt of the planet and orbital analysis says the days are short and the nights are long. So, let's get this done while we have some light left."

He moved closer to the ship. It was massive. 1677 meters long, vaguely arrow-shaped, with all sorts of fins and flaps for reducing speed and friction during a slow planetfall. The hull was ringed with flexible sections to allow it to settle onto uneven planet surfaces without breaking apart. That design philosophy worked pretty well, but there was an obvious fracture nearly amidships.

"They did a lot of repair work," said Collins, pointing to sections where plating from less important parts of the ship had been carefully welded over the break. "Must have been a bitch, doing all that while wearing those old-fashioned suits."

Our new pressure suits were like a second skin, allowing max flexibility and range of motion. The old ones were clunky, awful things.

We walked through the camp, looking for some sign of recent human activity. But everything we saw was overgrown and damaged by weather. It was a clear purple-blue sky now, but it was an ocean world, so there was a lot of rain and likely a lot of heavy storms.

Then we saw it.

Saw *them*.

It had been hidden by a copse of pines and some kind of rhododendron-looking shrub.

They were made from all kinds of materials. Plastic, thin sheets of metal, wood, and even stone. They formed their own grove, though nothing was ever going to grow there except weeds. Collins and I walked over and stood looking at them. Most were too poorly made and too badly abused by the weather to be legible. Others were in better shape. We read some of them. The names. The cities where they had been born. The ages they had been when they died.

We read the names of the dead colonists, and when we ran out of markers we could read we just counted them.

The oldest markers were in the back, and all of them had the same date.

"When they crashed?" mused Collins, and I nodded.

There were many hundreds of them. Maybe thousands, because we stopped counting.

The newer markers were a mix of dates, but the entire span— from first post-crash death to the most recent—covered a span of just under forty years.

And then nothing. No new markers. No new graves.

"Was that it, then?" Collins asked. "Did they all just die out?"

"Seems like it," I said.

"How? Why?"

"We'll have to do tests to figure it out, but if I had to guess ... it was some kind of infection. Terraforming changes a world, but you know as well as I do that worlds fight back. Bacteria, viruses ... stuff humans don't have any resistance to. Or maybe some Earth bug hitched along and mutated here. Or ..."

I trailed off because I noticed something written in small letters across the bottom of the closest marker. Twilight was deepening, so I aimed my light on it. We both read it.

I am sorry.

I had to.

God forgive me.

Collins tapped my arm and pointed to the marker closest to it. The same words were written there.

We looked closer at all of them.

Except for the headstones for the people who probably died in the crash, every other marker—hundreds and hundreds of them —bore the same three lines.

Collins and I exchanged a long look.

"What do you think happened here?" he asked, his voice hushed. "Maybe the pilot who crashed the ship?"

I shook my head. "He'd have written that on the oldest markers."

"Then what? Some biologist who let the wrong bug out of a jar?"

"Maybe."

"Or," continued Collins, "maybe it was something else. Maybe the soil here didn't generate the right kind of bacteria and the food became toxic."

I said nothing, but instead spotted a second, smaller cluster of markers forty meters beyond the big cemetery, and then headed in that direction. Collins trailed along.

"What is it?" he called, but I didn't answer.

The second graveyard was less orderly, a few dozen graves in a vastly more overgrown field. Oddly, the plants that choked this space were all of the same kind. There were thousands of meter-high stalks, some capped with pink or purple flowers. I squatted down and pulled on one thick stem, and the soil yielded a fat, pale bulb. The smell was strong and familiar.

"More garlic," I said. Then qualified it. "Only garlic. And see? It's not wild. These were planted here. There's some around each grave."

"Garlic? Why? Oh, I remember," said Collins. "It chases off rabbits and moles and ..."

"Do you see any leaves that look chewed?" I asked.

He did not.

"Look at the markers," I said. "Tell me what's different about them."

Collins frowned again, then looked around.

"None of them have that apology. No *I'm sorry* stuff."

I gave him a long, hard look. "And ...?"

"And what?"

"*Look*," I snapped.

He studied my expression for a moment, then looked. I saw his face when he realized the other difference.

"These markers ... they ..."

He didn't need to say it. Every grave marker in that field had symbols for whatever religion the people had believed in.

I got to my feet.

"Why'd they plant garlic on *these* graves?" asked Collins, a note of unease clear in his tone. "There's none on the other graves."

"No," I said. "There's no garlic over there, either."

We stood there in the gathering gloom and stared at the ship. I felt a slow, cold dread creep into my flesh. My blood turned to ice water.

"What did they bring with them from Earth?" I asked.

Collins could not answer. He couldn't speak. He stood there shaking his head as the sunlight thinned and faded and finally died over the rim of this world.

We did not see the hatch open. It was too dark.

We heard it, though.

Yeah, we heard it. Old hinges screeched in weary protest as a door somewhere opened.

But by then we were running.

Running.

Our ship was one kilometer away, beyond the overgrown fields. Beyond the cemeteries.

We ran.

God damn it to hell, how we ran.

MONK
A POEM

They call me Monk.
Real name's Gerald, but who cares?
Nobody calls me that anymore.
I'm not him anymore.

Monk.
More of a description, I guess.
I was a soldier.
I was a train wreck.
I was a drunk and a junkie.
I got lost.
Got found.
Hence ... Monk.

I see dead people.
Fuck you if you think that's funny.
Well ... okay.
Sometimes it's funny.
If you're drunk. Or high. Or an asshole.

The dead people need me.
Need what I am.
Need what I can do.
Need me to see them.
No one else can.

I take some blood from where they died.
Splashes on walls.
Puddles of it.
A few drops.
Mix it with holy water.
Take it to Patty-cakes.
She's the queen of ink.

Patty likes me to use a strap.
Something to bite down on.
While she works.
While she inks my skin.
Blood and holy water and ink.
I hate the strap.
She hates my screams.
So, I used the fucking strap.

She makes the faces.
Doesn't have to see a photo.
The blood tells her.
She's a freak too.
Not like me.
She's her own kind of freak.
She makes the faces.

The faces wake up on my skin.
They drag me down into the shit.

Into their memories.
Into the deaths.
Into the blood.
Through it.
Back.
Screaming all the way.
Them. And me.

I see the other faces.
The ones with the knives.
The ones with their dicks out.
The ones who take.
The ones who end.
The last faces the dead ones see.
Now I see them.

My name's Monk.
I see dead people.
They live on my skin.
We go hunting together.
They watch what I do to the ones who did things to them.

Afterward, they don't go away.
They live on me.
With me.
In me.
Always.
Day and night.
Some of them are quiet.
Some of them are screamers.

They call me Monk.
Real name's Gerald, but who cares?
Nobody calls me that anymore.

I'm not him anymore.
Call me Monk.

ROAD BEERS WITH NORM AND TANK AT TWITCHY'S HATCHET HOUSE

—1—

"Dead …?"

"Dead."

"How can you be sure?"

"Ain't breathing."

Tank considered that. He kept trying to light a joint, but he was five blunts in already and his hand-eye coordination was somewhere to the left of "for shit."

"He's moaning, though," he said.

Norm, who was nursing a sweating bottle of Stump Knocker like he was trying to bring it back to health, said, "So what?"

"Think about it, Einstein," said Tank, holding the match near —but not at—his dube. "Moaning is like talking. Can't do it unless you take a breath, right? I mean, you can't *just* moan."

"So?"

"So, they have to breathe if they're moaning."

Norm thought about that. There was a long line of dead soldiers standing around the blue plastic cooler. He had his ankles crossed on the white lid and was slowly peeling off the label with a thumbnail.

"Maybe the only time they breathe *is* to moan."

"Still breathing."

Norm cocked his head. "Is it, though?"

"The fuck else you'd call it?"

"Moaning."

The match burned down to his fingers and Tank whipped it out, cursed, tossed it into the campfire, lit another, but still failed to ignite the fatty. "That's still breathing."

"It's moaning."

Tank tossed the match away without realizing his joint wasn't lit. "Moaning *is* breathing, dumbass."

Norm finished the beer and set it with its companions. He considered another, decided that nine beers was one too many for an adult male on a work night, and opened one anyway. Kind of hard to say no to anything from Swamp Head Brewery. His favorite was Cottonmouth, but all they had at the store was the Stump Knocker pale ale. A little bitter, but then again so was he.

"Not sure it is, hoss," he said. "Moaning is moaning."

"Which involves breathing in and out," countered Tank.

"But not for the purposes of being actually alive. Breathing in and out regular—what they call respiration—"

"I *know* what they call it, for fuck's sake. I'm high, not stupid."

"My apologies," said Norm with a salute from the fresh beer. "Respiration per se is to keep you alive. Whereas *moaning* is just to make a statement."

Tank peered at him. "A statement? Such as ...?"

"Like 'I'm a hungry motherfucker and you look delicious.' Somethin' like that."

"Well, maybe, but that would be what they call a statement of intent. And these sons of bitches are brain dead. Any moaning they do, it would be more like reflex. Mechanical."

"Mechanical ...?"

"Well, sure, Norm. The body's a machine, ain't it? Made up of blood and bone and shit, but it still operates like a machine. Doctors are like mechanics, you follow me?"

Norm gave him a stare from the other side of too many bottles of Florida beer. "A bit."

"So," said Tank with the kind of confidence in a hypothesis only really good weed engenders, "breathing is a mechanical function. Like a car engine idling when it's turned on."

"Okay," said Norm, following so far.

"A car can't idle if it's dead."

Norm took a serious pull. "Dude, that's stupid."

"The fuck it is."

"The fuck it isn't."

"How's it stupid?" demanded Tank. He realized he was still holding the unlit joint, thought about having another go with the match, decided to quit while he was ahead, and pocketed it. Then he slapped Norm's ankles off the cooler, rooted around past all the Stump Knocker bottles, and found a can of Bud down deep in the ice. He preferred cans to bottles and preferred Bud to just about anything.

"It's stupid because you're saying that they have to be alive to moan."

"And ...?"

"And yet those bitey motherfuckers are walking around, grabbing people, biting the shit out of them, doing all that, and they're dead for sure. How does *moaning* change anything?"

Tank had a big explanation all locked and loaded, but he never got around to it because the thing that started the conversation finally reached them. It was a guy in orange coveralls that were slashed and stained. He staggered like *he'd* been the one drinking all night. Came out of the cut-road that went past Tank's double-wide all the way up to the manager's trailer.

"Shit on my shoes," said Norm, "is that Luke?"

The creature was in the spill of campfire light now.

"Hard to say," said Tank. "He ain't got a face."

"Yeah but look at him. Skinny as Luke. Tall as Luke. Wearing coveralls like he wore in the aluminum siding warehouse over in Lacoochee."

They watched the thing stumble forward.

"Okay," agreed Tank, "I think you're right. Might be Luke."

"Yeah."

"Could be his brother Caleb, though."

"Caleb works there?" asked Norm. "I thought he was still at Gary's Gulf down 'round Trilby."

"Nah, he got fired from there last November. No, wait, I'm lying. It was December."

"For what?"

"Fucking the wrong guy's wife."

Norm gave a philosophic nod. "Yeah, Caleb never could keep it in his pants. Whose wife did he fuck?"

"Gary's," said Tank, "so you can see why he got fired."

"Sure."

"Got his ass handed to him too."

"No doubt. Caleb can fuck, if the stories are true, but he couldn't win a fight with an old dog with a limp."

"Truth." Then after a moment, Tank said, "Long way for him to walk in his condition. I mean, he couldn't find his ass if his ass were in his back pockets at the best of times."

"Yeah. Maybe he got smarter dead," said Norm.

"Couldn't get much dumber."

"God's honest."

They watched as the thing—Luke or Caleb—tried to reach them over the fire. It hadn't yet sorted out the whole "go around it" thing.

"One thing, though," said Norm.

"Which is?"

"Whether these sons-a-bitches are alive or dead ...?"

"Yeah?"

"They're dumb as fuck."

Tank consider that. "To be fair ... neither Luke nor Caleb wasn't exactly a rocket scientist on their best days."

"Point."

"I mean, fucking Gary's wife when you're the only employee and she's home all the time. *And* with Gary being the size of a bridge support and Caleb being skinny as a stick."

Norm snorted. "That wasn't smart."

"Luke's no world-beater, either. Remember back in school when he *photocopied* Lily Mason's essay, whited-out her name, wrote his own in and tried to swear it was his?"

"Yeah. And was too stupid to be surprised when he got suspended. Thought he'd been taken advantage of."

They watched the dead thing.

"Shame what happened, though," said Tank after a pause. "I mean, stupid is stupid, but it don't mean you should die and turn into one of those things."

"Birth certificate doesn't make promises," said Norm in a wise tone of voice.

"Truth."

They clinked. Drank. Set their bottles down.

Tank looked at Norm. "You want to do the honors or are you too drunk?"

"I will and I ain't."

Tank frowned. "What?"

"I mean, I got this, dumbass."

"Oh. *Oh.* I got it."

Norm braced his palms on the armrests of the folding chair, took a breath, and heaved himself up. He was careful about it, because he wasn't near as thin as he used to be and sometimes his hips caught on the arms and lifted the whole chair. Do that enough times and people started saying shit. Tank was a friend, but he could be a dick now and then. He even kept his heel on one leg to provide counter pressure. Still, his knees cracked so loud Tank was amazed they didn't shine like glow-sticks.

"You're getting old," he said. "And don't give me any of that 'it's not the years' bullshit."

"Though it is," said Norm, shaking out each leg.

"You want me to do it?"

"You're as old as me."

"Sure," said Tank, "but I'm not an old, fat fuck with bad knees, a bad back, and a gut like Santa Claus."

"Two words," said Norm. "Fuck. You."

Tank considered. "You make a fair point."

Norm walked very carefully around the chair, the cooler, and the fire. He paused by the barrel where their stuff was, made a thoughtful selection, selected a Teton HXD driver from a set of clubs they found next to where a bunch of golfers had gotten chomped the night before. He hefted it, did some light practice swings, then walked all the way around to the far side of the big fire.

The creature—and they still weren't sure if it was Luke or Caleb—turned with him, dull eyes going wide, mouth snapping at the air like it could already taste rare Floridian served *au jus*. Norm took a line-drive hitter's stance, cocked the club back, and swung for the cheap seats.

—2—

That was Thursday.

It started the previous Friday.

—3—

Tank was coming off shift when he saw the first one.

He'd worked a double shift doing maintenance at Twitchy's Hatchet House and was dead on his feet. He'd had to sharpen a lot of blades because dumbass tourists couldn't hit the floor if they aimed straight down, let alone a big-ass target hung on the wall. Except that blonde gal from Clewiston who he wouldn't ever want to piss off if she was carrying anything sharp.

Point was, he was exhausted. He wanted a beer, a bed, and bad TV, and home was a ten-mile drive. He had his trailer at the

Seaview Mobile Home Park—which was a running joke because there was a *view* to *see*, but it wasn't the sea. You could see trees, cars, other mobile homes, fire pits, motorcycles, laundry hanging to dry, cords of split firewood, Fourth of July streamers so old they might have been hung by Thomas Jefferson, old Carol in a bikini because that's all she ever wore, and all of Tank's friends. His best bud was Norm, who lived next door and worked at the golf course driving that little Zamboni-looking cart that picked up balls and everyone at the driving range thought of as a moving target.

Norm was good for a late-night pizza and a movie. Maybe *Blues Brothers* for the five millionth time. Or *Blues Brothers*. Or, better yet, *Blues Brothers*. It was, after all, a cinema classic. Norm had a 1974 Dodge Monaco that the two of them had restored and christened the Bluesmobile.

He leaned against the side of his pickup, tugged his cell out the front pocket of his jeans where it was—according to Norm—giving him ball cancer with all that radiation, and hit the right numbers.

Norm answered on the second ring. Not with "Hello" or even "Yello." He answered with "Holy fuck!"

It was going to be a different kind of Friday night.

—4—

"What's up with you?"

"Holy fuck!"

"Yeah," said Tank, "you said that. What are you holy fucking about?"

"Christ, don't you ever watch the news?"

"I just pulled a double at Twitchy's."

"Nobody *told* you?" Norm bellowed.

"Told me what? You're not making a lot of sense, boy."

"About people eating each other."

"Dude, I was at work. It's a family place. Mostly, at least. People don't talk porn there."

"What? God, you're a dumbass. I'm not talking about that kind of eating. I'm talking about people *eating* people."

Tank took a beat. "Sorry, not following."

"Cannibals, man. People are turning cannibal."

"What channel are you watching? Is that a Nat Geo thing or—"

"The news, genius. Channel Nine. The. Evening. News." Norm leaned on each word.

"What?" asked Tank. "Where? Who's eating who?"

"It's all over."

"All over central Florida?"

"All over all over. Every damn where."

Tank looked at his phone to make sure he was having a real conversation. "Stop. Start over. What in the fifteen separate hells are you talking about? Go slow. Make sense."

He heard Norm drag in a deep breath. "Then freaking listen, man. It's on the news. It's on the Net. There's this plague or something. No one what knows what it is, but people have gone bug fuck nuts and have been eating other people. And I'm not talking meth addicts or dope fields eating Tide pods. I'm talking about real folks."

"*Eating* people ...?" said Tank, and all sixteen hours of his double shift stopped kicking his ass for a moment. "You're serious?"

"Dead serious."

"Like ... how bad is it?"

"Bad."

"*How* bad?"

"The guy on the news said the lieutenant governor ate the governor."

Tank had to stand and think about that for a few moments for the sentence to make sense.

"Like ... on TV?"

"Well," said Norm, "no. Apparently they were in the capitol building in Tallahassee. Right in the middle of a budget meeting or some shit. The governor was talking about cutbacks on something and the lieutenant governor—who wasn't even supposed to *be* at that meeting—just busts in, jumps across the table and begins chowing down on the governor's windpipe."

"You're shitting me."

"I shit thee not."

Tank turned in a full circle, looking at the parking lot, Twitchy's, a bunch of trees, the highway. It all looked normal.

"I'm having a hard time with this, Norm."

"Well *duh*. Imagine how the governor felt."

"No, I'm having a hard time believing this."

"Would I lie to you?"

"Dude," said Tank, "I've known you since third grade, you lie all the time."

"About people eating people?" demanded Norm, clearly offended.

"No, you lied about sneaking into my trailer last week and accidentally letting my dog out. You lied to me about screwing Cindy Miller in eleventh grade."

"Everybody screwed Cindy Miller."

"That's not the point. *You* lied and you're supposed to be my wingman."

"Okay, so I lied about some stuff," conceded Norm. "But why would I lie about this? Shit, Tank, you have a phone. It has Wi-Fi. Go check it out."

Tank did exactly that. Turns out Norm hadn't lied, but he wasn't accurate either. It wasn't all across Florida.

It was everywhere.

Every. Damn. Where.

Tank found out exactly how bad when Twitchy himself came out of the bushes behind the dumpster.

"Hey," said Tank. "You hear about what's going on?"

Twitchy grunted something.

"It's on the news," said Tank. "People are going off their nut and eating each other. And I mean in the bad way." He held out his phone to prove his point.

Twitchy staggered out of the shadows. That, in itself, was not what scared Tank. Twitchy was half in the bag 24/7. It's what got him dishonorably discharged from the Army. He wasn't an orderly drunk. He lost most of his hand-eye coordination when he was buzzed, which is where the nickname came from. And he just latched onto that name and even two of his three grown kids called him that.

So when he twitched and jerked his way across the parking lot, Tank didn't think there was anything weird.

It got weird when Twitchy tried to bite him.

He lunged forward, teeth snapping loud and nasty, and if Tank hadn't been quick enough to backpedal four steps he'd have lost the hand holding the iPhone. As it was, though, Twitchy bit the phone. Tank heard the *snap* as teeth crunched down on metal and plastic. He heard the sound of those teeth breaking. Twitchy was not the poster boy for dental health.

Tank said, "Holy shit."

Twitchy spat out the dead phone and tried for another bite.

Tank did what any tough, smart, self-respecting person would do. He screamed like a dolphin and ran for his life. He ran real damn fast.

He could have strolled, but he didn't know that. He was at the door, fumbling at the key ring on his belt, yipping and praying and making little dog sounds. When he looked over his shoulder, Twitchy was still about forty steps back.

That made Tank frown.

Fucker was taking his time about it. Between what Norm said and what was on Google, he thought the cannibals were fast. Or maybe it was just Twitchy. Maybe drunk cannibals were slow.

Either way, he got the door open, leaped inside, pulled the door shut—and had to wrestle it because the hydraulic thing that kept the door from closing was fighting him. He finally *got* it closed just as Twitchy reached for the handle.

Tank locked the door.

It took him a bit to realize he needn't have bothered. Twitchy clawed and pawed, banged and chest-butted, scratched and scraped. The only thing he didn't do was try the handle. It was like he'd forgotten what handles were or why they might have been useful.

"Are all cannibals that stupid?" asked Tank. "Or just you?"

Twitchy tried to bite the glass. Which made no sense because there was no angle to take a bite, even if it was USDA Prime.

Tank stood there, watching, fascinated despite his hammering heart.

"Well," he said, "that's not right."

—6—

"You're where?" asked Norm.

"At work."

"*Why?*"

Tank told him. Norm was distraught. He said so. He used that word because he liked it. It was the Word-of-the-Day word from last week and he always tried to use good words.

"That makes me distraught," he said.

"Makes you what?"

Norm, who wasn't all that confident he'd used the word the right way, said, "Can you get to your truck?"

"I don't know," said Tank. "Maybe. Let me look."

He looked and then went back to the office where the phone was. "No."

"Why not?"

"You know Larry?"

"Lawyer Larry or plumber Larry?"

"Plumber."

"What about him?" asked Tank

"He's out there too."

"And by out there ...?"

"Like Twitchy."

"Well shit," said Norm.

"Yeah. Larry's wife too."

"Awww ... no. Don't tell me Sis is one. I like Sis." Norm had dated Sis the year before she married Larry. Cute. Looked like Emily Blunt, if Emily Blunt made a lot of poor decisions in terms of moral compass and personal hygiene. Cute, but Tank tended to favor "sane and clean." Norm thought he was a snob.

"Yeah. Sis too," said Tank. "But you're not missing much. She's looked better."

"Please tell me the kids ain't there."

Tank said nothing.

"You still there?" asked Norm.

"Yeah."

"Why aren't you saying anything?"

"You told me not to."

"Oh, man ..."

"Yeah." Tank felt tears burning his eyes. Both kids were out there. The fifteen-year-old and the seven-year-old. He looked at them long enough to see what they were, and then couldn't look anymore.

The two of them were silent on the phone.

"You want me to come and get you?" said Norm.

"You cool with that?"

"Sure."

That part of the conversation was flat.

"I'll bring the F-250."

"I'll be ready."

When the call ended, Tank turned on the office TV and watched the world go nuts.

—7—

That was last Friday.
Now it was Thursday.

—8—

They went into Tank's trailer and rooted around for food.

"How old's this pizza?" asked Norm, his head and shoulders in the fridge, fat ass sticking up like a dog rooting in a rabbit hole.

"How would I know?" Tank called back.

"It's your fridge."

"So? It's not like I remember when everything in there was bought."

"But it's pizza. Can you narrow it down to a given week?"

Tank was playing with the remote, trying to find something on TV that wasn't the same emergency broadcast bullshit.

"Cut me a break, dude. It's not like shit hasn't been occupying my time. I go by color and smell," said Tank. "If it isn't green and you can stand the smell, then it's probably good."

Norm pulled his head out, looked at him for a minute, shrugged, and dove back in for the pizza.

The power was still on, which was something. Half the trailer park went dark on Tuesday. Norm nuked the pizza and brought it over. There were three and a half slices of double-meat, extra cheese, stuffed crust. He gave one and a half slices to Tank, kept the other two full ones for himself, settled down on the couch, and sighed.

"Find anything?" he asked with a full mouth.

"Not much."

"How much is not much?"

Tank flapped an arm toward the screen. "What you see is what you get."

They ate pizza and stared at the screen. All it said was *Please Stand By.*

Norm held out a hand. "Beer me."

Tank opened the cooler—which they had brought inside with them— and rooted around.

"Ummm," he said.

"Ummm ... what?"

"Ummm as in we're out."

"Well ... fuck."

"Yeah. What was in the fridge?"

Norm closed his eyes to refresh his memory and recited the contents. "Jar of mustard, jar of ketchup, jar of steak sauce, jar of hot sauce, jar of BBQ sauce, wrapped up piece of mystery meat, something I think used to be broccoli that looks like it's back there teaching its young, and a stuffed potato from Hardees."

"And ...?"

"And an empty pizza box."

Tank stared at him. "We drank all the beer?"

"Looks like."

"*All* of it?"

"Yeah."

"We had *six* cases."

"Had," said Norm. "It's been a week."

"Even so."

"And there's an actual zombie apocalypse."

"Sure ... but ... fuck."

"Agreed."

They stared at the screen.

"Well ... fuck," said Tank.

"Fuckity-fuck-fuck," agreed Norm.

The TV still wanted them to *Stand By*. It was polite. It said "*Please*."

Instead Tank got his laptop—one of the old ones that still had a slot for CDs and slid in the DVD for *Blues Brothers*.

Before they started watching, they did rock-paper-scissors to see who would say the line. Tank won. He cleared his throat and in his best Dan Aykroyd said, "It's a hundred and six miles to Chicago, we've got a full tank of gas, half a pack of cigarettes, it's dark and we're wearing sunglasses."

To which Norm, slightly but acceptably out of strict context, replied, "We're on a mission from God."

They watched the movie, ate the pizza, and shared what was left of Tank's beer.

"We need to do something," said Norm after the movie was over.

"We absolutely do."

The TV still insisted that they *Please Stand By.*

"Like ...?" asked Norm.

Tank looked at him. "What?"

"Like what are we going to do?"

"Fuck should I know?" groused Tank. "You brought it up."

"It's your trailer."

"So that makes me the boss of what to do?"

Norm spread his hands. "House rules."

Tank grunted and used a thumbnail to pry pizza gunk from between his teeth. "Wonder if Boo has any he'd be willing to share."

Boo Jenkins lived on the far side of the trailer park. The Hill. In the *nice* part, where they had covered carports and flagstone walkways. Only reason Boo—who'd come from nothing—lived there was because two years ago he'd won a metric shit-ton of cash from a scratch-off he bought at Twitchy's. Now he lived in one of the nicest trailers and drove a sweet new Jeep Gladiator with an all-aluminum Alu Cab camper body, a Clayton Offroad 2.5-3.5-inch overland kit, Falcon 3.3 adjustable shocks, an ARB full-width front bumper with a winch and offroad lighting package, and a roof-mounted solar package. Tank admitted to

Norm that he had truck envy, but Norm said he could be forgiven because Boo really had gone over the top and down the other side.

"Boo? Share?" Norm laughed. "That boy's so tight he wouldn't give a nickel to see Jesus riding a bicycle."

"Okay, fair," said Tank, "but these are different times."

"Boo was cheap before he got money," said Norm, making a face like he just sucked a lime. "Slowest man I ever saw picking up a check or buying a round."

"Times have changed," insisted Tank.

They thought about it.

"What if he don't share?" Asked Norm. "What if he's all bitey himself? What if he's one of them?"

"Well, not to be mean about it, but if Boo went zom I don't know that I'd have a lot of heartbreak bashing him and taking what he has left."

That thought was intriguing enough that they talked themselves into it. They got up, put on leather jackets and football helmets and thick canvas work gloves duct-taped to their wrists. They buckled on tool belts with every kind of blade and improvised cudgel slotted into the loops. Then they went out.

The biter Norm had bashed earlier was mostly ashes and charred bone now. They figured burning was easier than burying and less stinky than leaving to rot. They were wrong.

"Goddamn," gagged Norm. "Smells worse than your boxers after bean burrito night."

"Stop sniffing my underwear then," said Tank. It cracked them both up.

The trailers immediately around Tank's were a mixed bag. Some were empty shells from which everything useful had been scavenged—mostly by folks packing their car to drive anywhere but there. Some were burned-out hulks. Some were boarded and barricaded—not to keep people safe inside, but because in the first days after this all started, Norm and Tank locked up the zommed-out neighbors they liked in their trailers. That was when they thought this was a disease of some kind. Another flu or whatever. One or two had lights on but nobody ever answered the doors.

Far as Tank knew, the only part of the park with living people was the Hill. There was Boo, and some snooty neighbors who Tank knew by sight but not to talk to.

Norm had his golf club, and Tank had the top half of a really expensive hickory hiking staff he'd bought years back when he thought hiking sounded fun. But since Florida was flat as his own lean ass, there was no place to hike. The staff lived in a closet for a while and then he and Norm got high one afternoon and thought they could use it to pole vault. It broke because Norm was fat. The top half was about the length of a baseball bat. Because the thing had been expensive, Tank kept it in the big three-gallon pickle jar he used for umbrellas. Now it was his *weapon*. Like Thor's hammer, which he was pretty sure was called "My Yolner."

The golf club had a name too—"Forehead." Because Norm like bashing biters in the head and he yelled "Fore" real loud. He thought it was funny as hell. Tank thought the joke was stale the first time. Bad dad joke of the apocalypse.

They walked through the dense trees, wary of moans and movement. Stalking like they saw Special Ops guys do in movies. Silent as cats.

Norm peered into the distance and frowned. "What's that light? You telling me the sun's not down? I thought it was later than that."

"It's past nine," said Tank.

They stared at the fierce yellow glow behind the thick rows of shrubberies and trees that screened the Hill from the rest of the park.

"That ain't west neither," said Tank.

They hurried up the road, rounded the bend and stopped dead.

It wasn't the sunset.

It was the Hill.

And it was burning.

—9—

"I don't know about you, Tank," said Norm, "but that makes me mad as a box of frogs."

Tank looked at him. "Why frogs?"

"Why not frogs?"

"I mean, specifically, why a box of frogs? And what would make them that mad just being in a box?"

Norm just looked at the blaze. "Just a saying. Not sure it matters what's actually in the box."

"Yeah," said Tank. "Maybe."

They watched Boo's trailer burn. They watched his truck burn too.

"I mean," said Tank, "I can see a box of snakes. Or a box of hornets. Maybe a box of—"

"You might be overthinking things."

They saw Boo. He was missing an arm and most of his face, and his head was on fire.

"Well," said Norm, "that's unsightly."

Tank sniffed. "I'd be pretty upset if he wasn't always such a dick."

"Yeah."

The woods around them went quiet. All the crickets and night birds shut up. Then the sounds of moans drifted along on the breeze. Norm and Tank turned away from the blaze. Tank hefted My Yolner; Norm got a better grip on Forehead.

"As I see it," said Tank, trying to be reasonable, "we got no food, no beer, hardly any weed, no friends left around here, and there's biters everywhere."

"When it comes to stating the obvious, boy, you're a champion."

"My *point* is," said Tank, "I kind of feel we used up this trailer park all the way down to the grounds at the bottom of the cup."

Norm frowned. "Coffee reference?"

"Yeah."

"Ah. Can't stand coffee."

"So, much as TV says we got to *stand by*," continued Tank, "maybe it's about time we hauled a little ass instead."

Figures were beginning to emerge from the bushes. Some looked like people they knew—Jojo Waxwell, still in his suit from the insurance office; Mrs. Santos from the trailer park office; one of the Peabody Twins, though probably God couldn't even say which one because she'd been chomped pretty well. The rest were strangers. Not one of them was whole. All of them stank, and their skin crawled with maggots, flies, and other critters.

"I'm all for hauling ass, Tank," said Norm. "But where? Last I heard this particular apocalypse was everywhere. That's what the TV said when it was still saying shit. Net's down, and I don't think the power is going to stay on. Tell you the god's honest, I don't know why it's still on at all. So, if you have an actual plan, then trust me when I say I'm all ears."

"Kind of do," said Tank. "Check it out. There's a place with a big-ass beer cooler, a freezer full of food, a kitchen, pretty good doors and storm shutters, a generator, and enough fuel to keep it all going for at least long enough to at least give us breathing room to make a real plan."

Norm turned to him, a smile forming on his face. "Now ... would this particular place also cater to tourists who love throwing sharp wood-cutting implements at wall-mounted targets?"

Tank's grin was sly. "It just might at that."

"Then, by all means let's haul ass."

—10—

They hauled ass.

—11—

They took Norm's car. *The* car. The Bluesmobile. He lost the rock-paper-scissors to Tank, though, and had to ride shotgun. That was okay because Jake Blues was his favorite. John Belushi was halfway to being a god to him.

It was a normally twenty-four-minute drive from the trailer park—which was now burning with enthusiasm—to Twitchy's Hatchet House. The roads were a mess, though, so the actual trip was closer to two hours. They kept having to stop and push abandoned cars off the road or take bad side roads that were clearer but wandered around like the city planners had been drunk.

Halfway there, Norm sighed like he was deflating.

Tank cut him a look. "You okay?"

His friend shrugged. "Wish I knew if my sister Peg was okay."

"Peg? Really? I thought you hated her."

"Well, most of the time, but this is different."

"We're talking Peg who beat you up like every day until you were seven?"

"Yeah."

"The one who told you Santa Claus was a child molester? The one who took a picture of you once while you were sleeping drunk on the toilet, went onto your Facebook page and made that your profile pic? *That* Peg?"

"Okay, so she's not sister of the year," said Norm, "but she's the only blood kin I got."

They passed the pastor of First Somethingorother Church. He wore just his shirt and collar and was bent over busily eating someone.

"One thing about Peg, though," said Norm. "She's the meanest, toughest, take-*no*-shit woman ever walked the Earth. Remember what she did to Jimmy Joe Clock when she caught him peeking in her window? Chased his ass for half a mile, caught up to him, and beat him to tears on his own porch. Beat him so bad he missed graduation."

"Peg," said Tank. "She's scarier than any of these dead fuckers."

"That's no joke."

"Looks like Triple H with tits."

"Hey, don't say that."

"Sorry, sorry ... okay, she *doesn't* look like Triple H."

"No, she does. Just don't talk about my sister's tits."

"Oh. Right," said Tank. "Got it. Sorry."

"It's cool." Norm waved it away. "Anyway, she's all the way up at that fancy-ass trailer park outside of Jacksonville. That's like a hundred and forty miles."

Tank grinned and said, "Hey, Jake ... it's a hundred and six miles to Chicago, we've got a full tank of gas, half a pack of cigarettes ..."

Norm thought about it, shrugged. "Maybe, Elwood. Look how long it's taking us to get to where you work."

"You even call her since all this shit went down?"

"Nah. Bad enough with zombies without having her rag on me."

They lapsed into silence, watching the dying world go by.

When they were about a mile from Twitchy's, Norm said, "Not to piss on your shoes here, man, but how do you even know if that place is still good? I mean, it's been a week. Place could be overrun or looted or whatever."

Tank turned and looked at him for so long that he nearly rear-ended a crashed Amazon delivery truck.

"Don't look at me like that," protested Norm. "It's a reasonable question."

Tank veered around the truck. For the next mile, mile-and-a-half all he did was curse under his breath. Norm couldn't hear all of it, but he caught one phrase, "Slimy aftermath of a Costa Rican bunch-fuck."

They drove for a while.

"Okay," Norm said five minutes later, "I have to ask. Why 'Costa Rican' ...? I mean, specifically why? I mean, I can see Cuban, 'cause it's close and they're Commies. Or Bahamian if you wanted to get fancy. Or even any adjoining state. But I just can't see why Costa Rican."

"Because fuck you is why."

"Okay."

"Okay."

They were at Twitchy's fifteen minutes later.

It was not burning.

It had not been looted.

The establishment itself was not overrun because it was still locked up.

Parking lot was for shit, though.

Norm and Tank sat in the idling Bluesmobile, staring out the window at an overturned bus and what appeared to be the entire University of Central Florida Knights football team staggering around looking for something to bite.

Tank stabbed a finger at the dozens of living dead college athletes.

"You see? That's on you," he yelled.

Norm blinked a few times as he tried to make sense of that. He blinked a few more times and said, "How in the hell is that *my* fault?"

"You jinxed us."

"I ..."

"Things were going great until you had to ask a bunch of dumbass questions."

"But ..."

"So this is on you."

Norm said, "And none of this conversation has anything to do with you suddenly going completely out of your mind?"

Tank gripped the steering wheel so tightly his knuckles were bone white. "You just can't *say* shit like that, man."

"I'm sorry ...?" ventured Norm, unsure as to what the right response was actually supposed to be.

"Yeah, well you should be. Now we got to get through all of that shit."

They watched the football players.

Norm said, "Big for college kids."

Tank huffed.

"Could be worse though."

"*How*? How could it be worse?"

"They could be basketball players. They're all giants, and they're fast. Running up and down that court all day. Football players are beefy, but they ain't doing the same cardio."

"I thought you said the dead don't breathe."

"I never said they ... oh yeah. See your point."

"Got to be forty of them."

"Forty-six," said Tank. "I counted."

"Shit."

"You think we can get past them?"

"Maybe."

"How fast can you unlock the door?"

"Three locks," said Tank. "Under a minute."

Norm chewed on that. "Minute's a long time."

"Well, I'm sure as hell open to options."

The dead seemed not to notice them. Then Norm's phone rang. They both jumped. They both said, *"Yeep!"*

The zombies outside all turned toward the Bluesmobile.

The phone insisted on continuing to ring.

"Shut it off, shut it off," yelled Tank. Norm was trying to simultaneously unclip his seat belt, arch his back, and dig a hand into his pocket. Tank kept trying to help, which resulted in both of them having hands halfway into the same pocket, fingers scrabbling at the phone.

The ringing stopped.

The dead paused, looking confused.

Norm and Tank did not move or blink or even breathe.

Then the phone started ringing again.

They fought to get it out of that pocket. Somehow in the process one or both of them grabbed Norm's balls. He squealed. They *got* the phone, both of them fighting for it. The dead began lumbering their way. Moaning.

Norm finally took possession, but he was like a rookie wide receiver, juggling it from hand to chest to cheek to chest. It stopped ringing.

Tank leaned over and yelled in his ear. "Shut the fucking ringer off."

"Be quiet," snarled Norm.

"Why?" snapped Tank, pointing out the window. "They already heard us."

Which, of course, they had.

Dozens of football players were shambling across the blacktop toward them.

Tank threw the car into gear, backed and filled, turned around and drove the hell out of there. Every single zombie followed.

—12—

"Who in the fuck was calling you?" demanded Tank.

Norm looked at the missed calls and made a sound that was nearly as lifeless as the moans of the walking dead.

"*Peg.*"

Tank looked at him. "You are shitting me."

"I'm not."

"No, you're messing with me now. You're mad because I got mad and called you names."

"No, I'm not. Look." Norm held up the phone.

"Holy shit," said Tank. "Peg? Really?"

The screen flashed.

"Oh shit, she left a voicemail."

Tank looked in the rearview. The dead were still coming, but they were far behind. He made a few turns and then slowed to a stop behind a billboard for a senate candidate he hoped had gotten his nuts munched.

Norm raised the volume to half, and they both bent forward to listen.

"Norman," said the familiar voice.

"Even *sounds* like Triple H," said Tank.

"Unless you're drunk or high again, I should assume you at least know what's going on. If you ain't dead, then you better get your ass out of that shithole place you live and come up to fetch me. My car's blocked in by a crashed piece-of-crap Honda, and I'm running out of food. Down to my last roll of toilet paper too. And I'm having to use torn-up sheets for diapers."

Norm and Tank stared at each other. Both of them mouthed, *Diapers?*

"Since you never bother to even check my Facebook or Snapchat or TikTok then you probably don't know—or maybe you just don't care— but little Ronnie's almost four months. I can't watch him and go out foraging for stuff. Besides, I got that sciatica and all. So you need to get your fat ass out of where you are and come fetch me and the baby."

There was a pause, then in a voice that was somehow softer *and* nastier, she added, *"Just because you're a loser and I don't much like you, Ronnie's your nephew. It would be a sin against God if you let us get eaten."*

That was the end of the call.

They both sat back.

"Well goddamn," said Tank.

Norm was unable to articulate anything approximating human speech.

—13—

They sat for nearly ten minutes in the dark, engine off, minds blown.

One biter walked by, but he seemed focused on chasing a dog, who was clearly teasing the thing by running a few yards, waiting for it to catch up, then running more. Tank wondered if the zombie was his owner, or if the dog was just being a dick.

Then suddenly Norm jerked up in his seat like he'd been zapped by electricity. In the bad light Tank could see his friend smiling. A kind of weird, crooked, unpleasant smile, but still a smile.

"What?" asked Tank.

"Dude ..." said Norm.

"What?"

"Twitchy's."

"What about it?"

"All that food, all that beer ..."

"I know, that's why I said we should come here."

"No, no," said Norm excitedly, patting the seat. "The trunk of this car is big. Plenty of room in the backseat."

"Okay ... and ...?"

"It's fucking *obvious*."

"Not to the sane people here in the car."

Norm turned in the seat. "All jokes aside, man," he said. "Those biters followed us out of the parking lot, right?"

"Sure, so?"

"So, we can circle around and go back. Take that side road that comes up the back way past the Chick-fil-A. Come in quiet, lights off, going slow to keep the engine idle down."

"Okay, I get that part. Was kind of thinking about that myself," lied Tank. "How's that do anything about the fact that you have a baby nephew, and your sister wants us in Jax?"

"Stop being stupid for five minutes."

"Then stop being mysterious and straight up tell me."

Norm told him.

Tank goggled at him.

Tank laughed at him.

Tank told him he was out of his mind.

Tank said, "Well ... hell, son. I think that may be the best damn plan I ever heard. Mind you, it's batshit crazy and we'll probably die ..."

"But it's cool, though, right?"

They sat in the dark and grinned at each other.

—14—

They circled around.

They drove nice and slow and quiet.

There was a smaller lot in the back where Twitchy's took deliveries, but Tank didn't have those keys.

"We got to get around front."

"What if the football players came back?"

"Then we're lunch. But, since this is your plan, I'm going to let them chomp your balls while I make a break for it."

"You're a real friend," said Norm sourly.

"Hey, if we live through this, I'll buy you a beer."

"Make it a sixer."

"Done."

Tank drove very, very slowly around the building, lights off, trying to figure out how to make the Bluesmobile tiptoe. Hitting the corner of the dumpster was not part of the plan. Not that it was a head-on collision. Nope. The dumpster was just another patch of black nothingness. Tank knew it was there, but he thought he had the room to slip past.

He forgot that the lid was hanging down rather than closed on top. His error, because it was his job to close it to keep the damn trash pandas out. So, the right front wing hit the protruding edge of the hanging door. Didn't matter spit that the car was moving slow. Metal on metal in an otherwise silent night kicked up a banshee scream that scared the shit out of both of them.

"Fuck, I'm sorry," cried Tank.

"My *car*!" screamed Norm.

The lid caught on the door handle and swung the whole ass-end of the dumpster around, scattering raccoons, who fled with loud chittering that was undoubtedly foul language for a species of *procyonidae*—another Word-of-the-Day. The dumpster hit the rear quarter panel like the biggest bell in hell.

Then the Bluesmobile was past it, shooting into the front lot, half dragging the dumpster behind. The echo of that *karaaaang* filled the air, bounced off the line of trees, echoing through the night.

Tank stopped by the front door, killed the engine, bent forward, closed his eyes, and banged his forehead on the upper arc of the steering wheel.

"Fuuuuuuuuuck ..."

Norm jerked the door handle open, and it took effort because the whole door seemed to have been knocked out of true. He slammed the door. Not eased it shut. Slammed. Then he stood there, staring at the line of dents and deep scratches that began just behind the headlight and ended with a black hole where the taillight should have been.

"Get out of the car," he yelled.

"Give me a second," moaned Tank, who was feeling like the world's biggest damn fool.

"No! Right goddamn now."

Sheepishly, Tank got out and came around to look at what he'd done.

Which is when Norm punched him.

It was a very hard punch. Not a good one. Not very accurate. But it was hard. He was trying to break Tank's jaw but instead hit him squarely on the curve of his cheekbone. Tank flew sideways into the car, falling onto the hood with such force that he left a Tank-sized dent in it.

Norm began screaming.

He stuck his hand into his own armpit and began walking in a circle, making high keening sounds punctuated with comments about Tank's mother, his ancestry, his looks, and his personal hygiene. None of the comments were well-thought out. Retreads, really, from shit they used to say to each other when they were kids. But a broken hand will do that. It snaps you right back to the schoolyard when, in some similar fit of rage, a punch is thrown to punish but which is thrown with no real sense of the science of fisticuffs.

"You broke my hand!" he wailed.

Tank lay on the hood, staring up at the stars but really looking at the fireworks going off in his eyes. At that moment he wasn't really able to pay attention to anything Norm was saying. At that moment he couldn't have given his own name, his address, or added two plus two. His head felt like it had been stuck in a beehive, covered with cement, and then struck with a sledgehammer.

All he managed to say was, "Owww ..."

Norm kept screaming.

—15—

It was the moaning more than anything that made them each shut up.

In the space of a half second Tank stopped saying "owww" and Norm stopped screaming obscenities. They froze.

Then they turned their heads.

And saw the football team returning to the parking lot. Drawn by the many entertaining noises that were, for them, collectively the dinner bell.

Norm and Tank moved to the front of the car and stood side-by-side. As if they had rehearsed it a thousand times, they said— in perfect sync: "We are so fucked."

Tank whirled around and staggered toward the door, slapping at his belt for the keys. It took him a lot of tries to unlock the door. Panic and a newly-bashed head warred with each other to take the most credit.

Norm, his swollen hand still in the opposite armpit, jittered in place. It kind of looked like it was choreographed by a little kid who needed to go to the bathroom, but with overtones of interpretive dance.

All he managed to articulate was, "Hurryhurryhurryhurryhurryhurryhurry."

Tank, incapable of coherent thought let alone hurrying, finally managed to get the last lock open. By then the offensive line of the UFC Knights were really damn close. Grabby close. Almost bitey close.

"Get your stupid ass in," croaked Tank, and when Norm didn't —or could not—respond, he reached out, caught his friend by the back of the belt and hauled him through the door. Then he repeated that same tug of war against the door-closer's hydraulics. He was a little quicker getting the locks relocked.

Then the two of them collapsed.

Which was only fair.

They sat on the floor, their backs to the door. Norm was crying, though whether it was because of his car, his hand, the zombies, or life in general was anyone's bet. Tank had a case of the stares and blinked maybe three times each minute for a long time.

The only sounds were Norm's sobs and the soft, dull thuds of slack hands on the tempered glass of the door and front windows.

Maybe fifteen minutes later, Tank turned to Norm.

"Sorry about your hand," replied Tank. "And the, um, Bluesmobile."

Norm started to say something that would likely have burned the paint off a tanker truck. Instead, he said, "Sorry about your face."

"Yeah," said Tank.

"Yeah," said Norm.

Another five minutes passed.

"I don't mean to piss on the parade," said Tank, "but I always kind of figured the zombie apocalypse would be a lot more fun."

"Yeah," said Norm. "The end of the world should at least be entertaining."

They stared ahead, into the room.

At the beer coolers on the left, all of which hummed with juice from the generators. The insides of the glass doors were frosted in enticing ways.

They looked past the coolers to where a row of ten stalls had been set up, each with cup holders on one side near where people stood, and big targets on the back walls. Some of the targets were oversized bullseyes. There was one that looked like a Taliban guy with an AK-47. There was another that was a guy in a blue suit with a red tie, and, depending on who was in the White House, the face thumb-tacked to it changed. The last one, though ... made them both stare. It was a silhouette they'd both shot at on the gun range a million times. Very popular there. And it was a fan favorite at Twitchy's, though with all that had happened, he'd plum forgotten it.

"A fucking zombie."

And once more they both said it at exactly the same time.

And they both cracked up.

—16—

They got up.

Norm's hand was swollen and so red it looked like it was pissed off at both of them. But when he poked at it and flexed it, the hand worked. Not well, but not broken.

"Maybe our luck's changing," he said.

"Sure," said Tank carefully.

They walked through the place. While they did that, Peg called twice more. This time Norm took the call. He held the phone at arm's length to save his ear drum because Peg, God bless her, could yell. She could have won any hog-calling contests if they ever had such a thing in Florida. She could have stalled planes in flight. Even the zombies outside got louder.

Tank walked as far away as he could and still heard her screaming. Norm looked like a wolf in a bear trap thinking really hard about biting its own foot off. He even eyed the linebacker zoms outside as if wondering if they were a much better bet overall. As Tank saw it, there was an argument to be made.

The screaming ran down and Norm, sweaty and trembling, put his phone back in his jeans pocket.

"She's, um, delighted that we're, ah, coming to see her," said Norm.

"So I gathered."

"She said she's ... ummm ... looking forward to seeing you."

"Yeah, I heard that. Something about a skinny-ass cracker fucktard with no dick and a face like a map to Pimpleville, I believe?"

"That's Peg being amusing."

"Caught something about her shoving a tuning fork up your ass. Why a tuning fork?"

"Peg's a musical kind of gal."

Tank looked at him. "And we're sure she actually has a baby...?"

"Why?"

"'Cause if she ain't, my enthusiasm for this venture is going to bottom out right quick."

"Yeah," said Norm. "She has a rug rat."

"By ... *whom*?"

"I ... didn't have the nerve to ask."

Tank nodded. "Fair enough."

Norm dragged a sleeve across his face, looked at the blotted fear sweat, let the arm drop. "Baby," he said.

"Baby," said Tank.

They looked around. There were some cartons by the wall that Tank had left for the next day to break down for recycling.

"We can fit maybe four of them in your trunk. Fill 'em with anything we can eat. There's pork rinds, Cheetos, Slim-Jims, and all sorts of good, healthy stuff."

"Slim-Jims have protein, right?"

"I guess. I eat 'em all the time and I'm healthy as a horse."

Norm nodded. "We'll need that. For the trip and all."

They worked fast, pausing only now and then for necessary beers. When they were done, they had the boxes stacked by the door next to an improbable number of beer cases, and a cooler filled to bursting with crushed ice. There was a rack of cheap plastic sunglasses near the register, and they'd taken a pair each.

Then they stood looking out at the football zombies. They milled around the car.

"There's a lot of them," said Norm.

"Yeah."

"Did you count?"

"Yeah."

"How many?"

"Twenty-six."

"Shit."

"Yeah."

"Tank ...?" said Norm.

"What?"

"I left Forehead in the car."

"Well ... hell," said Tank. Then a moment later he said, "I left My Yolner there too."

"So, we got all this food, all those beers for the trip, and we got no way to bash those bitey cock-knockers?"

They stood for a long time sorting that out.

Then, because sometimes it takes exactly that long for certain synapses to fire in a moderately productive way, they turned around. Together. Perfect harmony.

They stood looking at the row of stalls with their various targets. Then they looked at the counter, over which was a big neon sign in red, white, and blue LED lights.

Twitchy's Hatchet House.

"Dude," said Norm.

"Dude," said Tank.

"It's like a sign," said Norm, his voice filled with awe.

"It *is* a sign."

"You know what I mean."

"Yeah," said Tank, smiling. "I surely do."

—17—

They sat in the front seat of the Bluesmobile.

They were covered in blood, bone chips, and bits of brain. They stank. Their clothes were torn. Tank's nose was broken. Norm's shirt was in rags.

All around the car were football players.

Dead ones.

Dead dead, not just bitey dead. Hatchet handles stood up at angles. Blades were buried deep. Norm, who was lousy at throwing hatchets, had used his undamaged hand to chop. He had good shoulders, and once he'd figured out the rhythm, he did pretty well. Tank had gathered a bunch of them in a cracker barrel he tucked under one arm and just threw. He was good.

Some of it got close. Messy.

Now they sat in the car.

"It's all about the baby, right?" asked Tank.

"Sure as hell not about Peg," agreed Norm. "I mean, let's be real here."

"It's one hundred forty-four miles to Jacksonville," began Tank, but Norm cut him off.

"No."

"No ... what?"

"That's not how we do it."

"What do you mean? You know a better route?"

"No, numbnuts, it's *not* how *we* do *this*."

He took the pair of cheap sunglasses from his pocket and put them on and just stared at Tank.

"You kidding me? It's dark as balls out here," Tank complained. "I won't be able to see shit."

"But it's how we're going to do this." Norm's voice had a

dangerous little tremolo to it. Tank looked at him. Then he put on his glasses.

They sat. Barely seeing a goddamn thing.

"Say it, Tank," said Norm.

Tank wanted to complain, to protest. But then he thought about it. It really *was* the way to do this. The world was fucked but somehow that made sense.

He put on the shades.

"It's a hundred and six miles to Chicago," he said in an Elwood monotone. "We've got a full tank of gas, half a pack of cigarettes, it's dark and we're wearing sunglasses."

Norm looked at him. "We're on a mission from God."

Tank grinned. "Yeah, we are."

He started the car and they drove off into the night.

SAINT JOHN

—1—

Saint John walked through cinders that fell like slow rain, and he found twenty-seven angels hiding behind the altar of a burning cathedral.

—2—

An hour before that he found a crushed and soiled rose.

He stole a wheelbarrow from a hardware store and filled it with the weapons he had collected since the plague began and wheeled to the cathedral. Saint John sang songs in his head while he worked. He did not sing them aloud, of course. God had told him years ago to sing all of his songs of praise in the temple inside his head. He left the barrow by the curb and walked up the stone stairs. The door was ajar, the lock chopped clumsily out of the wood by an axe.

There was an explosion behind the far row of buildings, and Saint John turned and stood on the top step as golden embers fell. He tilted his head face upward, eyes closed, tongue out, smiling as he waited for a piece of ash to find him. When it did he pulled it in with the tip of his tongue and savored it. The strongest flavor was the uninspired taste of charcoal that had to melt before he could enjoy the other tastes. Ghosts of flavors. There was sweetness there, like meat. A sharpness like ammonia. The tang of acid sourness. He did not know what this ash had been. Something alive, that much was certain, but that could be as true of a tree as of a dog, a pigeon, or the postman. He wished that he could discern which, but a learned palette was an acquired thing, its subtle perceptions honed through practice, observation, consideration, and repetition. Saint John did not believe that he would have the time to sample and catalog the many flavors and combinations of flavors of this apocalyptic feast. The fires would not last as long as his appetites.

Pity.

There was an explosion off to his left. He cocked his head and replayed the boom in his memory and then listened to the echoes as they banged off the building that surrounded the stone library. He smiled faintly. This *was* something he knew well. The blast was ordinary, not military ordnance. Probably a car gas tank rupturing from superheated gasses as the vehicle burned. Semtex or C4 each had their own unique blast signature, much like the calibers of bullets, weights of loads, and makes of gun. Each possessed a unique voice that whispered its secrets to him.

As if to reaffirm this there was a rattle of automatic gunfire followed by three spaced shots. A military M4 and a Glock nine. Unique in their way, but commonplace since the Fall.

The Fall ...

The concept of it was old in his mind. Saint John had expected it, prepared for it, *known* that it was coming ever since that day when he was reborn in the blood that flowed from the thousand cuts on his father's flesh. That's when the Voice began speaking to him in his mind, telling him of the Fall that would come. That was years ago and it was old and sacred knowledge to him. However, to the people around him, the panicked masses dwindling down to a scattered few, the Fall was immediate. It was their All, and in their panic they probably did not remember the world as it was before. Saint John was sure of that. He could see it in the eyes of everyone he met.

And yet the Fall, in societal terms, was only a few months old. A few weeks, if you start counting from the day when the offices of the CDC in Atlanta were overrun by mobs desperate for vaccines to the pandemic flu. Someone had begun a campaign on the Net saying that the CDC was hording stockpiles of the vaccine and selling it only to the super rich. The story was probably spurious, but the pulse of the nation had quickened to a fever pace. Atlanta had become a rallying point for protests, and the crowds surrounding the Centers for Disease Control had swelled to an ocean of angry, frightened people. Hundreds of thousands of them. Saint John had been among them; not because he believed the nonsense about the horded vaccines, but because the atmosphere of panic brought with it an apocalyptic flavor that he found delicious and uplifting. He was there on that Thursday morning when the temperature of the crowd had reached the boiling point. Like a field of locusts they went from sanity to insanity in the blink of an eye, and the National Guard were crushed under the sheer numbers. Shots were fired— shotguns loaded with beanbag rounds, TASERS, and finally bullets. Blood perfumed the air, but the crowd was in motion now, a mass mind bent on smashing down doors and walls.

In one of the last newscasts Saint John heard before the TVs all went dark, the authorities expressed fears that in an attempt to find the mythical stockpile, the mobs crashed into labs and hot rooms and viral storage vaults, inadvertently releasing many more diseases into the population. Saint John did not know how many viral vaults had been breached, but he suspected that there were seven of them. Seven seals were broken. As the plagues spread, the riot became a constant state of being, and it was then that Saint John revealed himself and walked among the diseased and dying, the murderous and the mauled, his knives in hand, a walker following in the hoof prints of the Horsemen.

He smiled at the thought and stretched out a hand to catch a soft piece of white ash. Then something closed out those sounds and drew Saint John's attention from the burning city back to the steps on which he stood.

A woman came running down the street, weaving and tripping and staggering under the weight of pain. She wore only a green T-shirt and one low-heeled shoe. Her thighs were streaked with blood. She screamed continuously in a red-raw voice. He watched her reel and stumble, but she was beyond the ability to focus her mind and muscles on the task of running. It made her clumsy and slow.

"There she is!" cried a voice. Male, out of sight around the corner. Saint John took a half step back, allowing the shadows of the entry arch to enfold him.

A moment later two men came pelting down the street after the woman, yelling and laughing. Saint John winced at some of the things they said. One man was completely naked, his semi-flaccid cock swinging and bouncing against his thighs with each step. The other, a college jock type in SpongeBob boxers and Timberlands, with distinctive lesions of the AL3 strain of smallpox blossoming on his face.

"Here kitty, kitty ..." called the Jock, laughing as his words drew a flinch from the woman. Her screams faded to a choked sob.

She turned toward a parked car and ran for it. Saint John wondered what sanctuary she thought it would afford her. The windows were broken out, the tires long-since slashed. But she stumbled and fell before she got within a dozen paces of it, her knees striking the asphalt hard enough to pull fresh screams from her chest. Her eyes were wild, and even though she looked briefly in Saint John's direction, it was clear that she did not see him standing in the shadows. She fell forward onto her palms and tried to crawl toward the car, but the Jock caught up with her and used his body to slam her to the ground. The naked man's cock was stiffening in anticipation as his companion used his knees to spread the woman's legs.

This was clearly the latest act in a play that had started hours ago. Saint John had no doubt. Intervening now could not save her. This woman was broken. If not by the rapes and abuse, then by whatever else she had lost. Whatever else had been torn from her. Family, safety, personal sanctity, perhaps even purity. Gone now, as most things were gone. What did not burn was plundered in the food riots, and what was not plundered rotted as the pathogens swept their way through the dwindling herd of humanity. This woman was a corpse whose ghost was still too shocked to leave its shell. That was sad, he thought, because to linger is to experience—with whatever sense and perception remained—all of the further indignities these monsters needed to inflict so that they could convince themselves that *they* were still alive.

Saint John did not like that. There was no beauty in this setting, and suffering without beauty was disgusting. It was crass and vulgar. Artless.

"You got her?" yelled a gruff voice and a third man emerged from the shadows. He was massive, a construct of anabolic steroids and overdeveloped muscle; he had turned himself into a freak even before time had decided that all of humanity should share in freakism. This one did not run. He swaggered slowly, his thick fingers undoing his belt buckle and zipper with the kind of deliberate calm that was itself a statement. An alpha to this small pack of dogs.

The Big Man was smiling, lips curled back from rows of white teeth. He came and stood over the woman and it seemed to Saint John that he was so into this moment that he did not blink. He grinned and grinned, and never flinched when bombs went off in the next street. He let his trousers drop and grabbed for his crotch, massaging hardness despite the limitations of steroids and other drugs. Saint John knew this type. If he could not rape he would brutalize, and it was all the same to men of his kind; his actions were completely unconnected to sex. Pain was the pathway to ecstasy for him.

Saint John knew that, and understood it from a height that gave him a much clearer perspective.

The Big Man pushed the smaller naked man out of the way and pawed at the woman, driving more screams from her.

Saint John stepped down. A single step, but it was his first movement, and the three men had not noticed him any more than had the woman.

Saint John took a second slow step, and the kneeling man looked up and snarled.

"Fuck off! This whore is ours."

Ah, and that is how worlds turn. On a word or phrase. Ill chosen and ill timed.

This whore is ours.

This whore.

Whore.

Saint John sighed. Such an unfortunate choice of words. Few words were less welcome to his ears. Not even the tough Aryan Brothers in the cell block had used that word around him—not after his first week in the SuperMax. One of them had, but their surviving members passed warnings down the line, to big stripes and little fish. Even though the word was tattooed on Saint John's own flesh in blue letters on his back, with an arrow pointing down between his shoulder blades to his buttocks. Burned there ages ago by an ex-con friend of his father; the act performed back when Saint John was the child Johnnie. Burned into him with a Bic pen, a lighter, and a pin while the boy who was not yet Saint John lay stretched out and bound with duct tape. *Whore*, it said. Branded fast while his father and the ex-con laughed and belched and spat on each letter as they waited for their dicks to get hard.

The ink had not even dried, the burns had not yet stopped singing their white-hot song when his father had shoved the tattoo artist aside to show why he had wanted those words put there. The tattoo artist had gone next. And then the other men. A pig roast, they had called it. Friends of his fathers. Men who shared the same appetites.

Men like these men.

This whore is ours.

And now these three men who crouched in the ash around the half-naked woman had conjured with that word.

Whore.

Saint John took another step.

There had been nine men back then, on the day the word had been fixed with boiling ink into his skin. The boy that he had been had survived it and the next day had fled. When he had come back in the night a month later and looked in through the window he saw the tattoo artist burning those same letters in another child's flesh. A girl, this time. Gender had not mattered to them. They coveted what they could dominate, what they could force.

Her screams made the men laugh.

As this woman's screams made these men laugh.

Whore.

Back then, on the day when he had been marked, it was not the first time he had heard that word. Not nearly the first.

But it was the first time that another voice spoke inside his mind.

The Voice had told him to go into a sacred place inside the mansion of his thoughts. The Voice guided him there, and with each inward step the laughter and grunts of the nine men diminished until they were no more than a faint and unimportant background noise.

The Voice had guided him back to the world later, when his body had been cut loose and thrown into the corner between the fridge and the stove. It was there to tell him what to pack and when to run, and schooled him on how to live after he'd fled. It brought him back to the house on the night the men had strapped the girl down, and it spoke great secrets to him when he begged for answers.

He had done everything exactly as the Voice instructed. Saint John later understood that it was the Voice of God, and upon that realization he had begun the transformation from Johnnie to the Saint. He was glowing with holy purpose when he returned to his father's farm. There were always gallons of gasoline in the barn, standing in a row beside the post-hole digger, near where a machete hung from its peg. When the Voice of God spoke, the lessons were always simple, always clear. The lessons were about clarity and simplicity.

And about fire. Ahh ... fire was such a beautiful doorway.

Saint John took another step down. The cathedral had lovely white granite steps and an archway carved with the austere faces of a hundred saints. Fellow saints, and Saint John wondered if each of them had been given the gift of the Voice. Probably. Why else would they be saints? How else could they be?

The Jock and the Naked Man looked up at Saint John. They looked up from what they were trying to do, shifting their eyes reluctantly from dirty flesh and bitten skin to this annoyance. This intrusion.

Saint John did not move with haste. Haste caused rabbit reactions, quick and defensive. He wanted to see the dog reactions. The jackal reactions. That happened best if he moved slowly, giving each of them the opportunity to make slight perceptual shifts as his personal bubble extruded outward and pushed against the outer edges of their self-confidence. It was very much like subtly shifting to stand too close to a person in a crowd—at first they think you're leaning in to hear better, to catch every drop of conversational juice, but then they notice that you do not lean away when they've finished speaking. That's when the hound that dwells in the middle of their brain raises its head and lifts its ears to tufted points, sniffing and smelling the wind.

First comes speculation as distances are judged and given value; then in confusion as those values are ignored. Then in defensive caution as the social bubble pops to demonstrate that it never really offered any protection. It was an abstract bubble after all.

Then comes alarm.

He watched for this in their eyes. The Naked Man was less focused, his eyes continually drifting down to what the Big Man was trying to do. He was more erect than the Big Man, and bigger, but he was not the alpha of this pack and he knew that he would have to wait. The Naked Man licked his lips in nervous anticipation.

The Jock was the one who looked up at the stranger descending the steps and briefly smiled. Maybe he thought that this newcomer wanted to join in and he was preparing a stinging rebuke. Maybe it was an uneasy smile. Maybe it was a smile that would include an invitation to be the fourth car in this train.

The Naked Man flicked a glance up, then down at the woman, and back up to Saint John. For a moment there was a fragment of shame in his eyes for what he was doing. Not for the woman or her humanity, but for his own participation in something they all clearly knew was wrong. Anarchy did not yet completely own this man's soul.

Saint John marked that one in his mind. A flicker of remorse in the presence of continued action was not a saving grace. It spoke to understanding, and complicity here was proof of corruption. A man like this would not initiate a rape, but he would always go where a door was opened. There had been men like him on the night that ugly word had been burned onto his skin. One of them had even whispered, "I'm sorry," as he had hunkered over and thrust. Saint John had spent a lot of time with him later on.

The Naked Man looked away. He was a loose-lipped slobbering buffoon. No muscle tone, skin like a mushroom. White and spongy.

It was the Jock who first realized the danger. As Saint John descended another step toward the screaming thing over which the men crouched, the Jock's inner hound finally came to point.

"Hey—jackass," he snarled, "what the hell are you doing? I told you to fuck off."

Saint John smiled. "You must stop this and go your way," he said. "Man's hand was not fashioned by God to lay waste to that which the Lord has made."

The Jock stared for a two-count and then burst out laughing.

"Who the fuck are you supposed to be? Church isn't until Sunday, dumbass."

The Big Man paused to punch the woman in the thigh, angry that he was having so much trouble getting hard enough to penetrate her.

Saint John descended one final step. Now he stood above the tableau. The woman's dirty-blonde hair cobwebbed the asphalt.

"It *is* Sunday," murmured Saint John, but the reply was lost beneath the woman's screams. Saint John wore white bedsheets as clothes, the material lashed to his limbs and torso with strips of white tape on which he had written crucial passages of scripture. Not from the Bible, but new scripture the Voice had spoken to him. The sheets were tattered now from all that had happened since the city had begun to burn, and the tatters floated on the hot breeze, like streamers of pale seaweed in a sluggish tide.

The Jock was still in dog mind, bolstered by the presence of the pack and the alpha. The others were too.

Saint John wanted to laugh, to kiss each of them for that ignorance. It was as delightful as it was false. So entertaining.

But he did not laugh. Instead he cast his face into the beatific smile he wore at such moments. Like Leonardo's model, his smile was a tiny curl of the lip that promised secrets but not answers. He spread his hands high and wide. He had long arms and longer fingers tipped with nails that each been painted a different shade of night gray.

The Jock nudged the Big Man, pack dog alerting the alpha to the possibility of something wrong. When the Big Man looked up, the smaller man bent and tried to kiss the woman. Even to Saint John such a kiss was strange and awkward. Obscene.

The Big Man growled deep in his chest as he saw Saint John standing there with his arms outstretched.

A ripple of explosions troubled the air close by and the three men looked over their shoulders. Even the woman looked.

That amazed Saint John, because he could not imagine in what way the destruction implied by those blasts could possibly matter to any of them. How could anything beyond the confines of this moment matter to them? Were these men in particular too stupid to grasp the importance of *now*?

Apparently so.

One by one they turned back to Saint John.

The Jock said, "Fuck off, you little faggot."

"Get your own," said the Naked Man.

The Big Man could not be bothered to pay a moment's further attention to the interruption. It's why he had a pack. Instead he glared down. "Lay still you bitch."

Saint John caught a flicker of movement and he looked across the street to see a fourth man standing by the corner. He was a shifty, nervous little thing. Clearly a junkie or a drunk suffering through D.T.s He shifted from foot to foot and grabbed his crotch, but he didn't cross the street. He was either too afraid of the three more aggressive pack members, or he had not yet crossed the line that separated social depravity from personal destruction. The man caught Saint John looking and immediately whipped his hand away from his crotch. He stood there, staring back, mouth open like a silent ghost.

The three men surrounding the woman laughed and told her the things they were going to do, and told her how much she would like it. And the penalties that would be imposed if she did *not* like it.

The predictability of this drama, and the triteness of the dialogue, began to wear on Saint John. He lowered his arms and said, "Let me share with you."

They all laughed, confirming that they were too stupid to understand what was going on.

"Let me share," repeated Saint John as he reached into the folds of his blowing white clothes and brought out his toys. They gleamed in the smoke-stained firelight. They were small and elegant, each polished to such a perfect shine that they seemed to trail sparks as he once more brought his hands out to his sides. A delicate blade extended the reach of each hand as he stood cruciform on the step above them.

The Jock and the Naked Man stared in awakening horror as everything froze into a bubble of time in which they all floated. The woman lay supine, her mouth strained open to cry out for mercy from a God who most of the survivors of the plague believed was either dead or mad. The Big Man knelt between her thighs in a mockery of a supplicant. On either side of him crouched the Naked Man and the Jock, their hands pressing the woman's wrists to the ground as above them an angel spread its glittering wings.

Saint John stepped down onto the pavement and two steps brought him to the curb. The Jock could have reached up to strike him. But he was unable to move. In his mind the pack was gone, transforming him from predator to prey.

"Thy will be done," whispered Saint John, and a sob of joy escaped his throat as his arms folded like wings and the knives flashed a crisscross before him. Rubies of hot blood splattered the steps and his clothes and his face as veins opened to his touch. Before the Big Man could look up again, Saint John swept his arms back and forth, each movement ending in a delicate flick of his artistic wrists.

The Big Man finally looked up as blood slapped him across the face. Saint John appeared not to have moved, his arms held out to his sides. But on either side of him the members of the Big Man's pack sagged to the ground in disjointed piles.

Saint John watched the man's eyes, saw the whole play of drama. The brutal lust and frustration crumbled to reveal shock.

Then there was that golden sweet moment when the Big Man looked into the eyes of the cruciform saint and saw the only thing more terrible and powerful than the portrait of himself as post-apocalyptic alpha that he had hung inside his own mind. Here was the sublime Omega.

"No," the Big Man said. Not a plea, merely a denial. This was not part of his world, not before or after the Fall. He had survived the plague, goddamn it; he had fought through the riots and the slaughters. He had become more powerful than death itself and he expected to rule this corner of Hell until the End of Days.

Yet the Omega stood above him, and the pack lay drowning in their own blood. So fast. So fast.

The Big Man tried to fight.

But before he could close his fists he had no eyes. Then no hands. No face.

No breath.

The Big Man's mind held onto the last word he had spoken.

No.

Then he had no thoughts and the darkness took him.

—3—

Across the street the nervous little junkie was backing away, one hand clamped to his mouth, the other still clutching at his crotch. When he reached the corner he whirled and ran. Saint John did not give chase. If the little junkie and these dead men had friends, and if those friends came here, then there would be more offerings to God. If it happened that the offering included his own life, then so be it. Many saints before him had died in similar ways, and there would be no disgrace in it.

Saint John turned suddenly, aware that he was being watched. He looked up the stairs to the church. The doors stood ajar, and the faces of saints and angels watched him. Stone saints from the carvings around the arch.

But the angel faces? They watched from the open doorway.

Cherubim and seraphim, hovering in the darkness. Saint John lifted a hand to them, but they were gone when he blinked.

Saint John wiped blood from his eyes.

Still gone. There were only shadows in the doorway. He nodded. That was okay. It was not the first time something had been there one moment and not the next. It happened to him more and more.

Even so, he let his gaze linger for a moment longer before turning away.

"Angels," he said softly, surprised and pleased. He had only ever dreamed of angels before. Now they were here on Earth, with him. And that was good.

—4—

The woman lay curled in pain, drenched in the blood of the three monsters who had hurt her, her faced locked into a grimace; but the scream that had boiled up from her chest was caged behind clenched teeth.

She stared at Saint John. Not at his knives, because even in her horror she understood that they were merely extensions of the weapon that was this man.

Saint John took a step toward her. Blood dripped from his face onto his chest.

"God," she whispered. "Please ... God."

Red splattered onto the cracked asphalt.

The saint knelt, doing it slowly, bending at ankle and knee and waist like a dancer, everything controlled and beautiful. The woman watched with eyes that were haunted by lies and broken promises. If she had possessed the strength, her muscles would have tensed for flight; but instead there was a weary acceptance that she was always going to be an unwilling participant in the ugly dramas of men.

Saint John bent forward and placed the knives on the edge of the curb with the handles toward her. Inches from her outstretched hands. Dead men lay on either side of her, but she watched this, darting quick glances from the bloody steel to Saint John's dark eyes.

He sat back on his heels, letting his weight settle. The movement was demonstrably nonaggressive and he watched her process it.

"What ... what do you want?" she asked weakly.

He said nothing.

"Are you going to hurt me too?"

"Hurt you?"

She jerked her head toward the dead men. "Like them. Like all the others."

"Others?" echoed Saint John softly. "Other men attacked you?"

A cold tear broke from the corner of one eye. She was not a pretty woman. Bruises, battering, and blood had transformed her into a sexless lump. The animals who lay around her had wanted her because of some image in their minds, not because she fit their idea of sexual perfection. She was the victim of smash and grab opportunism, and that was as diminishing as being the tool by which men satisfied their need to demonstrate control.

"How many men?" asked Saint John.

"Just today?" she asked and tried to screw a crooked smile into place. Gallows humor.

Embers still fell like gentle stars. Both of them looked up to see burning fragments peel off of the roof of the cathedral. The cathedral itself would be burning soon. Sparks floated down like cherry blossoms on an April morning.

The woman looked down and slowly pulled together the shreds of the T-shirt. There was not enough of it to cover her nakedness, but the attempt was eloquent.

"You won't hurt me, too, mister," she said softly, almost shyly, "will you?"

"No," he said, and he was surprised to find that his mouth was dry.

"Will you ... let me go with you?" It was an absurd question, but he understood why she asked it.

He shook his head. "I'm not a good companion."

"You helped me."

Helped, she had said. Not *saved*. The difference was a thorn in his heart, and he hated that he had allowed himself to care.

He said nothing, however. It would be impossible to explain.

The woman crawled away from the dead men and huddled behind a corner of the car. "What's your name?"

"What's yours?" he countered. He prayed that it would not be something symbolic. Not Eve or Mary or—

"Rose," she said. "My name's Rose."

"Just Rose?"

She shrugged. "Last names really matter anymore?" She coughed and spat some blood onto the street.

"Rose," he said, and nodded. Rose was a good name. Simple and safe. Without obligations.

"What's yours?"

She asked it as he rose to stand in a hot breeze. The sheets he had wrapped around his body flapped in the wind.

"Does that matter?" he asked with a smile.

"You saved my life."

"I ended theirs. There's a difference."

"Not to me. You saved my life. They'd have raped me again and made me do stuff, and then they would have killed me. The big one? He'd have killed me for sure. I saw him stomp another waitress to death 'cause she didn't want to give him a blow job. She kept screaming, kept crying out for her mother."

"Her mother didn't come?"

Rose shook her head. "Her mom's back in Detroit. Probably dead too. No ... Big Jack got tired of Donna fighting back and just started kicking her. It didn't make no sense. He'd have worn her down eventually. They had us for almost a week, so I know."

Saint John closed his eyes for a moment. *A week*.

Rose said, "I've seen what happened with other women.

There's only so long you can fight before you'll do whatever they want." She wiped a tear from her eye. "Donna was just nineteen, you know? Her boyfriend was in Afghanistan when the lights went out. He's probably dead. Everybody's dead."

"You said everybody gives in. You kept running. Kept fighting."

Rose looked away. "I got nothing left. These pricks ... this was all I had. They won."

"No," he said softly. "You have life."

She cocked an eye at him. "'Cause of you."

Saint John wanted to turn, to look up and see if the angels were still watching from the shadowy doorway, but he did not. Angels were shy creatures at the best of times, and he did not want to frighten them off. If "frighten" was a word that could be used here. He wasn't sure and would have to ponder it later.

When he noticed the woman studying him, he asked, "Would you have given in? Stopped fighting them, I mean?"

"Probably. If I did they would have treated me better. Given me food. Maybe let me wash up once in a while."

"Would that have been a life?"

Rose looked up at the embers and then slowly shook her head. "Don't listen to me, mister. They gave me some pills to make me more attractive. No—that wasn't the word. What is it when you cooperate?"

"'Tractable'?"

"Yeah."

"They gave you pills?"

"Yeah. I can feel them kicking in now. Oxycontin, I think. All the edges are getting a little fuzzy."

Saint John gestured to the knives. "Do you want these?"

She looked at the bloody blades. Embers like hot gold fell sizzling into the lake of blood that surrounded the three dead men.

Rose shook her head.

"Are you sure?" he asked.

A nod.

"These men," he said gently, "there will be others like them. As bad or worse. There are packs of them running like dogs."

"I know."

"Then take the blades."

"No."

"Take one."

"No."

They sat and regarded the things that comprised and defined their relationship. The embers and the smoke. The blood and the blades. The living and the dead.

"Not everyone's gone bad," she said.

"No?"

She managed a dirty smile. One tooth was freshly chipped and blood was caked around her nostrils.

"There are guys like you out here."

"No," he whispered. "There is no one like me out here."

They watched the embers fall.

After a while, she said, "You came and saved me."

"It was someone else's moment to die," he said, but she did not understand what that meant.

"You saved me," she insisted and her voice had begun to take on a slurred, dreamy quality. The drugs, he realized. "You're an angel. A saint."

He said nothing.

"I prayed, and God sent you."

Saint John recoiled from her words. He felt strangely exposed as if it was he and not this woman who was naked.

Then he felt the eyes on him again. Saints and angels from the doorway.

He stood. "Wait here for a few seconds."

"Where are you going?" she asked with a fuzzy voice.

"Just around the corner. I'll be right back, and in the meantime the angels watch over you."

"Angels?"

"Many of them."

Her eyes drifted closed. "Angels. That's nice."

Saint John hurried to the corner and around it to a side street filled with looted shops. He did not linger to shop carefully; instead he took the first clothes he could find. A black track suit made from some shiny synthetic material, with double red racing stripes and a logo from a company that no longer existed. There were no sneakers left, but he found rubber aqua shoes of the kind snorkelers and surfers used. No underwear, no medicine. The last item he selected was a golf club. A seven iron. He smiled, pleased. Seven was God's number.

With the clothes folded under one arm and the seven iron over his shoulder, Saint John left the store, stepping over the rotting bodies of two looters who had been shot in the head. It was impossible to say whether they had been killed by the police or other looters, and even if that information was known, Saint John doubted that there was anyone still alive who cared. Certainly he did not.

He rounded the corner and stopped.

The woman—Rose, he reminded himself. Her name was Rose —was gone.

Saint John set the clothes and the golf club down and ran the rest of the way, the streamers of his bedsheet clothes flapping behind him. The three dead men were there. His wheelbarrow of weapons was there. She was not.

Saint John looked for her for almost half an hour, but he could not find her.

As he walked back to the cathedral he found that he was sad. Saint John was rarely sad, and almost never sad in relation to a person. Yet, dusty and crumpled as she was, Rose had touched him. She had been honest with him, of that he was certain.

Now she was gone. He wished her well, and when he realized that he did, he paused and smiled bemusedly at the falling embers. It was such an odd thought for him. Alien, but not unwelcome.

"Rose," he said aloud.

—5—

Saint John gathered up the weapons—knives, a club made from a length of black pipe, a wrench caked with blood—and carried them up the stairs to the church. There were guns in the wheelbarrow, and even a samurai sword that the former owner had not known how to properly use. Saint John had obliged him with a demonstration. The wheelbarrow was heavy with them; it had been a fruitful week. He carried them, an armload at a time, into the church, counting out his ritual prayers with each slow step. He wanted to get everything right, however there was no need for haste. This was the end of the world, after all. To whom would haste matter? Inattention to details, however, could have a profound effect. Saints and angels were watching.

With his first armload hugged to his chest, he stood on the top step. The faces of the saints regarded him, and shadows cast by flickering flames played across their mouths so that it seemed as if they spoke, whispering secrets. Some of them Saint John understood, some were still mysteries to him.

He did not see the faces of the angels, however. The open doorway was a dark mouth, but it was filled with empty shadows, and so he entered with his armload of weapons. He paused in the narthex and looked down the long aisle that ran from the west doorway behind him all the way to the altar at the eastern wall.

The cathedral was vast, with vaulted ceilings that rose high into the darkness. The arches were revealed only by stray slices of firelight through the broken stained glass windows, and in this light the lines of stone looked like bones. Saint John walked to the center aisle and stopped by the last row of pews, bowed reverently, and then walked without haste through the vast nave toward the altar table.

"I bring gifts," he said. His voice was soft, but the acoustics of the cathedral peeled that cover away to reveal the power within, sending the three words booming to the ceiling.

As he walked to the altar the weapons clanked musically, like the tinkle of Christmas bells. He stopped at the edge of the broad carved silver altar table and laid his offering in the center. Then, taking great care, he arranged the blades and hammers and brass knuckles in a wide arc, the blades pointed toward the rear wall, pointing to the base of the giant crucifix that hung on the eastern wall. Jesus, bleeding and triumphant, hung from nails. Saint John knew the secret story of this man. Jesus had not died to wash away the sins of monsters like Saint John's father. No, he had allowed his body to be scourged and pierced as part of the ritual of purification, then he had ascended through the pain into godhood. He marveled that so many people over so many years had missed the whole point of that story.

Once the knives were arranged—seventeen in this armload—and the rest of the weapons, Saint John bowed and headed outside for more.

It was on his second trip into the church that he noticed the foot prints on the sidewalk. Small feet. A woman. Rose? Surely hers, but there were other prints; much smaller and many of them. They were pressed into the thin film of fine ash that had begun to settle over everything. Delicate steps.

Angel feet?

Saint John stood for a moment, his arms filled with bloodstained weapons, contemplating the footprints. Then he went inside.

However he paused once more as he approached the altar table.

On his previous trip he had placed seventeen knives on this very table, arranged by size and type, from a machete to hunting knives and steak knives to a lovely little skinning knife with which he had whiled away an evening last week. However there were not seventeen knives now.

Now there were two. Only the long machete and an unwieldy

Ghurka knife remained. The brass knuckles and clubs and guns were still there. Fifteen knives, though, were gone.

Saint John considered this as he laid his second armload down on the altar. He did not for a moment believe that he had only imagined bringing in those knives. Many material things in his perception were of dubious reality, but never blades. They were anchors in his world, not fantasies. The flying saucers he sometimes saw ... those, he knew, were fantasies. Knives? Impossible.

Nor did he believe that someone—perhaps the little junkie—had snuck in here and stolen the knives.

He was considering possibilities and probabilities when he heard a soft sound. Barely a sound at all. More of a suggestion, like the sound shadows make when they fall to the ground as the moon dances across the sky. Soft like that.

He cocked his head to listen. The cathedral was empty and still.

Were demons moving silently between the pews? Had demons come to take his knives?

Saint John was suddenly very afraid.

Could demons materialize enough to be able to lift a piece of metal? Before this moment he would have been certain of the answer to that question, but now he wasn't so sure. The knives were gone.

Had the demons made the footprints in the ash? Were the demons here in the church, maybe preparing to hunt him with his own knives? Had the Fall of man made the demons bolder? Had it given them more power? Had it, in fact, kicked open the door between Hell and Earth?

These were terrifying thoughts, and Saint John whirled, drawing two knives from sheaths concealed beneath the white rags that covered his thighs.

"This is the house of God!" he yelled into the dusty shadows. "You may not be here!"

He heard the soft sounds again. Louder this time, and more of them. A scuffle of invisible feet moving in the shadows behind the screen that separated the altar from the choir's chancel. The sounds were stealthy, of that Saint John was certain.

The fact of their stealthy nature injected a dose of calm into his veins. Stealth was a quality of caution, of fear. Predators are stealthy for fear of chasing off the prey they need to sustain their lives. Prey is stealthy to avoid being attacked. For both, fear was the key.

Fear, even in a terrible predator, revealed the presence of weakness. Of vulnerability. An invulnerable demon would not fear anything.

You are a saint, whispered the Voice inside his mind.

A saint. He nodded to himself. A saint in a church.

Saint John felt the fear in his heart recede. Not completely, but enough for strength to flood into his hands from the knives he held; and from his hands to his arms and the muscles in his chest, and to the furnace of his heart.

He could feel his mouth twist in contempt. He raised his arms to his sides, the blades appearing to spark with fire as they caught stray bits of light from the fires burning beyond the broken stained glass windows.

"I am Saint John of the Ashes," he cried in his booming voice. *"Exorcizo te, immundissime spiritus ... in nomine Domini nostri Jesu Christi!"*

A figure stepped out from behind the screen. He was dressed in filthy rags and held one of Saint John's gleaming knives in his fist.

"Go away!" said the figure.

Saint John had begun to smile, but his smile faltered and then fell from his lips.

If this was a demon, then it was a demon wearing the disguise of a cherub. The fist that was wrapped around the knife was barely large enough to encircle the handle. Its face was round-cheeked but hollow-eyed, dusted with dirt and soot, dried snot around the nostrils, tear tracks in the grime. And upon the shoulder of the T-shirt he wore was a single bloody handprint. A child's handprint.

The cherub pointed the knife at Saint John.

"Go away!" he said again. His voice was small and high, but there was so much raw power in it that Saint John was almost inclined to take a backward step. But he did not.

He asked, "Who are you to tell me to leave my father's house?"

The cherub's eyes were blue and filled with a fascinating complexity of emotions. His body trembled, perhaps with hunger or with sickness from one of the plagues; or fear. Or, Saint John considered, with rage barely contained.

This was surely no demon. He held a sanctified blade in a way that showed he understood its nature and purpose; and yet he appeared in the face and form of a child of perhaps eight. Or ... seven?

That would be exciting.

That would be wonderful, perhaps miraculous; and Saint John was now convinced that he was in the presence of the miraculous. Or on its precipice.

Saint John took a step forward. The cherub—or child, if it was only that—held his ground, but he raised his knife a few inches higher, pointing at Saint John's face and giving it a meaningful shake. He held the knife well. Not perfectly, but with instinct.

"I'm not messing," said the cherub. "Go away."

Saint John was close enough to kill this child. He had the reach and the knives; but he merely smiled.

"Why should I leave?"

"This is *our* house."

Ah. *Our.* A slip.

Saint John thought of the scuffle of footprints in the ash. And of fifteen missing knives.

"This is my father's house," Saint John said. "This is the house of God."

"You don't live here," insisted the boy.

"I do."

In truth Saint John had never been inside this particular church before, but that didn't matter. A church was a church was a church, and he was a saint after all.

"Who's there?" said another voice. A woman's voice. Vague and dreamy and slurry. Saint John smiled.

"Rose—?"

There was a stirring behind the screen and the hushed whispering of many voices. More than a dozen, perhaps many more. Male and female, and all tiny except for Rose. Shadows moved behind the screen, and then Rose stepped out. She wore a choir robe that was clean and lovely in tones of purple and gold; but her face was still dirty and bloody and puffed.

"You're real?" she asked as she stared at Saint John. "I thought I dreamed you."

"Perhaps you have," said Saint John, and he wondered for a moment if he, too, was dreaming; or if he was a character in this woman's dream. "I am sometimes only a dream."

Her face flickered with confusion. The drugs the men had given her held sway over her, however she kept coming back to focus. Saint John knew and recognized that as the habit of someone who was often under the influence and practiced at functioning through it.

"Are these your kids?"

As he asked that, more of the cherubs came out from behind the screen. Many of them carried knives. *His* knives. The cherubs were tiny, the youngest in diapers, the oldest the same age as the blue-eyed boy who still pointed his knife at Saint John's face.

Saint John counted them. Twenty-six. The firelight from outside threw their shadows against the wall, and their shadows were much larger. Did the shadows have wings? Saint John could not be sure.

"Go away!" growled the lead boy. "Or I'll hurt you."

"Hey," slurred Rose, "be nice!"

"He's one of *them*!"

Rose's eyes cleared for a moment. She studied Saint John and his knives, then she shook her head. "No, kid ... *he* isn't. He's the one who saved me. I prayed to God, and He sent him to save me."

The lead boy's eyes faltered, and he flicked a glance at Rose. In that moment of inattention Saint John could have cut the child's throat or cut the tendons of the hand holding the knife. He could have dropped one of his own knives and used his hand to pluck the knife from the boy.

He did none of those things.

Instead he waited, letting the boy figure it out and come to a decision. Allow the boy his strength. The boy refocused on Saint John, and his eyes hardened. "Where'd they take Tommy?"

"I don't know who Tommy is."

"You took him. Where'd you take him?"

The other children buzzed when Tommy's name was mentioned, and now their eyes focused on Saint John. He saw tiny fists tighten around knife handles; and the sight filled him with great love for these children. Such beautiful rage. They were ready to use those knives. How strange and wonderful that was. How rare.

How like him; like the boy he had been when *whore* was burned onto his back and he had first listened to the Voice and heard the song of the blade.

"I do not know anyone named Tommy," he said. "I have never seen any of you before, except Rose, and I met her only a few minutes ago."

"Bull!" the lead boy snapped.

"Shhh," said Saint John. He took a half step forward, almost within the child's striking range. "Listen to me."

The boy's eyes drifted down, and Saint John could see that he was assessing the new distance between them. So bright a child. When his eyes came back up the truth was there. He knew that he was in range of Saint John's blades and overmatched by his reach. Even so, he did not lower his knife—and it was *his* now. He had claimed it by right of justice, and Saint John was fine with that.

So, Saint John lowered his own knives. He slid them one at a time into their thigh sheaths and stood apparently unarmed and vulnerable in front of this cherub. He saw the child's eyes sharpen as he realized the implication of this, the threat unspoken behind the sham of vulnerability. Most adults would never see that. Only someone graced by the Sight could see *that*.

The boy hears the Voice, thought Saint John.

"Tell me who you are," he said, "and tell me what happened to Tommy."

—**6**—

The lead boy told the story.

They were orphans. They lived with four hundred other children at Saint Mary's Home for Children.

Mary. Ah. That name stabbed Saint John through the heart. *Her* name. His mother. Long gone. First victim of his father. She had tried to protect her son from the Devil in their home. She had survived a hundred beatings, but not the hundred and first. A blood clot. Mary.

Mother of the savior.

Saint John already knew where this was going. He wasn't sure he liked it, though.

The boy said that a line of buses set out from Saint Mary's two weeks ago, heading for a government shelter here in the city. There was a riot, fires. Gunshots. The driver was killed. The nuns were dragged off the bus. The boy did not possess the vocabulary or the years to understand or express what had happened to the nuns. He said that men did "bathroom stuff" to them. His eyes faltered and shifted away, but it was enough of an explanation for Saint John. He had been raped for the first time when he was younger than this boy. He knew every euphemism for it that existed in human language, and some spoken only in the language of the damned.

While the men were fighting with the nuns, this boy opened the back door of the bus and made the rest of the kids run. There had been forty-four of them on his bus. Last night there were only twenty-seven. Tommy had been playing on the steps of the church this morning, and men had come to take him away.

They heard him screaming all the way down the block and around the corner.

"Describe the men who took him," said Saint John. The boy did. Most of them were strangers. Two of the men fit the descriptions of the Jock and the Big Man.

Rose was fighting to stay awake, but when she heard those descriptions she jerked erect. "That's the same assholes who—"

Saint John nodded. "Tell me where they kept you, sweet Rose."

"Why?" she demanded. "The kid's gone."

"No!" yelled the lead boy. Others did too. A few of the younger ones began to cry. "I'm gonna get him back!"

Saint John shook his head. "No," he said. "You won't. You'll stay here and guard your flock."

The boy glared at him. There was real fire in the boy's eyes; Saint John could feel the heat on his skin. It pleased him. It was like being a stranger in a strange land and unexpectedly meeting someone from your own small and very distant town. He had not expected to see that blaze here at the curtain call of the human experience.

"Tell me your name," asked the saint.

"Peter."

Saint John closed his eyes and sighed. He smiled and nodded to himself. When he opened his eyes Peter was still glaring at him.

"I am going to find Tommy," said Saint John, "and bring him back here."

Rose snaked a hand out and grabbed his wrist. "Christ, are you nuts? They'll fucking slaughter you. There are like ten or twelve of those assholes over there."

Saint John said nothing, and his smile did not waiver.

Rose finally told him where the gang lived and where they

"played." Saint John nodded. To Peter he said, "Stay here. Stay silent. Stay hidden."

"You can't tell me what to do."

"No. I can only tell you how to stay alive."

Peter scowled. "You're gonna get killed. You're gonna leave us like the nuns did and the driver did."

Saint John could feel the weight of the knives hidden in his clothes. He said, "Doubt me now, Peter. Believe me when I return."

And he left.

—7—

There were sixteen men at the hotel that had been converted into a lair for rabid dogs. Sixteen men on three floors.

Saint John drew his knives and went in among them.

Sixteen men were not enough.

The skinny junkie was one of them. He was on the third floor, sleeping in a bed with a woman who was handcuffed to the metal bed frame. Her skin was covered with cigarette burns. Saint John revealed great secrets to the little junkie. And to the others. For some of them it was very fast—a blur of silver and then red surprise. For a few it was a fight, and there were two who Saint John might have admired under other circumstances. But not here and not now.

Saint John painted the walls with them. He opened doorways for them and sent them through into new experiences. He took the longest with the two men who were in the room with Tommy. They were the last ones he found. So sad for them that circumstance gave Saint John time to share so many of his secrets. The boy was unconscious throughout, and that was good; though Saint John wished that Peter could have been here to serve as witness. That child, of all of them, would probably understand and appreciate the purity of it all.

Saint John left the adult captives with keys and weapons and an open door. He set a fire in the flesh of the dead men and on the beds where the women and this body had been. As he walked away the building ignited into a towering mass of yellow flames.

Saint John carried Tommy in his arms. Halfway to the church the child's eyes opened. He beat at the saint with feeble fists.

"N—no ..." the boy whimpered.

"No," agreed Saint John. "And never again."

The boy realized that he was wrapped in a clean blanket, and when he looked into Saint John's eyes he began to cry. He tried to speak but could manage no further words. In truth there was no lexicon of such experiences that was fit for human tongues. Saint John knew that from those days with his own father and those vile, grunting men. The look the saint shared with the boy was eloquent enough.

Saint John bent and whispered to him. "It was a dream, Tommy, but that dream is over. Peter and your other friends are waiting."

When he reached the square where the cathedral sat, Saint John saw that the fire on the roof had failed to take hold. The tiles smoldered but the church would not burn. Not tonight.

The fire of the burning hotel lit the night, and as he walked, Saint John could see the other cherubs—the angels—and the dusty Rose standing in the doorway of the church, surrounded by the arch of caved saints, and every face was turned toward him.

Peter broke from the others and ran down the steps and across the street. He was crying but he still held his knife, and he held it well. With power and love. Saint John approved of both.

Rose came, too; wobbling and unsteady, but with passion. Her face glowed with a strange light, and she reached out to take Tommy from Saint John. Her brow was wrinkled with confusion.

"Why?" she demanded.

There was no way to explain it to her. Not now. She would understand in time, or she would not.

Rose turned, shaking her head, and carried Tommy toward the church as the other angels flocked around her.

It left Saint John and Peter standing in the middle of the street. They watched the others until they vanished into the shadows, then turned and watched the glow of fire in the sky. Finally they turned to face each other. Peter slowly held out the knife, handle first, toward Saint John.

Saint John was covered with blood from head to toes. He had a few bruises and cuts on his face and hands. He sank down into a squat and studied the boy.

"No," he said, pushing the offered knife back. "It looks good in your hand."

The boy nodded. "You didn't answer the lady," he said. "She asked you why you went and got Tommy."

"No," Saint John agreed. "Do you need me to explain it to you?"

Peter looked down at the knife and at the blood on Saint John's face, and then met his eyes. The moment stretched around them as embers fell from the sky. In the distance there were screams and the rattle of automatic gunfire.

"No," said Peter. Saint John knew that this boy might even have tried to get Tommy back himself. He would have died, of course, and they both knew it. Peter was still too young. But he would have tried very well, in ways the men in that building would not have expected. The boy would not have died alone.

Saint John nodded his unspoken approval.

They smiled at each other. Together they crossed the street and mounted the stairs and stood on the top step, watching the city die. There were fires in a dozen places.

"It's pretty," said Peter.

"It's beautiful," said Saint John.

The boy considered. He nodded.

The golden embers floated down around them.

SON OF THE DEVIL

His name was Nebuchadnezzar but everyone called him Neb.

When they were being nice, which was only when his pa was around. People were always polite if they thought Big Tom Howard was in earshot. Or any kind of shot, for that matter. That was the thing. That's what everyone was afraid of.

But Big Tom wasn't always around.

Then the kids had other names for Neb. Most of them weren't really names, they were words that Neb knew they hadn't learned in church or school. What Mrs. Carter from the next farm over called "barnyard words." The kind of words that would have earned every one of those kids a solid beating if they'd used them around the house or in front of grown folks. The kind of word Neb never used at all, even when he was alone and had to clean up the whole house by himself.

Well, that wasn't entirely true. He used one of those words—a really bad one—the day the sheriff and his men came out to arrest Neb's pa. All eleven of those men had come busting into the house with their ropes and chains and guns and fell on his pa while he was still sleeping off a drunk. They'd have never come out if Big Tom was even half sober. No sir.

Neb ran after the men when they rode off with his pa slung like a sack of beans over the bare back of a packhorse. He'd chased them all the way to the row of trees that separated the Howard spread from the Carter place, but by then Neb knew he wasn't going to catch them. And he knew there wasn't a blessed thing he could have done if he did. They were grown men, and he was twelve. There were a dozen of them, and he was all alone. They had guns and badges, and all he had was his fear and his anger.

So he yelled at their retreating backs.

"Goddamn you all to burning hell."

It wasn't obscene, but it was blasphemous.

That was not the really bad word Neb used. That was still percolating in his chest.

Mrs. Carter came running out and threatened to cuff those words right out of him. She said it was the Devil himself speaking out of him like that and she raised that little Bible she always carried as if it was the hand of God ready to strike him down.

"But they took my pa," he protested, trying not to sound like a little boy. Trying to sound like he was Big Tom's only son.

His plea hadn't softened Mrs. Carter much. She lowered her Bible, though, and gave him a pitying look.

"And the Devil's been in his soul since he was your age, young Neb," she said in a voice of iron. "Now I hear the word of Satan falling from your lips." She shook her head and pressed the leather-bound book to her skinny breast.

"They *took* him, ma'am," said Neb, and the tears were in his voice if not yet in his eyes. "They had no right to take him."

Saying that did something to Mrs. Carter. She lowered the Bible and walked up to him, standing face to face with him. Although she was a full-grown woman and Neb was young, he was two inches taller. Somehow, though, he felt much smaller and she seemed to tower over him. A thin scarecrow of a woman with sticks for arms and eyes the color of dust. Straw-dry hair pulled back into a bun that looked so tight it had to hurt, and a black dress with a white apron that flapped and snapped in the east wind.

"Listen to me, Nebuchadnezzar Howard," she said in a voice that was only slightly louder than the whisper of the breeze over the tall grass, "it's not your fault that you were born to such a family. A whore for a mother and a lawless devil of a father."

"Don't say that," he said, but his voice was nothing, too small to be heard.

"We are all sinners," she said. "We are born with the sins of Adam and Eve painted on our hearts. They betrayed the trust of God and therefore we are all born in the shadow of that crime. All we can ever hope for is to find acceptance in the Lord and to beg for him to rescue us from the Pit."

"N-no ..."

Mrs. Carter raised the hand holding the Bible and pointed with one bony finger at the group of riders that had dwindled down to specks.

"Evil is born unto evil as sin is born out of sin. Your father is a monster. A killer of men who has known the inside of every whorehouse west of Laramie. He has blood on his hands, oh yes he does. And as Adam's sins were passed down to his children so are the sins of Thomas Howard passed unto you. Your soul must bear that weight and it is up to you to find a way to expunge this guilt." She bent close and he could smell apples and bread yeast on her breath. "You stand at the very brink of Hell, Neb. Take one step and you will burn, like your mother burns now and like your father will surely burn when they slip that noose around his neck. Mark me, child. Mark what I say."

"You're crazy," said Neb. "Ma used to say you were and Pa said it all the time. You're crazy as a barn owl and twice as ugly."

Mrs. Carter's eyes flared as wide as an owl's right about then.

And before Neb could say another word of sass she slapped him across the face. Not with her hand, but with the black leather-bound holy book she always carried. She was as skinny as a hickory pitchfork handle, but she was as tough as one too. The blow caught Neb square on the side of the face and it sent him crashing against the post rail. He rebounded and dropped to his knees in front of her like a sinner in church.

That's when Neb said the bad word. The barnyard word.

"Fuck you!" he screamed.

The words seemed to roll away from his mouth, blow past Mrs. Carter like a hot wind, tumble all the way to the distant line of mountains and come echoing back. And as they did his shouted words sounded like they were in his father's voice and not Neb's own.

Mrs. Carter stared at him with eyes as wide as saucers, and as he watched Neb saw a strange expression come over her. Or, a series of them that pulled onto her face and then moved on, like cars in a locomotive. First there was blank shock, and then horror, then righteous indignation, and finally a smile crept onto her mouth. It was one of the ugliest smiles Neb had ever seen. Cruel and triumphant and delighted, as if she had waited all her life for just this moment, and now that it was here, with the proof of his sinful corruption still burning in her ears, her life's mission was complete. She seemed so incredibly pleased to have her certainties confirmed. Mrs. Carter pointed the Bible at him the same way his pa would point at someone with his gun.

"You are going straight to Hell," she said in a tight whisper. "You will burn in eternal hellfire where you belong."

Neb Howard got slowly to his feet. His cheek hurt and his face burned and tears stung his eyes. He wanted to break down and sob, and he knew there would be time for that, but he would die first rather than give her that kind of satisfaction.

"You're always telling people that they're going to Hell," he said. "I heard you say that to half the people in town. You think everybody's going to Hell. Or maybe you think they all deserve to go there 'cept you." He took a step toward her and there must have been something in his voice or in his face, Neb couldn't be sure, but Mrs. Carter flinched backward half a step. "If everybody you ever told to go to Hell ever did, then it would be full to busting. All the people down there and you up here. You'd like that, wouldn't you?"

She straightened and tried to reclaim her power. "It would be the fitting justice of the Lord. I pray for all you sinners every day."

"Well, I'll tell you this much," said Neb, "maybe you'd better pray real good because it'd be my guess that Hell's going to get mighty full. And all them sinners down there will be remembering who sent 'em down to burn."

He took another step.

"And I wonder what'll happen when there's no more room in Hell, Mrs. Carter." He smiled and Neb knew it was a bad smile. It hurt his face to smile like that. "What do you think will happen then?"

She held the Bible out between them as if it could protect her from him and his sinful words.

Neb looked from the book to her and back down at the book. Then he hocked phlegm from deep in his throat and spat at the Bible she held. It was a big green glop that struck the black leather and splashed on her bony fingers.

The woman screeched like a crow and immediately wiped the spittle off on her apron, then pawed at the leather to insure that it was clean. She made small mewling sounds as she did so. Neb stood there and slowly dragged the back of his hand across his mouth. He studied the glistening wetness for a moment, then he looked up at her again.

"It's getting dark," he said. "You better run home now."

It was still early in the day. The darkness, he knew, was in her soul and in his heart.

Mrs. Carter backed up all the way to the road, then she turned and ran home. Only when she was halfway up the footpath to her own front door did she turn and shake the Bible at him and shout something. But Neb turned away, shutting out the sight of her and anything she had to say.

—2—

It was a long, bad day.

For a long time Neb sat on a hard wooden chair in the kitchen, surrounded by the silence of an empty house, and waited for something to happen. A thought, an idea, a plan. A hope.

Nothing.

His heart hurt, and his head felt like it was full of hornets. His thoughts buzzed and stung him.

Ten different times he got up to head outside to saddle his horse, Dunders, and once even had the saddle on and the straps buckled. But then he unsaddled the old horse and trudged back to the house, knowing that his presence in town wouldn't do his father any good. There were a lot of stories about Big Tom and though many of them were wild, Neb suspected that most of them were true. Even if half of them were lies and the other half exaggerated it still meant that his pa was a bad man.

A sinner.

Neb thought of this as he sat in the house, wrapped in shadows that rose up, towered over him, and fell crashing down as the sun moved through the sky and threw light in through the windows. The truth was a hard thing to know. Knowing it made it hard for Neb to breathe sometimes. Not just then, but at nights in his bed when he heard Big Tom downstairs weeping or yelling, raving drunk. Telling bad truths to the night and whispering into his whiskey bottle.

Neb knew that it was what happened to Ma that turned his father bad. Ruined him. That was probably the better way to think about it. Mrs. Carter and the ladies at church had a lot to do with that. With what happened to Ma and what Pa turned into.

It was on account of the baby.

Neb's little sister, Hannah, had only lived long enough to cry once and then she stopped crying, stopped wriggling around, stopped breathing. Neb had been eight when it happened. He'd seen stillbirths before, it happened a lot on a farm. And there were

birthing deaths in town too. The Pederson twins both died, and
Mrs. Sykes died along with her sixth kid. It happens, and even as
young as he was Neb Howard was old enough to know that life
was hard and life was fragile. Dying came easy out here. Maybe it
was different in the big cities back East, but not out here. There
was sickness and there were all sorts of dangers. Fires and ranch
accidents, flash floods and all sorts of things. Death walked
everywhere and there was no one who didn't know the sound of
the Reaper's voice.

But with Ma it had been bad.

She'd been sickly for a long time, having never really
recovered from a sickness that cut through this whole region. The
influenza Neb thought it was called. That was the word people
used, though Mr. Flambeau who owned the livery called it the
grippe. It gripped all right, Neb knew. It grappled hold of people
from Sadler's Fork to Indian Pass, and by the time that winter
passed there were probably a thousand new graves dug in the soil
in the shade of these mountains. Ma had almost been one of
them, but even though she lingered there on the edge she came
back. It was Pa who brought her back. Sitting by her side every
night, holding her hand, praying to God and to her for her to
come back, come back, come back to him. That's what he said and
Neb was sure he heard his father say those words ten thousand
times.

Come back. Come back. Come back to me.

And even though she'd looked like death lying there with
sweat-soaked hair and gray skin and hardly no breath at all, Ma
came back. Slowly. Maybe reluctantly. But when Pa called her she
came back.

She was never the same after that, though.

Neb once heard Mr. Flambeau say to his wife that "Meg
Howard looked like death warmed up." And Mrs. Schusterman
over at the general store said that she looked like a ghost.

Neb thought she looked like an angel, and sometimes at night
he wondered if maybe Ma *had* died and it was her angel that had

come back. Ma was so gentle, so soft, so quiet after the sickness. And she was always fragile as butterfly wings. She rarely went out in the bright sun and could not abide loud noises. She left the heavy farm work to Neb and his pa.

Neb missed the old Ma. He missed her laughter and her energy. He missed the Ma who could bake a dozen pies at Christmas and decorate the house and the big tree in the yard and do it all with a smile. After the sickness he never saw that Ma again. Instead it was the angel.

Then she got pregnant. Even as a kid Neb understood about that. This was a farm after all. She got pregnant and every day, the bigger she got the sicker she looked. It was as if the baby growing in her belly was draining all the life force from her. Like a tick sucking on blood.

Neb grew to hate the baby.

At first, anyway.

Later he realized that he was just afraid of what the baby was going to do to Ma by the time she came to term.

Then that night came, and it was as if the doors of Hell had been cracked open. The midwife came and so did some of the ladies from town. Even Mrs. Carter came over, drawn by the sound of Ma's terrible screams.

Neb tried to hide from those screams. First in his room, then in the barn. The horses were spooked by the sound, and they screamed too.

It lasted all through the night and only around dawn did the screaming stop.

Neb, exhausted from a night of hiding and crying and praying for it all to end, heard the silence. That's how he remembered it. He *heard* the silence.

He crawled out from beneath the pile of hay he'd pulled over him, and crept out of the barn and stood looking at the house. He knew something was wrong. He knew that just looking at the house. It stood wrong against the dawn light. It seemed tighter, threatening. The gables and windows and everything seemed to be clutched into a fist. Ready to punch him. Ready to hurt him.

The silence was awful.

So awful.

Neb came up onto the porch and saw that the door stood open. It was never left open.

The living room was empty and messy. That was wrong too. Ma always kept the house neat as a pin. Everything dusted, everything in its place. Neat and tidy and snug and comfortable.

Now chairs were in the wrong place, and the hall rug was rumpled and there was a whiskey bottle standing nearly empty on the table. No glass. As if Pa had been drinking from the bottle itself. *Was that the haystack Pa hid under*, he thought. It was a thought too old for a kid, but he thought it anyway and knew it to be the truth.

Climbing the stairs was the hardest thing Neb ever did. So hard and it took forever. The effort of lifting his leg to place the flat of his shoe on each riser was harder than lifting fence rails.

Then he was upstairs, down the hall, standing at the open door to his parents' room. It was as far as he would go. It was as far as he could make himself go. He stood with his hands on the doorframe and stared into a scene from Hell itself.

The town ladies standing around, each of them looking sad or shocked or horrified. All of them looking worn down. Ma was on the bed, but the bed was wrong. So wrong. It was painted in red. Splashed in red. Drenched in red.

Pa stood holding something. A tiny form whose legs and arms drooped down from the edges of his palms. It, too, was red.

Ma lifted a pale, blood-spattered hand toward the thing that Pa held.

"My baby ..." she said in a ghost of a voice. "Give me my baby."

Pa did not move.

Ma pulled at the neck of her sodden dressing gown, tearing it open, exposing one breast. "I have to feed my baby. Give her to me. Can't you hear how hungry she is?"

Mrs. Carter said, "You should have called Brother Taylor when I told you to, Tom Howard."

Pa lifted his head and Neb saw that there was no trace of comprehension in his red-rimmed eyes. "W-what ...?"

"I told you that this would happen," said Mrs. Carter. "I told you that you needed the parson to come out here and baptize the child before ..."

She let her words trail off, the meaning clear.

"Where's my baby?" cried Ma.

"Only those baptized in the blood of the lamb can ever hope to go to heaven," said Mrs. Carter. "Only those blessed by the Lord can hope to escape the fires of Hell."

Pa clutched the still form to his chest and sank slowly down to his knees, broken as much by what had happened as by those dreadful words.

"Give me my baby," said Ma. "Little Hannah is so hungry."

He bent forward and laid the infant on the bed, let Ma take her, watched as Ma pressed the slack mouth to her nipple. Saw the smile on Ma's face.

"There she is," said Ma. "See how hungry she is?"

Those words beat Pa further down. He buried his face in the bloody sheets and wrapped his arms over his head. That's when Neb heard those words again.

"Come back," whispered Pa. "Come back. Come back to me."

But Hannah hadn't come back.

And as Neb stood there, he saw Ma's eyes close and her smile slowly fade. It did not go away completely. Not even when she stopped breathing. Not even when Pa began to scream.

That was how Pa went wrong. Neb knew it for sure.

The preacher came out at noon, but Mrs. Carter met him on the porch, and she had the same triumph in her eyes that day as she had this morning.

"I told Tom Howard to send for you while there was still time," she said. "Now look what he's done. That poor baby is lost for good and all."

Neb stood holding his Pa's hand, and he felt his father's grip tighten and tighten as they waited for the parson to refute those words, to say different, to say that Hannah was going to heaven. To say that it didn't matter that she hadn't been baptized.

But the preacher only took Mrs. Carter's hand and patted it. "I'll say a prayer."

That was all he said, and it wasn't enough. It wasn't near enough by a country mile.

Pa nearly broke Neb's hand by squeezing it so hard. If it had been a day later, Neb was sure Pa would have gone charging off the porch and punched them both. If it had been a month later he'd have taken a horsewhip to them.

If it had been this year, Pa would have shot them both sure as God made green apples.

Now Pa was gone. Dragged out of bed, beaten and slung across the back of a horse. Now he was in jail. And maybe he was going to wherever Ma and little Hannah had gone. Into the ground. Up to heaven? Or, if Mrs. Carter and the parson were right, then down to Hell.

Neb huddled inside the rough blanket of his own hurt and wondered what to do.

—3—

He summoned the courage to ride into town that afternoon. The sun was tumbling behind the hills, throwing long purple shadows in his path. Dunders, who was an old and trailwise horse, seemed uneasy by the coming twilight and Neb had to yank on the reins and kick him a few times to keep the horse headed to town. Though in his head Neb understood and even sympathized.

"I don't want to go, either," he told the horse when they were halfway there. "But we gotta find out what's happening to Pa."

Dunders blew out a breath that was almost a sigh of resignation and plodded on. It was nearly full dark by the time they reached the outskirts of town, and Neb knew at once that something was wrong. Bad wrong. There were lights everywhere. Torches and lanterns. He could hear voices shouting and even some gunshots popping. Mrs. Carter's rickety old dogcart with her rickety old horse, Ahab, was tied to a post. He saw the parson's half-breed Appaloosa tethered next to it.

Neb almost turned around.

Almost.

Dunders stopped at the edge of town, and Neb sat heavily in the saddle, knowing that nothing good was ever going to come of riding on. Nothing, no-how.

He rode on.

At a hesitant walk at first, then an unsteady cantor and finally a full gallop.

Knowing what he would see. The crowd clustered around the jail, swelling as more people ran in. He saw the fists shaking in the air, heard the guns fire into the night sky, saw the big tree in the center of town lit by torches. Saw the rope.

He knew all about lynch mobs. Who didn't?

Dunders caught his desperate terror and ran harder than ever all the way up the length of Main Street.

Just in time to see.

There were so many things to see.

The sheriff sitting on the wooden plank walkway outside of the nail, his left eye swollen shut, three townsmen holding his arms. Torchlight struck sparks off of the sheriff's badge, and off the badges of the men restraining him.

The faces of the people in town. People he knew. Mr. Flambeau, Mr. and Mrs. Schusterman, the milliner, the man from the hat shop, the two sons of the farrier, the parents of his friends. He knew those faces and didn't know them. He knew them as people in town, people he knew or kind of knew, ordinary people whose faces he saw at church or at the town fair or clustered together in front of the general store on every other Tuesday when the mail coach came rumbling in. The faces of the people in his life.

Except now they were different. Now they were screaming and yelling. Now their features were twisted into strange masks by the flickering torches. Now they were like the faces of monsters. Not human at all.

Monster faces.

So many monsters.

Neb saw those faces and didn't know any of them anymore.

The only face he knew—the only face that he recognized now —was that of his own Pa.

Sitting on a horse. No hat. Face bruised and bloody.

Shirt torn and filthy, hair mussed and hanging loose over his brow. Hands tied behind his back.

A thick loop of rope around his neck. The air was torn apart by the yells of the gathered monsters. They shouted his pa's name. They screamed aloud for the three burly men standing by the horse's head to do something bad. Something impossible.

"No," breathed Neb, though his voice was too small, too weak to be heard over the shouts.

He saw Mrs. Carter. She stood on a stump, shrieking as she shook her Bible at Pa. The parson was there, too, standing beside the stump, hands clasped together. For a moment—just one clear, sweet moment—Neb thought the preacher was calling for the crowd to stop, to step back, to not do this.

But then Neb saw the smile. A curl of his mouth that was too much like the triumphant smile on the twisted face of Mrs. Carter. That's when Neb knew it was all going to fall apart, that the hinges of his life had split from the frame and were falling off. He knew that as sure as he knew anything else in his life.

"No ..." he said, smaller than before. Faint even to his own ears.

And then it bubbled up from the bottom of his soul, boiling up past his breaking heart and tearing its way from his throat.

"*Noooooooooooooooo!*"

It was so loud that it stilled the crowd. It froze the moment. Everyone turned toward him, every face, every eye. Even the horse on which his father sat. They all turned to Neb Howard, but all Neb could do was look into the eyes of his father.

"No," he said again. Once more small and faint.

His pa said, "Neb, for god's sake go home."

He was crying as he said it. Neb hadn't seen his pa cry since that red day in his parents' bedroom. He'd heard him weeping in the night, but he'd never seen those drunken tears. Now, though, they ran down his cheeks like lines of molten silver. It burned Neb to see them. It stabbed him through and through.

As the moment stretched Neb saw how his presence began to change the faces of those monsters that used to be the people in town. Some of them looked angry that he was there. Others looked down or away, anywhere but at him. Some cut looks at Mrs. Carter, the sheriff, the rope; as if calculating how far this was taking them away from the people they were supposed to be.

And in that moment, Neb thought—wondered, hoped, prayed —that they were going to step back, cut him down, release the sheriff, not do this. They should. He knew it and they knew it, because this was a line that no one should cross. Not like this. Not when hate has turned them into monsters.

It was Mrs. Carter—of course it was her—who broke the fragile tension of that moment.

She yelled, "Damn you to Hell, Tom Howard. Your family is waiting for you in the Pit."

Neb heard the gasps from the people. Even the preacher recoiled slightly from her, his smile dimming.

Mrs. Carter stared down at them, looking around, disappointment and disapproval etched by firelight and shadows onto her face. And her face had never stopped being the mask of a monster.

"No, please," begged Neb. "For the love of God ..."

Mrs. Carter spat toward him and then she threw her Bible at the horse. The leather struck the animal's hip with a sound like a gunshot. The horse screamed as if scalded. It reared back, breaking loose from the men who held it, then it lurched forward, crashed into the people who were too slow and too shocked to move out of the way in time. The horse raced past Neb and ran down Main Street, the sound of its thudding hooves chopping into the air.

There was no rider on that horse.

Of course there wasn't.

No one watched the horse go.

They stood like silent statues and stared at the thing that swung slowly back and forth on the end of the rope. No one made a move to cut Big Tom down. There was no reason to hurry. Not with a neck bent and stretched like that.

The parson was the only living person who moved. He walked five paces and squatted down to pick up the Bible. He brushed it off on his black frock coat and then held it out to Mrs. Carter. She stared at him, at the book, and up at the man she'd killed for a long time, then she stepped down and took the book from him, smiling all the while, and giving a small *hmph* as she pressed it to her chest. When she walked away, no one said a word, no one tried to stop her.

Mrs. Carter paused for a moment in front of Dunders. She used her free hand to caress the horse's long nose.

"All sinners go to Hell, Nebuchadnezzar," she said. "And you will burn alongside the rest of your kin."

Then she walked away. She never stopped smiling.

No one could look at Neb. Not even the parson.

He sat there and felt his heart turn to cold stone in his chest. He could feel the weight of it as it tore loose from its moorings. It fell and fell, landing in a much lower place. Far too low.

He knew that even then.

—4—

They buried his pa the next day. Four men brought his body

out on the back of a cart and they set to digging in the front yard. They buried him next to Ma and little Hannah. The parson came out and tried to read some words over the grave, but Neb grabbed a pitchfork and brandished it at the parson.

"You take your lying words and that damn book and you *git!*" he snarled.

The parson was appalled. So were the gravediggers. "I am here to say a prayer over your *father.*"

Neb took a step forward, the tines of the pitchfork held at heart level. "Will your prayers keep my pa out of Hell?"

"You have to understand, son," said the preacher, "your father was a murderer. He gunned a man down in—"

"I know what he did. I hear people talking. But he was supposed to have a trial so the judge could hear both sides of the story. What happened to that? Did you speak up to protect my pa from those crazy people and their damned rope?"

"I—"

Neb sneered. "Where were your prayers last night? What did you do to stop Mrs. Carter? What did you do to stop all those people?"

"You must understand ... that was a mob. They were all whipped up and—"

"And what? Ain't you preachers supposed to stand up for what's right? No, don't answer 'cause I know you'd just lie."

"You ought to watch your tongue, boy," said one of the gravediggers.

Neb pointed the pitchfork at him. "And maybe you ought to hold yours," he warned. "This ain't about you. This is between my folks and his asshole of a god."

"By the Almighty," cried the parson. "Do you hear what you're saying? Do you not fear God's wrath?"

Neb nearly ran at him with the pitchfork. "Fear God's wrath? That's all I know of God. He took my ma and he took my little sister and you told me that she's burning in Hell because she died 'fore she was baptized. That's what your God does. And my pa may not have been the best man but he deserved to have a trial and he deserved justice, but last night I saw you standing right there when Mrs. Carter threw her Bible at that horse. Wasn't that the wrath of God? She stood there and said it was *God's* justice and I didn't hear you speak out against that."

Neb moved forward, the pitchfork's tines gleaming like a claw. All of the men, the parson, and the gravediggers, moved away. Neb stopped at the foot of the half-filled-in grave.

"You people ain't never done nothing but hate on my family. If you had even a shred of decency, you'd have told us that Hannah would go to heaven with all the angels. My ma too."

"God's truth is God's truth. I'm a man of God," said the preacher.

Neb didn't want to cry, but the tears came anyway. Hot as boiled water. "You could have had mercy," said the boy. "You could have lied to us. What you said, what Mrs. Carter said, that's what broke something in my pa's head. It's what turned him mean as a snake. He wasn't evil ... he was heartbroke. You're always preaching about saving souls—it wouldn't have taken much to save his."

The preacher said nothing.

"Go on and get off my farm," said Neb, his voice cold even to his own ears. "You're not welcome here. Not you and not your god. Now *git.*"

He jabbed the pitchfork toward the preacher and again toward the gravediggers. One of the men started to take a threatening step toward Neb, but the crew foreman caught his arm.

"Leave 'im be," said the foreman. "This here's his land now. He wants us gone then we best be gone."

The other gravedigger pointed at the grave. The corpse of Big Tom Howard was only partly covered and there was a considerable pile of dirt standing in a humped mound. "You want us gone, kid, then you best finish this your ownself. But bury him deep 'cause he's already starting to stink."

He turned away, laughing, and followed his companions back to where they'd left their cart. The preacher lingered a moment, looking like he wanted to say something else. It was the kind of expression people had when they wanted to have the last word in an argument. But the pitchfork had the last word, and both he and Neb knew it.

The preacher backed away, then turned and hurried to catch the gravediggers.

That left Neb all alone with the half-buried body of his father. They'd wrapped him in white linen and someone had tied some rope crisscrossed from neck to ankles. Neb figured it was the rope they'd hung him with. People did that because they wouldn't have to use a bad luck rope.

Neb jabbed the pitchfork down into the ground at the foot of the grave and pulled the small hunting knife he wore in a leather sheath on his belt. With tears flowing down his cheeks he stepped down into the shallow grave.

"I'm sorry, Pa," he said, sniffing to keep from choking on the words. He bent down and sawed through the ropes. It was a horrible thing to have to do. His father's body was rigid with death stiffness. Neb knew that this would wear off after a couple of days; he'd seen that with animals he'd hunted and livestock here on the farm. Knowing that his father would go through that process—that he was stiff as a board now—reinforced the fact that Neb was alone. That Pa was dead. That everyone he cared about was dead. He sawed and sawed. It was a task assigned in Hell, and he labored at it with the diligence of the insane. He knew it. He could feel parts of his mind cracking loose and sliding away into darkness.

He stopped abruptly, his face and body bathed in cold sweat, most of the ropes cut, his chest heaving. He felt as if someone was watching him. There was an itch between his shoulder blades. Neb straightened and looked around.

The house was still and silent. The horses in the corral stood with barely a flick of the ear or swish of the tail.

But he saw two things.

One chilled him, and the other set fire to something in his soul.

Above the yard, kettling high in dry air, were buzzards. A baker's dozen of them, swirling around and around. Here to feast on the dead. Neb wished that there was something like them that feasted on the living. Something he could sic on the parson and everyone who was there at the tree last night.

The sight of those birds chilled him.

But the thing that held a burning match to the cracked timbers of his soul was the person who stood watching him. She stood like a specter at the end of the road, her feet on her side but the weight of stare reaching all the way to the grave.

Mrs. Carter.

And she was smiling.

–5–

It rained that night.

He saw the storm clouds coming over the mountain. Big, ugly things, dark as bruises, veined with red lightning. The storm growled low in its throat. It sounded like laughter of the wrong kind. The bad kind.

Neb stood by his father's grave and watched the storm gather. And he was smiling.

—6—

Neb filled in the grave with his hands. He didn't bother to go get a shovel.

The raindrops began falling as he patted it down over his father.

"I love you, Pa," he told the dirt.

Lightning forked the sky and he looked up, gasping, as thunder boomed above him. The shock of it drove Neb down to his knees at the foot of the grave. He reached up to catch himself on the upright handle of the pitchfork, but his knees buckled and he slid down. He held onto the hickory handle, though, and laid his head against it, eyes closed as the rain fell.

"Come back," he whispered.

Come back.

He heard his pa's voice echo in his memory. There, kneeling much like this at the side of Ma's bed, holding out the little dead thing and Ma taking it, too far gone to accept that Hannah was dead. Too mad with her own dying to know that the babe she put to her breast was not hungry. Would never be hungry.

"Come back," said Neb. He *was* hungry. Not for food. Not for comfort. Not for peace.

He wanted to hurt them all. Mrs. Carter. The parson. All of them. Everyone who'd held a torch or raised a fist. All of them.

"Come back, Pa," begged Neb. "You don't belong down there."

He did not know if he meant that his father did not belong in the ground or in the hell that everyone said he was bound for.

The rain began to fall in earnest. Big, cold drops that hammered down on him and pinged on the leaves of the oak tree, and peppered the shingles on the slanted roof. Thunder rumbled and rumbled under a sky torn by lightning.

"Come back to me," cried Neb Howard. "You don't belong down there, and I need you here."

The hurt in his heart was so big, so deep, so unbearable that he could not even kneel there without caving over. He fell onto his chest, onto his face. He beat the ground as the rain turned the dirt to mud.

The storm kept getting bigger. Louder. Darker.

The clouds swirled and changed from purple to gray to a black so pervasive that it swallowed everything. Only the lightning carved edges and curves onto the things around him, trimming everything with cold fire.

The world seemed to be so huge and so dark and so empty of everything important. No love, no heat.

"Come back, come back, come back," he wailed. "*Please*, Pa, don't leave me alone. Come back."

A light flared in the darkness, and Neb stared at it. It was the Carter place, and Mrs. Carter was lighting her lamps against the darkness. He watched with hateful eyes as the house seemed to open its eyes, but then the woman began closing the shutters. The effect was like wide eyes narrowing to suspicious, accusing slits.

Neb did not even realize that he had clutched two handfuls of mud until the muck ran from between his fingers. He looked down at the mess. It was so soaked with rain that it ran like black blood down his wrists.

"Come back," he said. Then he pointed to the distant house with one muddy finger. "If you can't come back for me, Pa, then come back for *her*."

As he said it, the lightning struck directly above him, bathing him in so brilliant a light that it stabbed through his eyes and into his brain. Neb cried out and fell backward, flinging an arm across his face, screaming at the storm, hurling his rage, his curses, his damnation at the sky and all who lived under it. Hating Mrs. Carter and everyone in this damned town with a purity and intensity that was every bit as hot and bright as that lightning.

"Please," he whispered as he lay there. The rain fell like hammers, like nails. "Please come back to me."

Neb Howard lay in the cold mud and prayed his dark prayers as the heavens wept and the thunder laughed.

—7—

He did not remember falling asleep.

He did not know how long he slept.

Neb became aware of being cold. Of hurting from the cold.

It took him a long time to wake up.

When he did, the world was wrong.

He wasn't in the front yard anymore.

He was covered in mud, cold and sore, still dressed in filthy clothes, shoes and all. But he wasn't outside. He was in the house. Upstairs.

On the bed where his mother died. Where his sister never even got to live.

Laid out on the bed, but he knew he hadn't walked up here. He never came into this room. Never. He knew that he would never have gone to bed wearing muddy clothes. Never would have laid down with his shoes on.

Never.

Neb sat up very slowly. It took a lot to do it, his muscles hurt that bad. So did his head. As soon as he sat up, a cough took him and wouldn't let him go for five long minutes. It was a bad cough. Deep and grating and when he was done coughing there were drops of blood on the hand he'd used to cover his mouth.

Sunlight slanted through the window and outside he could hear the morning birds. A couple of cows mooed out in the field, needing to be milked. Dunders whinnied in the corral.

Neb got out of bed, moving carefully, afraid of that cough coming back. His feet were unsteady, and his body kept wanting to fall. He stayed up, though. And he got all the way to the top of the stairs before something occurred to him. He turned and looked the way he'd come. He saw the faint dried-mud smudges of his shoes on the floorboards, but they were coming out of the room. There were none of his footprints going in. There should have been, and his feet were covered in mud.

Not that there weren't footprints, though. It's just that they were too big. A man's shoes.

Like all the boys his age he knew how to hunt and how to track. He knew how to tell one set of footprints from another, animal or not. The shoes that made those prints were shoes he recognized.

"No," he told the morning.

No.

The prints remained, however.

Frightened, Neb hurried downstairs, clutching the banister

for support. The front door was open, and there was a pool of water in the living room. There was a line of muddy prints leading in through the open door, through that puddle, and on up the steps.

"No," he said again.

Neb walked wide of the footprints and had to step over them to get out of the door.

He walked across the front yard to the little family cemetery. The muddy mound over his father's grave was torn up and sunken in.

Neb backed away from it.

He stood halfway between the house and the corral, looking everywhere for answers, needing to find some that did not match the pictures in his head. The cough came again. Worse this time. So deep. So bad.

When it finally passed the whole yard seemed to tilt and slide sideways. It took forever for Neb to saddle his horse. Dunders kept shying away from him, and he kept dropping things. The blanket, the saddle, the reins.

Finally he managed to climb up onto the horse's back.

They rode away from the house.

The way to town took him past the Carter place. Neb stopped by the gate and studied the house. Their door was open too. He could see faint light inside, as if no one had bothered to turn down the night lanterns.

"No," he said one more time.

He turned the horse and walked Dunders up the lane to the Carters' porch steps. He could see how it was. The doorframe was splintered, the lock torn clean out of the wood. The porch rocker lay on its side. There was a muddy handprint on the door.

But Neb knew it wasn't mud. Blood turns chocolate brown when it dries.

He slid from the saddle and staggered up the steps. There was mud on the porch. Footprints in that familiar shape. Going in. Coming out. They were the only footprints on the porch.

Neb stepped over them and went in without knocking.

He stood for a long time looking at the living room. Seeing it yanked him out of that moment and took him back to his Ma's room and how it seemed to have been painted red. This room was painted red too.

Mrs. Carter sat on the sofa.

Some of her did, anyway.

The rest of her ...

Well it was gone. Even from ten feet away Neb could tell it wasn't a knife that did this. Nor a wood axe either. He'd seen animals in the wood that had been set upon and half eaten. He knew how that looked.

He knew what he was seeing.

Once more the world tried to tilt under his feet.

Neb hurried outside and vomited over the porch rail. Half of the vomit was red with his own blood. He gagged, coughed, gagged.

Dunders nickered and tossed his head, his big dark eyes rolling, alarmed at the smell of sickness and of death.

Neb shambled down from the porch and climbed into the saddle. He went back out to the road. Along the way, there in the center of the road, he saw those same footprints. One set of tracks coming here to the Carter place. Another set coming out and then turning, turning, not heading home. Heading to town. There were dark splotches of dried blood mixed in with the mud.

Neb sat on the horse as more of that awful coughing tore at him. He knew he was sick. Laying out there in the cold and the storm ... that had been bad. There was something burning inside his chest. In his lungs.

He sat astride Dunders, feeling lost, feeling sick, feeling like he was already falling into darkness. The footsteps went on ahead and vanished into the distance.

Neb did not follow them into town.

He knew what he would find there.

"No," he said one last time. But this time he knew that he meant "yes."

He turned Dunders around and let the horse take him home.

Once he was there he removed the saddle and bridle and let the horse go. Not into the corral. Just go.

Then Neb walked up the few steps to his porch and sat down on the chair.

And waited for his pa to come home from town.

THE SCREAM

—1—

In the spring of the year before, Jenny Mitchel went to war.

Bobby stayed home. This time Bobby stayed home.

He went with her all the way to the gates of the base when she had to report. He held her as tightly as he could, and she bent down to kiss his face. Then she smiled that smile of hers, hefted her duffle bag, blew him a final kiss, and went to join the others. Men and women. All so young. All going to war.

He told her that she didn't have to go. They could get married now. They could have a kid. Or, if the doctors couldn't help them manage it, they could adopt. It wasn't her war to fight. She couldn't change what had happened to him. She did not need to go and try to find justice over there, because this was war and there was no justice. No matter how hard she fought, no matter where in Iraq or Afghanistan or Syria she went, there was no chance she would ever find the person who built the IED. Wars were like that. It was as indifferent and unfair as the fact that the other three men with Bobby died and he did not. Only part of him died. The rest had come home to her. So why did she think that she had to go over and try and make it right?

What was "right" anyway?

Jenny walked away, her back straight and strong, moving well on good legs, the heavy duffle carried with ease. Bobby sat in his chair, feeling as cold as the chrome wheels, and watched her go. He kept his smile on his face for as long as he could. Until it broke off and the pieces fell and he had to turn away in case she looked back.

Jenny went off to war, and Bobby went back to their house. He wheeled himself up the ramp and into the living room. It had always been a small house, he thought.

Until now.

Now the goddamn thing was vast. Filled with noise and shadows and a complete and total emptiness of her. They had put up pictures of the two of them smiling. From before. One beautiful picture of her in a bikini top, straw-colored hair blowing in the Ocean City sea breeze. A photo that had been taken on the happiest day they'd had since he got out of the VA hospital. She looked radiant. Like a sea goddess, with her pale Irish skin that showed blue veins on the swell of her breasts. That dusting of freckles, the red of her smiling mouth, the white of her teeth, the bottomless green of her eyes. Bobby had taken the photo with the zoom function of his cell phone from the point of the beach that was as far as she could push his chair. He made a joke and Jenny had thrown back her head and laughed as if the whole world was theirs. A laugh that was as free as a child's but every single bit a woman's. *His* woman's laugh. Captured by his phone's camera, saved, printed, blown up, framed, mounted on the wall. Looking at him in the emptiness of the living room.

With every single day since she went away the laugh looked less happy to him. He sat and stared at it. Hour after fucking hour.

They say unexpected laughter can sound like screams if you don't know what it is.

Smiles were like that too. That was something Bobby came to understand as he looked at her open mouth. She looked like she was screaming.

Jenny screamed in his dreams too.

As did he.

—2–

Jenny was gone for five months.

Bobby got emails from her for most of that time. Emails, some actual letters delivered by the postman, and once a package filled with sand and a heart shaped rock she'd found.

Then there was nothing for a week.

Then a man from the Army came by the house. A very officer in a very crisp uniform. A lieutenant, but Bobby could not remember his last name. Or his face. The officer perched stiffly on the edge of the couch, holding a cup of coffee he did not drink, and told him what he was allowed to say. He was sorry he said. So sorry.

"How did she die?" asked Bobby.

"She died bravely," said the officer. "Serving her country."

"No ... *how* did she die? Was she shot? Was it a bomb?"

The lieutenant smiled the kind of smile that looks like a wince. "I don't know the full details...."

"What *do* you know?"

The lieutenant set his coffee cup on the table and stood up very slowly. He was very tall and there was a window behind the couch with a sunny sky that turned him to a dusky silhouette. Bobby thought he looked like the angel of death.

"What matters, sir, is that Jennifer Mitchel was a good soldier who laid down her life in the service of liberty. We should celebrate her sacrifice and honor her commitment to this great nation."

There was more. There's always more, but Bobby stopped listening. The picture on the wall kept screaming at him. The lieutenant couldn't hear it, but Bobby could. Jenny screamed and screamed and screamed, and Bobby closed his eyes and clamped his hands over his ears.

When he opened his eyes, the living room was as silent as it was empty.

Bobby would have taken the picture down and smashed it, but he couldn't quite reach it.

He tried, though.

He tried so hard.

—3—

Bobby dreamed of her that night.

Of course he did.

In his dreams he still had two working legs instead of useless meat and bone that was decaying to nerveless junk inside his burned skin. In his dreams Bobby could walk and he could run, and he ran and ran, drawn by the sound of her screams.

He was back in Afghanistan, in one of the mountain passes that are baked by the sun all day and turn to winter at night. Amid a nightmare landscape of deadfalls, box canyons, endless cave systems, valleys where no one goes unless they are dealing death or running from it, cliffs over which bodies are dropped and never found. Places where wind shears and gusts throw helicopters against unforgiving walls, where tanks won't go and Humvees go to die. Blighted lands filled with carrion birds, scorpions, sand snakes, and biting spiders that no one has yet named. A place that seems like it could only exist in bad dreams but which is more than real. As the Russians found out. As the US military found out. A place that is heartbreakingly beautiful from any distance but merely heartbreaking up close.

Alexander the Great conquered it once. Then the Muslims. Almost no one since. It breaks those who try as surely as it breaks those who fight to defend it. No one wins there because it isn't worth winning. That was a truth Bobby knew once he'd gone there for the first time as a young soldier. It was a truth everyone on any side of the fight knows with absolute certainty. And, for some reason no one that Bobby ever met or read about, its lack of importance was why people fought so hard for and against it. It was a philosophic point, a patch of ground sown with shell casings, irrigated with blood and yielding a hardy crop of pain.

That's how Bobby saw it.

It was part of the poetry he wrote when he was alone. It was in the lyrics of the songs he composed on his guitar during the long nights over there. And it was the secret whispered by the music of his dreams. It called to him.

She's here, it sang.

Come and find her.

She's here.

In his dreams Bobby could walk and he could run, and he never tired, even as he ran naked through the mountain snows or climbed the jagged peaks. In his dream he was not a broken, helpless man. In his dreams Bobby was something else. Stronger than a man. Less vulnerable. Angrier, hungrier, faster, relentless.

The thing he became in his dreams would never stop looking for Jenny.

How could it? Why would it?

So, in his dreams he ran and ran and ran. Calling her name. Screaming it as loud as her picture had screamed at him. The echoes of that scream punched into the sides of the mountains and flew back at him, cutting like knives. It startled dark night birds from their hidden holes, and they flung themselves into the air, all in a blind panic that made them collide and shriek and fall and swoop back up from the stony ground to go soaring over the crags and tors.

"Jenny!" he cried, but his voice sounded like those shrieking birds.

In the dream he saw a glow in the distance. A fire. A camp built into the shelter of a ledge of rock, hidden from the sky. There were camels and goats. There was a single spavined dog that was too old to be any use as a sentry. There were guards, but their rifles were slung, their knives sheathed, their eyes drawn to the cooking fire, their minds numb with the knowledge that they were in a place no one could reach. Not without making noise. Not without alerting them.

Except that Bobby ran without noise because this was a dream. No, because it was a nightmare and he was the thing in the dark. Even he didn't know what he was. Not an animal. Certainly not a man. Not anymore. Not even now that he had his legs back. He was something else. Less tangible, less real. A ghost, perhaps, or one of the *djinn* that haunt the legends of Iraq and Iran. Something like that. Maybe whatever he was had no name. No real name.

He ran and leaped and clawed and climbed and scurried and tore at the rocks with fingernails that were hard as iron.

Looking for her.

Looking for Jenny.

It did not matter that Jenny was dead. It didn't matter that her body was being shipped home to New Jersey. It didn't matter that the envelope of flesh that looked like the woman he loved was no longer here in these mountains. *She* was here. She died here, and she would always be here.

That was the secret known to the Bobby-thing that ran through the Afghan night. It's what made him run so fast and hard. It's what made him so hungry. It's what made him howl into the night.

These were the men who had taken Jenny from him. He knew that without knowing how he knew. Just as he knew what things had been done to her. To her flesh. These same hills had echoed with her screams, and somewhere here in this hell of ice and rock those screams were still trapped. That was how this worked. The screams of the dying are supposed to fly up into the sky, to disperse, to fade away and take the soul of the dying with them.

Except when they could not.

He knew—absolutely knew—that it was like that. He knew that there were houses whose walls could trap a scream as easily as these unforgiving mountains. A scream trapped likewise trapped the screamer.

Bobby knew that. When Bradley had rolled over the IED and half of him died, he screamed. As he lay there painted in the blood of his platoon, feeling his flesh melt, believing that death was about to lift him out of that wreckage and take him home, Bobby had screamed. And part of him *had* died there, so he believed that his screams haunted these same hills.

Part of him and all of Jenny.

These men had torn the screams from his Jenny and even though she died out here, her screams had never faded away. They had wandered, lost and desperate, into the open mouths of caves and become trapped. Forever trapped.

Hell was not an abstraction. It was a place. It was many places, and this was one of them. These mountains.

Jenny's soul had been torn from her and become lost here.

Bobby screamed out her name, and it roused everyone in the camp. The old dog began barking hysterically, but its eyes were as bad as its ears and it faced the wrong direction. The camels screeched and honked in panic, kicking at each other and at the men, and jerking their heads against the ropes that held them to a stump of a withered tree. Men kicked their way out of bedrolls and grabbed for their guns, standing back-to-back and pointing their barrels at the goat path while the goats themselves bleated and shrank back against the wall of the cave.

Bobby's scream had reached them long before he did. They were awake, alert, prepared.

But they were not prepared for him.

No.

The dream turned red and wet, and new screams tore the night.

—4—

Bobby woke in utter darkness, drowning in it, and he swam upward toward the light. He burst from the dream with a cry, his body bathed in sweat, stinking of the terror of that dream. His sheets were knotted around his waist and legs.

It took him a long, long time to understand that.

The sheets were knotted around his legs.

His legs, his legs, his useless dead legs.

How could the sheets be knotted around them? How could he have kicked and thrashed with ruined flesh and inert bone?

How?

How?

How?

He lay there, propped up on elbows, staring down the length of the bed at what he saw by moonlight.

In his mind he heard the echo of his scream and the paler echo of the screams of the men in that camp. Ghost screams, though.

Because he was here, and they were thousands of miles away and he was a cripple. And his woman was dead and lost.

But ...

The sheets were twisted around his legs.

"Jenny ..." he whispered to the night.

And the night, perverse and filled with possibilities, whispered back in her voice.

"Bobby ..."

—5—

There were dreams every night.

Only at night, though, because they were not daydreams. They were not nightmares either, but they belonged to the night. Bobby knew that and understood it.

It took him a month to go mad.

As mad as he needed to be.

It took six months to plan everything and then nearly a year to pay for it. He sold Jenny's car. He sold the house. He sold everything that was worth selling. This was going to be expensive, and he was not a rich man. The house was good, though. He got almost a quarter of a million for it. More than he thought. More than he'd need.

There were fees and equipment to buy. People to hire here, people to hire there. Hands to be greased, here and there. More there, though, because that's how it worked.

He got asked the same questions a lot. By friends, by relatives —his and hers; by people in the government, including someone Bobby was certain worked for Homeland Security. Eventually by the press.

"Why go back?"

At first he couldn't give a good answer, but because he was grieving and because he was disabled people cut him slack. Over time, though, they asked again and again, wanting a better answer. And Bobby realized that sketchy answers created obstacles. Good answers elicited support and opened doors.

"It's all about forgiveness," he told a public relations office from the Army. "I can't move forward with my life if I hold on to hate. I already lost too much to that. Now I have to accept what's happened and let it go."

It was a good answer. He'd rehearsed a dozen versions of it before he tried it out. It made the man from the Army go all glassy-eyed. When he used it on an old friend from his former unit, his friend tweeted it out.

And then it was all over the internet. Twitter, Facebook, Tumblr, even tagged to a picture of him and Jenny that wound up on Pinterest. He was *that* guy. The man who had lost everything and wanted to go to the place where it had been taken from him and find peace and closure.

The first book offer came in seven months into his campaign. The movie deal was closed less than a week later.

That almost made Bobby smile. A movie. The producer who optioned it and the screenwriter who became attached to the project both thought they were going to make an inspirational tear-jerker of a tragic love story. It would win awards, they said. It would win an Oscar. They were sure of it even though no one had yet written a word of the book or the script. The story was that good, they told him.

Yeah. The story was good.

But Bobby knew the producer and the writers were wrong about one big thing. This wasn't going to be a tender love story, even though love was the core of it all. It wasn't going to be a tear-jerker even though Bobby wept every day, and would probably weep all the way to the last. And it wasn't a heart-stirring story of forgiveness and closure.

Well, closure maybe.

Bobby knew that it wasn't that kind of story, and a movie would probably never be made. Not once the trip was finished. By then the producer and writers would know that it was a totally different kind of story. And, who knows, thought Bobby, maybe they would make that other kind of film.

A horror film.

Because that's what Bobby wanted it to be.

—6—

They threw a party for him.

That was funny. Bobby had to wheel himself into a toilet stall at the VFW hall so he could laugh without anyone hearing him.

A party? Really? A fucking party?

The mayor of Ocean City shook his head. The producer was there, along with a director and the actor who was going to play him in the movie. Ethan Hawke. Which was weird because except for them both being skinny white guys Hawke didn't look anything like Bobby. The press was there. Officers from his old unit were there.

Lots of speeches, lots of photos.

Bobby could not remember a single word of any of them. He couldn't remember what he'd said. It was a blur, and while he sat on the plane the following day, he let it all slide off of him the way mud will sluice off when you stood in the rain. It felt like that.

He dozed on the plane and dreamed of running in the hills.

Running.

Hunting.

He woke angry, as he was often angry. Scared, as he was often scared. Filled with doubt, as he was always filled with doubt. The dreams were always the same. The hunt, the chase, the red carnage, the taste of blood, the satisfying sound of bones breaking between his teeth, the texture of skin as it tore beneath his nails. All of that was good. That part of it was delicious and satisfying in ways that no longer made him feel strange or guilty or ashamed.

What made him angry about this dream—and all of the others—was that it ended too soon. It ended with death but not with discovery. It ended with him finding the camp with the men, the right men; but it ended before he found *her*.

She was there, though. So close. So maddeningly close. He could hear her screams on the wind. So close to the place where Bobby did his killing. So close to where Jenny died. That was her place, where she would be from now until forever. Bobby knew and understood that. He even thought that she heard him as he hunted and killed. Heard and came looking for him.

But the dreams always ended too soon.

Bobby pawed at the tears in his eyes and looked out at the night. The plane had so far yet to fly.

So did he.

—7—

After the movie deal was finalized, Hollywood location teams handled a lot of the more complicated logistics of the trip. They had the money, the experience, and the drive. They made sure he could get as close to the spot where Jenny died as they could manage. They hired private contractors—mercenaries—to provide security. It was all very exciting for everyone. Even Bobby thought it was kind of cool, though privately he was simply grateful that so many obstacles had been handled so easily.

It was like fate, or at least that's how he took it.

So much of the process was taken out of his hands, that for a while Bobby felt like he was floating on an outgoing tide. He was sure that during some of that process he wasn't quite there. He drifted in and out of himself. In and out of dreams. The heat and the cold of Afghanistan drew him away from his broken body in different ways. The heat pushed him into vivid memories of pain, of laying broken and charred inside the Bradley, of the hot taste of blood—not his own—in his mouth, the feel of it on his skin.

The cold took him somewhere else.

The cold sent him running deep, deep into himself. Into the nightmare landscape high up on the slopes of the mountains that now rose around him. To narrow passes and steep defiles and into the hungry mouths of caves. Chasing memories. Chasing dreams. Chasing a desperate hope of finding Jenny. Chasing her, while the demons of doubt and dread pursued him like dogs.

And then the day came when he was there.

Actually there.

"You sure this is what you want?" asked the producer. They were on a flat shelf of rock beside a path that whipsawed up through the hills.

"Yes," said Bobby. "This is great. Thanks."

The producer looked dubious, but he nodded. "You okay if we record this? We can let the cameras run. They're digital. We can leave you alone."

It was something they'd discussed. Background, they called it. So that Ethan Hawke could study the footage and reproduce the scene when they shot the movie. If there was anything worth using.

"That's fine," said Bobby. "But I want to be alone for a while? Let the cameras run, but nobody else up here until I call? Okay?"

The producer nodded and after a reluctant pause, turned and trudged down the hill to their camp, leaving Bobby alone. Night was falling over the mountains and already the day's heat was being leeched away. Cold stabbed him like a knife.

That was okay.

It was more than okay.

The colder it got, the sharper the stab, the easier this was going to be.

Somewhere in these mountains not too many miles from where he sat, the Taliban killers were making their camp. Tying up their camels and goats. Feeding the spavined dog, building a fire against the cold. Maybe they were aware of the Hollywood Americans down here. Probably. He hoped so. It seemed more apt.

The cold tore through his sweater and coat and found his scarred flesh. It really did feel like a knife. The pain was real, and he was too thin, too frail, too sick to have any resistance. This kind of cold could kill him, and he knew it.

So he took off his coat and threw it over the edge of the cliff. The sweater followed, and the shirt. He couldn't manage the pants, but that wouldn't matter. It was a few degrees above freezing and in half an hour it would be well below. His skin burned with the same intensity as it had when he'd been in the destroyed Bradley.

That was good too.

He shivered, his teeth chattering, his breath shuddering with each labored exhale. The cold was so intense up here in the brutal wind. He could feel a shriek, but he held his own cries inside.

It wasn't time. He wheeled his chair over to the very edge of the drop-off. The cameras, triggered by motion sensors, turned to follow like a host of silent witnesses.

The sun fell off the side of the world and huge shadows collapsed around him, bringing an even deeper cold. Inversion coaxed the winds into a howling storm of icy blades that slashed at him.

He risked a single word. Her name.

"Jenny..."

It came out hoarse and wrong and fractured. So he said it again. Louder. Needing the wind to take it from him and carry it to her. He opened his mouth and shouted.

"Jenny!"

Only it wasn't what came out.

Not her name. Not a word. The wind drew back and stabbed him with all of its force at the moment he tilted his head back to yell.

What came out was a scream.

A long, long scream. So long. So loud. So much bigger than he was. It was massive. A scream of pain, a scream of love. A scream of need.

As the scream slammed into the walls and flew back at him, Bobby fell sagging forward, nodding out of the chair, felt himself falling toward the infinite blackness over the edge. He fell.

And fell.

But the scream still rose above him.

He never felt his body land. He wasn't in it when it struck the rocks.

The scream rose and flew out into the darkness and it carried him with it. What there was of him. What was left of him. What mattered to him.

On dark wings of cold night air he flew through the mountain passes, climbing higher, calling out in a voice of darkness. In a scream.

There was a light below. A campfire in the mouth of a cave hidden in the craggy hills. Bobby saw it and swept downward. Then suddenly he was running. He had no idea where this new body had come from or what it was composed of. What did that matter? The answers might have mattered before his old body fell; it did not matter at all to this body. He had muscles to run, claws to climb, teeth to bite. If there was a name for what he was, it belonged to someone else's vocabulary. Maybe the Taliban soldiers would know. Maybe they would name the thing that came hunting them in the night.

Maybe.

But Bobby did not care.

He ran up the slope toward their camp and as he drew close

he screamed once more. The scream of what he was. The scream of something that lived now in these mountains. The scream of a thing that belonged in this nightmare landscape.

And far above him, coming from deeper in the hills, reaching him first as a whisper that escaped from a cave or some other hidden, lonely place, came a sound.

Another scream.

Higher, sharper.

Familiar. So familiar.

Answering his cry.

It sounded again. Closer now.

Hungry.

Coming to join him.

Coming to share the hunt.

WHEN YOU SEE MILLIONS OF THE MOUTHLESS DEAD ACROSS YOUR DREAMS IN PALE BATTALIONS GO

—1—

Alex had always been a ghost.

Long before he died.

Not before he went off to war. Alex was still fully alive then. Seventeen in the autumn of 1965. Dad signed the papers to allow him to enlist early. Mom screamed. Mom cried. We all cried. Except Dad and Alex.

He turned eighteen in basic training.

When he came home after that, he was still alive. Maybe there were some shadows in his eyes because by then, he'd heard the stories. The sergeants loved to tell those stories. They loved to make it real. Maybe they thought it would help, that it would toughen the kids they were training to be killers. Or maybe those sergeants were just malicious assholes. A case could be made either way.

Alex had enlisted in the Air Force rather than waiting to be drafted into the Army. Kids in our neighborhood always got drafted. Somehow poor kids in those parts of Philadelphia, where it was all crumbling homes in rows around factories, seemed to have numbers that always rose to the top. The sons of the factory owners must've had heavier numbers because they were never at the surface waiting to be scooped up. They stayed home, stayed safe, went to college, went to work for their parents. If they died, it was from wrapping their cars around the steel supports of the old El trains after nights of partying. That happened, and maybe it was sad. More ghosts. But none of the factory workers shed tears that I ever saw. Not with everyone's son, uncle, older brother, cousin, or friend getting shipped off to 'Nam.

Alex thought he was playing it cool. Being smart. Gaming the system.

"The Air Force is safe," he told everyone. "Soldiers are in the damn thick of it. Wading through swamps and mud and shit. Soldiers get their asses blown off or they step on punji sticks or toe-poppers or bouncing Betties. Soldiers are just meat for the grinder. But *Air Force*? Shit. They stay the hell out of the way."

He told that to the recruiting sergeant in that little shitty storefront place on Kensington Avenue. I remember standing outside with my buddy, Bob. We were seven. We saw Alex shake hands with the sergeant. We saw how that sergeant grinned and grinned. He never once stopped smiling. I think that's why I don't like people who smile too much.

Not after what happened.

Alex told us about it later.

"I *told* you it was the smart play," he said that afternoon. He was sitting on the top porch step, a sweating bottle of Coke dangling from a loop made from his index finger and thumb, a cigarette bobbing up and down as he talked. Alex in a white T-shirt, jeans with patches and scars, a pair of Chuck Taylor All-Stars that were stained and scuffed exactly the right way. He'd used a Magic Marker to draw music notes all over the white rubber toe caps. His buddies were on the steps, too, or standing around like a pack of lean jaguars. All of them with hair that was more 50s holdover greased-back Doo-Wop shit than the longer hair some of the other kids wore.

I was standing on the pavement with Bob and a couple of

other kids. Listening to Alex talk about how he played his game with the recruiting sergeant.

"I told him straight up that I was no soldier," said Alex.

"You're a lover not a fighter," said Chick, right on cue. If Alex ever took to doing comedy movies, then Chick would be his straight man. Or side man. Not sure what you call it. The guy who feeds you lines and backs what you say. Not sure I ever heard Chick ever speak up first, but he was always there to back Alex's play.

"You damn right," agreed Alex. "And I told him that. I told him I was a mechanic too."

"Yeah, you are," said Chick. "It's got a motor, you can fix it."

Alex pointed a finger at him. "You damn right. I told that sergeant that. I said my dad was a mechanic and my uncle and my cousin."

"It's in the blood," said Chick.

"Born to it," said Alex with a nod. "He said that the Air Force needed mechanics."

"Does that mean you'll be working on jet engines?" asked Bob.

Alex grinned but shook his head. "Naw. At least not yet. Going to start with trucks, Air Force has a lot of trucks."

"Cars too," added Chick.

"Shit-load of cars," said Alex. "And get this ... the sergeant says that there's such a big need for mechanics right now that he was willing to make me a deal."

"Deal?" I asked. "What kind of deal?"

"That's what I'm trying to tell you," said Alex. He took a long pull on his Coke. "Y'see, they need mechanics for bases right here in the States. Maybe over in Jersey. Close, you know? Well, he said that if I could get some of my buddies to enlist, then they'd guarantee us all a stateside gig working on trucks and cars."

"Really?" asked Bob, looking interested. His uncle Bill worked at the same garage where my dad worked. Where Alex hung out after school most days.

"Hand to God," said Alex. "So, I talked to the guys in the band, and they're all down."

The band was the Six Saints. One of the Philly a cappella groups. They'd cut a couple of sides on a promo album that featured ten groups. One of the sides, "Sugar Sweet," even got airplay last fall. Local stations, but even so. How cool was it to turn on the transistor radio and hear Alex singing lead on a love song? The other guys singing harmony that would make you cry. You'd never think six tough cats like them could sing like angels.

"What'd the guys say when you told 'em?" I asked.

"What do you think they said?" my brother replied, looking me dead in the eyes. "They said 'hell yes.'"

"Hell yes," agreed Chick, nodding.

"So ... you're really doing it?" asked Bob.

"Doing it? Shit, son, it's *done*."

That was on the last day of October 1965. Halloween, but in Philly that's not cold and blustery. The sun was nine inches above us. The blacktop on the streets was melting, and no matter how still you sat, the sweat just popped out. Boiled out. No one was out trick-or-treating yet. Hell no. Way too hot. We'd all wait for dark and then we monsters would be out in force.

Old Man Raynor down the street was fiddling with a wrench, trying to open the fire hydrant. The conversation kind of died then. We watched Mr. Raynor and maybe everyone was doing what I was doing. Thanking God for good-hearted sergeants at enlistment offices.

—2—

I wonder sometimes whatever happened to that sergeant.

That office closed in 1968. Well ... not closed. Someone threw a brick through the window and then tossed in a Molotov cocktail. Happened on Mischief Night, October 30. I saw the blackened shell of the place the next night when my friends and I were running around in costumes knocking on doors and taking candy

from strangers. I was dressed as Sergeant Saunders from *Combat!*
Bob went old-school cheap with his sheet and eyeholes. We stood
there, fists knotted around the handles of bags heavy with Clark
Bars, bags of M&Ms, boxes of Dots, sticks of Pez, and—God help
us—apples. Me and Bob threw our apples into the burned-out
building. Tricks, not treats. We ran away as if someone would
chase us.

Police never found out who torched the place. Happened in
the middle of the night, and the papers all said it was Mischief
Night gone too far.

I never thought so. I think it was someone's dad. Or mom. Or
brother. Someone who maybe had a folded flag at home,
graveyard dirt on his hands, and a heart so filled with burning
grief they just had to do something.

If I was older and bigger and braver, it *would* have been me.

I wanted to.

I needed to. We all did.

The ones who were too old or too young to go to 'Nam. The
ones who stayed home and watched it on TV. The ones who went
to graveyards or vet's hospitals. The ones who visited rehab and
brought books and candy and empty words.

Us.

—3—

There was a rumor it was Chick who did it.

He enlisted with Alex and the other Seven Saints, but he never
made it past the medical. Perforated eardrum and feet flatter than
snowshoes. I remember him sitting in the park under a sycamore,
crying so hard that it made me feel like screaming. Crying because
his friends went, and he didn't.

I remember him crying another time. When Alex wrote to say
that he and the others were going straight from basic to a base
out west, and then from there to Vietnam.

At funerals where we all stood looking stupidly at cheap

coffins while airmen in uniforms folded flags in weird slow motion. Where officers handed those flags to mothers and saluted and turned away to hide their dead eyes.

We went to a lot of those. For the Army families. The infantry kids.

But we also went to funerals for the Angels.

Mickey.

Jimmy.

Ricky.

Big Greg.

Dan.

Five of them.

The ones who didn't come home alive.

And, no, the irony was lost on no one. In fact, it was a lot of fucking salt in everyone's wounds. Fucking angels.

Chick and Alex were there, but I saw how they couldn't even look at the families of their friends. Chick because he couldn't go. Alex because he got them to go.

Everyone cried. Everyone was so fucking mad.

The fathers—the ones who fought in World War II—wore their medals and saluted the flag and sang the songs the loudest. Telling themselves it mattered. Adding worth to the coin their families spent. Trying to, anyway. Telling everyone their own war stories at the luncheons after each of the boxes were lowered into the ground and covered with cold dirt. They talked about their battles, their scars, their friends who never made it home. Trying to get everyone to feel proud, to sell the story that Vietnam was Anzio or the Bulge or Midway. Which it goddamn well was not.

The fact that they all had to lubricate their throats with Wild Turkey or Canadian Club in order to squeeze those words out was telling. Even to little kids like me.

Their wives drank too. A lot. Quietly, in corners. Looking at one another but too destroyed to look at anyone else while their husbands told those stories over and over and over again. One funeral after another.

I lost count of how many people squeezed the hands of the parents and said, "If there's *anything* I can do ..."

Maybe they meant it, but I doubt it. Not because people are unkind, but because, really, what *could* they do? The boys were dead. No kind words would bring them back. No actions they could take would seal the cracks in broken hearts. There was no way to rescue anyone from the images conjured at closed coffin funerals. I mean ... most of Ricky wasn't even in the box. They brought home what they could find, and from what I heard, that wasn't much.

My folks went to the luncheons. Dad brought a bottle of whatever he could afford. Mom made a casserole. At Dan's funeral there were twenty-two casseroles on the dining room table. There had been twenty at Big Greg's. Seventeen at Rick's, sixteen at Jimmy's, and ten, I think, at Mickey's. I think people brought them as props because they'd already run out of things to say.

Once, years later, when I was drunk after someone else's funeral and I'd counted twenty-five casseroles, I wondered if they were some kind of charm, or talisman, or whatever the right word was. Bringing something, not just to feed the grieving family, but to appease the ghosts. To keep them from getting angry.

We all believed in ghosts.

We had to. For a lot of the families in my old neighborhood, ghosts were all we had left. Maybe that's why I stopped going out on Halloween even before I aged out of it. Some kids—the ones who didn't have anyone older who went to 'Nam—would wear mashup costumes. Zombie soldiers, vampire soldiers, werewolf soldiers. Like that. They scared the shit out of me.

Then.

And now.

—4—

Alex and I drifted.

We were ten years apart, with four sisters between us. Well, three, now. One died of cancer a couple years back. Alex was haunted, and I think at times he resented the fact that I never served. Vietnam was in the rearview mirror by the time I got out of high school. And even if it was still on, I'd have skipped it because I got a full ride to Temple University. Journalism. I was going to be the reporter that broke the big story. Woodward or Bernstein. Maybe both.

Not really sure why he'd be mad at me for skipping war of any kind. It hadn't done him any damn good. It killed most of who he was. It turned him into a ghost—just one with a heart that still beat and blood that pumped. But the resentment was there. We both felt it. At times we saw the color of it in each other's eyes, but that wasn't a conversation we could ever have. Not then.

He stayed in Philly. He became a mechanic and worked that until it ground him down. Or at least contributed to that process. Every year, on the anniversary of his last day in country he'd go to Coney Island Joe's tattoo parlor and get more ink. He'd gotten his first—a tiger—in 'Nam. Back when it was cool, back before 'Nam *became* the tiger and his friends the meat. Now Alex was covered in tattoos. Full sleeves on his arms, nearly every inch of his torso. Most of his legs. I used to know each from the days when we were still family, still friends. Not anymore.

The ink was his scripture, but I was not a member of that church. Maybe Chick would have been if he hadn't skated sideways from whiskey to horse to a single-car accident while high. I wonder how many casseroles his mother got when they buried him. I'll never know. I'd moved away by then.

I live outside of LA.

Never did become a reporter. Instead, I wrote scripts for crime dramas on ABC. Sometimes on CBS. My most recent stuff is on Hulu. Got some awards for it. One Emmy that the whole writers room shared for a TV movie spinoff of *CSI*. Plaques on the walls. Two ex-wives, and one giving that some real thought.

I hadn't seen Alex in the flesh for years. Like ... fifteen years? Give or take. When people asked, I said it was because of politics. I've always been somewhere on the left, and he went hard right. These days you can float that explanation and people accept it without asking questions. No one wants to talk politics these days except when they feel the need to preach to their own choir.

So, yeah, I was really surprised when I got a call on a late Sunday afternoon. Another October 31. Another hot Halloween. I was slouched on a loveseat on my porch, looking at the parents who *insisted* on dragging their kids around in costumes while the sun burned. I even had a bag of candy. First time in I don't how long. Full-sized Three Musketeers because there is no real fun in "fun-size" bars. Let's be real.

Then the phone rang. The caller ID said, "ALEX."

Alex didn't call me. Frankly, I couldn't remember even adding him to my contacts. But I guess I did. I answered after three rings, right before it would have gone to voicemail, and damn me if I nearly let it go there.

"Hello ...?" I asked, surprise in my voice.

"Joey," said the voice. Pale and ghostly, like he was calling from another planet instead of three thousand miles east.

"Alex?"

"Yeah," he said. "It's been a minute, I guess."

"Really has." Neither of us wanted to do the math and say how long. That was one of those landmines you can see poking out of the dirt.

"You got some time?" he asked.

"Um ... sure ..." I said. "What's up? Is Joan okay?"

"Huh? Oh. Sure," he said. "She's good."

"Great."

"And ... is it Cassie? How's she?"

"We got divorced seven years ago," I said. "I'm with Audrey."

With being a tricky word. Audrey was staying with her sister in Sacramento while we "figured things out."

"Oh," he said again. "Right. Audrey."

A bit of silence on the line. Cell phones don't have that soft white noise the old landlines used to have. There was nothing to listen to except silence.

"What can I do for you, Alex?" I said, trying to make it kindly. Trying to mean it.

"Can we get together? Maybe for coffee or a beer?"

"Next time I'm in town? Sure ... but I don't know when that'll be."

"No," he said. "I mean now."

"Now?"

"I'm here."

"Here ... *where*? In LA?"

"Down the block, actually," he said with a small laugh. "I'm in town."

"You're in LA? Why?"

"Funeral," he said.

I didn't ask. All of Alex's friends were vets. He was in a dozen veterans groups. They were all aging out too. The war ended in 1975, close to fifty years ago. I was in my sixties, and Alex was in his seventies. Between Agent Orange, PTSD, and old injuries, they were prime candidates for hypertension, diabetes, suicide, cancer of every kind, strokes, and heart attacks. Funerals were a regular thing.

I haven't been to one since I moved away from home. Not even the funerals of my friends and work colleagues. Can't do it. Too many ghosts. Too much hurt hung like garlands. And even being a writer, I never know what to say. Maybe that makes me a coward. Could be. Better that than spending time with the dead.

"Wow," I said, meaning that. "Sure. I'm on the porch."

"I saw you when I drove by. Be right there."

—5—

He looked old. Not just older—*old*. His brown hair was snow white, his skin wrinkled in ways that distorted the shapes and meanings of a lot of his tattoos. His goatee was sparse, and he looked shrunken, somehow. We were both the same height—a bit over six feet—but while I still looked it, he did not.

He came to the foot of the porch steps and looked up at me. His smile was small and nervous. Maybe mine was too.

"Come on up," I said, and he did.

We didn't shake hands.

He went and sat on a rattan chair in the corner of the porch, out of the direct California sun. I sat down on the wicker love seat. I opened the cooler next to my chair and lifted out a beer, cocking an eyebrow. He nodded, and I handed it to him. Alex twisted off the cap. There was a pause and then we clinked bottles and drank. I sipped mine and watched him gulp more than half of his. Adam's apple bobbing. Drinking like he'd just come out of the Sahara.

We sat and watched a pair of mothers herding a group of six-year-old Jedi and Sith. I saw Alex smile a little. Just a little, but it was there.

"What brings you to LA?" I asked.

He looked down the mouth of the beer bottle as if there was a script for him in there.

"It's been a long time," he said.

I waited.

"I guess I'm sorry for the way things went between us."

I sipped my beer. Said nothing.

"Life got weird, you know?" he asked, looking at me.

"Life's always been weird," I said.

He shook his head. "We never really had much of a chance to be brothers, Joey."

"Ten years difference in age," I said.

"Yeah. That was part of it," said Alex. We paused as the Star Warriors tromped up and held out their bags. I plunked candy into each. They looked down, assessed, and moved off. The mothers tried to get them to say thanks, but all we got were wordless grunts. Alex watched them go to the next house. "Was a time I'd have been royally pissed about that," he said, using his bottle to point to them. "Fuck, man, I don't even remember getting old, but I started doing the 'you kids get off my lawn' shit."

"I'm feeling it too."

"What's that about, you think?" he asked, then before I could say anything he answered his own question. "Envy."

"Envy?"

"Sure. Those kids are alive. They got everything ahead of them. They got no scars, no ghosts haunting them. None of that shit. We see them running across the lawn or up and down the street and we get mad. We *say* it's because they should watch out, look both ways, respect property. All sorts of shit, but it's envy, 'cause *we* want to be running like them. Yelling like them."

I tapped my left knee with the bottom of my bottle. "Titanium," I said. "Had it replaced in '06."

He grinned and nodded and tapped his chest. "Pacemaker, five years ago. One of my buddies gave me a T-shirt that says, 'Battery Operated.' It was funny for like two seconds."

"Surprised it was funny that long," I said.

We drank. We watched the kids. A couple of older teens— three boys and five girls in their late teens—were working the far side of the street. Costumes were bullshit. Whatever they could grab. Not really costumes at all. No theme. Just part of their grift.

"That's where it starts," said Alex. "When you're really too old for trick-or-treat, but you try to cling onto it."

I thought about that and nodded. When they came to us, I didn't bitch at them and let them each grab bars out of the bag. One girl took two and looked me right in the eyes when she did it. I smiled and nodded, and there was every chance she took it the wrong way because her face turned sour. But it was because of what Alex just said.

We finished our beers and opened two more.

Out of the left corner of nowhere, he said, "Been seeing a shrink."

I said something clever like, "Oh, yeah?" You can tell I write TV dialogue for a living.

"Yeah." He was using his thumbnail to peel the label off the bottle. Doing it carefully so as not to tear it. Years of practice. "You know how it is. PTSD and all that shit."

And all that shit.

I was not dumb enough or clueless enough to act surprised that he had *those* kinds of ghosts in his head.

I said, "Doing you any good?"

He looked up from his work, studying me with brown eyes under white eyebrows. "You ever see a shrink?"

"Up to and including yesterday," I said. "Been in and out of therapy most of my life. Out here, and in this business, it's kind of a requirement. Nobody I know's *not* in therapy."

He thought about that, nodded. "What for? I mean ... you didn't ..."

The rest hung there, but I didn't take offense. "Didn't serve? No. Didn't want to wear anyone's uniform."

There were old arguments hanging in the air between us. Military service makes a *man* out of you. Or, woman, if he was arguing with one of our sisters. Or, duty to the flag. Stopping the spread of—fill in the blank anything we Americans don't like, don't want, can't own, and doesn't look like us.

But he didn't go there. Not that day.

We gave out some more candy. Even had a kid with a really good Transformers costume that turned into a truck when he knelt down but must have been eight thousand degrees hot. Kid was maybe eight and he was pouring sweat. I gave him two bars.

"We all have our ghosts," I said, picking up the thread of the conversation.

"Yeah," he said. "I guess we do."

"Therapy doing *you* any good?"

He took a really long time to answer that one. He sat looking out at the kids, taking micro-sips, eyes unfocused.

"We covered some ground," he said at last. "He got me to a place."

"A place?" I asked. "What kind of place?"

"Understanding the nature of my guilt," said Alex in the way people do when they are quoting or paraphrasing someone else's comment.

"Because you feel guilty about talking the guys in the band into enlisting?"

"Kind of," he said. "Mostly. Partly."

"How'd that get you to Los Angeles?"

He sipped. "Needed to close things out between us, Joey."

I leaned back and studied him. "This a twelve-step thing? What's the phrasing? *'Make direct amends to such people wherever possible, except when to do so would injure them or others'...?* Something like that?"

He waggled his beer bottle. "I'm not in AA," he said, "but it amounts to the same."

"You don't need to make amends with me," I said. "And even if you felt you had to, they have these newfangled contraptions called cell phones."

I hated surprises. Especially when they felt like ambushes. Confrontation always felt that way to me. Our sisters always wanted some of kind of Hallmark Christmas movie thing where one of us would show up unexpectedly to surprise the other, bury the hatchet, make it all right as the music swells and we hear Bing Crosby and David Bowie singing a holiday duet. The naivety of that always staggered me. As if a dramatic appearance could change anything. As if corny dialogue, familiar tears, and a shared belief that happy endings were part of the calculus of dysfunctional family dynamics.

If I thought that encounters like this *could* do some good, I'd have written a script for it and let some Lifetime Channel actors sort out the inflections for me. But this is the real world and people don't get happy endings just because they want them. I *know* this, and it's one of the many, many reasons I loathe surprises. So, yeah. This was beginning to piss me off.

"Some things you got to do in person," he said. "I wanted to put things right between us."

"The thing is, Alex, you could have saved the airfare," I said coldly. "Why waste your time coming all the way out here. It's all fine. I don't hold grudges."

"Fuck that," he said. "Yes, you do. Everyone does. Maybe you're not aware of it, but you do. I did. I mean, let's face it, neither of us picked up a phone in years. Fuck, we never even sent an email."

Yup. That's a line of dialogue I knew one of us had to say. Cliché as balls.

"It wasn't about holding a grudge," I protested weakly. "We just lived different lives. Different—"

"Politics and shit," he interrupted. "Yeah, I know. But none of that really matters anymore, does it?"

"I haven't changed my political views," I said.

"I have," he said.

"You have?" I asked, greatly surprised.

"I left all of that behind," said Alex. "I shouldn't have carried that freight all these years anyway. And to be straight, little brother, I think it was deflection. Or maybe projection. Not sure which term applies. Point is, I got deep into my side of politics— or ... one side of politics—because it was something to get mad about that had nothing to do with the Angels. I could get mad at borders and social security and who was in the White House and what color they were and feel like there was a *reason* for being mad. Good reasons, with ways to argue about it."

I said nothing.

"But it wasn't real," he said. "It was shadows and phantoms and all that."

He looked at me, and this time I could see miles deep.

"Joey," he said, "I was so mad at you for so long. Do you know that?"

My mouth went dry. I didn't even try to reply.

"You were a kid when 'Nam was happening. It was all around you, but you were bulletproof. Flame resistant. Invulnerable. You were too young to fight, too young to be drafted. And then there was no draft at all, and you skated. Fuck, man, I hated you for that."

I said nothing.

"Really hated you," he said. "Then you moved out here. Became a big time TV writer. Hollywood friends, all those hot actress chicks. All of that. And I was growing old in Philadelphia, dragging around all my shit."

"I'm sorry," I said.

"Sorry? Aren't you listening, Joey? You got nothing to be sorry about. I put that on you because I couldn't bear to carry it myself. I mean, you saw what happened to Chick. If he hadn't hit that El support, he'd have found another way out, and he hadn't even *gone*. I'm the last of the Angels, and every year it got harder to *be* that. So, I dished out the shit to everyone I could reach. You. My wife. Some friends from back then who went into the Army or Navy or whatever and, luck of the draw, never went to 'Nam. I went twice, and some of the guys from the neighborhood never got farther away than New Fucking Jersey. They went home for Christmas and Thanksgiving while I was in the shit. And, hell, I was a combat engineer. They dropped Agent Orange, and before the smoke even cleared, they sent me and the guys in to build helicopter bases in forward areas. That's where we were when the Angels started dying. And you know what? It was a goddamn Halloween the night Mickey got killed. Took a round in the throat. Voice like he had, and a VC bullet blew his whole throat out."

I stared at him. How does one write dialogue to respond to that? Hell if I knew. My heart was hammering and each beat felt like a separate punch.

"You know what we were doing when he got shot?" asked Alex, his voice still filled with surprise although the memory was decades old. "We were near a vil. Not VC, far as we knew. We had some time, and we were making benches and desks for a school. It was Halloween—they didn't know shit about that—but you remember how much Mickey was into it. He and Dan could speak the language. Not great, but well enough. They told the kids a bunch of ghost stories and made costumes and we all shared our chocolate bars and other shit. Trick-or-treat, but really just treats. Kids were laughing even though they had no real idea what the crazy Americans were doing. Everybody was having a good time. Then a sniper's bullet took Mickey in the throat. We all hit the deck, but the sniper got two kids too. Punishment for them having fun with us, I guess."

He paused. There were tears in his eyes.

"There were a lot of things like that," he said. "Funny how it always seemed to be a holiday. New Year, Christmas, Good Friday. And fucking Halloween."

We sat for a very long time.

Alex said, "When I came back the last time ... I mean came home for good ... you were growing up. Going to junior high by then. Reading everything you could. Talking about writing books. Even talking about college in seventh grade. God ... I was so *mad* at you. Want to know why? The real reason?"

The writer in me was already writing the script for this. Including all the self-recrimination about how I might have at least sent an email, left a voicemail, sent an emoji-heavy text message. It's not like I was unaware of PTSD. Shit, I'd written it into four or five TV scripts and one feature. Only on my denser days did I convince myself those insights came from watching the news. I grew up with everything anyone needs to know about what happens when the innocent go to war and no one prepares them for coming home. Another cliché, but a real one. I knew this stuff. I knew it and I never sent those messages. Never once picked up a phone. Fuck. I could *feel* my therapist getting richer by the moment. And here was my brother, having flown all the way across the country to do what I hadn't done with a couple of taps of thumbnails on cell keys.

"Sure, what reason is that?" I asked, and braced myself for the kick to the nuts I knew was coming.

"Because you had a future and you knew it," said Alex, pawing tears from his eyes. "You shined brighter than me. As bright as I did when the Seven Angels recorded those sides. What's that old line? Future's so bright I gotta wear shades? Like that. When I came home, I was still in my twenties. Still young, but I felt so damned old. Too old. Older than you've ever felt, even with divorces and all that. You know it too."

I felt my eyes burning.

"I hated you and everyone else," Alex continued. "Not our sisters, though. Women couldn't be combat soldiers then. Not in 'Nam. But when I looked at you, I saw what I wanted to be and never would be. I was broken. Dirty. Fucked up. And there were six ghosts haunting me."

"I ... I'm sorry, Alex," I said.

"You don't have to be," he said. "I'm sorry for letting the war win. That's what we talked about in therapy. I wish I could go back and change things. I wish I could be the older brother you wanted, the brother I wanted to be. If I could fix it, I would. I'd give anything."

I wanted to run. I wanted to yell. I wanted to cry. I needed to pull him into my arms and hug him and tell my brother that it was *me* who was sorry. If this was a script I'd be all over it. Slick, polished, with the right words tumbling out so that some TV actor could start rehearsing his Emmy speech. Writing that kind of dialogue is easy, it's how I make my living.

Saying those words ...? Even conjuring a reasonable reply to this ... goddamn. I was blank. I was scraped raw.

"Look, Alex," I began, fumbling for *any* useful words, "there's no—"

And my cell rang.

I glanced at the screen, then frowned. "You came out here alone?"

"Yeah. Why?"

"It's your wife," I said, waggling the phone.

He sighed and wiped the tears from his eyes. "Better take it."

"Why?" I asked. "Are you two breaking up or something?"

"More or less," said Alex. "There are some kids coming. I'll give out the candy. You take the call. It's cool. Better you know."

"Um ... okay. Whatever."

I stood up and walked to the far end of the porch, turning away from him as I pressed the green button.

"Joan," I said, "good to hear from you."

Her answer was a sob. Not even my name. It was big and broken and ugly and filled with jagged glass.

"Whoa, whoa," I soothed, immediately imagining all kinds of very bad scenarios. Alex always had a temper. "Just take a breath and tell me what's wrong."

I could almost feel her gathering herself. It felt like a massive undertaking, and I wondered what kind of damage Alex had left behind. He'd been talking about rage and there was an icy chill in my stomach because I kind of knew what this was going to be. The polite phrasing is "domestic violence." Alex, even wasted as he was now, was big and strong and Joan was petite. I began bracing against the bruising violence of her explanation.

She said, "Oh, my god, Joey ... it's so awful."

I lowered my voice and kept my back to Alex, not wanting to see the guilt on his face. Fighting the rise of my own rage.

"Tell me what happened," I said very slowly and carefully.

"I was downstairs making dinner," she said. "And I heard it."

"Heard what?"

She said, "The shot."

"The *what*?" I demanded.

"He did it in the shower ... oh, my God, Joey. There was so much blood. I tried to help him, but ... but ..."

She said more. Probably. Certainly. But I wasn't listening.

I turned around.

The bag of candy sat on the top step next to an empty beer bottle.

Alex wasn't there.

Of course, he wasn't.

Some kids were walking away. I could see the Three Musketeers bars in their hands. They were laughing, like kids do.

The step was empty. There was no car parked down the street. I was alone there.

Joan was still talking. But I couldn't listen to her. I sat down on the loveseat and stared at the laughing kids in their Halloween costumes. The happy parents herding them along. The sun shining down.

"Alex," I said to the empty air.

I knew he could hear me.

I was certain of it.

JONATHAN MABERRY'S PUBLISHED WORKS

SERIES

The Joe Ledger Thrillers

1. Patient Zero (2009; St. Martin's Griffin)
2. The Dragon Factory (2010; St. Martin's Griffin)
3. King of Plagues (2011; St. Martin's Griffin)
4. Assassin's Code (2012; St. Martin's Griffin)
5. Extinction Machine (2013; St. Martin's Griffin)
6. Code Zero (2014; St. Martin's Griffin)
7. Predator One (2015; St. Martin's Griffin)
8. Kill Switch (2016; St. Martin's Griffin)
9. Dogs of War (2017; St. Martin's Griffin)
10. Deep Silence (2018; St. Martin's Griffin)
11. Rage (2019; St. Martin's Griffin)
12. Relentless (2021; St. Martin's Griffin)
13. Cave 13 (2023; St. Martin's Griffin)
14. Burn to Shine ((2024; St. Martin's Griffin)
15. Joe Ledger: Special Ops (2014; JournalStone; short story collection)

16. Joe Ledger: The Missing Files (2012; Blackstone audio collection)
17. Joe Ledger: Secret Missions (2021; Blackstone audio collection)
18. Joe Ledger: Unstoppable (2017; St. Martin's Griffin; anthology)
19. Joe Ledger: Unbreakable (2023; JournalStone; anthology)
20. Joe Ledger Companion (nonfiction; with Dana Fredsti and Mari Adkins)

The Rot & Ruin Series

1. Rot & Ruin (2010; Simon & Schuster Books for Young Readers)
2. Dust & Decay (2011; Simon & Schuster Books for Young Readers)
3. Warrior Smart (2015; graphic novel; IDW publishing)
4. Flesh & Bone (2012; Simon & Schuster Books for Young Readers)
5. Fire & Ash (2013; Simon & Schuster Books for Young Readers)
6. Bits & Pieces (2015; Simon & Schuster Books for Young Readers)
7. Broken Lands (2018; Simon & Schuster Books for Young Readers)
8. Lost Roads (2020; Simon & Schuster Books for Young Readers)

Bewilderness

1. Threshold (Audible 2020)
2. What Rough Beast (Audible 2020)

3. Destroyer of Worlds (Audible 2020)

Kagen the Damned

1. Kagen the Damned (2022; St. Martin's Griffin)
2. Son of the Poison Rose (2023; St. Martin's Griffin)
3. The Dragon in Winter (2024; St. Martin's Griffin)

The Dead of Night Series

1. Dead of Night (2012; St. Martin's Griffin)
2. Fall of Night (2014; St. Martin's Griffin)
3. Dark of Night (2016; novella; JournalStone; with Rachael Lavin)
4. Still of Night (2018; JournalStone; novella and short stories; with Rachael Lavin)

The Pine Deep Trilogy

1. Ghost Road Blues (2006; Pinnacle)
2. Dead Man's Song (2007; Pinnacle)
3. Bad Moon Rising (2008; Pinnacle)
4. Darkness on the Edge of Town: Pine Deep Stories (2015; Blackstone Audio)
5. Ink (2020; St. Martin's Griffin)
6. Long Past Midnight: Tales of Pine Deep (2023, Kensington)

Stand-alone Novels

1. The Wolfman (2010; Tor)

2. Deadlands: Ghostwalkers (October 2015; Tor)
3. Mars One (2017, Simon & Schuster)
4. X-Files Origins: Devil's Advocate (Imprint/Macmillan, 2017)
5. Glimpse (2018; St. Martin's Griffin)
6. The Unlearnable Truths

The Sleepers War (with Weston Ochse)

1. Alpha Wave (2023, Aethon Publishing)
2. #2 The Dreaming Gods (2024, Aethon Publishing)
3. #3 Title TBD (2025, Aethon Publishing)

V-WARS: Chronicles of the Vampire Wars

1. V-Wars (editor and principle writer; 2012; IDW Publishing)
2. V-Wars: Blood and Fire (editor and principal writer; Fall 2014; IDW Publishing)
3. V-Wars: Night Terrors (2016; IDW Publishing)
4. V-Wars: Shockwaves (2016; IDW Publishing)

Weird Cosmos (*Weird Tales Presents*)
1. Necrotek (2024, Weird Tales Presents/Blackstone)

The Nightsiders

1. The Nightsiders: The Orphan Army (2015; Simon & Schuster Books for Young Readers)
2. The Nightsiders: Vault of Shadows (2016; Simon & Schuster Books for Young Readers)

John Henry Gallo series—details under NDA

1. The Long Walk of John Henry Gallo (Alcon Entertainment; all data TBD)
2. The Road to Damascus (Alcon Entertainment; all data TBD)

ANTHOLOGIES (as Editor)

1. Aliens vs. Predator: Ultimate Prey—with Bryan Thomas Schmidt (2022; Titan Books)
2. Aliens: Bug Hunt (2017; Titan Books)
3. Baker Street Irregulars Vol 1—with Michael Ventrella (2017; Diversion Press)
4. Baker Street Irregulars Vol 2—with Michael Ventrella (2018; Diversion Press)
5. Don't Turn Out the Lights (2020; HarperCollins)
6. Double Trouble: A Media Tie-in Mashup (with Keith R.A. DeCandido; IAMTW)
7. Hardboiled Horror (2017; JournalStone)
8. Joe Ledger: Unbreakable (JournalStone, November 2023)
9. Joe Ledger: Unstoppable—with Bryan Thomas Schmidt (2017; St. Martin's Griffin)
10. Nights of the Living Dead—with George A. Romero (2017; Griffin)
11. Out of Tune vol 1 (2014; JournalStone Publishing)
12. Out of Tune vol 2 (2016; JournalStone Publishing)
13. Scary Out There (2016; Simon & Schuster)
14. The Good, the Bad and the Uncanny: Tales of a Very Weird West (Outland, 2023)
15. V-Wars (editor and principle writer; 2012; IDW Publishing)

16. V-Wars: Blood and Fire (editor and principle writer; Fall 2014; IDW Publishing)
17. V-Wars: Night Terrors (2016; IDW Publishing)
18. V-Wars: Shockwaves (2016; IDW Publishing)
19. Weird Tales Magazine: 100 Years of Weird (Blackstone/Weird Tales, 2023)
20. Weird Tales: Best of the Early Years 1923-25—with Justin Criado (2022; WordFire Press)
21. Weird Tales: Best of the Early Years 1926-27—with Kaye Lynne Booth (2022; WordFire Press)
22. X-Files vol 1: Trust No One (2015; IDW)
23. X-Files vol 2: The Truth is Out There (2016; IDW)
24. X-Files vol 3: Secret Agendas (2016; IDW)
25. Double Trouble (2023; International Association of Tie-In Writers)

COLLECTIONS

1. A Little Bronze Book of Cautionary Tales (2017; Borderlands)
2. Beneath the Skin: The Case Files of Sam Hunter (2017, JournalStone- print; Blackstone -audio)
3. Darkness on the Edge of Town: Pine Deep Stories (2015; Blackstone Audio)
4. Empty Graves: Tales of the Living Dead (2021; WordFire Press)
5. Hungry Tales (2013; Blackstone Audio)
6. Joe Ledger: Secret Missions vol 1 (2021; JournalStone – print, eBook; Blackstone Audio –audio)
7. Joe Ledger: Secret Missions vol 2 (2021; JournalStone – print, eBook; Blackstone Audio –audio)
8. Joe Ledger: Special Ops (2014; JournalStone –print, eBook; Blackstone Audio –audio)
9. Joe Ledger: The Missing Files (2011; Blackstone Audio)

10. Long Past Midnight: Tales of Pine Deep (2023, Kensington)
11. Strange Worlds (2015; Blackstone Audio)
12. Tales from the Fire Zone (2012; Blackstone Audio)
13. Whistling Past the Graveyard and other stories (2016; JournalStone)
14. Wind Through the Fence and other stories (2017; JournalStone)

NONFICTION BOOKS

1. Counterstrike Kenpo Karate Student Handbook (indie published, 2004)
2. ESM: Effective Survival Methods (Vortex Multimedia, 1984)
3. Judo and You (with Charles E. Rinear; Kendall Hunt Publishing, 1991)
4. Martial Arts Student Logbook (Strider Nolan Publishing; 2001)
5. Shinowara-ryu Jujutsu Student Handbook (Vortex Multimedia, 1985)
6. The Cryptopedia (with David F. Kramer; Citadel, 2007)
7. The Joe Ledger Companion (with Dana Fredsti and Mari Adkins; JournalStone, 2016)
8. The Vampire Slayers Field Guide to the Undead (written under the pen name of Shane MacDougal; Strider Nolan Publishing; 2003)
9. They Bite (with David F. Kramer; Citadel, 2009; reissued 2021)
10. Ultimate Jujutsu (Strider Nolan Publishing; 2002)
11. Ultimate Sparring (Strider Nolan Publishing;2003)
12. Vampire Universe (Citadel, 2006)

13. Wanted Undead or Alive (with Janice Gable Bashman; Citadel, 2010)
14. Zombie CSU (Citadel, 2008; reissued 2021)

COMICS AND GRAPHIC NOVELS

1. Age of Heroes (Marvel Entertainment, 2011)
2. Bad Blood (Dark Horse, 2014)
3. Black Panther: Doomwar (Marvel Entertainment, 2017; reprints)
4. Black Panther: Power (Marvel Entertainment, 2009)
5. Captain America: Hail Hydra (Marvel Entertainment, 2011)
6. DoomWar (Marvel Entertainment, 2010)
7. Karl Kolchak
8. Klaws of the Panther (Marvel Entertainment, 2011)
9. Marvel Universe vs. The Avengers (Marvel Entertainment, 2011)
10. Marvel Universe vs. The Punisher (Marvel Entertainment, 2011)
11. Marvel Universe vs. Wolverine (Marvel Entertainment, 2011)
12. Marvel Zombies Return (Marvel Entertainment, 2009)
13. Pandemica (2019-20; IDW Publishing)
14. Punisher vs. the Marvel Universe (Marvel Entertainment, 2016; reprints)
15. Punisher: Naked Kills (Marvel Entertainment, 2008)
16. Punisher: The Complete Collection Vol 6 (Marvel Entertainment, 2017; reprints)
17. Road of the Dead (IDW Publishing, October 2018)
18. Rot & Ruin: Warrior Smart (IDW Publishing, 2015)
19. V-Wars: All of Us Monsters (IDW Publishing, 2015)
20. V-Wars: Crimson Queen (IDW Publishing, 2014)
21. V-Wars: God of War (IDW Publishing, 2018)

22. Wolverine vs. the Marvel Universe (Marvel Entertainment, 2017; reprints)
23. Wolverine: Flies to a Spider (Marvel Entertainment, 2009)

BOARD GAMES

- V-Wars: A Game of Blood and Betrayal (IDW Games)

ABOUT THE AUTHOR

Jonathan Maberry is a *New York Times* bestselling author, 5-time Bram Stoker Award winner, four-time Scribe Award winner, Inkpot Award winner, editor, and comic book writer. His vampire apocalypse book series, V-WARS, was a Netflix original series. He writes in multiple genres including suspense, thriller, horror, science fiction, fantasy, and action; for adults, teens, and middle grade. He is the editor of many anthologies including *The X-Files*, *Aliens: Bug Hunt*, *Don't Turn Out the Lights*, *Nights of the Living Dead*, and others. His comics include *Black Panther: DoomWar*, *Captain America*, *Pandemica*, *Highway to Hell*, *The Punisher*, and *Bad Blood*. He is the editor of *Weird Tales Magazine,* and the president of the International Association of Media Tie-in Writers.

Website: www.jonathanmaberry.com

facebook.com/jonathan.maberry.5

x.com/@jonathanmaberry

instagram.com/jonathanmaberry

threads.net/@jonathanmaberry

OTHER WORDFIRE PRESS TITLES BY JONATHAN MABERRY

Empty Graves

Our list of other WordFire Press authors and titles is always growing. To find out more and shop our selection of titles, visit us at:

wordfirepress.com

"The Door Between Us" © 2024; never before published.

"A Small Taste of the Old Country" ©2016 Jonathan Maberry Productions; first published in *Haunted Nights*, edited by Ellen Datlow and Lisa Morton; Anchor, 2017.

"The Queen of Thorns—a poem" © 2024; never before published.

"Being Emily-Claire" ©2018 Jonathan Maberry Productions; first published in *A Secret Guide to Fighting Elder Gods*, edited by Jennifer Prozek; Pulse Publishing, 2019.

"Calling Death" ©2011 Jonathan Maberry Productions; first published in *Appalachian Undead*, edited by Eugene Johnson, Apex Publishing, 2012.

"Cooked" ©2011 Jonathan Maberry Productions; first published in *Death Be Not Proud*, edited by Thomas Erb, Dark Quest LLC, 2011.

"Gavin Funke's Monster Movie Marathon" ©2020 Jonathan Maberry Productions; first published in *Movies, Monsters, and Mayhem*, WordFire Press, 2020.

Doctor Nine ©2024; never before published.

"Lullaby" ©2018 Jonathan Maberry Productions; first published as an Audible Original, 2018.

"The Things That Live in Cages" ©2013 Jonathan Maberry Productions; first published in *High Stakes: A Vampire Anthology*, edited by Gabrielle Faust, Evil Jester Press, 2013.

"Invasive Species" ©2023; published in 2023 PhilCon souvenir booklet.

"Monk—a poem" ©2024; never before published.

"Road Beers with Norm and Tank at Twitchy's Hatchet House" ©2022 Jonathan Maberry Productions; first published in *It Came From the Trailer Park, Volume 2*, edited by William Joseph Roberts, Three Ravens Publishing, 2022.

"Saint John" ©2011 Jonathan Maberry Productions; first published in *The Monster's Corner*, edited by Christopher Golden; St. Martin's Griffin, 2011.

"Son of the Devil" ©2015 Jonathan Maberry Productions; first published in *Weird*

Wild West, edited by Misty Massey, Emily Lavin Leverett, & Margaret S. McGraw, eSpec Publishing, 2015.

"The Scream" ©2016 Jonathan Maberry Productions; first published in *Drive-In Creature Feature*, edited by Charles Day and Eugene Johnson, 2016.

"When You See Millions of the Mouthless Dead" ©2022 Jonathan Maberry Productions; first published in *Literally Dead*, edited by Gaby Triana, Alienhead Press, 2022.

www.ingramcontent.com/pod-product-compliance
Lightning Source LLC
Chambersburg PA
CBHW050522110726
47899CB00005B/1553